by vanessa zhan

Dog Tags & Lace Series

Midnight to December

Ruby in July

Mine after October

March becomes Dawn

Standalone

The Lifecycle of a Crush

ruby in july

vanessa zian

Cover Design - Lori Jackson Designs
Design Concept - Willow Winters
Editing - Jacqui Muller
Proofreading - Catherine Elaine

For my mom, the original queen.

———

And for the Ruby and Mama Z's of the world—may you find your dagger, if you haven't already.

content notice

My books weave in subplots of trauma and may be triggering to some, but there's good reason for it. I'm all about the happily ever after, so you will absolutely get that. But my aim is to leave the reader with the ultimate narrative full of truths, no matter what the trauma. We all have experienced some at some point, whether it be "small t" or the "Big T" kind.

We learn by sharing stories. We heal by tweaking the narrative. And we soar when we can join forces and journey together. It's what I'm here for, and I'm so glad you are too.

love lost

. . .

Present Day

one

. . .

joey

PINK. THE WALLS in this bedroom are actually pink—I can just make it out in the darkness. I'm not sure how I've never noticed it before; it's not my first time in here. Though with a snap of the fingers, I know it could be my last. But pink. What an odd paint color choice for a grown ass woman.

I hear the bedside lamp get clicked on and the wall shade suddenly changes. "You must be colorblind, Joey, because my walls are really more of a purple than a pink," Lila says.

I blink as my eyes adjust to the new flood of light.

"I...I didn't realize I had said that out loud," I say with a firm head nod. Shit. I hate when I do that. But hopefully, Lila Ray will view my honesty with chivalry.

I mean, to Lila's credit, it's not a *bad* pink. Or purple. Kind of rich in a way. The whole bedroom has that feel to it. Girly and luxurious. Opulent, even—I think that's the word. The kind of place a guy like me could never in a million years decorate, but I have to say, it feels real nice in here.

Or maybe it's just the company that I like.

"Well, you did say it out loud. And if the walls are not to your liking," she says with one perfectly arched eyebrow, "then may I remind you you don't in fact need to be here. Being in this room is a privilege, babe." Lila pats my cheek twice before rolling over to climb out of bed.

"Whoa, whoa, whoa. Get that ass back here and let me make it up to you." I grin and wiggle my brows. "With my tongue." Truth be told, I'm not sure my dick can go again after three rounds, but I want to make her happy. And I'm out of condoms. I grab her hand to pull her back to me, but Lila waves me off and climbs out of bed anyways.

God, she really does have the body of a model. Tall, tan, and slim. Not much for tits, just a handful, but that's really all you need. That *ass* though. A perfect bubble that I can never decide if I prefer the look of with clothes on or without.

I'm kidding, it's without.

"Aw come on, you usually love what my tongue can do." I lay back to stretch out on her insane amount of pillows and lace my fingers behind my head. Rest against the headboard in an effort to look calm and collected, because I know she's about to kick me out. The girl is committed to not committing. Dreams of being a model and getting the hell out of here, apparently. Which I understand, so I'll take what I can get.

Lila tosses my jeans to me. Damnit.

"Up you go, dimples. That's enough fun for one night." She grabs my shirt and tosses that at me too. "And quit flexing, show off."

Reluctantly I groan and grab my clothes. "Why won't you ever let me stay the night? Or take you out or cook for you or something?" I hate myself a little for even trying. Girls usually have no problem falling for my irresistible charm, but I guess we want what we can't have. "You just use and abuse me, don't you?" I say with mock hurt.

She pauses the buttoning of her jeans and looks at me. I see a little hesitation in her eyes mixed with consideration of my proposal. That pause fuels my hope. I'm a romantic at heart, what can I say? So I go in for the kill. Let out a little growl.

"Or better yet, let me whisk you away for a weekend—wherever you want. Your choice."

Yup, I fucked that one up. Just as quickly as it came, her consideration vanishes. She shakes her head. "No, no, no. Stop that. First off, you and I both know you'd never take a weekend away from your restaurants." (She's got me there.) "And second, once again I remind you, this is just sex. That's it, all it will ever be."

To clarify, I really am okay with that, despite my little pleading act. I just like to push her buttons.

"Oh, come on, baby. Lucy would be so happy to see us together," I say, striking for the right balance between playful petition and perfect persuasion.

Lila raises an eyebrow at me. I'm expecting her to yell at me for calling her baby, but she brushes past that. "Lucy would have your balls on a plate because she'd be convinced that you were the one to seduce her sweet little sister, not the other way around."

"You wouldn't let her believe that, right?" Lucy and her husband Justin are two of my best friends. But it's true, Lucy would never believe that it was actually Lila that seduced me. Lila bartends for me a couple nights a week, and I tell you what, having gotten to know her recently, I think we've all underestimated the sweet little girl we used to think she was.

Though I'd probably marry her in a second if she'd give me the time of day outside of this bedroom. Lila Ray is a Five Star, a perfect Ten. The whole package.

And unfortunately, she knows it.

Lila shrugs a shoulder before popping her shirt over her head. "You being on the receiving end of Lucy's wrath might be fun to watch." I'm convinced Lila might have a bit of an evil streak in her. Which I find hot as hell since her sass makes her fun to fuck with.

I groan and climb out of her bed though, dejected. Step into my jeans, pull them up and tuck my dick in. I look down at it, say, "Guess we're done for the day, man. Good work, though." I give it a salute before zipping up and buttoning. Shirt on, a quick scan for my shoes, and I feel Lila's hand on my back, pushing me towards her bedroom door.

"You need to hurry. My roommate will be home soon."

"Maybe *she'll* appreciate a good meal with me," I say.

"Paws off. She couldn't handle the likes of you. She'd fall madly in love, and then watch. *That* would be the one girl's heart you break," Lila warns. I know she's right. Cici is cute, but not my type.

Just as Lila's about to grab her doorknob, we hear the front door to the apartment opening. I look down and see what I think might be actual terror emanating from the unshakable Lila's gorgeous green eyes.

"Relax," I whisper to her as I give her a kiss on her cheek.

I open the door and step out into the living room just as Cici walks in. She's dressed in scrubs, juggling a lunchbox, a water bottle fit for a desert hike, mail, keys, a small package and an overall look of exhaustion.

"Let me know what you think of the book, I found it *riveting*," I say over my shoulder to Lila with all the ease in the world. I wink as she stares back at me wide-eyed and likely furious. "Though I do want it back. I have notes in there."

I turn back towards Lila's roommate. "Oh, hey there, Cici. Back from work? So late? Shit, let me give you a hand with all that." I reach for her and help unload what can only be described as a travel pack of belongings, minus the pack. "You know I really don't like the idea of you walking through that parking lot alone late at night. You must be tired after a long shift, and what with the recent car break-ins around here? I wish I would have known you were coming home." I turn back towards Lila. In a scolding voice I say, "Lila, why didn't you tell me Cici would be coming home soon? I could have met her out there."

Cici sighs and pushes back a stray strand of hair from her eyes.

"Thank you, Joey. Had I known you were here, I would have," she says. "There was no one there tonight to harass me though, thankfully."

"You keep pepper spray or something on you?"

"Always," she confirms, and that makes me feel better. I have two little sisters and know too well the shit they gotta deal with that I would never even think about.

"Good," I say. "Don't be afraid to use it."

"We done here?" Lila interjects.

Cici pushes a playful finger into my shoulder. "Hey, you maybe want to stay and share an after-work drink with me?" she asks, eyes hopeful and smiling.

I think about it for a second, then catch Lila glaring at me, cat eyes narrowed, subtly shaking her head no. A warning. Actually, from her, more like a threat.

I run a hand through my hair. "Gosh, you know you make it hard to resist, Cici, but unfortunately I have to head out. It's late, Lila and I were just closing down the bar, and this book I love came up in conversation," I lie and with any luck, convincingly. "I promised I'd drop the book off to her real quick, so I'm just here for a pop in, but I gotta head to bed." I try to eke out a yawn, and a real one thankfully manages to escape.

Cici looks hurt, and I instantly feel bad. She's a sweet girl. I gotta offer her something. "You know what though, I'm gonna take a guess and say you work too hard, Cici," I say. "Bet you could use a night out."

"You'd be guessing right," she confirms.

"Late hours, taking care of patients," I soothe. "You gotta balance that out with a little fun, so how 'bout you come into one of my restaurants when you have a night off? Hang by the bar, let me treat you to a meal and drink?" I smile at the light brought back into Cici's pretty eyes, though I can practically feel the daggers darting out of Lila's.

Lila clears her throat obnoxiously. "Oh, I'm sure Mr. Restaurateur is way too busy to attempt to host Cici, right?"

Cici glances over at her, confusion on her face and then looks back at me. "Congratulations, by the way. I've been dying to see one of your places. I hear they're both great and have rave reviews. A couple of the nurses were just talking about it."

I put a hand over my chest. "Are you seriously telling me you've never been in? Cici, shame on you. Second one's been open for almost two years now," I say.

Cici covers her face in embarrassment. "I know, I'm sorry. I've been meaning to, but I've been adulting too much."

Lila snorts. "Cici, do not let him guilt you."

"All's forgiven," I say, ignoring Lila, "if you do me one favor."

Lila rolls her eyes. "Here we go." But Cici seems more than happy with a little coaxing from me.

"You and your coworkers come have a night out. Text me when and you'll get nothing but the star treatment." I grab the glittery cellphone out of Cici's hands. I type in my number, then hand it back to her. "Maybe my future bride is in your group of nurse friends, and it'll all be meant to be," I say with a mischievous wiggle of my eyebrows.

Lila pushes me towards the door. "Alright, Don Juan. Out you go." I say my goodbyes to a deflated looking Cici and allow Lila to push me out into the hallway of their building. She closes the door behind her and punches my shoulder.

"Ouch," I say, grabbing the abused spot. "What the hell was that for?"

"Please. You know damn well you're not finding any brides anytime soon."

"Ouch again, Lila. You're on a roll. Why would you say something so mean?" I give her an exaggerated frown of hurt.

She looks at me with raised eyebrows. Like I'm an idiot.

"Well?" I prompt.

She sighs and crosses her arms over her chest. "Because you're already madly in love with someone."

I pull my head back in surprise. "Reggie? No, no, no, kid. You've got that all wrong. She and I are friends. That flame is long over," I say. And I mean it. Reggie is my ex, by the way. She's now married to my uncle, they actually just had their second baby, but that's a story for another day.

Lila shakes her head. "I know that. Not Reggie, you beautiful fool."

"Who then?"

She bites her lip as if debating whether or not to say.

I cock my head to the side in frustration. "Lila, if not Reggie, then who the hell do you think I'm madly in love with?" As soon as the words slip out, I already know what she's going to say.

She sighs dramatically before saying, "Why, none other than the famous Ruby Francesca." She adds a satisfied smile.

Well, fuck, I think.

Because she's absolutely right. I am.

I'M WALKING OUT TO MY car with thoughts of Ruby now circulating in my head. Damn Lila, ruining my distraction from my heartbroken soul.

Ruby, Ruby, Ruby. My Nightingale. You gotta understand. This girl is everything—and I mean *everything*—good in life.

And I let her go. Had to. She had long outgrown our little town of Garden Springs, PA, suburb of Philly. Too many dreams lay waiting for the beautiful singer-songwriter. I had no choice. I had to let her chase them.

And now she's a star, just as I knew she would be from the start.

I guess you could say I'm the guy that helps women find their path in life. Always the stepping stone, never the groom, it feels like. I don't know if that's even a saying, but it's pretty spot on for me.

Not that I struggle with the ladies, mind you. Just the ones that really count.

I get to my car, unlock the door to step in and hear my phone go off. A text. I tense up as I see it's from my mom, which can only mean one thing at this hour—something's wrong.

M: Are you awake? Mama Z is taking a turn for the worse.

J: I am, you need me?

M: I hate to ask, but your father's in the middle of a long shift.

J: Be right over.

two

. . .

mama z

I SUPPOSE IT is natural to begin to reflect upon one's life choices when you in fact find yourself struggling for your last breaths. Oh yes, I'm on my way out (in style, with any luck), though still very much here and present. But in this last chapter of my life, I cannot exactly sit up and demand that everyone in the room shut the hell up, now can I? I would like to, though. Only *my* family would actually be loud and chattering and *arguing* over nonsense when their beloved matriarch is quite literally on her deathbed.

But who am I kidding? I would have it no other way. I would smile in this moment if I could, delighted as I am to have the majority of my loved ones all here in my room in my home, but the energy to do so is slipping away from me more and more. It has been for a few days, now.

I do not want anyone to feel sorry for me, so you can go ahead and drop the "Oh no!" act because there's no need for it. Death is a part of life, and mine has been a damn good one. I designed it that way. So please, enough with the "so sad" dramatics. It's unbecoming.

"Your leg! It's crushing her foot, get off the bed, Stella."

"I want a snack, Mommy. When can we leave?"

I do believe that's one of my great-grandchildren making pesky demands for a snack. She's a chubby girl, that one. Her mother should watch that. But that's one of the things I'll have to let go of, I suppose. They will miss my advice when I'm gone, but I'll try and find a way back into their dreams, and if that doesn't work, fiddle with a light switch or two, perhaps. This is not the last they'll be hearing from me.

"Joey, is she coming? Mama Zabel specifically asked for her."

There it is, the thing I have been holding out for. I hear my eldest daughter Isabella asking her son, my beloved grandson Joey, for just the thing I want.

I cannot quite make out Joey's voice, though. He must be in the back of the room somewhere. Can I manage a noise of some sort? A groan or whimper—something to get their attention? I am making efforts, and I tell you, it may just be the hardest thing I have ever done. And I birthed four baby girls, all naturally, of course.

"Did you hear that, Mom? She said something!"

"Get your head out of your ass, she hasn't spoken in days."

"No, I heard it too!"

Alright, well apparently I'm making something happen then, am I not? Come on now fools, I urge silently. Hush up and pay attention! Of all the times to find it in your hearts to be quiet, *now* is it.

I hear shushes coming from across the room. Good. They're listening. I try again to articulate my request.

"I hear it, I hear—"

"Move," booms a male voice.

Yes! That was my dear Joey! Yes, tell them, Joey! Clear these fools out of the way and tell them to listen.

"Mama Zabel, it's me, Joey." His voice is smooth and rhythmic

in my ear as he grabs my hand. A delightful tune. Perhaps his presence alone can bring me the extra few days that I need. *"My oh my, you are a beauty still, even now. How is it that you make even death look good, the Real EmZee?"*

And that right there, my dears, is why Joey is my favorite. I am allowed to have a favorite grandson, and I shall not be shy in admitting that. Can you see why he is mine? Aside from giving me the best nicknames, that boy knows not to bullshit me and dance around a word like "death." We are all well aware that is what is happening, just as it should be. Who would want to live forever? No need to fear the word. Death at this point will be a gift.

I just need one last thing before I slip away. One last mission. And Joey is key to making it happen.

I try again and focus on my belly, just like in my singing days. Slowly, I push from deep within. I can do this.

I'm close now, I can feel it.

And finally, the word slips from my mouth, and I know that my Joey will hear it.

"Ruby," I breathe out, with an effort fit for moving mountains.

One more time. For the people in the back. I can do this. I'm Zabel Derian, for God's sake.

"Ruby."

three

. . .

ruby

THE ROAR IS unshakeable, a steady hum of electric energy outside the confines of the dressing room. Like a roll of thunder, it is commanding and awe-inspiring. A welcome purr to her ears. The audience is awaiting the performance of the rising star, Ruby Francesca. *Her*. In mere minutes, she'll be on that stage, and give them what they want.

But Ruby wills herself to focus on her visuals. On what she sees, and so she tries to ignore the intoxicating rumble of the crowd beyond. She looks around at all her eyes can register, humming as she keeps her voice warmed up.

So many visual experiences to take in, existing all in one small space. Her eyes dart to her left, catching blings of sparkle, both on fabrics hanging on the rack, and sparkle on the table top of the vanity. The more sparkle the better. Sequins adorned garments and studs of flashy rocks for jeweled accessories. The dazzling square of multiple globes of light, surrounding the mirror.

As her eyes cross to the edge of the vanity, the shine from the beads of condensation of her water further capture her attention.

Ruby only drinks water during her shows, nothing else. No drop of caffeine, electrolyte restorers, or other self-proclaimed elixirs will enter her body until the show is complete. She insists on it, despite recommendations to fuel with something more substantial. Her voice is better this way, clean and pure.

Besides, she's got energy enough to light up all of New York City if she wants.

A glance up and Ruby sees the flat texture of the white paint. Shiny and smooth.

"I see glitter, I see sparkle, I see shine," she murmurs out, halfway into her pre-show ritual, her meditation routine. She's igniting her senses with the practice. It begins with naming five things she sees, five things she hears, five things she feels, five things she smells. Then she moves to four. Then three and eventually she will lose track, but her senses at that point will be more alive and ready. Fired and charged, yet her nerves calm and steady. Ready to take on the pending task at hand. The task of performing.

And now she listens.

Listening is her favorite part of the senses meditation routine, a practice long ago learned in therapy. In listening, she absorbs the rumbling of the crowd, out there waiting for her. She hears the music of the opening artist, someone even newer than she is to the music scene. He's wrapping up, and she knows the crowd is anxious to see her.

To see Ruby Francesca.

But she remains humble. She remembers that it wasn't long ago when she would have killed for the chance to be so much as the opening act for someone. Three years ago that opportunity would have seemed like a dream come true. Three years ago she was a nobody.

Now she's the main show.

"I hear the crowd," she whispers, nearly choking up at the magnitude of their roar. It bellows and bounces off the walls, a comforting steady hum of noise. "I hear the thud of the music."

She squeezes her eyes closed, wanting to take in the sounds with maximum fervor. "I hear footsteps outside my door." The anticipation in their steps, the team waiting for her to finish, so they can whisk her away and on stage to begin.

With reluctance Ruby takes a deep breath in to leave the sense of what she hears so she can move to the next sense—what she feels. She focuses her mind on the feeling beneath her palm. "I feel the scratch of rhinestones. I feel the heels of my boots. I feel the squeeze of my toes." The constraints of her opening costume a welcome embrace, a reminder of just who she is and what she's capable of.

On she continues until her mind is in a beautiful trance, and she is jumbled up, lost in which sense comes next or how many she is supposed to say. But that's the point of the practice. Because now she's ready. Now her nerves are calmer than any Xanax could possibly make her. Xanax would dull, and Ruby doesn't want dull. She wants a unique cocktail of static energy. This state is how she best manipulates her gift of music and connects with her fans.

She doesn't like to know the numbers before hand, the tickets sold and the total number of people in the crowd. But it's nearly impossible to escape it. She's already giddy from the earlier sight of the snaking line of people on the street, her driver slowing down as they passed. People with custom shirts with her name, or "Dog Tags & Lace," the name of her album and the tour. People all waiting to see her. The words "sold out" inevitably escape someone's lips, and her stomach inevitably flips at the knowledge of this. Another show sold out. For Ruby, a brand new artist (or brand new as far as the world at large knows), already selling out shows. Sure, the venue is on the smaller side, a capacity of 3,000 or so. There's room to grow yet. But still. That's 3,000 people right here in New York, waiting to see *her*.

She flutters her eyes open and looks down at Rebel.

"We're ready now, aren't we?" she asks, patting the fluff ball Pomeranian. At sixteen years old, Rebel is mostly deaf, but he senses his mama. He raises his head in quiet acknowledgement, then drops it back down to rest on his nest of a blanket, content to sleep while his owner performs. He knows her routine, and knows the snuggles and love he'll get when she returns after the show.

Ruby takes one last gulp of her water before preparing to walk out to let them know that she's ready.

But a knock beats her to it.

"Ruby, I'm sorry to interrupt," says the muffled British accent of her assistant. She frowns because everyone knows of her one pre-show request to have five minutes of peace to complete her meditation. And everyone knows they can count on her to keep it to four-and-a-half minutes. She'd long ago sworn she'd never be that kind of artist, the diva mandating everyone cater to her timeline in panic.

"I'm finished, Grayson. Come in," she says.

The door opens and a cacophony of sound rushes in from the crowd beyond, but is quickly dulled again as Grayson shuts the door behind him. His face is etched with concern and Ruby knows to trust it. She immediately tenses.

"What is it? Just tell me," is all she says. Rebel lets out a low rumble of a snore, already asleep again.

"He made me promise not to talk to you until after the show, love. But I knew you'd want to know first."

"Who?"

"Joey."

"My Joey? I mean, Joey Conti?" Ruby confirms. Grayson knows who Joey is, as Grayson held the role of friend before becoming Ruby's assistant. He knows their history, their fling three summers prior, and what she had mistakenly believed to be something more. But that was before her life changed.

Before a famous musician happened to see Ruby singing in a small Philly restaurant. Singing in Joey's restaurant.

"Yes. He rang, not long ago. It's his grandmother." Ruby watches Grayson shift his body weight from one foot to the other, clearly uncomfortable. "I know you two were close."

"Mama Zabel?" Ruby confirms, her fear growing.

"Yes, Za—?" he asks.

"Za-BELLE, yeah. Is she…" Ruby can't get the word out. *Dead.*

"No, she's still alive."

"Oh, thank God."

"But not for much longer, I'm afraid. According to Joey, she has mere days left."

Ruby nods, calculating her next plan of action. Should she try and see her? Would Mama Z want her to? She'll be in Philly tomorrow, just thirty minutes or so from where she knows Mama Zabel is.

Another knock comes in with a call for Ruby to be ready. Grayson responds for her, assuring them she'll be right out. He returns his attention back to her.

"Do you think I should try and see her? Would that be appropriate, or is that weird?" she asks her friend.

"Actually, Ruby," Grayson says, stepping closer to her. "That's exactly *why* he rang. Apparently Joey's grandmother is asking for none other than you."

four

. . .

joey

"TOMORROW," I SAY to my mom as I end the call with Grayson and put the phone back in my pocket.

"You spoke with her?" she asks. Her dark hair is streaked with gray, and I look at her and see just how much more gray it's gotten these past few years. I see the toll it's taken on her to care for her mother, for Mama Zabel. My mom stands there, uncharacteristically immobile with her arms crossed over her chest, a red shawl the size of a small blanket draped loosely over her arms. Her eyes have a strange distance to them. She's looking at me, but it feels more like she's staring *through* me. Like she doesn't even see anything at all.

I walk over to my mom and pull the shawl tighter around her neck and shoulders. "Not directly to her, but I spoke to Grayson," I say, and I wrap my arms around her. She keeps her own arms crossed though, locked between us. Like a small little statue, the usual fierce and almighty Isabella now feels frail in my arms, and I realize she's lost some weight. I wonder when that happened. I'm consumed with guilt. Wonder where the hell I've been that I've missed the fact that she's obviously not been eating enough. I'm pissed at my aunts, too. They've thrown all the burden of care on my mom, escaping their own responsibilities.

My mom's muffled voice whispers between us. "Good. That's good. Tomorrow then," she says, still remaining frozen between my chest and arms.

I know what she's thinking, what we're all thinking. "She'll make it another day," I reassure her, hoping I'm not lying.

"You don't know that."

I drop my arms to grab my mom by the shoulders. Pull her back to look her in the face. "Ma, hey. Look at me," I say, giving her a gentle shake. "Yes, I do," I say with a smile. "Mama Z wants to see the great Ruby Francesca. And you and I both know that Mama Z gets exactly what she wants."

My chest feels just the smallest bit lighter as I see the flicker of a smile escape the corner of my mother's mouth. She finally uncrosses her arms, steps forward, wraps her arms around my waist, and I resume my embrace. Shit, I can feel the damn ridges of her ribs and spine beneath my grasp. And I sure as fuck better deliver on my promise that Mama Z will in fact make it another night.

"Well you're right about that, Joey," my mom sighs. "She sure does."

"'Course I'm right. She'll go when she's good and ready. Not a damn thing that can change that." I release her frail little body, usually far more sturdy than it is now, and kiss her head before walking over to the kitchen. My chest is tight all over again and I need a distraction, and clearly my mother needs to eat.

"Oh, no you don't," I hear her call after me.

"What?" I say as I make my way behind the peninsula and take a peek in the pantry.

"I know what you're doing, Joseph Conti Junior. I'm not hungry," I hear her voice follow behind me. I close the pantry door, disappointed by its contents.

"Did you stop to consider that maybe I am?" This woman's

going to eat something, and if I have to eat five dinners in one night to make that happen, then I will.

"Don't bullshit me," she scolds.

I place a hand over my heart. "Ma, I would never," I say, before reaching for the fridge door. I open it and scan across the glowing shelves of glass for something to work with. Even the fridge is looking unusually empty. I make a mental note to have groceries delivered in the morning.

I'm now fuming with every passing second. This house has never been known to have sparse looking shelves. While us kids are all grown adults now, my little sisters have kids, and my cousins are all known to take full advantage of my mom's offers to help with their kids too. The woman practically runs her own day care around here. Something I know she loves, but I can't imagine it's been easy with my grandmother's health going from stable to a quick and steep decline these past few weeks.

My mom's now on my tail in the kitchen. Says, "Well let me make you something then," and I damn near tackle her to push her out of the space.

"Take a goddamn seat and relax. You've barely left that room," I say, pointing to the in-law suite around the corner where two of my aunts are sitting with Mama Zabel, "and I know those tiny little bird bones popping out of you aren't because you've been hitting the gym too hard." I raise an eyebrow at her and dare her to continue to fight me.

"Fine," is all she says, but she cracks the slightest of smiles. She takes a seat at the raised counter, and I allow myself to relax.

I get busy, pulling out some peppers and onions, a cutting board, a knife that makes me wince. I can at least scrounge together something basic with the chunk of frozen ground turkey I stumbled across. It'll have to do.

I get to work, chopping and taking in the state of the kitchen. Piles of who knows what in the corners, crumbs scattering the counter tops, a half full pot of coffee, and a sink full of dishes that look days old. This is not my mother's usual kitchen.

I try and lighten the mood a bit. "So you think Mama Z wants a personal concert from Ruby or what?"

Music to my ears, I do actually get a little laugh from her out of that one. "I wouldn't put it past her."

"Maybe I should arrange for a band. I bet the high school marching band would lend us a few members. I know the director there."

"Naturally."

"Who doesn't love a steady drum cadence and white gloves?"

"I'm starting to worry you're not joking."

"Good," I say. "Because Mama Z would love a parade."

My mom exhales a sad little huff of a chuckle. "You're right. She would."

"Seriously though," I say. "What do you think the Ruby request is all about?"

While I can't blame my grandmother for wanting to see Ruby, (Ruby has that kind of quality about her that just draws you in), it does seem odd. See, she and I were only seriously together for a little while, three years ago. A hot and heavy summer which ended with her getting her big break. Late September, a guy walks into my restaurant—except he wasn't just any guy, he happens to be a famous rockstar. He sees Ruby performing and boom—Ruby's discovered. Go figure. Her career catapulted, she moved to LA, and we spent the next two years back and forth, pretending we weren't together but falling into a familiar rhythm any time she was back in town.

Until last year, that is. Let's just say, things didn't exactly end well.

"Mama Z has her reasons," my mother says, to my surprise. I pause my chopping and look back at her. She has that distant look on her face again.

"She does?" I ask, incredulous. "You say that like you expected this request."

My mother turns to face me again. Gives me a look so direct, I'm caught off guard. "I did expect it."

"Huh? You *expected* Mama Z to ask for Ruby? Why?"

"Your oil is burning," she says, waving a hand at the stove. I look back at it and quickly lower the burner before lifting the chopping board. I scrape the onions down the slide and into the pan.

She continues. "I think she has a few wrongs that she'd like to right."

"Okayyy. Interesting given that Mama Z is barely even talking now. And how does Ruby play into this anyway?" I ask. I shake the pan around before looking back at my mom, still perched in her seat. But she remains silent. "I mean, I know they got along well, but I gotta be honest, I was kind of surprised when Grayson didn't even hesitate to say Ruby'd be here tomorrow. She's mid tour, things must be insane for her right now."

My mom tilts her head side to side. "Chart-topping Billboard hits will do that for you."

I try not to cry out in horror as I throw the chunk of ground turkey into the frying pan. This is all wrong, everything feels off right now.

As if on cue, I hear a theatrical sob come out of the in-law suite. I know the old bird didn't croak yet, so I'm guessing these are the excessively dramatic cries of my aunts. I point to the stove. "Watch that," I say to my mom as I round the corner and throw open the door.

I take in the scene. My aunts Ani and Malia are hysterically crying with one another. I keep my hand held on the doorknob but throw them a glare. Whisper, "Will you two get your shit together?" I nod my head towards the hospital bed where my grandmother continues with her steady, slow breaths. "She can hear you. She'd be furious seeing you react like this. Make her laugh for Christ's sake, and stop crying like idiots."

And hand to God, I swear I hear the whisper of *"thank you,"* in Mama Z's voice, and I'm suddenly covered in goosebumps. I look back at the bed, at her face and open mouth, but she's in the same position. A sleeping beauty, knocking on death's door, but still here in the flesh.

I step back out in the hallway and slam the door shut behind me with more force than I really meant. Lean my head back against the closed door and try and get ahold of my spinning thoughts. I'm pissed at my aunts for being conveniently absent these past few months, yet now having the audacity to sit here sobbing like babies, which their mother would *despise*. I'm sick at the thought of my mom being run into the ground with caring for her mom all on her own.

But most of all, I'm confused as fuck at this whole Ruby thing. No clue what's going on there.

Look, I admit, I'm pretty damn thrilled to have this excuse to see her. Not gonna lie. I'm half pinching myself wondering if she really will come through. She's a good person, and I'm sure in different circumstances, if she weren't caught up in the midst of fame and finally living out her dreams, she wouldn't give it a second thought.

But she's living a different life now. The one she was always meant to live.

And it's not only that. You see, the famous Ruby Francesca, the lost love Lila was so on point with calling me out on, the one person my *dying* grandmother wants to see (which I still don't understand), well—

She hates me. That's right, Ruby hates me. Spit in my face, in fact, the last time she saw me.

And she had every right to.

five

. . .

ruby

YOU'D THINK IT would unsettle her, having news like that come in right before going on stage to a waiting crowd of fans. But not Ruby. Despite Joey's fear of disturbing her, Grayson was right to inform her of the call before the show. Hell, he probably even waited for that exact moment, which is why Grayson is absolutely everything in life to Ruby, and the perfect person for Ruby to have in her corner. He understands how she works, and how the gift of her music and emotion can combine to create a powerhouse of show-stopping perfection.

It's what makes her a star.

It wasn't always like this of course; this hasn't been her life for very long. An "overnight success," that's what they're calling her. But for Ruby, she's been a star her whole life, waiting for her moment.

But truth be told, for years Ruby held back. She quieted, and withdrew, always keeping her talents in a small, dark corner of the universe. On YouTube and SoundCloud, she shrouded herself in a mask, never revealing herself, never fully opening up the well inside her. Safely hidden. She told herself it was better that way, though looking back now, it's clear she was lying to herself.

She hadn't quite blossomed yet back then, she didn't hold the confidence to realize all she was capable of. All she needed to do was let the emotion open up and take over. And that's when it all came together—when her writing improved, her musicality reached a level no professors could ever teach. It's when she came alive.

So yes, she's glad Grayson gave her this news of Mama Zabel's request now, just as she's getting ready to join her band, walk on that stage, into the lights and into the echo chamber of electrified energy. Because that news is just the type of thing that gives her another level-up of sensation, which she'll allow to soar and shine as she connects with the crowd through her performance.

Together, Ruby and Grayson pound their way down the dark hall, the noise beyond increasing with each step.

"Tell him I'll be there tomorrow," Ruby tells Grayson.

"I already did," he says.

Ruby smiles. "Of course you did. Thank you," she says, pointing a finger to her cheek. Grayson responds as requested, closing in for an air cheek kiss next to her face, as they both know direct contact while all dolled up is off limits.

"Go take that, soak it in and kill it out there, love," Grayson says as Ruby nods.

She joins her band. They collectively bring their hands in for their pre-performance ritual, and she climbs the stairs to the awaiting darkness on stage beyond. Bodies blurt out updates, accolades, mic checks, what to watch for, what to expect, someone throws her mic at her. But she is laser focused now, on the music and her opening notes. Those first moments to connect with her crowd more important than most any other.

It's this moment right here that is her heartbeat of life. The moments before she sings her first notes. The crowd beyond, in the dark, chanting, begging for the song they expect to hear. It sets her soul on fire.

She steps to her first position. Armed and ready, mic in hand, an extension of her face.

She hums a few notes into her microphone and into the darkness, to land on the ears of the crowd beyond.

And the crowd quiets. The occasional cheer escapes, but largely they are silent in their anticipation of more from her voice. More from the shadow on stage.

Ruby repeats the tune...

Mmmm la hmmm la hmmm

The simmer of the snare drum is her only accompaniment at this point. The lyrics dance silently in her mind, swirling and fueling her emotion, but she only allows the hum to escape.

Louder this time.

Mmmm la hmmm la hmmm

Ruby is rewarded with excited whistles, pops of squeals from various points among the crowd. She feels the tingle on her skin in tandem with the rising energy contained within the confines of the theater.

And finally, it's time now—she allows her voice to release, to fully open up and be freed as she sings her first words. The song her fans know and love her for—"The Good-est of Girls." The lights turn to illuminate her and she's enveloped in the flame of them.

Ruby opens her eyes to greet her audience. She loses herself in the endless pockets of darkness dotted with glowing lights from phones swaying to the still subdued music.

A chill consumes her and her heartbeat increases. Though she's lost count of how many shows she has done nearing the last leg of this tour, she still relishes in the nerves of these exact first few moments. Before the dancing, before the music unleashes and she becomes ignited with the connection with her fans.

And the show begins.

six

. . .

mama z

WELL, BY NOW, something better be happening. Ruby had better be on her way. I need to hear her voice one last time. And I need something else, as well.

Though I must say I've rather been enjoying myself in this in-between state of existence. Good drugs will do that to you.

Because in my reality, you see, I am not on that God awful hospital bed, but instead I'm floating in a garden somewhere. Odd, as I've never been one for gardening, but here I am. I can deeply inhale and smell the lush greenery. There's that nurturing compo-nent to it—rich and warm as the scents of various blooms make their way through my nostrils. I float between rows and rows of tulips, reminding me of Holland. My husband and I lived there for a bit back in our teens, you know. We were two displaced, orphaned Armenians, tumbling through our childhood throughout post war Europe together. Trying to survive. Holland was our last home on that side of the ocean. Right before we both decided to take our chances, marry on a whim, hop on a boat across the Atlantic and sail our way to the good old lands of the United States of America.

Oh, and what do you know, looking down I realize I'm in one of my favorite cocktail dresses. How perfect! I had no idea I'd get to revisit my youth like this. I always loved this dress; I wore it originally back in the 60s.

To a certain gentleman's party.

A male suitor, you could say, though I shall never be able to tell you who. He's famous, even to this day, I'll go ahead and brag. But revealing his identity would be a sin, so get that out of your mind this instant. I'll never tell.

We were fantastic lovers, though. We'd long ago agreed that our affair would always be kept secret. We kept many secrets back then; we had to, given that he and I were both already married. And no, never to one another. He was good to me though, my Gentleman, as I shall refer to him for the sake of avoiding scandal.

But this *dress*! My God, I feel just as I had that night. I was a sexy siren, in my fitted, blood-red cocktail frock. A sleeveless boat neck top, cut to a deep V, with little rosettes at the top of the shoulder straps. I could barely walk in it, tight as it was. But I'd be damned to hide my glorious body in some A-line hag-gown nightmare like the other wives of my day. To hell with that.

How my husband let me out of the house that night, I'll never know. But I suppose we had an understanding, he and I, didn't we? Our marriage was one of convenience. A partner in crime with which to escape our tumultuous childhoods.

Well, that's how Artem spun it to me when I learned of his first affair.

Oh, I was mad as hell at first. *Crushed.* How could I have been so naive? I felt like a fool, thinking he and I had something special. Only to learn "special" was a rather flexible term for dear Artem.

But I buried down the pain. If Artem wanted to fool around, then two could play that game. I sure as hell wouldn't be the one left standing in the dust.

So yes, there I was at The Gentleman's home, at his party, by his own personal invite. I remember being thrilled, and I loved that he treated me no differently than anyone else. He ignored my accent, my too-tan skin that was neither white nor black. He was of Spanish decent himself, and so perhaps we had a little more in common than one might have imagined, him being the success he was, and me being a young immigrant trying to find her place in the world.

He looked so handsome though, in a tuxedo with a smile that could charm the brassiere right off any gal. He had this way of looking at me like he wanted to do exactly that. It was different than the way my husband looked at me.

Well, what do you know, the garden I was just surrounded by is now gone, and here I am back at that very party. And I have the sole attention of my tuxedo-clad charmer. Whisked away in a cozy corner. Sharing a cigarette and a head buzzing full of naughty dreams.

Suffice it to say if anyone was looking carefully enough, they'd see The Gentleman's hand up and between my legs, and see mine gripping the lapel of his suit jacket, our mouths mere inches away from one another. We had been bold that night. Blame the booze.

Knocking on death's door is not so bad after all, I suppose.

seven

. . .

ruby

"MY OH MY, this is gorgeous," Grayson notes with a whistle as their driver pulls up to the house.

"Mmm," is all Ruby can say, patting Rebel's back as he rests in her lap. There's a strange pit in her stomach, or maybe it's more like a little gremlin, gnawing its way from the inside out. *Damn that little ridiculous gremlin. Damn him and his insatiable hunger.*

Grayson scoffs dramatically. "That's all you have to say? Goodness, this is not exactly the Philly suburb house I was expecting. There's a fountain. And columns. I'm surprised there was no gate."

Ruby shrugs. "Joey's dad is a surgeon. Or was. I think he might be retired now? I can't remember." She frowns as she realizes this. There's a distance that happens when you become catapulted into an industry of entertainment. Basic things like the career status of those once in your world now become background noise, hushed and indiscernible.

She looks back up at the house—beautiful stone, encased by a garden of reds, pinks, and greens. Ruby notes with curiosity an overgrowth of weeds, in stark contrast to the impeccable garden of her memories. Her mind flashes back to an image of fireworks over the house. An end of the season Labor Day celebration three summers ago. Brilliant bursts of color lighting the sky, Joey and his father bursting with pride, amateur pyrotechnicians. She remembers how warm she felt that night, with this family that had wrapped Ruby up in their gregarious arms in just a few weeks.

Grayson turns to face Ruby. "Want me to go in with you?"

She shakes her head no. Nope, she knows she can do this. Last night she was in the company of thousands, all singing her songs right back to her. She's freakin' Ruby Francesca. She can handle this.

"Good, because death creeps me out," he says.

"You ready?" the driver asks her.

"No. But yes. But no, but yeah, go ahead," she replies, and the driver gets out to open Ruby's door. Ruby hands Rebel over to Grayson. "Wish me luck," she says to the pup, nuzzling his downy head.

Grayson grabs the dog and tucks him under his arm. He grabs Ruby's arm before she steps out. "Hey. You look hot," he says. He looks down at Rebel. "Mama looks hot, right, little one?" At this Ruby laughs, grateful for the comic relief Grayson always knows how to provide.

"Not too...dressed up?" she asks. She had felt panicked while getting dressed at the hotel. What do you wear to see your ex-boyfriend's dying grandmother on her deathbed? In the middle of June? Grayson had decided on a simple, white tunic-style dress, pointing out how it would contrast perfectly with her long, dark curls. Cut just above the knee, the dress cinched in at the waist with a brown leather belt. And Grayson insisted on her signature red lips.

"You're perfect, doll." He kissed her cheek. "We'll be just around the corner, waiting. Text me for an update and we'll go from there."

"Sweet cheeks, I'd be lost without you," Ruby says as she steps out and faces the house.

She remembers the first time Joey brought her here. It feels like a lifetime ago. He'd broken his way into Ruby's heart, and she couldn't help but fall in love with not just him, but his family. She'd met them all within a couple weeks. Caught off guard by the chaos of the household at first, she remembers how quickly she felt right at home.

And Mama Z. She had just moved in to the in-law suite of the house back then, and Joey seemed so happy and relieved at the arrangement. He told Ruby she'd meet his grandmother, and Ruby remembers being taken aback when she first laid eyes on the woman. Ruby had expected an old and fluffy lady, with a house-dress made of small florals, maybe a smear of flour on her face. The way her own grandmother had looked when she was alive.

But Mama Z was nobody's Gam Gam. Not at all. Instead, Ruby was introduced to a woman that looked more like an Armenian Jane Fonda than anything else. She exuded the energy of a fierce survivor with a history that fascinated Ruby. She had no idea at the time the impact Mama Z would go on to have on Ruby. The wisdom she would impart, the way she would teach Ruby how to scoop up all the shit she had encountered, and use it to fuel herself to propel her to the goals of her dreams. Most importantly, Mama Z taught Ruby she was nobody's victim.

She smiles at the memories of their talks, and prepares to take her first steps to the house. She is wondering whether to knock or ring the doorbell when the front door opens. A woman in black leggings and a black sweater too warm for the season steps out, arms wide and awaiting an embrace. Ruby warms at the sight of Isabella, Joey's mom.

"I can hardly believe it. You're here." A welcoming smile spreads across Isabella's face.

"Of course I am, there's no saying no to Mama Z," Ruby replies as she steps into Isabella's arms.

"You've lost weight," Isabella says.

"So have you," Ruby retorts.

"I'll warn you now, Joey has been on a mission to feed anyone he deems too thin."

At the sound of his name, Ruby's heart sinks. She was half hoping he'd have the courtesy to not be here. While Ruby has maintained contact with Isabella and Mama Z on and off over the past three years, she has had zero communication with Joey since last year.

Isabella grabs her hand and leads her inside. "Come on in. Are you thirsty or anything?"

"I'm fine, thank you."

"How much time do you have?" Isabella asks, and Ruby notes that the usually fierce Isabella looks a bit nervous herself. She gestures for Ruby to take a seat in the plush chairs of the living room.

"I have until the afternoon," she says, sitting in her chair, but remaining perched towards the front. "No show tonight, but performing tomorrow, then Baltimore, then a few other stops and then finished this leg of the tour."

"Are you exhausted?" Isabella asks, reaching a hand out to hold hers.

Ruby pauses, unsure how to answer. Until a smile slowly works its way across her face, and she shakes her head. "I...am...more and more energized with each and every show," she says, grinning now. "Just—I don't even know." She sits back in her chair, hand remaining in Isabella's. "It's wild. Absolutely wild. It's like this surreal dream when I'm performing. I'm on a cloud, I'm singing my heart out, dancing around with a confidence I never knew I had. Talking to the audience between songs, feeling like I'm surrounded by old friends. We're connecting, and they *cheer* and there's applause and I still find myself wanting to look behind my shoulder, sure they're cheering for someone behind me. But it's all for me. And I'm in shock."

"You come alive when you talk about it," Isabella notes. Ruby notices the initial nervousness she perceived now is gone. In its place, a motherly warmth. The only real motherly warmth Ruby has ever known, aside from her own late grandmother.

"I wish you could come see," Ruby says, the words surprising her as they spill out. She rushes to explain, "I know that's not possible right now, but..."

Isabella nods with understanding. "I will. When I can, I'll be front and center, if you'll have me."

Ruby leans forward in her chair, as if to share a secret. "Well you know, I'll have to talk to my people," she says with mock seriousness.

Isabella laughs. "I would expect nothing less. Good to see you in your element."

"I'm kidding, I'm kidding. But man I have had some fun messing with people, saying things like that. You'd be amazed how many people think I'm serious. Lots of fun to watch."

"You're a star. People aren't going to be sure how to handle you, what to expect. It's hard I imagine, if someone didn't know you before." Ruby can only nod at this, as the words are hitting pretty on point. "They see you as this entity now."

"And forget that I'm just a person like anyone else," Ruby finishes for Isabella.

"Well," a male voice interrupts, and Ruby looks up to see Joey leaning on a square column in the foyer, just outside the living room. "Not exactly like *anyone* else."

She's stunned for a moment at the sight of him, here in the same space as her. Typical Joey, poised in calm confidence. He's in jeans, a gray tee that says, "Not Today," and bare feet. His dark hair has grown out a bit and curls around his neck in a subtle flip. The early stages of a beard accompany his face, though she's never known him to have facial hair. She guesses it's due to a lack of time to shave. His dark jeans hang low on his hips, and she wonders if he still prefers to go bare, or if he's made a switch to wearing underwear of some sort. Her eyes instinctively drop to his crotch, and she catches herself and looks back up to meet his eyes.

"Meaning?" she asks, attempting to remain cool and collected.

He peels himself from the column to take a step closer, but remains just outside the space of the living room. Crosses his arms over his chest with a twitch of a rounded bicep. "Not everyone can do what you do, Ruby," he says. "Not everyone has your presence. It's magnetic."

Though his words are warm, there's not the slightest hint of Joey's usual sunny demeanor reflected on his face. His eyes remain dark and stern, unlike the smiles she remembers from him. He gives nothing away, and her head is screaming to want to know what he's thinking. Is the sight of her doing the same things to him that it's doing to her? Again, her eyes betray her, and she scans the length of his body. Down his jeans, to his bare feet, then back up again to his bronzed and corded forearms, his sculpted shoulders. His jawline remains square and sharp, in contrast to the softness of his eyes, his curly lashes. The dimples she knows are lying in wait beneath this cold facade.

Ruby remembers those dimples when they were reserved for her. She hates that she misses them.

"Such magnetic presence deserves a hug, at the very least," Isabella says, interrupting their moment.

Ruby looks back at her and realizes she had nearly forgotten she was here. "Right," she says, as she rises to her feet, legs a little wobbly.

Joey uncrosses his arms and moves towards Ruby and she tries to think where to place her arms in order to hug. She's petite, and their typical embrace would usually involve her arms around his waist. That seems inappropriate now, somehow.

Yet that's exactly what she does anyway.

She feels his arms wrap right back around her, like no time has passed. As if they are just the same two lovers with all the hope in the world ahead of them. She inhales and breathes in his familiar scent of fresh cotton. The feel of his back muscles beneath her palms stir up more than she'd like.

"I'm so glad you're here," he whispers, and she can feel the vibrations of his voice in his chest, beneath her cheek. It feels so comfortable, and she's consumed by the confusion of feeling so safe with someone who hurt her so badly.

On the other hand, that hurt helped her write one hell of an album.

eight

. . .

joey

FUCK, SHE FEELS so good in my arms it's insane. My Nightingale. I don't dare try and use my old nickname for her now, though. She'd probably kill me.

Her hair smells like strawberries. This is a lot harder than I thought it'd be. And she's even smaller than usual, which pisses me off. I wonder what's with the women in my world not taking care of themselves. This better not be some shit marketing scheme telling my Ruby she's gotta lose weight. Mine or not, she'll always be my girl and I'll fucking lose it on someone if they've made her feel less than perfect.

"Joey, you're squeezing me," she says beneath my grasp, and I snap out of myself and release her.

"Sorry, I just...why are you so small?" I pretty much shout at her.

"Joey!" my mother scolds. But I see her look at Ruby and smile. "See? I warned you."

"Warned what?" I ask. I don't like the look they're giving each other. Like they're in on something and I'm not.

"Don't worry about it," Ruby says with a mischievous look. She sucks in those pillowy lips of hers, pops them back out again and snaps those baby blues right at me. She has this wickedly innocent looking face with her button nose and full cheeks—yet I know the playful fire that's inside her. She's a work hard, play hard, kind of girl. And not in a partying kind of way, she barely drinks thanks to her alcoholic mother. But she's just *fun*. Silly fun. It's part of what made me fall for her in the first place.

"Ruby doesn't have all day, Joey. Want to go take her?" my mom prompts.

"Yeah, sure. Come on, she's in her room," I say to Ruby. I look down at her, and my usual spitfire gal looks a bit pale. "You alright?" I ask. I want to put my hand on her cheek, give her a comforting stroke like I would have before. But I know I don't have that right anymore. Instead I clench my fists by my side in an attempt to keep it together.

"What should I expect in there?" she asks.

I'm not sure how to answer her. I've gotten so used to the hospital bed, the machines, the aides constantly in there and the overall stench of disinfectants mixed with impending death. But I guess it would be jarring for anyone not used to it.

I try to answer as honestly as I can. "Like the queen is being locked up against her will, but she's going down with a fight."

It seems to work, and Ruby smiles. She shakes her head and says, "Perfect," and I lead her through the house and to the back.

We enter the room and I feel myself walking through it as if for the first time. I'm trying to see it through Ruby's eyes. Strange how the cloud of death feels thick in here, though I've not really noticed it until now. There's machines beeping, Mama Z laying under her favorite fuzzy red blanket. I notice someone put lipstick on her, and I look to my aunt Malia. Point to my own lips, then back to Mama Z in question.

"She said, 'lipstick,' so I put some on her," Aunt Malia shrugs, like it's the most natural thing in the world.

"Okay. Lipstick, huh? Mama Z, you're barely communicating, but lipstick is what you wanted?" I ask my all but lifeless grandmother.

"It's probably the dry lips," Ruby says. "When you're...you know," and she gestures in my grandmother's general direction, "your lips are dry from dehydration and open mouth breathing."

A groan escapes Mama Z's otherwise still body, and I'm left with another chill, the inner whisper of *"she gets it"* invading my skull.

Ruby steps right on up to my grandmother, and I watch in awe as she sits down on the edge of the bed. Grabs my grandmother's hand. So strange, just earlier today I was on my phone stealing glimpses of videos of Ruby. Interviews, performance clips, behind the scenes snapshots. And now she's here, in the flesh. The brightest light in this dreary room.

Ruby shifts herself and swings her legs up to tuck beneath her. "A little bird said the great Mama Z is about to make her grand entrance into the afterlife and happened to ask for me," she says. "So I'm here now, and gotta say, I'm pretty flattered."

I shoot a look to Aunt Malia, nod my head toward the door to signal to step out, give them some privacy. She rises and follows me. I hear Ruby continue talking to my grandmother, and I'm amazed at how natural and at ease she seems. It's like there's a whole connection there, and I'm getting the sense that there's more to the story than I realize.

Back out in the light of the day (that room feels like a cave), I drink in a big, deep breath. Aunt Malia looks at me all stunned-like.

"I can't believe she's *here*!" she whispers.

I frown at her. "Yeah. Neither can I, actually."

"You think she'd be okay if I ask to take her picture? Or should we take a picture of her in there with Mama?" There are stars in my aunt's eyes, and it's irritating. The woman is fifty something years old and looks like a deranged school girl fan that just met Barbie.

"She's mid-tour, Malia. I bet it took some convincing for her to even be here. Let her feel normal for a quick second, not have to showboat the whole affair."

She grabs her purse and keys from the kitchen counter. Gives me a look of raised eyebrows and judgment as she swings the purse over her shoulder. "Fine. I don't know how you ever let that girl go. Bet you're regretting that now."

Nope, not gonna fall for it. I'm keeping my cool. "You heading out?" is all I say.

"Yup, I have some errands to run and need to get my nails done."

Don't let the door hit you on the way out.

But instead I say, "Drive safely, Aunt Malia," in my most syrupy voice. Not that she catches the tone anyways. I hear her say a quick goodbye to my mother and out she goes.

I take a peek into Mama Z's room, confirm that Ruby seems to have a comfortable groove of one sided conversation going, and I walk out to rejoin my mother in the living room.

"She in there with her?" my mom asks, looking up from the magazine in her lap. She removes her reading glasses and puts them on her head.

"Yeah. And looking like a natural. Like she expected this." I shake my head. "I don't understand."

My mom just shrugs her shoulders. "They've been close."

"What?"

"You really don't know?" my mom asks me, and I feel like I walked into the wrong classroom or something. Lecture discussions going on all around me and I have no idea what anyone's talking about.

I pull my head back in surprise. "Don't know what? That Ruby, my Ruby that I barely even dated for more than a summer, and haven't spoken to in a year, that she's been, I don't know, *friends* with my grandmother?"

"Yes," my mom says with one firm nod. "Well, and me too, I

suppose. But apparently Mama Z and Ruby spoke even more frequently."

"About what?!" I'm dumbfounded.

My mom mindlessly grabs the glasses off her head and puts one arm in her mouth to bite. And then, unnervingly, she *smiles*. Like this is all funny and amusing or something.

"You got something to say?" I ask.

"Sweet boy, you can be such a people person, everyone's favorite guy, yet completely blind sometimes, can't you?"

Oh man, that hurts for some reason. It's like I'm missing something massive here, and I have no fucking clue what. I've been blindsided once or twice in my life before (e.g. the whole ex-girlfriend Reggie thing) and it's really a shitty feeling.

"Will you, or someone, please tell me what the fuck is going on?"

"Joey, the cursing!"

"Sorry," I mumble half-heartedly.

My mom sighs. "Look, they both have a love of music and are similar artistic spirits. Is it really that surprising?"

"But we broke up!" I don't know why I'm getting so riled up about this. It's like I'm jealous or something. Of my fucking grandmother having a connection to a girl that I chose to let go.

"So?" my mom says, eyebrow raised. "That means no one else was allowed to talk to her?"

"No, that's not what I mean. It's just weird, that's all."

"Joey, I don't know what exactly happened between you and Ruby, but if she still finds comfort in a little communication with a woman she adored, what's the problem?"

The problem is that it's communication that I'm not a part of. *I* want to be on the receiving end. *I* want to hear directly from my girl instead of being locked out and stuck with the information I get online.

"Nothing," I grumble, defeated.

My mom glances behind me. I turn around to see Ruby now

joining us. Looking like an angel in that white dress. Legs bare from the knees down. Hair curly and tempting and I just want to reach out and grab it to pull her close to me.

"Hi," is all she says.

My mom rises out of her chair. "Hi, Ruby. How'd it go in there?" she asks as she walks over to Ruby and grabs her hands.

"I love that woman so much," Ruby smiles. I watch them hug and once again, I feel like an outsider looking in.

"I'm pretty sure she loves you too."

Great. All this beautiful fucking love floating around that I'm not a part of.

"Thank you so much for coming, Ruby," my mom says. "I know you have to go. Is your car here?"

"Yeah, it is. Back at it!" I watch as Ruby gives my mom one final squeeze. "I'll be in touch, okay?" Ruby assures as she releases my mom.

They hug and cheek kiss, exchange a few other words and I'm just standing there like an idiot watching. My mom tells me to walk Ruby out, and then she vanishes, leaving just the two of us.

Me, Ruby, and my heart. An anchor in my chest, threatening to drown me.

nine

. . .

ruby

"I NEED TO see you again," he says, steely dark eyes looking down at her as he walks her out the front door and into the June heat. "Soon. When," he says with authority. A statement, not a question.

"Excuse me?" Ruby responds. "Need to see me again? Joey, last I recall, I was hardly a priority in your life, remember?"

"That was different. That was…"

"What, before I got to the level of fame I am now? Is that it?"

"No, what? That's not it—" Joey starts to say, but Ruby has had enough.

"—I'm sure, whatever. Look, a lot has changed in a year. You'd be amazed the random 'old friends,'" she says with air quotes, "I've had coming out of the woodwork, wanting to reconnect. But I expected a little better of you, Joseph Conti Jr."

"I'm not after your fame, Ruby. Shit. I more than *anyone* wanted this for you. Don't you know that? It's…" He stops and raises his arms up to the back of his head to grab his hair in fists. "Fuck!" He glances over to Ruby's waiting car, the back window rolling down revealing a sober looking Grayson. Rebel drapes his paws over the open window, tongue out and panting. Ruby can't help but smile at the sight of the two. The men in her life. The mismatched pair of her makeshift family-on-the-go.

Her constants.

"Hi there, Joey," Grayson says with a small wave. "Everything okay out there?" he asks.

"All good—" Ruby says.

"We're not done—" Joey says at the same time.

He drops his hands and turns back to her. He tentatively reaches toward her hands, brushes his fingertips against hers. She looks up at him and sees the question in his eyes. *Can I?* Without thinking, she grazes her fingers further along his, to his palms. She hates the natural comfort she feels.

Joey intertwines their fingers together, lifting their locked hands up and to his chest and pulling her closer. With their hands locked between their two bodies, she's amazed at how good it feels to slip right back into this kind of closeness with this man.

His hands are warm. There's a soft tenderness in his touch, in contrast to the roughness of his callused skin. The electric zing she once knew and loved from him zips through her. "Please," he says. There's a beautiful sincerity in his eyes that Ruby struggles to ignore. "Please, I can't...I want," he says, stumbling over his words. His eyes well with tears, and Ruby looks down past their clasped hands and to the ground below. She can't look in his eyes and see his sadness.

He's just sad over his grandmother. He's upset to lose Mama Z, she reminds herself.

"I know I hurt you, Ruby. And I don't deserve a chance to make it right, I know that. But, I just wish you knew how much I care about you."

She snaps her head up. "Care about me?" She breaks free of his grasp, welcomed anger taking the place of confused longing. "Oh please, that's rich, Joey. To say that you care about me seems odd."

"Odd or not, it's true. I do."

"Interesting, since when we last spoke, I seem to remember you telling me something along the lines of you don't love me, never have, and never will. Remember that?" She clasps her hands in front of her chest in a dramatic love-sick pose, joking, "Oh, imagine how I swooned at that," then drops her hands to her hips. "But now you care about me?"

Joey's eyes squeeze shut, hurt etched onto his face as a tear rolls down his cheek and into the stubble of his beard. He presses the heels of his hands into his eyes. "I didn't mean that," he says. "It was so fucking wrong, and this is all messed up."

"You're telling me."

"Listen to him, Ruby..."

Mama Z's voice whispers in Ruby's head. *"Trust me and listen to him."*

"Did you hear that?" Ruby says, eyebrows pinched together.

"Hear what?"

"Listen to him..."

"You don't hear anything?" Her eyes dart around in confusion.

"The, uh...the dog, you mean?" Joey says, looking over to a house down the street, and Ruby registers the sound of barking.

She looks up to the sky. "I'm exhausted, I think. I'm zapped and losing it. Clearly! I need to recharge before my next show." Her eyes drop back to meet Joey square in his. "Look. I came here today because I love your mom, and I love Mama Z. And she's an impressive old bird because she somehow picked now, while I'm in town for two freakin' days, to be on her deathbed asking for me. Yeah. So I came.

"But my connection to your family no longer includes you, Joey. You hear? I gave you a chance, remember? Against all my better judgment. I did. And I fell. Fucking. Hard. For you. Like an idiot."

"He loves you too..."

"And now I'm hearing things!" she shouts, raising her hands in the air. "What the fuck?!"

"Are you alright, love?" Grayson asks from the car. "Lots of cursing happening. You can't lose it yet, you know."

Joey takes a step closer to her, tenderness in his eyes. "Ruby, you okay?"

"Fine! Fine," she says, dropping her arms back to her side. "I have seven more cities, seven more shows and I'm going to focus my ass off on that. And then collapse for a while.

"Please keep me posted on Mama Z. Call Grayson and stay in touch with him." She looks over to the car and sees Grayson give a wave of acknowledgment.

"I will," Joey says. "I can't thank you enough for coming."

Ruby sighs. "If she holds out another two weeks, I'll be back. Alright? I want to visit my dad after the tour, so I'll be back."

As soon as the words slip out of her mouth, Ruby is both surprised, yet curiously relieved. And she swears she hears Mama Z tell her she'll hang on.

"You are something else," Ruby mutters under her breath. "Better be good."

"I didn't catch that, what?" Joey asks in confusion.

"Nothing," Ruby says, and she turns to walk to the car. "I need a nap. *Now*."

The driver hops out and opens the door just in time for Ruby to hop in. She scoops Rebel into her arms, needing his comforting softness and warmth. He situates in her lap, and Ruby looks up and out the window to see Joey standing there. All alone in the yard, next to the dominating fountain.

"You alright? That seemed like an odd bit of interaction at the end there," Grayson notes.

"Well, it was," is all Ruby can say. They drive away and she watches as Grayson turns around, giving one last wave to the distant figure of Joey.

ten

. . .

mama z

WELL, WELL, WELL. She came through. My little singing star, Ruby Francesca, came through.

I knew she would.

And yes, we had a good chat, she and I. My words are mostly limited to the sound waves beyond, but she heard them alright.

Now, I imagine you are wondering about all this nonsense. And you will understand soon enough, don't worry. These things take a little time to explain properly, you see. Have a little patience. I have some orders of business to get through before I can fully make my way to the other side.

You need to understand something here, so listen carefully. Ruby Francesca is a gem, through and through. Oh yes. It's a unique thing when someone holds the right combination of—well, it's hard to say, really.

What I'm referring to goes well beyond basic talent. It's so much more. Don't let Ruby fool you, she is a Rubik's Cube of perfect design. Complex and disorderly, downright *impossible* to most. But in the right hands, with the right knowledge and resources, the cube reveals itself to be a thing of pure genius and beauty.

And that is Ruby. But she and Joey are no longer together, I'm afraid.

It's amazing what we can learn when we look backwards, I always say. You would think lying on one's deathbed would grace you with numerous profound insights. Epiphanies and grand, new wisdoms.

And yet, the only wisdom I am finding is something I have always known, and that is the power we can have when we meet certain people. We are all unique souls in this world, moving around in our own directions like the dots on an air traffic control screen. Committed to getting to our next destination. Desperately trying to keep from crashing before arrival, only to find yet another destination, another goal taunting us again and again.

But there are a handful of people we will be lucky enough to meet in life that simply are *our people*. Fellow suffering souls, doing the best we can, yet with an uncanny ability to understand one another. When we stumble across them, we can find that their very presence in our lives helps us flourish. Their love breathes power into our otherwise weak bones, and we can achieve so much more simply due to their faith and acceptance of us, flaws and all. When we are tired and uncertain of ourselves, they can swoop in and be our strength for us. They teach us all we are capable of and aid us in reaching the destiny of our dreams.

I do believe that is what I was for Ruby.

Just as it was The Gentleman for me.

And now I need to make sure that Ruby can be that for Joey.

IT'S TIME YOU LEARN JUST a little bit more about The Gentleman. Judge all you want, but it seems he is floating into my consciousness non stop these last days here on earth. So there you have it. Nothing I can do about that, so we might as well have a little fun walking down memory lane.

Before I had my first daughter, Isabella, I was keeping myself busy working at a small local radio station. It was always music for me. Art and creative expression breathe life into everything, and when you've lived a hard life as I had in my early years, you get good at finding ways to cope through it.

Let me rephrase—you do if you're clever. Otherwise you get sent off to a loony bin, and no saying what happens in a prison like that.

So yes, I did all I could to surround myself with music. My husband Artem and I were dead broke when we first came to America. I was lucky to get the job at the station. I came bursting through the door like I owned the place, prepared to sell my talents of creative problem solving, bookkeeping, whatever they might need, but The Gentleman simply stopped and smiled at me. He was a charmer capable of melting the ice of any glacier. And my cold little heart needed some melting at the time, you see. Having no real home to speak of your whole life will do that to you.

It was late one evening when he first kissed me. He had recently landed an interview with one of the hot new bands of the time—I'll leave you to guess which one—and I imagine The Gentleman was feeling rather proud of himself. He was making fast gains within his career, and that momentum tends to bleed over into other areas of one's life.

We were alone one night at the station, as was often the case. He offered me a drink. Mind you, I rarely drank in those days. Could scarcely afford food and rent, let alone spend extra on a mind altering substance that tasted of the poison of death. Or rather, the garbage I had tried up to that point struck me as such.

But The Gentleman had a private stock of Scotch, and when I balked at his offer, he only smiled at me and told me to close my eyes. Well, I could not say no to that smile of his, now could I? So I obliged, and my heart skipped a beat as he grabbed my hand. He raised the glass in front of me, and I felt the ridges of crystal beneath my fingers and palm. He gently guided my hand with the glass to the spot under my nose. Instructed me to breathe in, pay attention to the smell.

I told him I smell the bullshit of a man that was up to no good, and I think he got a kick out of hearing me curse. He said I had good instincts, because his intentions were far from good. I said I didn't mind, that I never knew anyone to have truly good intentions anyway.

"Breathe, Zabel," he had said, redirecting my focus. I loved how he said my name, how he would stretch it out, like he could hear it as a chime. The "Zaaahhhh Beeellle" escaping his lips would sound like a bar of music. Then again, he had the instincts for great music. A Midas touch not of gold, but of a Siren spell to one's ear.

I listened to him, and inhaled as deeply as I could, taking in the scents beneath my nose.

"And?" he asked.

"Bullshit smells awfully delicious. Spicy," I said with a wicked grin, eyes still closed.

I delighted in hearing his frustrated groan. "You tempt me, Zabel," he said.

"As do you tempt me," I said.

He lowered the glass from under my nose to now be pressed against my bottom lip. Nudged it in a tilt, prompting me to take a sip. I braced myself for the bite of the liquid. But this bite was a welcome one. It swam in my mouth, a vibrant charge. An igniting flame. I swallowed and felt as the flush of warmth traveled down my throat, rolling its way to my belly. It spread to my arms and legs, a blanket of heat, leaving a tingle in its wake.

"And what do you taste?" he asked.

"Smoke," I said. "Vanilla."

"Mmm, like you and me."

"I'm the smoke and you the vanilla?" I asked with a smile as I opened my eyes. I was feeling brave at that point, and took another sip, one much too big.

"Careful now," he said as I swallowed with a cough. He took the glass from my hand and raised it to his own lips, draining it. He placed the glass down on the table beside us.

"What does your husband think of you working these late nights?" The Gentleman asked, the pupils of his eyes growing.

"Nothing. He works late anyhow," I said.

I did not know how much to share. Did not know if I should explain that Artem and I were friends more than lovers. That we had an arrangement, that he was content to run around on me and leave me to my own devices.

It's not that I didn't trust The Gentleman with this information. It was that I worried it would take away the appeal of me. The enchanting spell between us might be broken if he knew Artem couldn't care less who lay in my bed. We want what we cannot have, you know. And I wanted The Gentleman to feel as if he could not have me.

So that he would. So that he would find he *had* to have me, and therefore take me as a result of his pent up lust.

"He's a fool," The Gentleman said. "If you were mine, I would never let you out of my sight."

"If I were yours, if you said such words to me, you would never live to see the light of another day."

And with that he grabbed my rear, pulled me hard straight into him, and kissed me. Took the breath right out of me as his tongue parted my lips, slipped its way right past and beyond, into the depths of my mouth. Invading me.

His other hand yanked my blouse out of my skirt and snaked its way under, his hands pressed on the skin of my belly. I clung to his shirt, my fingertips still buzzing with the remnants of the Scotch. I wanted this man, this powerhouse of a man to enter into my body. I needed to know if he could give me real pleasure, pleasure that I had not yet experienced in my lovemaking with Artem. I wanted him to consume me completely.

It was not long before we were both naked, lying on the filthy floor right there in the station. Surrounded by buttons and gadgets and equipment, no mind to what was being broadcast or the consequence of our abandonment of the job. It was only the heat of our two bodies, pressed against one another that mattered.

I clawed at his back, arching my hips into him as he kissed my neck, my chest, brought my nipple to his mouth with exquisite force. I cried out in pleasure as his mouth explored every inch of my torso. It was as though he was insatiable for the taste of my skin.

And then his head was between my legs, and my eyes popped open in shock at the sensation of his mouth on my sex. His tongue slipped between and all around, firm in its devour of a part of my body now on fire with need. I cried out his name in ecstasy, squeezed my eyes shut as I focused on this exquisite new feeling, his mouth a force of its own, devouring me, my body merely an instrument at the mercy of his destruction.

Soon a quake between my legs threatened to undo me, my body trembling with this pleasure beyond belief. A drug of deliciousness like nothing I'd ever felt before. His mouth, my gift. My key. My answer to everything I had been missing so far in my hard life. The answer had been all right here between my legs, this whole time.

When my trembling had stilled, The Gentleman climbed back on top of me. Looked me in the eyes and said, "I'm going to make love to you, Zabel," and all I could do was nod, because the only other thing I could think of ever needing at that point, the only thing missing from my otherwise perfect bodily existence was to be filled by him.

He spread me apart when he did, his shaft so immense I thought I might split in half at the force. "Ah!" I had cried out, and he kissed my forehead and apologized. I could not imagine why on earth he was apologizing, as welcomed as the pain of him was inside of my body.

He told me I needed to relax if he was going to be able to fully enter me. I said, "You haven't yet?" and he laughed and told me no, that once I relax he'd keep pressing. So I did, and centimeter by delectable centimeter he pressed on, further into me. Eventually our bodies were pressed as tightly as they possibly could be. And he moved on top of me, my breasts pressed against his chest, my arms pushing against his back as I worked to allow him to consume me as fully as possible. His thrusts were everything I needed.

When he trembled on top of me, when I knew his seed had shot inside of me, no barrier between us to mask the sins of what we had done, I did not care. Not one bit. I felt only the satisfaction of our act, of a new pleasure I had never before experienced. I knew too that even if The Gentleman discarded me after having me, it did not matter. Because this act alone was enough to light a fire of life inside me that could carry me to my dying days. I felt that with all my heart.

Thankfully, that first night with me was not nearly enough for my Gentleman.

messy meet cute

. . .

3 years ago

snacks with oj

. . .

O. JONES MEETS NEW RESTAURANT OWNER J. CONTI

And the reviews are in! The Guilty Olive, one of the newest Philly restaurants proves to have "potential," one blogger raves.

Interview with owner Joseph Conti, by Octavia Jones.

O: What was the inspiration behind your restaurant?

J: Wanting to be my own boss.

O: Well, I guess that'll do the trick then.

J: Except no one warned me I'd really, really like being the boss.

O: You're wiggling those eyebrows pretty enthusiastically.

J: (laughs) Kidding, kidding. Let's see, the inspiration was the love of food, naturally, but also the love of hosting and entertaining.

O: I have heard you're known for being the life of the party.

J: Oh yeah? You must have good sources.

O: I do. So tell me, where does that party spirit come from?

J: Baby, I was born this way.

O: I have no doubt. So that's it, then? Just a natural entertainer?

J: That and my big and chaotic family. You know, the type where dinners are everything, we show love with food. I wanted to bring that spirit in along with my grandparents' roots. They're from Armenia originally, both orphans, and during their childhood they bounced around throughout Italy and Greece, so Mediterranean dishes were always at their dinner table.

O: And the plant-based focus?

J: In culinary school I learned a lot about the farming industry prioritizing animal feed and the strain that puts on the planet, that kind of thing. I was young and at the time had no idea that something like a cow had such an impact on emission outputs. It stuck with me. I started focusing on plant-based diets, and thankfully, that marries really well with Mediterranean foods.

O: And yet, you have beef on your menu.

J: Ah, you caught that, huh?

O: Well, it seems a little like a

half-hearted attempt. Why not go full fledged?

J: Greed, Octavia. Greed. I still want to make money.

O: You don't strike me as ruthless enough.

J: Should I be insulted? Or was that a compliment?

O: There go those eyebrows again. No, not insulted. It's a compliment.

J: Why thank you, darlin'. No, I don't really consider myself money hungry. Just don't want to go under and cost my employees their jobs, that's all. Trying to cater the menu to a variety of tastes seemed like the smarter move.

O: Can't argue with that. But I have to say, having burgers on the menu seems like a cop-out.

J: What's your favorite fruit?

O: Huh? My favorite fruit?

J: Yeah. Name one, what's your favorite?

O: Oh, I don't know. Strawberries.

J: Strawberries. Nice. Okay, so imagine this…a fresh batch of locally grown strawberries, beads of water glistening on them, begging to be enjoyed. Turn it into a compote. Some rose water and mint, delighting the senses. The compote is spooned over roasted veggies, eggplant and caramelized onions. Punctuated by tart labneh cheese dollops. The flavors lit up by the touch of sweetness from the compote. You place this on crisp endive petals with a gorgeous mint leaf garnish. Accompany it with a rustic barley bread and voila! Pure magic.

O: Uh-huh. Sounds like you should have my job. Sounds incredible.

J: It does and it is.

O: And?

J: Octavia, darlin'. Now tell me you still have any interest in the damn burger on the menu.

eleven

. . .

ruby

ANOTHER SONG FORMS in her mind, and she struggles to remain focused.

It isn't easy when you're stuck, stuck, stuck
It isn't easy when all you can say is fuck

Maybe it's the clanging of the keyboard happening next to her that's getting under her skin. After a while, she found that you get used to the banging, the abuse of such a beautiful instrument. You learn to tune it out, dig deep and tell yourself that you love music, you love kids, you love your job. She was reminding herself that she loves getting *paid* to do her job. And by extension, she was teaching herself to love the horrific sounds elicited by the horrific hands of the kid sitting in her living room.

Ruby was pretty sure her dad was a freakin' saint to endure this in his home. She could only hope his office walls are thick enough to muffle the product of the kid's relentless attack. She looks down at Rebel and thinks that now is one of the rare times where his minimal hearing is a beautiful gift.

With some effort, she allows a smile to work its way across her face as Ruby looks at the little boy sitting at her piano bench. "It's sounding really awesome, Miles," she says. "Keep it light, though. Remember to lift your wrists." She gently helps readjust his hands and posture, then winces as he quickly drops the weight of his hands right back to where they had been. *At least he's trying,* she thinks.

Ruby would be lying if she said she loved teaching private music lessons to tone deaf little kids whose parents insisted on raising a piano player. Probably to try and live out their own failed dreams. Even though the kid has zero actual interest or musicality. Sure, she's stumbled across the rare kid or two that picks it up with a natural grace, but there's a price to pay for those far more fun lessons, and it turns out that price is a zillion excruciating ones in between. There are moments Ruby worries she herself might lose her own ears if she keeps this up.

A quick glance at the clock and she's rewarded with the confirmation that the lesson time is up. She tells Miles so, but all he can say is, "When do we get to play fun stuff? This stuff's boring."

Never, kid. Give up the hope because with your lack of practice and, I don't know, talent, you're never going to be rocking it out with the fun stuff you want, she thinks to herself.

Instead of verbalizing that thought, Ruby remains professional and digs deep. She evokes her most compassionate smile and says, "Oh you're getting really close. I can feel it. You're getting better and better each week. We'll do cool things real soon."

With a depressed sigh, she walks Miles outside to where his mom is waiting in their car. Ruby stays standing in the doorway, praying the mom doesn't want to talk to her.

Aaand the driver's side window rolls down. *Fucking, great,* she thinks. Unfortunately she doesn't have another lesson afterwards to conveniently walk up and save her from whatever Mama Dreamer possibly has to say.

"Ruby! Ruby, honey, can I talk to you?" the mom calls from her SUV. With mischievous intent, Ruby wonders how terrible it would be to smile real big, wave and turn around as if she didn't hear her. She could do that, right?

But then she remembers that she needs the money. As much as Ruby loves her father, she certainly has no intentions of living with him forever. It was humiliating enough for her to have to move back in a few weeks ago after graduating college. Twenty-two and living with her dad again. No thanks. She's given herself six months—six months of saving and planning with the intention of getting an apartment on her own.

And so she walks over to Mama Dreamer with her professional face on. Ruby decides to try her best to rush the conversation by selling her a dish of false hope. "I gotta say, Miles is really getting the hang of it," she says to the sunglasses clad woman sitting behind the wheel.

"He is? Oh, that's a relief. I'm so glad, I really can't thank you enough, Ruby. He seems to like you a lot."

"The feeling is mutual," she replies.

And it mostly is. While teaching wasn't her first choice, Ruby does in fact like kids, and Miles in particular. There's a sweetness to kids, a carefree spark that she both admires and envies. As an only child, she's always had a playfulness that was lost in a crowd of grownups. While mature for her age, she was often burning with spitfire energy ready to burst. Younger kids around her had gravitated towards her. A kind of hybrid between the adult world and kid world, and she liked the role.

But she's also itching to play some *real* music. Teaching lessons has a way of making Ruby starved for it.

"Okay, well see you next week," she says to the mom, attempting to shut the conversation down.

But no such luck, apparently. Mama Dreamer waves a diamond adorned hand in Ruby's direction. "Wait, honey. Just one more thing."

Ruby attempts to hide her annoyance. Please the customer.

The mom seems completely unaware of the fact that she's

eating into Ruby's coveted personal time. "You see, his sister has a birthday party in a couple weeks and I was really hoping Miles could show off his skills by learning the happy birthday song. Any chance you two could work on that?"

"I don't want to learn that song! I wanna do something fun," Miles chimes in from his booster seat in the back.

I got you, kid. Don't worry. "As fun as that sounds," she says as calmly as she can, "there's actually some big jumps in the birthday song, so it's a bit advanced for where we are at this point."

"Jumps?" the mom asks, saucer-like sunglasses hiding what Ruby imagines is disappointment. For some reason the fact that she has left the damn things on while talking to her pisses Ruby off.

"Yeah. As in, the notes aren't all close together, so he'd have to change hand positions, and the geography on the keyboard can be a bit hard to master so early on in his musical career." Her use of the word "career" was a bit of her own little joke, but the mom doesn't seem to catch that.

"Oh, I see. Well is there a way you could alter it or something? Like an easier version he could do?"

Ruby smiles at Miles' protests, trying not to full fledged laugh out loud, and she reassures his mom that she'll try and figure out something. It seems to appease her, thankfully, and she and Miles roll away down the street.

Which means Ruby can finally go do what she wants to do. And that's not just play, but *perform*. Thankfully, that's exactly what's on the agenda for tonight.

twelve

. . .

joey

I LOOK AROUND my surroundings and think about the difference from this dive bar and my restaurant. My baby, The Guilty Olive, is a dream I've had for most of my life, and one I fulfilled just a few months ago. It's fantastic with its Mediterranean-style city flair, and I'm not above bragging about it.

But this spot out here on the patio feels homey too, in a way, with its standard fries and burgers. And shit, for all my love of cooking and the art of fine foods, I'm not too good for the classic dive bar scene. So here I am, looking around, and I'm kind of turning my wheels on a gastro pub concept for my next restaurant. Yeah, could be cool.

"Jesus, you just opened your place a few months ago," my uncle Xavier says as I share my thoughts.

I grin at him because I see the panic in his face. "Exactly. I did it. It's a success, and so now what's stopping me from doing it again," I say, slapping him on the shoulder.

"Capital?" he fires back.

I wave him off. "Nah, I'll figure it out. A little creativity and these things have a way of turning out just the way you need."

He shakes his head and sips his drink.

"You're one of those guys, aren't you?" our friend Justin says.

"What guys?" I ask.

"The guys where shit just works out for you."

I dramatically place a hand on my heart. "Gentleman, I'm surrounded by pessimists, it breaks my soul and spirit," I say. "You all just need to have a little faith, a little optimism," I wave my hands gesturing to the space around us, "and the world too can be your oyster." I love messing with them, I know they both think I'm nuts, but I'm telling you. You gotta be able to manifest what you want. That's what it's all about.

I mean here I am, turning twenty-nine today. But I don't feel a day older than sixteen, and I don't plan on ever changing that. Life's good. Real good.

"Well, it's a small world, shit," my uncle Xavier says. I follow his gaze across the restaurant patio to a table with a lone guy, sipping a beer. A little older than Xavier, I'd guess. This guy is a trim and fit early-fifties maybe? Casually dressed, but he doesn't look familiar to me.

"What, you know him?" I ask, nodding my head in the guy's direction.

"If it's who I think it is, yes. Dom Francesca, was an Air Force guy." Xavier was in the Army for twenty-one years.

"Nice! You could use another old man friend." I'm partially joking on the "old" part, since Xavier is only twelve years older than me. But I really would love to see Xavier reconnect with some friends of his own. Since he retired from the Army and moved back home, I don't think he's really done much socializing beyond our family circle and my friends. "Go say hi, see if that's him," I urge.

"I don't know, it's been too many years. Doubt he'd remember me," Xavier says. My uncle's not exactly the rubbing elbows and making your acquaintance type. He's more an earn his trust and then maybe we'll talk, kind of guy.

"No problem, I'll go find out," I say, rising out of my chair.

"Joey, don't—" Xavier starts, but I'm already out of my seat and halfway across the patio. I side-step my way between a couple tables and chairs before pausing in front of the man in question.

"Excuse my interruption, but you wouldn't happen to be the notorious Dom Francesca, would you?" I ask.

The man looks up at me, eyes all friendly and I'm already glad I approached him. He nods towards Xavier and says, "I don't know who you are, but I'm guessing that is in fact Xavier Derian then?"

"Sure is, he recognized you right away," I say. "Didn't want to be rude and interrupt your evening though." I look back towards Xavier, cup my hands around my mouth and yell, "Dom recognized you too!" I'm met with a glare since I know Xavier hates that I just shouted that across the crowd of diners. God, I love embarrassing him.

I return my attention back towards Dom and offer for him to join us at our table.

"Oh, that's okay," he says. "I'm just waiting to see my daughter, she's up there getting ready to play." Dom points in the direction of the small stage up ahead.

I look up to see the back of the head of a dark haired woman in a baggy tee and cutoff jean shorts, crouched down, unzipping a guitar case. "Nice, here with the band then! So does your daughter get her musical talents from you?" I ask. I'm not particularly interested, I just want to see my uncle reconnect with an old friend, and I know he needs a little help with that kind of thing.

"Not me, her grandmother had pipes on her though. And Ruby—that's my daughter—she's always had a knack for music. Just graduated from Temple, working to be a music teacher in the fall, hopefully," Dom says. "Though I'm still holding out hope she'll make it big. She does cover songs at these little gigs, but she's written probably a hundred songs of her own."

"No shit?"

"Oh yeah. Maybe more. Ruby wrote her first one at just six years old."

"Well how 'bout that," I say. "Just tell her with a little faith and optimism, the world can be her oyster." I laugh to myself at my own little inside joke. Life is good.

I look over to watch as Xavier makes his way over to us. *Good*, I think to myself. This is good for him. Dom rises to shake his hand. "Hey, old friend! Looking good, you're clearly with me in the retirement stage of your military career," he notes, pointing to Xavier's long hair and beard. "Like the 'do."

Xavier runs his hand over his head with a quick tug on the messy bun-thing at the nape of his neck. "Turns out, not having to get your haircut every six weeks saves a lot of time," he says. I look at him with amusement. I think that might be actual warmth on his face for his old friend Dom here.

"I guess I do remember you saying you were also from the Philly area," Dom says.

Xavier looks over to me. "Dom and I crossed paths from time to time over the years. He was one of the good ones."

I grin. "Well, that's saying something, my uncle doesn't like anyone," I tease. I reach out a hand to Dom. "Hey, I'm Joey, by the way."

"Nice to meet you, Joey."

"Seriously though, come join our table. We have a better view of the stage anyways."

"Alright, what the hell," he says. I'm all grins, loving my birthday so far already.

NOW LISTEN, MY CREATIVE TALENTS may be pretty firmly fixed within the kitchen, but as I'm sitting here listening to Dom's daughter Ruby sing her little heart out, I gotta say. I'm in awe. She's got a voice on her, and she's bravely sitting up there all by herself, in front of the patio guests here at the Moon Lounge. It's impressive.

Her eyes are closed, she's lost in the music and her voice is carrying through the space like raw honey. It's scratchy and smooth all at the same time. Her sound is distinct, and I'm mesmerized by it. I don't know if it's the birthday shots, the warm July heat, or Ruby herself but I'm a little hot and bothered.

Of course also screwed now, if this is Xavier's friend's daughter. That might complicate any chance of me trying to get to know this girl if he's the "hands off my daughter" kind of guy. I'll just have to put a pin in that idea and see if I can earn the good dad's favor.

"Hey, birthday boy. Sorry we're late," says Reggie as she walks in with our mutual childhood friend Lucy and Lucy's sister Lila.

"Happy birthday, Joey," Lucy says, kissing my cheek. "Last year of our twenties, better make it count." She hands me a small gift, says it's from both her and Reggie.

"Ladies, too kind. Not necessary though."

"Good, because I brought nothing," Lila jokes.

I wave her off. "Perfect, because I'm not sure I've ever gotten you a gift either."

Xavier introduces Dom to Lucy and Lila, then introduces Reggie as his fiancé, and I try to ignore that their relationship still sits a little weird for me. Guessing that'll never really go away, seeing how it's been over a year since the whole thing went down. It was the fall before last when Reggie broke my heart and proceeded to run into the arms of my uncle.

I shake off the thought—all in the past now—and focus on unwrapping my gift. A framed photo reveals itself, and I laugh as I stare down at a shot of me, Reggie, and Lucy as kids. We're probably eight or nine in the photo, on the front steps of someone's house, eating watermelon. "Where the hell did you find this?" I ask.

"I know, right?" Reggie says. "She gave me one too, I couldn't believe it when I saw it."

The three of us grew up in the same neighborhood together.

Reggie, I could have sworn, was destined to be the great love of my life, and we did date for a while there. Until good old Uncle Xavier turned out to be more the apple of her eye than me. You can take a guess the scandal that it was when he came back to town after retiring, and somehow stole Reggie's heart right out from under me. Twelve year age gap between them and all.

Water under the bridge now. Family comes first, and nothing is worth wrecking those bonds, I remind myself. My mom would have my ass if I ever forgot that and let my pride get in the way. And I gotta say, hard as it is to admit, Reggie and Xavier seem good together. Don't feel too bad for me though, 'cuz I've learned the single and dating life is pretty damn perfect for me.

Still, I love to tease the two of them any chance I get.

I look down at the photo, say, "Well, if it isn't me, Lucy, and my aunt Reggie. How sweet!"

Reggie covers her face with her hands, a look of stress I recognize well. "Fuck...Off." She looks back up at me, determination in her eyes. "You are *not* to call me that, Joey," she says, gaze held firmly on me and I'm reminded of being a kid in school, in trouble for some offense I swear I never meant to commit.

"But soon that's exactly what you'll be," I say, all devilish smiles as I watch the blush creep up her neck.

Xavier's shooting me a look that I know he's trying to make look mean, but ultimately I've always been his favorite nephew. He can't be mad at me. He shakes his head with a poker face, radio silent, and I'm satisfied.

"One of the many reasons we're eloping," Xavier mutters.

"Like hell you are. Mom would never let you marry without the family," I say.

"Try me."

"The family will be invited," Reggie says, putting a hand over Xavier's hand while giving him a look that I'm guessing is a bit of a warning, though in a way it looks like it softens him. Not sure I've seen Xavier with that kind of look on his face. I can't place it—happy, I guess?

It's funny to watch them interact. I mean look, a piece of my heart will always belong to Reggie, it's true. I'd be lying if I said it didn't still hurt. You don't just pop right out of a love that dates back to your childhood. I mean, I can sit here and still strip off her clothes in my mind, imagine every curvy inch of her body with perfect accuracy, a body that was once mine, and I'm guessing that'll never change.

But I'm not the type to wallow in self pity. It does no good. Mistakes be damned. And they're happy, I can see that.

And like I said, the single life has been real fun for me. Like, *real* real fun. Didn't even know what I was missing. Turns out I'm not a romantic—I'm the dating type, no strings attached—who knew?

But now I'm thinking about that voice crooning away in the background and my eyes are drawn up to the stage where Ruby quietly plays. I know I've seen her perform before. Garden Springs, PA is a pretty small town on the outskirts of Philly. You get to know the local usuals. I wonder why I hadn't ever paid more attention.

I gently elbow Reggie's arm. "Hey, you know Ruby, right? She's done open mic night when you've done poetry readings, hasn't she?"

Reggie furrows her brows together. "Know of her, yeah, but we never really hung out. She's a little younger than us."

"Dom here is actually her dad," I say, pointing towards Dom.

"No way, I love that! Ruby's your daughter?" she confirms to Dom.

"Yeah, my one and only," he says.

"I can see it now, she looks a little like you. The blue eyes, dark hair," Reggie says.

"The girl can sing," Lucy notes, an impressed look on her face. "What's she doing here?"

Dom keeps his gaze on the stage, but shakes his head slowly. "Don't I know it," he says. "Talent like that, you'd have no idea she has stage fright, would you?"

"Stage fright?" I ask. "But she's up there now, isn't she?"

Dom nods. "She says if she's doing cover songs, it's easier. But she refuses to do her own."

Huh. I look back to the stage, now even more intrigued. I zero in on Ruby's face, partially blocked by the dark curls spilling over. Her eyes remain closed, and I'm suddenly feeling pretty damn curious to see those allegedly blue eyes for myself. Her lips are a full, ruby red and I think how perfect her name is. Button nose. She's a tiny little thing from what I can tell, slim and narrow, hiding in an oversized shirt. My dirty mind wanders, and I can't help but feel curious to know if she's clean shaved. Or maybe there's a little landing strip, that'd be fun. I find myself wanting to run my fingers up the exposed skin of her legs, slip under the hem of those jean shorts and explore. Oh yeah.

But that *voice*. It's something to hear, that's for sure. Seems too big for such a little body. I've always had my own love of all things music and can actually belt out a halfway decent number or two. Give me a couple lines of Panic! At The Disco's "Death of a Bache- lor" and I'm going to give you a decent show. Nothing to write home about, but I can make it work.

Ruby, though. I mean, there's no real describing it. I scan around the room and notice most people aren't even really listen- ing. It kind of pisses me off, what the fuck is wrong with people? She's got a real gift and no one even seems to hear it. Guess they're all tone deaf.

"You're looking uncharacteristically grumpy, Joey." Lucy's long arm stretches out and nudges my elbow.

"What? Am not."

"Birthday blues?" Lucy pulls her dark hair behind her ear. She's got one of those looks that's always sort of shiny and perfect, never a thing about her out of place. She and Reggie have both always been kind of polished like that, though Reggie's got more the wild and wavy hair that I like.

But I'm thinking I like dark curls even more, and I can't help but glance back up at the stage.

"Wait a sec," Reggie says. "All of this Ruby talk, your gaze glued to that stage, might I be seeing stars in your eyes?"

"Ruby the singer?" Lila asks, pointing to the stage. "You into her?" she asks, and I catch the littlest bit of disbelief in her tone.

"He looks more mad than smitten," Lucy says.

"Oh but that's the thing. Joey's never mad," Reggie teases.

Lucy joins right along in the fun. "My gosh, you're right, Redge. Smiles For Days Joey *does* do the grumpy look when he's smitten."

"Huh," Lila says with a shrug, crossing her arms and looking back up to Ruby.

I keep my gaze firm as I look back at them. "Merely calculating, ladies." I look back over to Dom, and clear my throat to interrupt the guys' conversation. Turn on my smile and charm.

"Dom, I hope you don't mind me asking, but your daughter wouldn't happen to be single, would she?"

thirteen

. . .

ruby

S HE HAD BEEN curious about the medley of table mates her dad had acquired while she was on stage. Always the supporter, her dad was there to see her, though she told him it's nothing exciting. Ruby had been doing little gigs here for years, since before she could even drink (though drinking's never been her thing anyways). Grayson, her friend from college, might join her now and again. Overall though, it's a pretty chill affair. Considering her dad is a single, retired guy with a lot of down time, he naturally insists on going to her gigs whenever he can.

It actually warms her heart. As a military brat having lived all over the world, Ruby's not one to have a major collection of friends. The closest thing she has to a best friend is Grayson. Also a recently graduated music major, Grayson has the unique quality of being, well—*decent* as opposed to being a competitive ass like many of the other students.

She sneaks out back to the parking lot to pack up her gear in her hatchback before heading back in to find her dad. She's not really in the mood for being social though, so she hopes he doesn't insist on staying much longer. Truth be told, she's itching to get home and write. Maybe pour some tea, take a hot bath, and let the creative juices flow. Playing gigs like this usually sparks that for her.

Ruby pops open her trunk and tucks her guitar in before noting the unwelcome sounds of footsteps behind her. She's suddenly aware of how alone she is in the parking lot, how vulnerable. She regrets parking in a secluded spot, away from any other vehicles. The hair on the back of her neck stands as the volume of the footsteps rises. Each step indicating proximity, closer and closer to her.

Too close for comfort. Why is this person walking towards her? She contemplates what to do. Is this person a threat? She wonders if she's being paranoid, but finds herself reaching for the random flashlight in her trunk she knows is floating around. Just in case. *This could work as a weapon*, she thinks to herself. Ruby has always been nothing if not resourceful. She braces herself, preparing to spin around, hoping to catch the intruder off guard.

"Can I help you with that?" a male voice says, cutting through the air and Ruby startles at the unexpected vibration of his voice. On impulse, she clocks him upside the head with her makeshift weapon.

"Fucking Christ!" the man yells, grabbing his face and bending at the waist.

Her heart is beating at a thousand thumps per minute as she looks down at her victim. "Stay the fuck away from me," she says, hoping her voice comes off as terrifying, strong, and in control.

The man backs up, covering his now bleeding temple that sports a cut just above his right eyebrow. "Ruby, my God. I'm sorry, shit."

"I don't need any fucking stalkers, so I'll say it again. Stay the fuck away from me, you hear me?"

To her relief, the man continues to back away from her, but she's still unsure what to do next. Should she get in the car and drive away? She can't run back inside or she'll have to pass the stalker. Her phone's in her back pocket; she could call 911.

But then she recognizes the man's shirt. It's an alarming orange color that jogs her memory—it was the shirt on one of the guys from the table where her dad had moved to at the Moon Lounge patio.

"Are you a threat?" she asks him, now unsure.

"You sure as fuck seem to think so. And if I was, do you think I'd actually admit it?" he points out, rising to a stand.

"What I mean is," she stammers, "I think I saw you sitting with my dad."

He drops his hand, revealing his face. Yes. Definitely the guy. He speaks slowly and calmly. "Hi. Yes. Hi." He puts his arms and hands out to his side in the "I'm cool" gesture of innocence. "Let me explain. I'm Joey. My uncle and your dad used to be in the military together. We ran into your dad and were sitting with him." He slowly nods, as if trying not to scare off a wounded animal. "Okay? I'm not sure why you felt like I was—what was it you said?"

"Stalking me."

"Right. Stalking you. But," the alleged Joey moves his hand over to his chest, covering his heart, "I really thought you heard me tell you to wait up, so I could help you carry your stuff out."

Did she hear that? She vaguely recalls someone calling after her, though Ruby gets so caught up in the zone of thinking about her performance after she's done, she tends to tune out the world.

"Oh," is all she can say.

Joey raises his eyebrows in a look of complete and total apology, says, "I am so, so sorry I scared you. Shit, I was really just hoping to make a good impression on you and help you carry your things out here, that's all." He shoots his thumb back towards the Moon Lounge. "I told your dad I'd give you a hand."

Ruby sucks in a deep breath, holds it for a moment. She takes another look at the bleeding wound above his eyebrow. She leans back to perch on the edge of her hatchback, the trunk still open. "I see."

"You see? Does that mean we're cool?" He has a look of both question and maybe a little amusement on his face.

"For now." She crosses her arms over her chest. "But don't go sneaking up on girls in parking lots, maybe."

He smiles with relief. "Noted. Definitely was going for more good-guy helping out than actual stalker, but noted." Joey brings a hand back up to his cut. "Nice defenses though."

"Thanks."

"You're welcome?" he asks tentatively with a look of uncertainty. He clears his throat. "Right, well I think I better get inside and take a look at the damage here."

Ruby stands back up, satisfied in trusting that he's not a threat after all. She closes her trunk and grabs the keys out of her pocket. Locks the door and starts walking back, passing the immobile Joey. After a moment, she hears his footsteps on the pavement.

"Hey, wait up," Joey calls after her.

"For what?" she says over her shoulder. He's jogging to catch up to her.

"For...well hell, now I don't know. Who are you? I mean I know who you are, but why are you so—"

"So what?" she snaps before he can finish his sentence. *This guy is not seeming to get it.*

"Aloof."

"That a problem?"

"I mean, I guess not. Hey wait, seriously, stop for a sec," Joey says. He starts to reach out for her arm, but then thinks better and pulls it back.

Ruby stops, though, and puts one hand on her hip and gestures towards him with the other for him to say his piece. "Yes, Joey?"

He grins, like he finds something funny. "Look, I'm really a nice guy, I swear." She hates that he's grinning at her, though she can't say why. "Ask anyone in there, alright? I just wanted to come help you out. Introduce myself."

"Well you've done that. Nice to meet you, Joey."

"You don't say that like you mean it."

"Great to meet you Joey?" she says with question in her tone. A sliver of a smile escapes out of the corner of her mouth, despite herself. She quickly recovers and replaces it with what she hopes to be a stern and straight line of her lips.

"Ohhh, okay. No, I get it now. Hey, cool, alright."

"Get what?"

"You're, um. You're not into guys," he says.

"What makes you say that?"

"You know, like the whole, ummm..."

"Aloof thing?" she offers for him.

"Yeah."

"I see."

"So..." he starts. "Are you?"

Ruby stares at him, this Joey guy, and takes in his demeanor. The guy may not be getting the hint, but he's cute about it, she'll give him that.

She decides to have a little fun with him. Innocently places both hands behind her back, looks down at the ground and sways around a little. "Oh, I don't know. I mean if the right girl came my way, I doubt I'd say no."

"Right, okay," he nods, hand back up to cover his cut.

Ruby rolls her eyes. "Yes, I'm into guys. However I'd never pass up a chance with Taylor Swift. Always holding out hope for her."

"I'll keep that in mind. Watch out for the competition."

"It'd be no contest."

He clears his throat. "So to clarify, yes to guys? Just not...?"

"Just not," she waves in his general direction, "the 'let me help you with your things, because I'm so great' type of guys."

"Would it have been better if I just went straight for the stalking instead?"

She shrugs a shoulder. "Maybe, who knows." Ruby turns back around to head into the building. "You really should get that cut cleaned up, though."

"God, you're a fast walker for being so little," he says.

"I have to be. Too many people underestimate me. And I gotta stay one step ahead." *That could be a song,* she thinks.

"Well seriously, what can I do to start over, make a better impression, Ruby?"

She stops walking again. Turns to look at him. Ruby takes in his face, strong jaw, his chocolate brown eyes and curl of his lashes. His dimples steal the spotlight as he smiles at her. *Alright, fine, he's attractive,* she admits to herself. Obviously a gym rat, his short sleeves are tight around bronze biceps that clearly have been given some dedication. He has this whole sweetheart vibe that she'd love to be all for.

Just not right now. She has too many goals and too much going on in her life to risk it on losing herself with some guy. No guy is worth the distraction of her focus.

"Sorry to say, Joey. But absolutely nothing."

fourteen

. . .

joey

"SARAH, SWEET SARAH," I say with a grin to the Moon Lounge bartender.

She pours my beer and slides it across the bar. "Yes, Joey? Why are you saying my name like you want a favor?"

"Because that's exactly it. I need a favor."

"And what's that?"

I motion to the table behind me. "Put in a good word for me with Ruby, the singer."

"Okay," Sarah says with hesitation. "I don't really know how much my word would mean to her. I don't know her like that."

"Well, how do you know her?" Sarah's brother owns the Moon Lounge, so I figure Sarah's gotta have some kind of in with Ruby.

"Beyond scheduling and giving her her check? That's about it."

"Sarah, the girl's been singing here for how long?" I scold.

"A few years. What's your point?"

"And you don't know her beyond a few logistical exchanges?"

"May I point out that you, Joey, the man who knows everyone, also hadn't paid her much mind until tonight."

I wince at that, because it's true. "I'm a loyal man. I was with Reggie up until a little over a year ago. I've been busy with my new restaurant. And now it just so happens that Xavier knows Ruby's dad from their days in the military. Satisfied?"

"It's kind of funny, you know?" Sarah says with a smirk.

"What is?"

"Reggie. Ruby. Poet. Singer."

"Uh-huh."

She shrugs. "Seems you have a type."

Another customer comes up, waiting for Sarah's attention. I tell the girl to go ahead. Watch as Sarah takes her drink order, a round of lemon drop shots.

"Celebrating?" I ask the cute blonde.

"It's my birthday!" she gushes at me.

"No kidding, mine too," I say, and she beams. I see Sarah rolling her eyes as she arranges the shots on a tray.

"Really?" The girl turns towards Sarah, says, "Can you get him one too? It's also his birthday!"

"Oh, that's not necessary," I say. "But let me buy you this round. A birthday twin gift."

The blonde leans into me, eyes a little hazy, and whispers in my ear with alcohol fueled breath, "I'm thinking it definitely is." She pulls back and gives me a look that I'm guessing is slowly undressing me.

I throw her a wink, hold her gaze while I tell Sarah to bring a water along with those shots. Looks like this girl could use one. Out of the corner of my eye, I catch Ruby watching me. *Shit.* I really hope she doesn't think I'm flirting with this girl. I quickly pull my gaze away from the blonde. I'm not giving up on my chances with Ruby, and this chick suddenly feels like a major inconvenience in that plan.

"What's your name?" the blonde asks, but I'm preoccupied with what's going on at my table. Namely, Ruby rising out of her chair and doing what looks like the "I'm heading out," gesture to her dad.

I raise my index finger to the blonde, say, "So sorry. Would you excuse me for a second?" and I practically sprint my way across the patio and over to the table.

"Hey! You're not leaving, are you?" I ask Ruby. I have the attention of everyone at the table, including her dad Dom, but I don't care.

"I am actually, yeah," Ruby says.

"Well let me walk you out, at least."

"Oh, Joey. Turning on the charms," Lucy chides.

Lila adds in, "You better watch it, Ruby. Girls fall hard for this one, and Joey eats it up." I glare at her with a look that says "what the fuck?"

I snap away from Lila and smile over at Ruby. "I'm just trying to be a gentleman here and walk a lady out," I explain to Ruby's unblinking eyes. Blue like a cloudless, summer sky.

"Appreciate it, but I'm good. Don't need any help. I'm perfectly capable of walking myself," Ruby says.

"Clearly," I say and I point to the cut on my head. I hear some giggles from Reggie, Lucy, and Lila, who had been more than a little amused by my recounting of the incident.

Thankfully, Dom seems to have taken a liking to me, and he chimes in. "Let the guy walk you out, Ruby. It's late."

"Nice. Bring my dad into it," Ruby says. "Fine, you can walk me out." She waves to the table, says her goodbyes, and starts off.

I follow after her. We make our way into the building, through the main dining area and back outside again. I jog ahead of her to swing open the door for her, and she rushes past me. I catch a whiff of something sweet in her wake. Wonder if it's perfume or shampoo or what, but it smells real nice.

The air is a little cooler now that the sun's gone down and we're no longer in a crowd. A breeze picks up and I see her wrap her arms around herself.

"You cold?" I ask.

"Please don't offer me a jacket."

I laugh and tell her I don't have one to offer her anyways.

"Thank God," is all she replies.

"You really don't like nice guys, do you?"

She's quiet for a moment, drops her arms back down to tuck her hair behind her ears and reaches in her pocket. "Nice guys are usually masking a hidden agenda," she says as she pulls out her keys. "That's what I don't like."

"I get that."

We walk a few more steps in silence. Get to her car and she presses her key fob to unlock it.

I'm not ready for our conversation to be over before it even started though, so I continue. "How do you date then if you aren't willing to buy into the nice guy thing?"

She shrugs. "I don't."

"At all?"

"It's a rather recent arrangement, but currently, no. I'm not dating, nor do I plan to."

I'm tempted to press, to ask who this nice guy was that clearly broke her heart, but I don't want to push her. This feels like my chance, like I have these few minutes right here and now, out in this dark parking lot under a sky full of stars, and I better make it count. I need to choose my words wisely.

"It's a good plan," I say.

She raises an eyebrow at me. "You think so? I figured I was about to get some sales pitch from you on why that's a terrible idea, why I should give you a shot, how my eyes are beautiful and blah blah blah."

I laugh and put my hands in my pockets. Slowly start taking a few steps backwards, walking away. "You think you've got me pegged, huh, Nightingale?"

"Nightingale?" she asks. Her hand is on her car door handle, but she turns her body slightly towards me.

"Yeah. Apparently you're a nightingale. While you were up there singing, I was asking your dad about you. And he said you've written over a hundred songs of your own. That you post them online. That when you were a teen, he'd find you up in the middle of the night, singing in the dark. Singing songs of your very own. A nightingale," I repeat.

I pause my backward walk to gauge her reaction. Her hand is still clinging to her car door handle. I see her chest rise and fall under her shirt. I try not to focus on the fact that I'm pretty sure she's hiding an exceptional rack under there. Full and in total contrast to her otherwise small and slim frame.

Her fingertips slowly glide off the car handle, and I'm given the littlest bit of a smile from her. I gain a little hope. I try not to stare at her mouth, at those full lips that just an hour ago I was lost in watching sing. But fuck, I want to feel that mouth on me.

"Nightingale," she says, looking like she likes the name. Or maybe that's just my optimism. "What's your favorite song, Joseph Conti?"

"Shit. That feels like a loaded question coming from a singer-songwriter."

"No pressure."

"I feel all the pressure," I say, laughing. I think of a few, but none of them feel like a good enough answer. I try to deflect. "It depends on my mood. How 'bout you, what's your favorite song?"

She grins, and I feel like I won the lottery, getting a grin out of her. Finally, a real smile. "Annie Lennox," she says, "'Little Bird.'"

"No shit? Nightingale loves Little Bird," I say, nodding.

"Do you know it?"

"I really, really wish I did, but no," I admit. As soon as I walk away from her though, that's the first thing I'm doing, looking up her song. "What makes it so good?"

"It's upbeat, all about picking yourself up from the ground and taking charge. Carrying yourself away from the old. From the shit that happens in life." She shrugs. "Annie Lennox is a badass, and that particular song helped me through some tough times.”

“Well now, sounds like it’s going to be my new favorite song,” I say with a wink.

She rolls her eyes and I worry that landed wrong. But then she smiles at me. *Again*. I decide I’m officially addicted to her smile.

“You’re brave, you know. Talking to my dad,” she says with a quiet softness. I see her armor coming down, just a little.

“I told you. I’m a good guy. And I have no hidden agenda. In fact, I think I’ve made my agenda very clear.”

“And what’s that?”

“Don’t you know? I want to take you out on a date, Nightingale Ruby.”

She huffs, incredulous. “Just a date, huh?”

“Just a date. So I can get to know you.”

The distant sound of the crowd in the restaurant behind us raises up a notch. Some cheers pierce through the air.

Ruby nods her head in that direction. “Think that’s your blonde and her friends?”

I close my eyes and make a dramatic grimace. “Oh, Bar Blonde is no Taylor Swift.”

“Obviously.”

“So obvious. And that girl in there is definitely *not* my blonde. No. She came up to me. I don’t even know her.”

“She seemed like she knew you.” I can’t help but smile. Call me crazy, but I think I catch the slightest jealousy in Ruby’s remark.

I take a careful step towards her. “No interest in that girl. I assure you. I’m not that guy.” Another step towards her. We’re inches apart now, but she’s not backing away. I take a gamble and reach for a handful of her dark curls. “And I’m definitely more into brunettes with blue eyes.”

She licks her lips, and I feel my dick respond. It’s enough for me to want to drop to my knees in torture.

“I can’t believe you were talking to my dad about me,” she says, and at the mention of her dad, my dick's shot right back down. I release her hair and drop my hand.

"Fathers and big brothers. Gotta respect them."

"Oh yeah?"

"Fuck yeah," I say. "I have sisters. I have, and will again, beat the shit out of anyone that hurts them."

She grins. *Yes. I love that grin.* She shakes her head slowly. "Such a good guy, aren't you, Conti?"

"The worst good guy." We hang in silence for a minute, locked in a stare down. I catch her eyes do a once over on me, then back up to meet mine. "Like what you see, Nightingale?" I ask.

She shakes her head back in nonchalance. "I've seen worse."

"You're warming to me, admit it," I dare, and I earn another grin and laugh from her. "Trying so hard not to like me, but you're warming to me." I run my hand along my jaw, like I'm taking in this fantastic news.

"Maybe a little," she says.

Fucking fireworks shoot in my chest.

"Well, that's a start. Please. Just give me a chance."

"A chance?"

"One date. Not even a date. A non-date. To hangout," I say, but we both know I'm full of shit. I want a full fledged date with this girl. My Nightingale. I need to get to know her.

Ruby smiles and licks her lips. Fuck I want those lips on me. I try and stay focused.

"Fine. A non-date. Where?" she asks.

"Wherever you want."

"Nuh-uh. You want a non-date with me, then you gotta plan it, Good Guy."

"Okay. I'll plan it." My eyes can't help but keep dropping back down to her mouth and those ruby red lips.

"That's it?"

"That's it," I confirm. "What more is there?"

"Do you want my number or something?" she asks, looking at me like I'm an idiot.

"So is that a yes?"

"It's a 'fine,' because you talked to my dad, and he obviously liked you, probably because he knows your friend—"

"My uncle," I clarify.

"Uncle, whatever. And so now he's going to be on me to give you a shot and go on about how he wants me taken care of and all that. So I'm screwed."

"Wow. That might be the saddest way I've had to get a girl to go out with me. For a non-date," I rush to add.

"A tale for the grandkids for sure," she says. Then looks at me all startled. Points a finger at me. "I did *not* mean that how it sounded. Don't get any ideas, Good Guy. This is a non-date, and I'm not having kids. Just, forget that right now."

"Nightingale, how 'bout we just start with dinner?"

I'M SO FUCKING EXCITED I'M like a kid finding out he's meeting his favorite baseball player. I'm at work, trying to focus on the stack of bills in front of me, the cruel reality of numbers yanking me from what otherwise was a fantastic month for the restaurant. I should be crying at the money we seem to hemorrhage, but I'm grinning from ear to ear.

I've got a date with Ruby Francesca, my Nightingale.

It's the first time I've felt truly into a girl since my breakup with Reggie. Not gonna lie, I've had a hell of a year and a half learning all about what "playing the field" means. No better way to lick the wounds of heartache than having random girls literally licking— well you get the point. It's been good. Fun. Between opening my restaurant and diving headfirst into casual hookups, I haven't had a chance to even think about a girl in any serious way.

But there's something about Ruby. That voice. I could listen to her sing all day and all night and still be starved for more. Raw honey, that's the sound. That voice with those pouty lips of hers.

I did some digging and found her YouTube channel. I know now why she was worried about stalking, based on some of the comments. She doesn't show her face on there, often the videos just have an image. Occasionally she shows herself playing, but that only offers up a distracting front row view of her body. At one point I had to look away because I was starting to feel like a fucking creep. The girl is *mesmerizing*.

And her dad wasn't kidding, she's got more songs than I think emails I've ever written in my life. Ever since we met, I've been listening to them nonstop. So much soul in her music. I can't believe she actually wrote all that. I had my grandmother listen to some. She's always had a great ear for music, and Mama Z confirmed—this girl has got something.

So now I'm hell bent on coming up with the right setting for our date. Sweet, but not so sweet it scares her off. I don't know what happened to her that's got her guard up so high, but I know I need to make the best of this chance.

I think I've got it, too. The perfect plan—something simple, something personal. I'm the king of perfect surprises. No need to worry here, because I've got just the perfect one for her.

fifteen

. . .

ruby

MIDNIGHT.

YOU'VE GOT to fucking be kidding me, she thinks to herself. *The guy wants a date at midnight?*

Ruby is fuming when she sees the text from Joey. There it is, his not-hidden but totally bullshit agenda. He's asking for a date at midnight. A booty call.

She's surprised to find just how disappointed she is by this. Ruby was starting to soften to Joey, little by little. They had been texting for the past week, little bits of banter that she was enjoying. He'd check in, ask how her day was. She'd tease him that he was putting in a lot of communicating for a non-date. He'd counter by challenging her to imagine what he would be like if she actually gave him a real chance.

It was sweet. Light and fun. He wasn't your average college boy that she was used to. She was sick of the immaturity and game playing that she'd encountered so far in her dating career. Talking with Joey felt so much more natural. She'd find herself getting a little flutter of excitement when she'd hear a text from him. (Of course she also set her phone to chime in a dark and ominous tone designated for him.)

But the truth is, a teeny little part of her had actually been starting to like Joey.

"Why the frown, love?" Grayson asks from his chair as she steps out of the dressing room. He had insisted on taking her shopping for a first non-date outfit. Said he was sick of Ruby hiding her body in "frumpy frocks and parachute tops," as he called her usual wardrobe. If anyone else said that to her, she'd have been wildly offended. But Grayson was good people. And she adored and trusted him, a rare thing for Ruby.

She catches a glimpse of herself in the mirror—the high waisted jeans with an impossibly large bow at the center. The strappy black tank that barely contained her ample breasts. The tags hanging off the sides, only working to make her feel like an absolute imposter. And now this text, an anvil crashing down from the ceiling.

"Look at this bullshit," she says, throwing the phone at Grayson. He fumbles, just barely catching it in surprise.

"Bloody hell, warn me before you throw a phone, would ya?" He spins the phone around to the upright direction. Scrolls through, and she watches as his eyes skim through the text exchanges. "Ahhh. I see. The midnight booty call?"

"I feel like an idiot!" She pops a leg out, putting a hand on her hip. "Do I ghost him now or what?"

Grayson raises a finger at her, says, "Hang on," and rises from his seat. He presses something into Ruby's phone, and puts it to his ear. She bites her lip, curious as to what he's doing.

"Yes, hiya. This is the honorable Grayson Simon Atkinson of Cambridge, and this message is for Joseph."

Ruby hurls herself onto Grayson's back, attempting to steal the phone away. "Give me that," she whisper-shouts, but Grayson manages to wave her off and continue his message.

"I'm here to judge the merits of your intentions with our doll, the effervescent Ruby Francesca. It seems you have requested a date at, let me look at my notes here, midnight."

"I'm going to murder you so good they will need dental identification," Ruby mutters, relinquishing and dropping off Grayson's back. He signals for her to shush while stifling his own laughter.

"What you fail to realize is that this is not a suitable time for a date, or non-date, as I understand. And one would question if you were in fact not seeking a date at all, but rather a mere hookup. In which case, you've got the wrong girl.

"I look forward to hearing back from you with what I hope to be a riveting explanation." Grayson recites his own number into the phone before closing out the message and hanging up. He hands the phone back to Ruby.

"You're going to drive me to drink," she says with a glare.

"Now there's an idea. How about I get you a Coke, me a vodka tonic, and we decide how we're going to pull revenge on this bloke."

Ruby shrugs. "Fine." She stares down at her bare feet, feeling deflated.

"Awww, come on now, love. It isn't all bad." Grayson cocks his head to the side to take in the defeated sight of Ruby. "You liked him, didn't you?"

"No."

"Ahhh, so you did. I wish I had had a chance to meet him, then. Too bad." Grayson starts to walk out of the dressing room, but pauses and turns back around. "I'm buying you that outfit though. No sense in denying these poor, innocent clothes that hot figure of yours."

"Excuse me, sir, this is the ladies dressing room. No men in here," says the sales lady as she walks into the area, startled at the sight of Grayson.

"Well, love," Grayson says, thumb and index finger to his chin as if deep in thought. "Good thing all you will find in here are queens."

NOW, NORMALLY RUBY WOULD NOT have given someone like Joey a second thought. He would have received the silent treatment from Ruby, a full ghosting, followed by blocking on any forms of social media. This would have given Ruby incredible satisfaction—a feeling of beautiful control of the last word—and the brief chapter of Joey would have been closed.

If it weren't for Grayson. Apparently, Joey had called Grayson later that day after the infamous phone message. And Joey in all his wondrous charm, somehow convinced Grayson that his intentions *were* in fact good. Evidently he had a perfectly good reason for requesting such an odd date time, and that it was all part of some master plan, yet to be revealed.

In fact, Joey pled such a good argument, that Grayson had promptly reached out to Ruby and insisted she "pop on that trouser-dropping black tank, find some suitable footwear, and be at this address at midnight." Ruby was floored at first. But then curious.

He had creativity and balls, this Joey dude.

So here she was, at midnight, in the outfit (though flat sandals were the best either Grayson or Joey were going to get out of Ruby). As promised she was sharing her location with Grayson, and she assured him she'd text promptly at the agreed upon time so he knew she was still alive and well.

"How will you know it's me texting, and not Joey while standing over my lifeless body?" she had asked over their video chat.

"You're right. We need a code word," Grayson said, very serious.

"Hmmm, how 'bout 'this was a bad idea,'" Ruby suggested.

"No. Too confusing."

"I hate you?" Ruby offered.

"My broken heart, Ruby, when all I do is love you."

"You're right, I apologize."

"I've got it," Grayson snapped his fingers on the other end of the screen. "Nightingale sings."

Ruby groaned. "I should not have told you about that."

"It's perfect. Text me 'Nightingale sings' at 12:30, and I'll know we're good. No wait! Make it at one instead."

"Why one?"

"Because you need a full hour at least to know."

"I could be dead by then," Ruby had said.

"If he is planning on killing you at all, thirty minutes really won't make a difference."

"Good point. Fine. I'll text you at one, and we'll see just how good of a guy this Joey really is."

So that was the plan.

But she's nervous as she pulls into a spot on the hilly side street in Manayunk, the Philly neighborhood of the address she was given. As promised, she texts Joey once she parks, though he must have been waiting for her because he appears not five seconds later.

She watches as he jogs up to her and waves with a flash of those dimples. She opens her car door, and he steps over to help her out.

"You actually came, I'm relieved," he says as he leans in to kiss her on the cheek. The gesture throws her off and she tenses.

"Oh, hi," she says.

Joey rolls right on past her awkwardness. "You look—" he starts. "Wait. Now I'm scared to say anything. Am I allowed to say you look great?"

She laughs, thankful for his playfulness. It calms her nerves, and she closes and locks her car door behind her. "You're allowed. Let's hear it."

Joey grins. "Good, then I'm not gonna lie. You look fucking hot. In a very respectful way," he rushes to add.

"Better not be in a booty call way," she says, shaking her head. But she's smiling. Joey has a way of putting her at ease. Even here, on a dark city street at midnight, she feels comfortable. She catches a whiff of his laundry detergent. Fresh and clean and comforting.

He grabs her hand and she mindlessly hangs on. He leads them up the hill. "Do I get to know where we're going now?" she asks.

"To my restaurant. The Guilty Olive. Ever heard of it?" he asks.

She shakes her head no. "*Your* restaurant?" she clarifies. She thinks back to their texts, and her social media stalking. She knew he worked in a restaurant, but it never dawned on her that he actually owned the place.

"Yeah, I just opened it not too long ago."

"Wow. Here I am fumbling through music lessons and mini gigs, hoping for a teaching job, and you like, run a business."

"Barely. I'm making my share of mistakes, don't worry."

"Is that supposed to make me feel better?" she asks.

"It's supposed to assure you that I'm human. But I had wanted to do this for a long time. Had a vision of a plant focused Mediterranean spot, and eventually I just said 'fuck it,' took the plunge and here we are. And it's working, by some crazy luck."

"You seem like the kind of guy that will figure out a way to make just about anything work if you really want to. Optimistic determination wrapped in a winning smile," she jests lightly.

"Oh wow, thank you. I mean I don't know about that, but that might be one of the best compliments I think I've ever gotten, Nightingale." He gives her hand a little squeeze and looks down at her with the aforementioned smile.

Her heart skips a little beat, hearing his appreciation. She likes that she was able to say something of any semblance of meaningful significance to him. For a guy that oozes a lot of confidence, it makes Ruby feel wonderfully valuable, in a way. Like what she says matters to him, she can have an effect. It's a good feeling. "I call it like I see it," she says.

"You're gonna give me a big head."

"I get the feeling you already have one."

"True. I landed a date with you, didn't I?" he says with that grin of his. "You saying yes blew up my ego by about a thousand percent."

"I barely said yes," she points out.

She should have corrected him. Should have reminded Joey the Good Guy that this was a non-date. Yet Ruby finds she doesn't want to. Yes, she realizes. She absolutely wants this to be a real date. There's something so right about walking down the dark street with him, hand in hand. Him guiding her while teasing her with flirtatious conversation. Fully transparent about liking her and wanting to get to know her better. It feels like home, like he's been a piece missing in her life that she hadn't realized was missing in the first place. Her attraction to Joey Conti Jr. is quickly rising to new levels.

They round the corner and he releases her hand to open a back door.

"After you," he says, arm out for her to step past him.

She walks in and takes note of her surroundings. A world of steel, an empty kitchen all closed up for the night. The distant sound of music coming from the dining area beyond. "Where is everyone?" she asks.

"Right. So that's why I asked for you to meet at midnight," he says. "When everything would be closed up, and I could do this."

"Do what?"

"You'll see," he says, and he grabs her hand again. Her pulse quickens at the feel and warmth of his grip. It's comforting, having her hand held like this. She looks up and notices his hair looks a bit shorter. A fresh haircut, neat and tidy. She thinks about what it would feel like to run her fingers through it, mess it up, or grab a fistful while he kisses her neck. She squeezes her eyes shut, surprised at the places her mind is wandering with a guy she barely knows. A guy who might very well be planning to murder her tonight, she laughs to herself, thinking of her call with Grayson.

Joey leads her through the kitchen, down a small hallway of brick walls and modern art. "That's my office," he says, pointing to a partially opened door. Ruby tries to push down the feeling of being impressed. She's twenty-two, but suddenly feels like a kid, painfully out of place with the grown-ups.

They enter into the restaurant area and pass a small corner to the right with a booth of a gray tufted suede material. Books on wooden shelves stacked high above, creating the atmosphere of a miniature library, nestled away. To the left, a long line of tables, anchored along a brick wall. She notes with appreciation some of the music themed art adorning the walls. Towards the front of the restaurant, a concrete bar wraps around. The whole place has a feel of urban warmth and sophistication. She feels completely out of her element, knowing Joey actually *owns* this place.

But the thing that stands out the most to Ruby is not the atmosphere itself.

It's the music.

Her music.

Playing softly from hidden speakers, her very own songs. Her lyrics, her voice, her creations. Accompanying the otherwise still and silent space. Her stomach flips at the realization, and suddenly she feels naked and exposed.

Ruby turns to Joey, pointing up towards the ceiling. "You?"

She studies his face as he smiles sheepishly, puts his free hand in the pocket of his jeans, bounces on his toes for a beat. "Yeah, I hope it's okay. I did a little digging, found you online."

"How? I don't even have my full name out there." She's dumbfounded and stunned. Drops her hand from his and raises it to cover her mouth.

"I may have recruited help from your dad," he says guiltily. "Is that okay?"

She's not sure how to answer, for some reason it all feels like a lot to take in. Is it okay?

First, Ruby's consumed with the vulnerability of having her music play throughout the entire space. She's never heard it like this before. Leaking out beyond the confines of her own headphones, where it's usually quietly contained.

It's surreal.

Second, should she be worried that this guy went through all the trouble to do this? Track down her music, bring her here after hours, blast it through the place?

"Say something, Ruby. Is this okay?" Joey says in a whisper, reaching for her elbow. She can hear the concern in his voice. The worry, even, that maybe he messed up.

She looks up at him. Notes the sincerity in his eyes. Takes in the black button down dress shirt he has on, rolled up on his forearms. The muscles of his chest and shoulders bursting through it. The gray jeans, the dress shoes that present an overall look of stylish masculinity.

His fresh hair cut. The clean shave. The dress shirt.

The midnight plan. Her music.

He put effort in here. All for her. She's stunned and not sure what to say.

"I wanted to do something special for you," he explains, his voice gentle. Her heart and pulse race each other, threatening oblivion. "I love your voice. I found that out when I met you." She watches as he licks his lips, the movement causing his dimples to make a flash appearance. "But then I wanted to hear *your* music." She watches the movement of his lips as he says the words. *Your music.* Like her music is an entity in and of itself. A thing with its own rightful place in the world, worthy of appreciation and admiration.

He steps closer to her and starts to reach out to touch her, but then pulls back. Grabs the back of his neck instead. "You got me strangely nervous here, Ruby."

"My music?" she stammers, still in complete disbelief.

"Your music, yeah." There it is again.

Your.

Music.

"Not just cover songs," he says as if cover songs hold no value whatsoever, "but the songs *you* actually wrote. And I got lost in it."

"You did?"

Ruby isn't used to this and she finds she's completely off balance. Guys she's dated have either discarded her music as a silly little hobby, or downright cracked jokes about her songs, her lyrics, all in a cheap attempt to be funny. She'd play along and laugh, determined to never show her disappointment.

Her mother, too, would do the same back when Ruby still lived with her, after her parents divorced. Her mother would cackle in drunken fits, especially if she got a hold of Ruby's journals. Page after page bursting with Ruby's creations. She'd long ago given up on showing her mom any. She'd given up on the hope to make her mom proud.

Eventually Ruby learned to put her hurt into her lyrics. She'd write about her mother's behavior, her snaps of rage, her disregard for her one and only child. As a kid, Ruby referred to her mother in songs as "the witch."

The witch is at it again
Lava in her veins, taking a spin
Stealing all joy from any grin
Drowning in the potion of her spells of sin

Ruby used music as her escape in those dark couple of years. With her dad still active in the military, stationed all over the world, she was all alone with no way out.

Until the day her dad found out how bad her mom's drinking had gotten. What that had led to, and how bad *everything* had gotten. It's when he retired, a little earlier than planned, all so he could move back to Garden Springs, PA. Settle and find a home for Ruby to finish out her high school years. Her mother didn't even put up a fight, zero regard for her daughter.

And Ruby's never looked back since.

She looks back up at Joey and sees the worry on his face.

"Ruby, I really hope you're not mad or hurt by this."

Mad or hurt, she thinks? She laughs as she realizes the absurdity. There have been many times in her life that she's been mad and hurt and then some.

This is not one of them.

This is…this is kindness in a world where she's known cruelty. She can feel a bubbling in her, an excitement and attraction to this guy quickly becoming consuming. It gives her hope.

"I meant for this to be a good surprise. And I know, I know. You don't trust the Good Guy—"

Ruby steps forward, closes the space between them. Presses her body into his and steps on her tippy-toes to throw her arms around Joey's neck. Without hesitation she pulls his head down to her, feeling the stubble beneath her palms of the fresh shave on his neck.

His mouth meets hers with satisfaction, and she drinks him in, relishing in the subtle mint taste of this beautiful Good Guy. That did all this just for her. Dug around, found her music, set it up to play proudly in his restaurant.

It's incredible to her, and she can't believe the ways her body is responding as a result. She's attracted to him and feels actual *need* in this kiss. She wants this from him.

He groans and grabs her waist, deepening their kiss. Ruby allows her hands to roam in his hair, grabbing it in her fingers. He spins them both around and backs her up, pinning her up against the brick wall, pressing his hips against hers. She feels his tongue explore hers, sucking and tasting. He removes his arms from around her waist and brings his hands up to her cheeks, cradling her face in his hands as he continues to consume her mouth.

And then he stops and pulls back.

He releases her and puts both hands on the wall behind her, on either side of her head.

"Fuck, I did not see that coming," he says, his gaze to the floor.

Ruby smiles to the ceiling above. "Can't say I did either."

"I swore I wouldn't kiss you tonight. That I'd be the perfect gentleman."

"I kissed you," she points out.

He looks back up at her, and she meets his eyes. "So I guess my plan landed well?" he asks.

She grins. "Uh, yeah. It lands. Real well. Yeah." She bites her thumb nail in attempt to contain her smile. And then remembers something. "Wait, though! Hang on just a sec," she says as she maneuvers herself under Joey's arm, still leaning on the wall and encasing her.

She steps out of his cocoon with reluctance, and grabs her phone from her bag.

"Everything okay?" Joey asks behind her.

"Yeah, real good. Just gotta do something real quick." And she furiously types away to Grayson, though it's not even close to one yet.

> R: Nightingale sings. Fucking Nightingale nightingale nightingale sings.

She looks down and sees the three dots and waits for Grayson's response.

> G: It's about bloody time.

sixteen

. . .

mama z

THINGS ALL STARTED to fall into place when I had first met Ruby. It was in my early days of illness, I had just completed my surgery and come out of the fog of treatments. I had a fresh wig, a decent prognosis, and an extra boost of motivation. On some level I was aware that I was on borrowed time. And truly I was alright with that. As I have said, who wants to live forever?

So. There I was, yet again revived and given the gift of life for a bit longer. Determined to use it wisely, I wanted to ensure I would make my mark in all the necessary ways. Joey had been telling me all about this girl. She's gorgeous, she writes her own songs, she sings like the sweetest of sounds of a damn harp or something like that. On and *on* the boy went. I was floored at his infatuation! "My God, Joey," I had said. "Don't be such a lovesick fool."

The look he gave me though. I could see he wanted me to understand. And so I said, "Alright, let me hear about this girl."

He told me they had been seeing one another for a few weeks, they were taking things slowly, as this girl is young and perhaps naive (or so was my line of thinking). Joey played me some of her music. It was good, her voice lovely, I did have to agree. But what's so special about that? We all have talents. That's easy. Dig deep, take the right lessons to grow your strengths and voila! Talents can be obtained.

But I could see he was falling for her.

So, I looked into her, naturally. Did a little of my own digging. And that's when things really got interesting. *My, my, my. Ruby Francesca,* I remember thinking. Once I learned a thing or two, I knew I absolutely had to meet this girl. It seemed Joey had in fact found someone worthy of infatuation.

I just needed to know if what I had learned about Joey's new love interest was in fact true. If I had connected the dots accurately.

And if so, was she as fierce a survivor as I?

"BRING HER TO MY ART STUDIO," I said to Joey through the phone.

"Aw, come on, Mama Z. Wouldn't a coffee date or something be better?"

"Coffee conversation is a bore, Joey. I would much prefer an afternoon of painting if I am to get to know this new girl."

"Why painting?" he had asked. "I don't even know if Ruby likes painting."

"Because, Joseph," I said, my voice slowing down and lowering to convey he had better understand. "There is no better way to get to know someone than to see what their mind can do with some paints and a blank canvas."

"The Real EmZee, at it again. You are up to no good, aren't you? Testing my Ruby, is that it?" He was not cross with me, as his voice was smooth and teasing. I knew he was getting a kick out of this even through his desire of my approval of this girl.

"Life is one enormous test. A test of survival, and if painting with an old lady is too much for her—"

"—It won't be," he had interrupted.

"Good."

So that's how I came to meet Ruby. One impossibly hot and sunny afternoon at the end of July or early August, painting with one another.

She had walked right on in, her own canvas and supplies of paints and brushes in hand. Joey had tried to make introductions, and Ruby waved him away, telling him to leave us be. "Mama Z wants to know if I'm good enough for you, so let me show her," she said with a clever glint in her eye. *Maybe not so naive after all,* I had thought. I was warming to her instantly as I watched this girl.

She reminded me of myself.

We had gotten right to work, with the peaceful notes of Bach providing our ambiance. She shared with me her knowledge of Bach's history and her appreciation for the composer's innovation. I told her I could not agree more, and explained that Bach had been an orphan like me.

We both remained focused on our canvases, eyes darting back and forth between them and the still life set up I had arranged for us. A poppy flower display accompanied by pomegranates.

"You're an orphan?" Ruby asked.

"That's right," I said. Another test passed. I set the bait with Bach, and she stepped in rather nicely.

"Interesting," she said. I appreciated that she did not give me pity. "Joey did mention that you're not sure of your exact age. That you have a birthday that was chosen for you, but not necessarily accurate."

"Oh yes. My exact age is a mystery," I said, pleased with her questioning. Most people shy away from things that are uncomfortable. Not Ruby. "Many Armenians fled home in those days in favor of refuge in other European countries. I had been sent to live with distant relatives at a very young age, but had no birth certificate. I was too little to talk much, so papers were forged for me with a date chosen at random."

"Do you ever wonder about the real date of your birthday? Or have a feeling of an astrological sign that feels right?" she asked.

"No. I know who I am and what I want. The day I appeared on this earth has nothing to do with that."

She only nodded, continued her work, and I mine. But I knew she had more questions. I had questions of my own as well.

At some point, Ruby asked me about my name, Zabel, which I thought curious. I happily told her what I had been told—that I had been named after the medieval Queen Isabella of Armenia, also called Zabel. Whether that was in fact the inspiration for my name or not, or just a nice story told by my guardians, I shared how I liked the idea.

"What do you like about it?" Ruby had asked.

"Queen Zabel had resilience," I explained. "She had been forced into multiple arranged marriages for one political gain or another, as was common for the time. But in her final marriage," I said with conspiratorial enthusiasm, "she managed to find respect and equal power held with her husband, as is depicted in their placement on either side of their coat of arms."

"A real progressive badass," Ruby nodded, and I beamed. I went on to share the history of the queen's passion in education for the arts. Ruby listened with quiet interest. If she was bored with the brief history lesson, she did not show it.

I continued to stab away at my painting, creating texture in the dark centers of the poppy blooms and the pomegranates. I thought about what to ask her next, glad we had entered into a comfortable conversational rhythm. "Tell me about your upbringing, Ruby," I said. "I hear our Xavier and your father knew one another from their time in the military."

"So it seems," she said with a sadness. Her eyes flashed over to me, catching herself and hoping to recover, I imagine. She was used to the weight of a vault, locked up tight. One could see that.

"I was a military brat, mostly," she explained. "New bases every couple of years, so I lived all over the place."

"'Military brat' is a terrible term. Don't use it," I said. I watched as she switched paint brushes. A thinner one. She dabbed it in some white paint.

"Okaayyy," she said with a frown. "You know it's a fairly common term."

"It's trivial. 'Brat' implies one is stupid and spoiled."

"I don't know about stupid, but living all over the world could be considered spoiled," she pointed out.

"Yet you do not seem thrilled with having that history."

"I think I'm indifferent. I've seen beautiful places that many never get to, but nothing ever felt like home because we just weren't there long enough. That part could be tough."

"Home is a concept, not an actual place, Ruby. *I* had no home, if we are to get technical. Removed from my country. Hopping from one makeshift home to another," I said.

"Doesn't that make you sad?"

"Absolutely not."

"Maybe sad isn't the right word."

"Sad is easy. It is gratitude in the face of darkness that is hard." I waited for my words to sink in. I was hoping to soften the girl up. Get her to see I could be trusted.

"I suppose that's true. Gratitude can be a double-edged sword, though."

"How so?" I asked, hoping to keep my voice innocent.

"When it's used against you. When you're gaslighted and told you need to be grateful."

Now we're getting somewhere, I thought.

I knew I needed to tread lightly. "I guess we've all had to experience things we would rather not," I said, carefully watching her body language out of the corner of my eye. She remained firmly rooted to her place in front of the canvas, focused on her work. I decided to back off and allow a little break in conversation. We continued our work, the music filling the room with notes fluttering through the air, waiting to drop and shift the mood.

Eventually I picked up conversation once again. "And your parents?" I asked. "What are they like? I know your dad was in the military. What does your mother do?"

"As a kid she did odd jobs on base, usually. Administrative work, that kind of thing."

"Are you close with them?"

"With my dad. My parents divorced when I was in middle school. I lived with my mom for a little while, but then my dad retired and moved here, so I moved in with him."

We were getting closer, now. Closer to the history that had made Ruby so intriguing to me.

"How old were you when you moved in with your father?"

"Fourteen."

"A fourteen-year-old girl that did not want to live with her mother?" I pressed, knowing I might be pushing too far. I felt I had been using incredible restraint in my questioning, but the flutter in my chest was eager and persistent. My words seemed to obey to that flutter more than my own reasoning.

Ruby looked over to me, and we locked eyes. I could see then the wall she had put up, my last question the button to signal locking of the vault. The firm tiles of the floor beneath me were starting an ache in my feet. I ignored them.

"Well you sure don't beat around the bush, do you?" she said.

I kept quiet, afraid my words would ruin any chance of her continuing. Thankfully she eventually spoke again. "It's hard to explain," she said with a sigh, her attention firmly focused on her painting.

I tried to build a bridge. "Forgive me," I said, "I do not mean to be intrusive. You see, I had a rather tumultuous childhood, and I get the sense that you too must have had some difficult decisions to make at that point in time." I searched her face for signs of a reaction, but she gave none. *Strong girl.* Again, a flutter in my chest as I saw even more in Ruby that I liked.

I continued. "I learned early on the power in crafting your own destiny. I find the best strength of character can be obtained from our rise above the hardships we have endured."

"Painting and a life lesson, today then, huh?"

"Grandmotherly wisdom, perhaps."

"Sure. It sounds real nice," Ruby said, stretching the word "real" out. I was frustrated with her sarcasm. I had thought we were getting somewhere. She needed to know I was a friend, here. Then again, I suppose I might have reacted in a similar way when I was that age. In our youth of early adulthood, our self identity is like a newly sculpted clay figure, soft and precious. We react to perceived threat by sprouting spikes so as to keep out potential harm, aware of our fragility.

I let us go on for a while in silence. I had the feeling she was not going to reveal herself to me willingly, so I focused on my painting, determined to let that be enough for today. If she and Joey really were going to continue seeing one another, then there would be plenty more time to earn this girl's trust.

After a while, Ruby broke the silence and informed me she was finished.

"May I see?" I asked.

She tilted her head to the side and said with an absolute straight face, "Of course. How else will you get to judge me, otherwise?"

I smiled at the girl. Oh yes, a real Rubik's cube, albeit still in its jumbled form, I could see. I took a few steps over to Ruby and her canvas. I paused before rounding my way in front of it, leaving it just out of my line of sight. "I do not have to look if you would prefer," I offered.

"It's poppy flowers, not a nude self-portrait. You're free to look, Mama Z."

I liked how she called me Mama Z without hesitation, even though she appeared on guard with me. It was as if she wanted to like or perhaps trust me, despite her bristly reaction to my inquisition. I wondered if that was because of her growing relationship with Joey, or if she, too, felt a kindred spirit in me.

She turned the canvas toward me, and I remember being rather pleased at what I saw. "You could say there is a bit of a self-portrait in here, isn't there?" I said. "Lovely."

On her canvas was not an attempted replica of the still life arrangement between us, but Ruby's own interpretation entirely. One large oversized poppy flower in the center, with a pattern of black music notes scattered throughout the edges of the canvas, framing the center bloom.

She crossed her arms. "Well?" she prompted, and I had to admire the boldness in her attitude. "Do I pass the test?"

I turned around and took the few steps back to my own canvas. "You do not care for me very much, do you, Ruby?"

"I hardly know you to say whether or not I like you."

"We've spent a lovely afternoon painting together. What more do you need to make a decision?"

"I get the sense that it's *you* that is trying to decide whether or not you like *me*," she countered.

"What makes you say that?"

"You don't like that I chose to move in with my dad." She said it as a statement, and I was disappointed that I had conveyed that to her.

"Not at all. Quite the contrary," I tried to explain. "See to me, a fourteen-year-old girl no longer wishing to live with her mother tells me there is something with that relationship with her mother that forced the child to make such a choice. I'm curious to know what that is, especially as you and my grandson are getting close. I like to know the skeletons the people getting close to my family might have." As soon as I said that last sentence, I regretted it. It was not the way to earn one's trust, and I knew better. And yet, it had spilled out anyway.

Ruby dropped her jaw, said, "Wow. Skeletons? Like I've got something to hide? Some guilty conscience you just have to know about?"

I watched as she gathered her brushes in quick movements. She walked over to the small sink at the other end of the room and turned on the water to start washing. I looked over to my own painting, nowhere near complete. She grabbed a paper towel from the roll next to the sink and wrapped her brushes up like a blanket swaddling a baby. Ruby walked back to her canvas and started packing away her supplies in her carrier, her movements sharp and abrupt.

She finally spoke as she pulled the strap of her carrier over her shoulder. "My mother was an alcoholic," she said with admonition. The statement rolled out of her mouth with minimal inflection, but the bitterness was laced in its sound nonetheless. The words were quick and to the point, just as someone might say, "We're completely out of milk." And yet, there was no denying the somberness in the underlying notes.

Ruby continued. "Still is, I'm guessing, though I don't see her anymore." Her tone remained clipped. "At some point, living with her became no longer an option. So I moved out, and have been here in Garden Springs ever since. Happy?" she said, a sharpness in her eye.

I struck a chord, that was for sure. And if she informed Joey of my questioning, I knew he would be disappointed in me.

She turned around with her things, leaving the canvas on the easel. As she got to the doorway, she paused and turned around. "I'll leave that here to dry and have Joey come get it. But next time you want to grill someone about their past, there's no need to butter them up with all this set up," she said, waving her arm around to indicate the studio.

And with that, Ruby Francesca walked right out. And my wheels began churning out a plan for this girl. This Rubik's Cube that had a similar fire in her I knew within myself.

She did not need to like me. But I was going to help her anyway.

seventeen

. . .

joey

"SO IT WAS a good time? You like her?" I ask Ruby. She's sitting at my bar, sipping her water and sharing about her afternoon with Mama Z. Work has been insane the past few days and we haven't communicated beyond a few texts and quick phone calls. I've been dying to hear how their time together was.

"Let me try a sip of that," Ruby says, pointing to my beer.

I look at her in surprise. I'm behind the bar, so I gesture over to the tap. "My beer? Do you want one?"

She laughs, "No, I do not want one. I just want to try a sip of yours, if that's alright. Unless you'd rather not exchange germs."

"I want to exchange all the germs with you," I say, sliding my glass across the bar and towards her.

"I'm so flattered," she says. I watch her lift the glass, inhale with curiosity. Take the slightest of sips. Then make the most adorable scrunch up of her nose like she just tasted motor oil. "No, don't like that one," she says with a firm head shake.

"Do you like any beer?" I ask. It's strange being a restaurant owner and dating someone that doesn't seem to have a ton of interest in food or drinks. I wouldn't call Ruby picky, exactly. Just selectively indifferent.

She shrugs. "You're not going to find me chugging from any kegs, but I like to try a sip now and then just to know what the fuss is about. I like the fruity ones, they're all right."

"That's the lowest of the low," I tease.

She throws her head back in a laugh, and the skin of her neck and throat taunt me. "Gee, thanks. Good thing I don't really give a shit either way."

Reluctantly, I leave her side for a bit to work. Take care of some deliveries coming in, sweet talk a customer or two, all the while fighting the pull to get back to my girl. She never did say how her afternoon with my grandmother went, and Mama Z was cryptic in her response too when I asked. I don't know why I care so much, I guess I just trust my grandmother's opinion. My mom can learn to like almost anyone, or at least put on a game face when she needs to. But it's a little more difficult to earn my grandmother's favor, which makes this interaction all the more meaningful.

At some point, I notice Grayson join Ruby, and I'm grateful she has some company. Lucy and Lila trickle in later too, and my quick check ins prove they're all having a good time together.

It's funny this urge I have to make sure Ruby's okay. Logically I know she can hold her own. I guess I just want everyone to love her as much as I do.

Yeah, I said it. Love. I think I might actually love this girl.

Not that I can admit that to Ruby herself yet; it's way too soon, even I know that. Not even been a month, and she's made it clear we'll be taking things slowly. We haven't even slept together yet, but hell if I'll be rushing her when I'm just thrilled she's even giving me a chance. She's worth the wait. And she's met my family, so that has to mean something.

Although shit, now that I'm thinking about it I'm wondering if she's one of those no sex until marriage girls.

What if she's a virgin?

The thought scares the shit out of me, catching me off guard, and next thing you know I'm getting shoved aside by my own staff in the kitchen, looking at me like I'm hopelessly in the way.

But fuck, I'm pretty sure I love this girl. I'm wondering how soon is too soon to know.

After what feels like an eternity, my head now clouded with the thought that Ruby's a virgin, we finally are slowing down for the night. I go to join the crew, all laughing and looking right at home at the bar.

"Did you miss me?" I whisper in Ruby's ear before making my way around to the other side. I see the chill it gives her and my dick's twitching. I clench my jaw, now realizing I may be flying solo for a lot longer if I want to make Ruby officially mine.

I know I'm fucked when I realize I'm okay with that.

"Ruby was just telling us all about painting with your grandmother," Lila says. "How sweet."

"Quite the formidable force, your grandmother," Grayson grins.

My heart race picks up a little, and I look at Ruby to explain. "What do you mean, what happened?"

Ruby waves her hand around, dismissing me. "Don't look so worried. She was just doing what she thought needed to be done."

Lila leans forward on the bar. "Asking about skeletons in Ruby's closet."

Ruby throws a balled up straw wrapper at Lila. "Hey, I said not to tell him, it's fine. She called, we met up again for coffee and she apologized. Don't go stirring the pot."

"She did what?" I'm scanning their faces, hating that Ruby was telling them something she didn't want me to hear. And pretty fucking pissed that that thing was Mama Z being rude. "Skeletons? That's what she said?"

"Relax, Joey," Lucy says. "Sounds like your girl gave Mama Z a run for her money."

"I handled it," Ruby assures me. "I told her next time to just be up front instead of luring me into her lair with innocent painting." I look at Ruby, search her eyes for anything else she's not telling me, but thankfully she seems at ease. She looks over, catches my gaze, and grins. A silent assurance that everything really is all good.

"See?" Grayson puts his arm over Ruby and gives her a little squeeze. "Tough girl, right here. Held her own just fine."

"She must have, because that woman doesn't apologize to anyone for anything," I mutter. I still don't like that Ruby was trying not to tell me about that, but I'm glad it seems like it all turned out okay.

My grandmother really can be a piece of work, I realize with a little bitterness.

AT THE END OF THE night, Ruby and I are the last ones there, and I'm locking up. I shut off the last of the lights in the kitchen and look down to my gorgeous Nightingale, smiling up at me like sunshine and fucking rainbows.

"What's got you so happy? I know it wasn't my IPA," I say with a little poke to her stomach.

She works her hands up my chest, around my neck and says, "Just had a good day today."

I wrap my arms around her waist, heart so full seeing her look so happy. "You deserve every day to be a good day." I press my lips to her forehead. Sway with her a little to a soundless music.

"It's Sunday night," she says.

I nod, not sure why she said that. "Yes, and?"

"Tomorrow's Monday. The restaurant's closed. You have off."

Please tell me she's suggesting what I think she's suggesting, I think.

"Now who's stalking who? Didn't realize you were tracking my schedule so well, Nightingale."

We sway together a little bit more, me trying not to get my

hopes up, but really getting my hopes up here. I fucking *need* this girl. I'm not gonna be able to think straight until I have her.

"I'm ready to spend the night," she whispers.

I half release her, victory punch the air with my fist as she giggles.

"I think those are the most beautiful words I've ever heard. Because holy fuck, I can't stop thinking about you and I need you so badly." I should try to play it cool, I know. But what can I say, this girl is my undoing.

I press her against me again, crash my mouth down to hers and take in every bit of it I possibly can. Ruby, Ruby, Ruby, mine for the taking.

And then I pause, breathing heavy and trying to collect my thoughts.

"You alright, Good Guy?" she asks, breath just as heavy as mine.

I lean my forehead against hers, pressing her into the back door in the kitchen. "Are you sure you're ready? I don't want to pressure you."

She laughs, like I'm being ridiculous. "Yes, I'm really ready."

I lean back to look at her, trying to study her face in the darkness. "Ruby, have you...have you slept with anyone before?"

"Oh my God," she says, pulling away and raising a hand to her mouth, hiding a smile. Blue eyes, wide with amusement, peeking over the cracked glitter polish of her nails. "Wow, you really aren't used to girls making you wait, are you, Conti?"

I open my mouth to speak, but then close it again. I'm not sure what to say. I don't know if that was a yes or a no. That was a yes, right? Yes, she has slept with someone before?

Next thing I know, her hand is on my crotch, cradling what is probably the hardest my dick has ever been. I groan at her touch, not sure how we're ever going to make it back to my place. "Is this your way of answering me?" I ask. She only purrs out a little hum though, and I look down at her teasing eyes, see her watching me.

I'm a reckless mess, and as much as I know I shouldn't, I can't help but react to her touch. I need her. *Now.*

I shake my head, slide my hand down the front of her body, down to her thighs and grip the hem of her dress. I yank her dress up and over her, dropping it to the floor. Squeeze the fabric of my own shirt around my neck and pull it off, needing to feel my skin on hers. I'm kissing her, absolutely ravishing her, and she's fumbling with the button of my jeans.

"I'd like to explore a little," she says, and I grumble out something along the lines of "be my guest."

Before I know it, she's on her knees, and those ruby red lips of hers are on my dick. *Holy fuck.* I'm blind with the feel of her fucking me with her mouth. I have one hand on the back door, the other gripping her silky curls, holding on for dear life.

Well *this* sure as hell isn't new to her.

Nope, not at all. This mouth knows exactly what it's doing, and with her working like she is, I might just survive a car ride home with her. Then I'll take her to my bed and make love to her, slow and proper. Just need this little release, and then I'll be able to think clearly. I run my fingers through her hair in appreciation, grateful she understands just how badly I need her.

And then, like the little tease that she is, she stops. Rises back up to a stand. Says, "Condom," and hell if that's not the end of my ability to think straight.

I work to step out of my jeans, still pooled at my feet. Stumble and damn near fall over as I work to take my shoes off and kick all these unnecessary barriers away. She's laughing at the sight, and I tell her she better be ready to get fucked so hard for that sly little teasing mouth of hers.

She nods her head through her laughter, tells me it's too bad she's not a virgin because she's pretty sure I'm about to claim her as mine no matter what, and that's music to my ears.

Because I'm not about to be gentle.

No fucking way I can be.

I rip the wrapper with my teeth, roll on the latex and rip her panties to the side. Hear her giggle, "Oh, so we're doing this," right before I lift her up and slam my cock into her like it's the most important mission in the world. Her legs are wrapped around me and I'm pressing her against cold steel, dishes rattling, dropping to the floor in sharp-pitched shatters. The pristine kitchen is going to be obliterated thanks to my recklessness, and I can't even begin to give a shit.

I should be more gentle with her. It's our first time after weeks of dating, and I should have made it more romantic.

But all the shoulds go right out the window with this girl. All reason, all sensibility, completely gone.

Probably never to return, because she's right—I'm claiming her. "Mine," I growl with several more thrusts, and feel the bite as she sinks her teeth into my shoulder, whimpering and clawing at me, crying out my name.

Never knew just how right my name could sound coming from someone else's voice. I lightly put my hand around that gorgeous and gifted throat of hers. Kiss below her jaw, and think about how my Nightingale will forever be the love song of my life.

***

WE'RE APPROACHING THE START OF the new school year, and I hate how miserable Ruby seems looking into teaching jobs. She wasn't able to find anything music specific, so she's having to resort to expanding to other options.

It's all wrong, she deserves so much more than music being confined to her playing covers, and weeknight music lessons to halfway interested kids.

That's when I get the idea to approach Mama Z for help with Ruby's music. Strange to think I'm asking a seventy-nine year old woman something like this, but I know she has a friend in the local music world somewhere. Every now and then if you happen to mention wanting tickets to something, Mama Z magically makes them appear. I'm guessing it's one of her friends in her long time art group she's been a part of. I think she mentioned that at one point, who knows. But I'm wondering if maybe this chick knows someone, can make a call. You know, maybe see if we can get Ruby into some bigger spots in Philly or something. Or at a minimum, audition for one of the more established local bands around here.

"I'll see what I can do," Mama Z says as I share my ideas with her.

It's a quiet afternoon, no kids running around the house. No meals being cooked. I'm with Mama Z in the back conservatory, a room boxed with French windows, flooded with light. My grandmother's art studio. She's working on an abstract painting, red and orange mixed with charcoals. An S pattern snaking its way across the mural-sized canvas, dotted with small pops of color that might be flowers. Might be something else, I'm not sure.

"But I'm warning you, my sweet Joey," she says, and I'm a little on edge waiting for what Mama Z is about to say. She's giving me a look that I'm not used to. One that can freeze oceans. I know she's completely capable of holding a fierceness for anyone that crosses her path, but I'm not used to being on the receiving end of it.

"Alright. Let's hear it," I say, a mix of amusement and nervousness hitting my veins.

She pauses her painting. Puts the brush down and looks at me again, that expression of intensity as strong as I've ever seen. "Once the world discovers your Ruby, you will be opening yourself to constant risk of losing her."

Okay. Let's just go ahead and clarify that this was not what I expected to hear my grandmother say. I expected a warning about her not being able to do anything, maybe. Or about potential rejections. That the rejections may hurt her, how putting herself out there is hard and I may have to help Ruby through that. To be ready to scoop her up, kiss away her tears, reassure her that her talents are real and encourage her to keep at it.

But never that I might lose her.

"Aww come on now, Mama Z. What do you mean?" I ask, trying to lighten the mood. I glance back at her painting. Notice the strokes of red and gray intertwined. What had appeared to be an uplifting image of a wave just a minute ago, now I'm seeing as a dark and menacing cloud. Red blood bleeding from it in drops of warning.

"This is not a joke, Joey. I love you, and I can see how much you love that girl. Rightfully so. Ruby is, I believe, the only girl I have seen to truly match your spirit."

My mind goes back to Reggie. Mama Z liked Reggie. But never *loved* her for me. In fact, I remember when she learned about Reggie and my uncle Xavier, (Xavier being the illegitimate lovechild of none other than my grandfather Artem and his secretary. Mama Z took to Xavier as if he was her own son, scandalous as it all was).

When she learned Reggie and Xavier were together, I fully expected a response of rage to pass through Mama Z. Even my mom had an initial reaction of anger before eventually calming down and helping me get my bearings. She helped me see that what Reggie and Xavier had was obviously something bigger, and outside of me.

But Mama Z didn't have any of that kind of reaction. Instead, all she ever said was, "Good. A good fit," like we were talking about damn shoes or something, instead of the love of my life making off with my uncle.

I remember being floored and hurt. I was her favorite grandson, I wanted to know where the fire and anger were for me. When I had confronted Mama Z, hoping to see the hurt and anger I was feeling reflected back to me from my beloved grandmother, all she said was, "Reggie wasn't the one for you. But she is the one for Xavier." Just like that. Like it was all very natural, nothing to be surprised by. The strangest fucking thing.

So you can understand why I'm a little thrown off by this declaration about Ruby. A girl I've been dating for mere weeks. In some ways just getting to know, in other ways I've felt like I've known her my whole life.

I mindlessly reach for Mama Z's paint brush, but she slaps my hand away. I retreat. "If you're so sure Ruby is the one for me, then what makes you think there will be an issue?"

"Because, sweet boy." She picks up her paintbrush and resumes her work. I watch as she presses down, the brush seamlessly melting into the canvas, a fan of pigment left in its wake. "Neither you nor her have any idea the monster of the industry she's about to throw herself into.

"And that monster will give you highs so high, you forget there was ever an earth down below. And lows so low, you question if you even really exist. And all the while, you're clinging to your own identity, not sure where it ends and where the world's perception of you begins. So at some point, you allow it to swallow you up. You close your eyes and hope when you have a moment to pause, when you can open your eyes again, that you can see something grounded and still."

I blink back at her blankly. Like she has two heads.

And wonder what the fuck that all was that she just said.

second chance

. . .

Present Day

the glitter & notes press

. . .

INTERVIEW TRANSCRIPT WITH R. FRANCESCA
PRE-SHOW ON HER U.S. DOG TAGS & LACE TOUR

Interview by S. Right:

S: It's been a hectic couple months, with sold out shows on your tour, yet you are looking dazzling as always, Ms. Francesca.

R: You should see me at home in my onesie pajamas.

S: You're kidding.

R: Maybe I am. Maybe not.

S: They warned me you like to joke.

R: Warned you? That seems extreme. I'm not a wild animal.

S: Interesting, as "wild" is exactly the buzz surrounding your show. Care to share your take on it?

R: Alright, yeah. Wild might be about right. My crew has some real talents that they like to indulge.

[Muffled British voice in the background, "Tell him it's untamed delight!"]

[Laughter from Ruby] Fine. You hear that? It's untamed delight.

S: So this is your third album you've put out. Would you say it's your best yet?

R: Well, I haven't hit that platinum mark yet, but I think word's catching on.

S: And is it true that rockstar Jamison Spencer discovered you? At your boyfriend's restaurant, the The Guilty Olive?

R: Discovered me? I mean I'm not an ancient fossil.

S: Fine, what do you prefer to say?

R: Let's say it was right time, right place when Jamison heard me playing.

S: At your boyfriend…[papers ruffling] Joseph Conti's restaurant.

R: You're really committed to confirming that storyline, aren't you?

S: His restaurant just got featured on the show "The Best Thing I Ever Ate," and apparently has a reservation waitlist that requires your first born as collateral, so you can see the interest in the potential connection with you.

R: Are you hoping to get a reservation? Is that what this is about?

S: Would you be able to make that happen? Do you have the in?

R: Babe, I'm Ruby Francesca. I write, I sing. I play music. I'm an artist, first and foremost, but I don't play into the whole "hottest of the hot" thing. And if a restaurant is so hot that it needs collateral in the form of small children, then maybe that restaurant is skating on thin ice. Because the higher the rise…

S: The further the fall?

R: The bigger the head that bangs that much harder when it falls.

S: Ouch, okay. Am I sensing some fire in those words? A hot spot touched?

R: Just stating an observation. I've seen it happen.

S: Interesting, coming from someone where she herself is rising high rather fast.

R: I'll tell you what. If my head is so big, my ego so out of whack that I start requiring donations of family loved ones in order to get tickets to my show, then you can start to worry.

S: Ooo. Well I will state it best I can, then…Be warned, Joseph Conti. Whether or not Ruby Francesca really is a former love interest, she sure seems to hold some harsh opinions of you.

eighteen

. . .

joey

SEEING RUBY AGAIN after all this time has got me so fucked up I can't even see straight. It was bold of me to reach out for her hands like that, after her visit with Mama Z, but she surprised me when she let me. Shit, unless I'm remembering it wrong, in some ways I think she leaned into it. I'm really hoping that's the case. Maybe she doesn't hate me.

Maybe there's a chance, here.

Or maybe it's all just pity for a guy consumed with grief for his dying grandmother. I really fucking hope that's not it.

We were so good together, me and my Nightingale. After Reggie broke my heart, I didn't think I'd get serious with anyone ever again. Felt like it just wasn't the thing meant for me, like I wasn't a relationship guy after all.

Until Ruby. With her, the things I thought I felt for Reggie suddenly felt like puppy love. Made me realize Reggie was just a convenient security blanket from my childhood. But with Ruby, I felt something else. Something way bigger. The real deal, soulmate connection, sing it from the rooftops kind of love. The way we'd have *fun* together, just silly and stupid and easy. Ruby matched my sense of humor in a way Reggie never did.

Ruby. I'm losing my mind thinking about her, it's torture. It took every ounce of strength in me to let her get in that car and drive off. I'm guessing kidnapping her and locking her in my closet would be too extreme though. But shit, not having her by my side feels a thousand times harder now that I've seen her again.

In some ways she's exactly the same. Same ice blue fire in her eyes, same playfulness (or as playful as you can be when talking to a dying woman).

Then in other ways it's like she's a different person. And I don't know if that's just me, if I'm putting that in my head because my interactions with her have been limited to the one-sided online stalking I love to torture myself with. It's easy to let that cloud my concept of her when she's not right in front of me.

But to hold her again. To touch her again. When I had her hands in mine, right before she left, back to her crazy new world.

It's like every time my skin met hers, it came loaded with flashbacks of us from before. Us from that first summer we got together.

Her sitting on my bed. Me naked, lying across from her, watching her with blatant admiration. Sheets a wild mess, Ruby in one of my t-shirts. Drowning in it as it was about a thousand times too big on her.

Me brushing her hair away from her cheek, coaxing her to sing one of her songs in front of me. Closing my eyes to help her feel more comfortable, because she said she was nervous. Telling her that I was the one that was naked and exposed, her laughing at me and saying that I looked anything but nervous.

And listening as she got up out of bed, grabbed my own guitar I had in the corner, collecting dust. Leaning myself back, eyes still closed, but listening as she tuned it. Her teasing me for abusing my instrument.

I had asked her when she learned to play. She told me her grandmother taught her when she was young. It was her dad's mother, and after her parents divorced she would only see her dad and grandmother in the summer. Every July.

"It's when I'd feel most comfortable, most like myself. Those July nights, with those two. I didn't have to pretend or play any games, I could just be me."

"Ruby in July," I had said. "I've been loving Ruby in July." And I caught myself. Was it too soon to say "I love you?" I already knew I did, though, even just a few short weeks in.

I tried to move the conversation past my accidental declaration. "Your dad told me your grandmother could sing too," I said. The look of surprise she gave me.

"You sure did your research on me," she had said.

"You should be careful. I was obsessed right from the start." I can still remember the look of my shirt, falling off her shoulder. Leaning over to kiss the exposed skin, just a quick taste, before moving myself back to my eyes-closed position. Laying on my side, arm bent at the elbow, head propped up in my hand.

She laughed. "Fucking Stalker Good Guy," she said under her breath, barely audible.

But then she started playing.

I kept my eyes closed as promised. Found myself humming along in harmony. "You can sing," she had said, "despite the horrifying conditions of your guitar." I shushed her, eyes still closed as promised, told her it was because she was so inspiring, but that I knew my limits.

I remember at one point deliberately opening one eye with a grin when she was mid-song, and she threw a pillow at me, whacking me square in the face.

"You really love hitting me, Nightingale, don't you?"

"Good Guys sometimes need to be brought down a peg from their mighty high thrones."

"I think you're thinking of Kings," I said.

And she had paused her playing. Bit her thumb nail in concentration. I had started to interrupt, and she shushed me. Said, "wait," and she closed her eyes again.

Started playing a new tune. One with a little more soul than what she had been playing a moment ago. And then she started singing it.

Good guys often buy
Thrones in the sky
Thinking that they're kings
Yet I know why
It's to break past the armor
Guilt like a charmer
Sitting high tryin' to break
The good-est of girls...
Like me.

"Did you just make that up?" I asked.

"Yeah." She started looking all around her. "Where's my phone? Let me record it." She looked up at me. "Did you like that?"

And I crawled my naked ass right across that bed over to her, grabbed the guitar and tossed it aside. She laughed at the sad, startled noise of the instrument hitting the floor, said, "See? Abuse."

But I just grabbed her face in my hands and pushed her back on the bed. Kissed those amazing lips, her cheek, her forehead, her mouth again, drinking her in. "You're gonna be a goddamn star, Ruby Francesca."

"No I'm not," she said, but she was giggling. "I can't even play my own songs on stage. I'm too scared."

I held her face and looked in her summer sky blue eyes. "You're gonna get past that."

"Oh yeah? How?"

"You'll see. I'm going to help you." And we rolled around again for more ecstasy and I don't think I had ever felt happier in my whole life.

She did end up pausing to write down that song. And that

song, written right on my bed, with my horrible excuse for a guitar, that song became "The Good-est of Girls."

Her first hit single.

"YOU'RE GOING TO THROW YOUR back out if you're not careful," Xavier says to me as he watches me add more weights to the barbell.

"I know my limits, old man. I got more in me than you," I say to him with a smile. "Watch me." I lay back on the bench again, ready to destroy this next set.

He rolls his eyes and comes behind me, ready to spot. It's 270, so I know he's worried I'm going too hard. But I'm fucking bursting out of my skin lately, and I need this. I haven't been able to get Ruby out of my head. Work has been in such a groove lately that not even *that* has provided the distraction I need.

I grab the bar, solidify my position, and let the reps roll.

One.

Now that I've seen Ruby again, there's no way in hell I can let her back out of my life.

Two.

I fucked up with her. She didn't deserve what I did. I hate what I did. Hate that I hurt her.

Three.

She has no idea how much I love her, and I'm not sure if I can ever convince her that I do.

Four.

I had my reasons. She needs to know that I had my reasons. I need help in making her understand.

Five.

I got nothing to lose in doing everything I can to try.

Six.

Mama Z—there's something there, I can feel it, I just don't know what.

Seven.

"Christ, how far are you going, Joey?" Xavier frowns down at me. "Thought we were just clanging and banging here."

Eight.

"Until I'm fucking done!"

Nine.

She's mine. Ruby's mine, she's always been mine and I will not stop until she's absolutely mine again.

Ten.

"Enough!" Xavier shouts as he helps my shaking arms put the bar back on the rack. "Is there a camera here watching or something? What the hell are you trying to prove?" I look up at him, face upside down in my view, towering over me with a glare.

I try and deflect with a grin. "I got two of the hottest restaurants in town. You never know who might be watching." I sit up and blink away the stars threatening to swim across my vision.

Xavier shakes his head as he walks back to his machine. I get up, grab my water and towel. Unscrew the cap and let the liquid pour down my throat. Finish and wipe down the bench and weights, walk back over to where Xavier is pumping out leg presses.

"You ever feel like the women in this family are all in on something that you don't know about?" I ask.

"Every fucking day," he says, completely monotone.

"Even with Reggie?"

He pauses and raises an eyebrow from the spot on his angled bench. "The mother of my two children? She's more of a mystery to me than ever," he says. He keeps going with his presses.

"Yeah? How so?" Xavier doesn't usually talk to me about shit like that. Then again, I guess I never ask.

"I don't know. No time to talk, really. Just tossing diapers at each other after long days at work. Kids clingy because they've missed us all day. We're both exhausted with the baby. James slept like a dream. But Veronica is giving us a run for our money. Ornery Ronnie, living up to her name already."

"Thought I noticed some bags under those eyes, old man," I tease.

"Fuck off. Just wait 'til you have kids."

"Gee, I can't wait. You make it sound like such a thrill."

Xavier stops his presses and sits up, straddling the V of the press machine. Grabs his towel and wipes down his face and beard. "It is fun—James especially, it's amazing hearing him finally talk now. We're just tired, that's all."

"Maybe you need a night out."

Xavier looks up at me. "You watching the kids for us?" he asks with sarcasm.

"What about Lori?" Reggie's mom, Lori, lives in the guest house on their property.

Xavier shakes his head. "Nah, she helps so much during the day as it is."

I raise my forearm and lean against a nearby machine. "Yeah, okay. If it's a Monday night when I can be away from work, and you put them to bed first and I don't have to change diapers or cut up grapes and shit to avoid choking," I say.

"Done. We'll take it," Xavier says with basically the most amount of enthusiasm he's capable of showing. Watch out, folks! He's practically giddy. He swings his leg around the bench, rises up and faces me. "But why are you asking about the women in the family?"

I drop my arm down and pinch the bridge of my nose. "This whole Ruby thing. It's wild, when she came to see Mama Z, I got the sense that she and mom have had a whole lot more communicating going on this past year than I realized."

"And?" he asks. He cleans his machine and we walk through the rows of machinery, head toward the locker room. "What's wrong with that? Sometimes we find friends in surprising places."

"But my mom and grandmother? Even long after Ruby and I

broke up?" *Even after what I did to her,* I think. But Xavier doesn't know about all that.

"Her dad and I are friends. She knows that."

"So what, you're saying you are the connection now and not me?"

"That's not what I'm saying. I mean that there's a general connection between her family and ours," he emphasizes that last word and circles his hand between the two of us, "and that maybe made her feel more comfortable to keep contact with your mom and grandmother."

"Makes sense, fine," I say. But I still feel like there's something else there.

"You don't look convinced," Xavier says, reading my mind.

I open up my locker and pull out my gym bag. Unzip it and drop my towel and water bottle in. "I guess you had to see it. When Ruby came by she just...I don't know. She popped down next to Mama Z like she had things she wanted to say to her too."

Xavier shrugs as he throws the strap of his bag over his shoulder. "Ruby doesn't talk to her mom, right?"

"Yeah."

"So that could be it. She found her female role models, and since you two ended things, maybe your mom and Mama Z just didn't want to tell you about it. Maybe they didn't want to throw it in your face."

"Maybe. Whatever, either way, I'm getting her back."

"Ruby?" he looks at me, eyebrows raised and looking obnoxiously skeptical.

"Yes, Ruby. She feels it too, I'm telling you. There's still something there between us. Fucking chemistry. It's there."

"Alright," Xavier says as we walk out. "Just don't go doing anything stupid, like running up on stage at her show or something and getting yourself arrested."

"Nah. She's all the way in Chicago now. Too far."

"Oh the relief."

"I'm just praying she actually comes back after her tour." I get to my car and throw my bag in.

"When does she finish?" Xavier asks. And I laugh at the sight of him standing next to his SUV, two car seats packed in the backseat.

"Next week. And I'm going to be ready if she does make her way back to town."

"Naturally. I'd expect nothing less from you."

nineteen

. . .

ruby

"WHAT DAY IS it?"

"Wednesday, doll," Grayson says, handing over her tea.

"And what city are we in?" Ruby says from her spot on the hotel room floor. She starts laughing and falling forward, curling her upper body carefully around the startled Rebel in her lap. "Oh my God, I'm delirious."

Grayson grabs the tea from her, saving it from sloshing around. He places it on the desk and takes a seat. "Talk to your man Gray, what's the matter?" he asks. He looks over to Rebel, still squished in Ruby's lap, licking her cheek as Ruby remains bent in half, her face to the floor. "Rebel, what's wrong with your Mummy?"

Ruby pops back up to an upright seated position, and Rebel readjusts himself in her lap. Her eyes are bright and wide, sapphire gems sparkling with a light Grayson knows all too well. "I've got a new song. I need your help. I want to perform it at the last show."

"Ahhh, creativity bug has bitten, I see." He looks down at Rebel. "Why didn't you tell me Mummy was in the zone?"

Ruby nuzzles Rebel's fur and kisses his head. "He's always my best inspiration," she says. She looks up at Grayson. "Seriously though. Grab a guitar, help me out. I want you to play it with me on stage for the last show." There was an evil glint and devilish smile on Ruby's face. "I haven't slept all night. It just came to me and I've been working on it."

"Okay…"

"But I want you, my dear, sweet Grayson, to be the one to play." She bats impossibly long eyelashes at him.

"Me?" Grayson balks in surprise.

"Yes, you. Just the two of us. Seated and chill, like the old days of small gigs."

Grayson frowns back at her. "What is this about, Ruby?" he asks. Ruby is daring in her hope to persuade him to do this. She knows that Grayson felt he had found his knack for everything behind the scenes of music as Ruby's right hand. But he has no interest in performing. For Grayson, teaching was always his goal as a music major and he never expected to take it anywhere beyond that. His friendship with Ruby had obviously changed his plans, but Ruby knew Grayson still preferred off stage more than on.

"If you play with me, instead of the band, it's personal. It's emotional. I can introduce you as my long time friend, my ride or die who has been there through so much with me."

"I thought Rebel was your ride or die."

Ruby looks at the now closed-eyed Rebel, peacefully resting in his mama's nest of fuzzy blue pajama pants. "Of course he is, right muffin? My ride or die *fur* buddy." She looks back up at Grayson. "But you're my ride or die everything else. And I need you. Please?" She gives him her best wide-eyed and innocent face. "You wouldn't say no to lil old me, would you?"

Grayson rolls his eyes and gets up. He grabs the guitar in her room and gets himself settled. "You ran this by Jules and the team I'm assuming?"

Ruby nods with the enthusiasm of a bobble head doll on a

dashboard of a car careening off-road. "It took a little convincing, but after explaining my vision and your role, they were all in. They love it. We got the go."

"You're exhausting."

"You're magical."

"Alright, let's hear it," Grayson says, closing his eyes.

Ruby clears her throat, straightens her back, and begins. The honey of her voice floats through the space, and she feels the mellow notes surround them in a hug.

See my July
Weightless in the soar, and you and I know
it glides, it carries all
See it be the answer of my cry

She sings with soul, lowering her voice and dragging out "cry," to the point of it fading out to a quiet nothingness. Grayson begins playing, accompanying and filling the spaces in between.

She continues, the next notes deep and heavy from her abdomen.

Carry me home since I've been so far gone
Hear it in the blanket of night sky

Ruby opens her eyes now. She pauses and looks at Grayson, a small smile escaping her lips, as she knows he'll understand once he hears the next lines.

Your Nightingale
In July

She grins at Grayson, and he shakes his head at her with a huff and soft smile in response. But he likes it—she can tell. Soon his head shakes shift direction, turning to affirming nods.

Ruby continues with her new tune, singing of the adventures of the July nightingale, seeking cozy spaces but making mistakes. Grayson's hands on the guitar create a sound that rides along with her voice. Waves of harmony and movement that are the exact match and feel she knew he could create.

They work together, stumble and pause in some parts, re-work others. Grayson grabs his phone to record at one point, and they run through and fine tune. With each pass at it, each new bit that they hit just right, a warmth floods through Ruby's belly. It's a coziness that rises up and through her chest, swims up her throat, and escapes out of her lips to encase the lyrics of her latest creation.

When eventually they get to the end, they look at one another in a frozen moment. The silence creates a vacuum in the static air. Though no sound fills, the essence of their song remains in a buzz around them.

Ruby eventually grins, saying nothing.

"Fuck, that's good," Grayson says, matching her grin.

"I know," she says. "I know."

"I can see why you couldn't sleep."

"I don't even feel tired."

"Just a couple more shows."

"I can't freakin' WAIT to do the last one and play this," she says. "It's perfect."

Grayson gently sets the guitar down and moves over to the floor across from Ruby. Gives Rebel a little pat.

"What? Go ahead, say it," Ruby says.

"It's just—you know he'll hear it."

"Why...I haven't the foggiest idea what you're talking about, mate," Ruby says in a mix of a British accent and a yipping dog.

"Well shit, now, ma'am," Grayson says in what is supposed to be an American accent. "That right there is the sorriest attempt at an accent I here ever heard."

"I'm not southern," Ruby says, falling to her side in fits of giggles.

"That's the only American accent I can do," Grayson says, his voice back to normal.

"Maybe we'll just stick to our day jobs and not try impressions then. Our musicality makes us too good. We over act." Ruby grabs Rebel, pulls him to her chest and falls back onto the floor. Grayson joins her, and together they stare up at the ceiling.

"Seriously though, Ruby."

"Uh-oh. You said my actual name."

"Are you trying to send him a message?"

She's quiet for a minute while she thinks about this. So many emotions have been stirring up for her since seeing Joey again. She missed when she could simply hate him. When she could write him off as an asshole and call it a day. Even Mama Z and Isabella were gracious enough to rarely mention Joey in their few exchanges they'd shared with Ruby over the past year.

Then again, Ruby wonders if a part of her reasoning for even remaining in contact with those women was more for the link to Joey than anything else.

Ruby raises her hands, presses the heels of them into her eyes at the thought. "I'm stupid. I know."

"Stop that," Grayson says, nudging her shoulder with his.

"I can't help it. I can't help but still think of him, Grayson. I don't get it."

Grayson sighs. "He's not a bad guy, that's why."

"Ha! Right. Good Guy after all, is that it? Even after what he did?"

"Maybe there's more to the story that you don't know."

"I hate that I want to believe that," Ruby says, raising her head to Rebel and speaking in her high-pitched talking-to-a-dog voice. "I really, really do, Rebel! Why do I want to believe that? So stupid! So, so stupid, yes it is. But I want to believe that."

"So believe it then, love."

"What exactly am I believing? That he's a good guy?"

"More than that Ruby," Grayson says softly.

They both know what he means, but she's not sure she can hear it. She can't hear Grayson say the exact thing she hopes for.

Ruby groans. "I'm just not sure that's the answer here. I mean not even Mama Z ever tries to sell me on Joey. Isabella will throw in the occasional 'Joey saw your interview and loved it,' email now and then. Mama Z seems to believe her grandson is unworthy though."

"But here you are, up all night thinking about him. A few more shows left and you know you'll be back near him again," Grayson points out.

"It's just my broken heart," Ruby mutters through a frown.

"Nah, your heart, Ms. Francesca," Grayson says, grabbing her hand, "is much too strong to break."

"Okay. Then a sprain."

"Very temporary."

"Easy to fix," she says.

"Quick Band-Aid."

"Healing vibes."

"Back to normal." Grayson raises her hand to his lips, gives it a chaste kiss. "Good as new."

"Good as new," she whispers.

And she hopes it's true. Because truth be told, she does want Joey to hear this song. So many times she considered writing a song with his nickname for her. Any time before, she'd push the lyrics down with all her might. She'd be damned if she gave him the credit of thinking he inspired her.

Clearly though, that strength was impossible when he was in her presence. All the old feelings resurrected. More than that, the way he looked at her—like he truly did care for her. Even as she had thrown the accusation to him of seeking her fame, she knew in her gut that it couldn't be further from the truth.

It's why what happened last year didn't make any sense.

While they had decided to no longer label their relationship after that first summer three years ago, when her career catapulted overnight, they had remained friendly. Okay, more than friendly. Anytime they reconnected, it was clear that flame had not dissipated. The sweet and single public image might be what her team wanted for the rising star, and she'd play along with the knowledge that she was paving the way to the career of her dreams. But the exchanges with Joey in those following months were so much more than ones of platonic friends.

And he was always, always supportive. She would tentatively tell him over a phone call she was going on a date with the latest TV heart throb and would explain that it was all a setup to help her image. And Joey would go, "That's good, Nightingale. Play your game, do your thing. This is your time." She remembers being nervous to admit those incidents to him. It felt weird talking to him about dating, if that's what you could even call it. Joey would joke, saying, "Okay, rub it in my face, why don't you?" and Ruby would instantly feel guilty.

If she apologized, though, Joey would ease her mind and say, "You don't owe me an apology, Ruby. We're friends, right?"

"Friends," she'd say, though they both knew that's not what they wanted. Or at least not what she wanted, anyway.

"Yup," Joey would say. "Friends. But yes, I'm jealous as fuck, and I can't say that'll change," he'd say through a laugh, and she'd smile and laugh too.

Until it all came to a head last year. When he blew it all up, just like that.

She had been back in town, prepared to throw in the towel of pretending they weren't together. Ruby wanted to ask him to join her because this life of living her dream was nothing if he wasn't living it with her. It seemed so obvious—even though their actual time together had only been a couple months, the past two years had felt like Joey had become a critical part of her life. She didn't care what her image needed to be, she needed him by her side more.

So why did he have to fuck it all up? And with that painful memory of what he did to her fresh in her mind, she's fueled with anger all over again. An endless torment of confusion, love for him, hope, hurt, and anger.

She's sick of the cycle—it has to stop. Not even the busyness of the tour can shut her brain down of the monstrous replays of memories of Joey Conti Jr. What she needs now is closure so that she can end the cycle and turn off the thoughts of him once and for all.

At least, that's what she tells herself.

Because if closure was what she really wanted, she wouldn't be putting out this song.

the glitter & notes press

. . .

Ruby Francesca's Dog Tags & Lace tour—electrifying! But her last show?

The buzz is that it was her best performance yet. So, what gives?

"It was that surprise new song she did," gushes a fan fresh out of the theater post-show in Orlando, FL.

That's right! A surprise new song, apparently written only days before. Francesca performed the new number on stage with her longtime friend and associate, Grayson Atkinson. The Glitter & Notes Press reached out to Atkinson for a comment, but received no response.

"It was beautiful. So simple with just the two of them up there," says another fan. Taking a quick peek on social media, you'll find praise for the song and its performance trending all over. Critics are calling the move "ballsy," but fans seem to be screaming for the official release.

The new song, titled "Nightingale in July," seemed to evoke a raw level of lost love that could bring even the strongest to their knees with its emotionally charged pain. With rumors circulating that the song is about Francesca's ex boyfriend, we had to know more.

Rest assured readers, we here at GNP did all the digging for you, and guess what we found? A source confirms that Ruby Francesca and Philly restaurateur Joseph Conti Jr. were in fact an item. And it only gets better—

Francesca and Conti were reportedly together just a few weeks prior, all in the name of saying goodbye to Conti's ailing grandmother.

"She seemed upset when she came back," our source confirms. "And not just for the old lady. It seemed like more than that. Like she was heartbroken. She was late for sound check, she tripped during a run through—something was definitely off."

Well one thing is clear—Ruby Francesca dusted off whatever it was she was experiencing, and used it to her advantage. Word in the industry is that "Nightingale in July" might just be the key to getting

Francesca not just to the very top of the charts (a barrier she has yet to breach since her first hit single, "Good-est of Girls")—

But maybe even her first Grammy.

twenty

. . .

joey

"I'M GUESSING YOU heard?" Reggie asks as I walk into her and Xavier's house. She's looking at me with so much kindness on her face I want to puke. I try and ignore her look and walk into their kitchen. Prop an elbow on the island.

"About the ego comment? That I demand a first born child to get into my restaurants? Yeah, I heard," I say.

I don't want Reggie's pity, that's for damn sure. I'm here to help them babysit so they can get a night out, and that's already feeling pretty sad. I'm a thirty-two year old man with a successful restaurant business and on a rare night off I'm babysitting little people. And for some reason, that's got me feeling pretty low right now.

Especially since those little ones were supposed to be asleep when I got here and clearly aren't.

"Right, that too, but I mean the other thing," Reggie says. She's balancing baby Ronnie on her hip when James comes up to tug at her.

"Mommy, up—ee," he says, pulling on her shirt.

I grab the baby from Reggie so she can pick up James. Stare at Ronnie's giant green eyes and even larger bow thingie wrapped around her red, peach fuzz hair. "Ronnie, tell your mom that I don't want to hear what the other thing is, okay?"

"I think you're going to want to hear this, Joey," Reggie says.

I turn away and throw Ronnie up in the air. Mostly to avoid that look of obnoxious pity that I know is still on Reggie's face.

"I really, really don't!" I say, throwing the baby up and laughing at the squeals I'm getting in return.

"I'm going to warn you that I just fed her," Reggie says. "You might want to think twice on that."

"Appreciate that," I say, stopping and pulling the baby back toward me.

"Seriously though, Joey. She put out a new song. You have to have heard."

"Huh?"

"Seriously? Ruby's last show. It's all the rage right now—shit's gone viral. And I think you need to be aware of the fact that people are saying the song is—"

"I *do not* want to hear it, Reggie. Doesn't anyone fucking listen to me?" I look over at James, say, "Sorry, buddy," but he just has his head on Reggie's shoulder. Staring at me. The kid kinda creeps me out, actually. Very serious for a two-year old.

I'm an asshole.

"Okay," Reggie says, hand held up in the air in surrender.

Then I feel a little bad for snapping. Though from the look on Reggie's face, she's more amused than anything else.

"Are you laughing right now?" I ask. "Why doesn't anyone take me seriously when I'm trying to get mad?!"

"Alright, alright, fine," she says, shaking her head with a smirk. "I'm taking you seriously. I just know that when you hear this song, you'll be wishing you weren't caught off guard, that's all."

"Where is your husband?" I ask, changing the subject.

"Uh-huh, okay. I see what you're doing there. We're moving

on. Noted." She looks at James. Pokes his belly and the giant bear on it, says, "Go pick out your bedtime stories."

James nods and slithers down from Reggie's hip.

"He was helping me with some things at the office and got home late and is now rushing in the shower and of course we're off schedule, as usual," she says. She grabs Ronnie from me.

"I don't do bedtimes," I say. "Unless they can stay up late eating candy and watching scary movies," I say to James, winking.

The kid just stares at me, wide-eyed.

"I see he has his father's sense of humor," I say.

"Some humor is more subtle than others," Xavier says, coming down the stairs, beard long and dark hair loose around his face.

"I'm going to change Ronnie and put her and James down real quick," Reggie says. "Wish me luck."

"Good luck," Xavier and I both say as she and the kids make their way up the stairs.

I look at Xavier with a smirk. "Your buttons are off."

"What?" he asks, frowning.

I point to his shirt and the sad attempt at lopsided buttoning. "Look, you skipped one."

"Shit," he says, moving his hands to his chest to fix the error. "That's what I get for rushing."

"Take it easy, there's no rush. As long as kids are actually asleep before you abandon me, I'm good."

"We really appreciate it."

"Not that I'm ever having kids, but if I get some girl in trouble then you can return the favor then," I say.

"Any luck on the Ruby front? Speaking of girls."

"She's back in town. I've been texting with Grayson."

"Grayson...but not her?" Xavier asks, leaning back on the kitchen counter. He crosses his arms over his chest. "Is she officially too big for regular people to text her or something?"

"Not exactly. Just me, I think."

"Why, what happened with you two?"

"What makes you say something happened?" I say, unsure of how to explain.

He looks at me for a hot sec, and I swear he's studying me. I'm consumed with guilt, like he knows my shameful secrets.

"Never mind. I don't want to know," he says. "Not if you don't want to tell me," he explains, and I'm given the littlest bit of relief.

He walks over to the fridge and grabs two beers. Pops off the caps and hands me one.

"Am I allowed to drink on the job?" I ask before taking a sip.

"Kids get cuter with beer goggles on. As long as you're not taking shots in a corner somewhere while waking up the kids to be your dance buddies, I think you'll be fine."

He takes a sip and I take in the scene before me. Here he is, in this house that he shares with Reggie, kitchen full of baby bottles and a high chair with toys scattered around. It looks like my parents' house with all the grandkids running around. I suddenly realize how busy life has been and how little I'm actually over here. Xavier looks so strange standing in this domesticated space.

Strange and tired. But also happy.

And shit, my heart hurts for Ruby. Grayson's assured me over the course of some of our texts that she doesn't hate me. But after hearing what she said about me and my alleged big ass ego, I'm thinking he's just trying to be nice.

On the other hand, I have nothing to lose.

"You're awfully quiet for a change," Xavier notes.

I rub my hands over my face. "Just busy with work, checking in on Mama Z who seems to be a cat with nine freakin' lives. Trying to help mom out with the house at least, since it's been looking like a bomb went off. Making sure she's eating and taking care of herself. Yelling at my sisters and cousins to keep their damn kids somewhere else now and then to give my mom a break. And ya know, generally trying to distract myself from the fact that the love of my life is running around town right now after finishing a tour. But I'm not sure she has any interest in talking to me, though she did say she'd come back to visit with my dying grandmother." I take in a deep breath, exhale and sip my beer.

"You've had a lot on your mind," is all Xavier says.

I let out a sarcastic breath. "Yeah. I guess so."

"What makes you say she'd have no interest in talking to you? Ruby, I mean?"

"Let's just say I fucked up with her. Last year when she was in town. Said some hurtful things that I didn't mean, but now it's out there and I can't undo them."

"That's not like you," Xavier says, frowning.

We hear a muffled wail of a cry come from upstairs and we both look up at the ceiling.

"Moment of truth," Xavier says, still staring up.

"What's that mean?"

He looks back down at me. "We rock Ronnie almost to sleep and try and put her down just before she's completely out. To try and get her acclimated to being able to settle herself. She always cries right when you put her down, you just don't know if it'll be thirty seconds of fussing, or if she's going down with a fight and then you have to start all over again."

"That sounds fucking awful," I say. And then I grin. "Look at you and this sweet little family life."

The cries stop, and he joins me in a smile. "Looks like it's gonna be a good night," he says.

"There's hope in the world," I agree.

Reggie eventually comes downstairs and she and Xavier look like two kids heading out for prom, they're so damn excited. I tell them to make good choices, they roll their eyes at me and then they're gone.

And that's when my loneliness creeps in. Like a crippling fucking bullet. Sharp and unexpected.

I live a pretty busy life, and I'm starting to realize that still moments are not good for me. Way too easy to get in my head and think about what I'm missing.

I'm looking around this house, full of the signs of chaos and family, and I'm in physical pain thinking about Ruby. The words from that interview. She seemed so casual and smug about it. I'm torn between thinking I have nothing to lose in trying to get her back, and feeling like she deserves better than me. Shit, I know she deserves better than me, I'm just too fucking selfish to give up.

I need her. That's all there is to it.

THE NIGHT WITH THE KIDS went down without a hitch, by some miracle. Reggie and Xavier came home glowing, thanked me profusely even though all I really did was sit and watch baseball and bask in my loneliness like a pitiful asshole.

So we'll blame that for what I did next, and why I am in fact, in a jail cell right now.

It started out innocently enough. I just wanted to drive by her dad's place. See if that's where she was staying, not that I even really would know how to confirm that. I could text Grayson to ask, but I guess I was feeling dysfunctional in all my self-pity, what can I say?

And then I don't know why, but next thing you know I'm parked out front of the house, watching. By now, it was after midnight, but I didn't even think about that. The street was quiet, the house was dark. I looked up at what I knew was Ruby's old bedroom window. I'd only ever been there a couple times—usually if Ruby needed clothes or something. We'd always be at my place when we were together. I wondered if she was there now, sleeping. Hopefully getting what I would guess is some much needed rest after her tour. I wanted to know when she was due back out in LA, but I was on a strict No Looking Up Ruby plan, and I'd gone cold turkey since the interview about me.

It's been a tough forty-eight hours.

The light in her bedroom window clicked on.

I could make out the silhouette of her through her curtains. I had a gut punch feeling when the thought, "Is she alone?" popped in my head. I punched my steering wheel at the thought. Screamed a little in frustration.

And then I got out of the car. I swear to Christ I was moving completely involuntarily, just floating on over towards the house. Found myself climbing up the side of the house, grabbing hold of whatever I could until I got to the small roof of the wraparound porch. I maneuvered to the side and got to the spot right under her window. It was still a little too high though, I could only tap at it.

So I did. A couple of light taps, no big deal.

And then her light went off. Fuck. I figured I probably scared her.

It was the moment of truth. I had to text her. Grayson had given me her latest cell number, but I had no idea if she blocked me or what.

J: It's me. Under your window.

Nothing.
A minute went by.

J: It's me, Joey, by the way.

Figured I'd add that in case she didn't have my number anymore.

Another minute.

I sat on the porch roof, tried to get comfortable while not sliding off.

Another minute.

It was around this point that I started to feel pretty fucking pathetic and miserable.

But then the most glorious glow of my phone happened. I rushed to open her text.

R: What are you talking about? How?

> J: I climbed onto the porch roof, but I'm stuck here.

R: Oh my fucking God, Joey. You mean at my dad's OLD house?

Oh shit. And about forty-seven seconds later, I was arrested.

I'M SITTING IN MY LITTLE local jail cell, and I've got nothing but time. Thankfully, I'm on my own in here, so that's a plus. Cinderblock walls are my only real accompaniment for the night. I hear some strange sounds around me, but nothing too crazy. Made my call and all that, and hopefully I got someone on the way. Not much I can do now but sit here and wait.

You know you really don't think about how much you value the concept of time until you have no way to know what time it actually is. My phone, watch, and wallet have been collected, so I'm stuck here. Staring at the bumps of these goddamn cinderblock walls. Thinking about the bumps in my own life.

I mean shit, life's good on paper. Even Ruby's recent interview was a strange blessing—it only increased our calls for reservations, so that's something. I'm being asked to consult for other restaurants, offering me amounts of money that I'm pretty much laughing at. It's not that I'm known for Michelin star quality food, just that my food is creative and trendy and my restaurants never without customers. Which is fine, really. Less pressure but all the success I could want.

But Ruby, Ruby, Ruby is consuming my mind in this literal jail cell of timeless torture.

I think back to three years ago when I really started to fall for her. That for me was a *moment*, if you know what I mean. I think we can all agree that there are certain moments you go through when you think, "Yeah, things are happening." And I don't just mean the big stuff, like the first job you land that you actually wanted. Or the first time you have sex and realize you're not exactly a kid anymore if you're doing acts that all your life had been expressly described as reserved for "When you're older."

I'm talking about the little moments, here. The first home run you get as a kid. Or to be a little sweet about it, the first time you play through a piece of music with no mistakes. The types of moments that leave you with a high, and you can ride that high for days on end.

I know exactly when that moment was with Ruby. My heart felt like it could burst right up and out of my chest with that girl, and I figured that out early on into our relationship.

We had dinner at my parents' house one night. It was maybe only Ruby's third or fourth dinner there, but she was quickly becoming what felt like one of us. She and Mama Z had apparently become fast friends with a mutual love of everything music. Ruby fit right in with my chaotic family.

She had been working on getting over her stage fright, and we were talking about it over dinner. Kids were running around and screaming in some chasing game, and my poor cousin Ava was looking exhausted, holding her four-month-old with her eyes closed right there at the table.

"Ava, you're dropping your baby," my mom had said to her. "Malia, grab your granddaughter for me before she slides off her mother's lap and the dog thinks it's leftovers for him." She took a sip of her wine and I saw Ruby giggling, hand held over her mouth to try and hide it.

"That's ridiculous. The dog's a snob and only likes lamb. And besides, I'm not going to drop my baby because I worked much too hard to birth this thing," Ava had said, eyes still closed and head still back on her chair. She adjusted the baby in her lap, though.

Aunt Malia had popped up, grabbed baby Arabella from Ava's lap, and handed her to Ruby.

And no, it wasn't some fatherly instinct I'm talking about here that made me feel this thing I'm doing a terrible job of describing. I don't think, anyways. You'll see why in a minute.

Ruby reluctantly took baby Arabella, and that girl of mine looked so damn awkward holding her I could have sworn you'd think she'd never held a baby before.

I told her so, and Ruby rolled her eyes. "I have. Just not one this little."

My mom was shooting glances at me from her seat at the head of the table, and I was trying to ignore them. I remember what Ruby had said—that she had no interest in having kids. The conversation had come up again, and Ruby still maintained that it just wasn't something she was sure would be in her future. We were way too new to be talking about future planning, but I liked that Ruby felt she needed to give me the heads up. To me, none of it really registered. I figured see what the future brings, and if that meant kids? Cool. If not? Then more freedom, money, travel time and less diapers seemed like a good life to me.

But there she was, holding Arabella even though I knew she was nervous to, and I loved that she was here in this mayhem of a household all for me.

"You're cute, I guess," Ruby said, bouncing Arabella on her knee. The baby was grinning and doing those little baby laughs. "Oh, look at you! You've got the Conti dimples, don't you?" she said, pointing to the mini divots on Arabella's face.

"Not the Conti dimples," Mama Z said from across the table from Ruby.

"Oh, right. Derian then?" Ruby asked, looking to Mama Z.

"Actually, Ava's husband has dimples," my mom said.

"Yes," Ava confirmed from her mini catnap. "Maybe one of these days he'll actually be around for you to meet and not traveling and leaving me exhausted and open to judgment from my aunt." Ava opened one eye and stared down to my mom.

"Be happy he works and provides for you, Ava," Mama Z scolded.

"Please. *I* provide. I'm back to work and juggling both full time working and full time mom. No one's giving me props for that though."

"You want credit? Credit is for the insecure," Mama Z said.

"Alright, subject change!" my mom said with a bright smile and purple stained teeth. "Ruby, we all have been listening to your music and have decided we want to hear you perform. When can we do that?"

Ruby stopped her bouncing of the baby and looked up at my mom. "Oh. Well, I actually struggle with performing my own songs on stage. I'm working on it, but I have terrible stage fright."

"Didn't you go to school for music?" Ava half mumbled.

"Yeah, and I stuck to the sidelines there too and performed anyone and everyone's music but my own."

"You know, Cher had stage fright too. Gosh I remember it," Mama Z said, leaning forward and resting her elbows on the table, chin in her interlaced fingers. "She needed Sonny to go on stage with her." She looked over to Ruby. "Lots of musicians have stage fright, you know."

"Well rest assured, I'm working on it. Not giving up yet," Ruby said, pulling her eyes away from Mama Z and looking right at me.

Something passed between us then. There was something in her eyes that said to me, "*You, babe.*" Like I was breaking down my Nightingale's walls, and in their place feeding her hope. "I'm getting more comfortable by the day with the idea of having my music heard." And we smiled at each other, knowing the moments we'd been sharing with her playing for me.

Later that night, I took her to the restaurant—my only one at the time—The Guilty Olive. Lucy and her sister Lila joined us, as well as

Grayson. The past few weeks of Ruby and I dating had forged a new little group between us with lots of nights like that, hanging at my bar. Formerly, it would have been Reggie and Xavier as well, but lately they had been feeling more like the parents of our group. I didn't mind, I was enjoying the new friendship circle we had been finding that summer.

At one point I left the group at the bar, safely in the hands of my bartender Katrina. Pulled myself reluctantly away from Ruby's presence. Went to the back to get some work done, since I'd been spending more and more time with Ruby, and was falling behind.

I had been spinning around an idea for a while. Something I was hoping Ruby would go for, because I was committed to helping her get over this stage fright thing. I wanted to see her at least doing bigger gigs than the damn Moon Lounge, for fuck's sake. Hell, even at my place she'd be in the city, and maybe have more of a chance of building a following. I'd had my marketing guy take a look at her social media, minimal as it was. Tasked him with spinning up some ideas to help her get her name out there, build a website, drum up some interest.

But I needed my girl to sing her songs for an audience first.

After the restaurant officially closed for the night, there were a handful of my employees left keeping our group company. Drinks were being passed around in the low light of the now empty bar. Ruby and I were in our own little corner, laughing at the memory from earlier in the evening of my cousin practically falling asleep at the dinner table.

Ruby was in white shorts and a blue tank, I remember it like it was yesterday. Hair loose and curled around her face. Smelling like strawberries and sunscreen, though we'd been inside most of the day. Her legs were crossed, and I pulled them apart, lifted them up and rested them across my thighs. I had half a mind to kick everyone out of the place so I could throw her on top of my bar and do all the things I wanted to do to her.

Instead, I placed my hand on her cheek, my other soaking up

the silky skin of her thigh. "You tired?" I asked, as I watched her close her eyes and lean into my hand.

"I've had like three Diet Cokes. I think I'm more wired than tired." She popped open her eyes and laughed. "Wired and tired."

"You can't help yourself, can you?" I said.

"Guess not." She gripped my shirt at my waist, and I had to dig real deep to focus. Not get lost in what my dick was doing in reaction to her legs spread across mine.

I cleared my throat. "So, I have an idea."

"Uh-oh," she said, but she was smiling and looking up at me from the corner of her eye. I pushed my hand back from her cheek. Dragged it behind her ear, through her hair. Down her neck and along her collar bone. She moaned and I had to adjust myself in my seat. Try not to look at the way her tits were rising and falling with each slow breath she was taking.

"I hope this idea isn't to put on a show for everyone," she purred. I glanced over to the rest of the crew. Of the five that remained, I gathered at least two were probably having similar inappropriate thoughts, though I didn't think the feelings were reciprocated. Katrina without a doubt had a fierce "no dating the 'Bar Bods,'" (as she called them) rule. Though she probably had no qualms with some play. I may or may not have found myself in her bed once or twice. And Kevin, one of my waiters, I knew had been making multiple failed attempts with Lila.

"Oh, no show. What's under these clothes is for my eyes only," I said to Ruby, running a finger along the neckline of her shirt. Dipping a finger in that cleavage. Wanting to dip my cock in her mouth. "Fuck," I said as I grabbed her legs and removed them from their spot on my thighs.

"You alright there?" she said with the most wicked of looks.

"I'm trying to do a thing here, and you are frustratingly distracting, Nightingale."

She crossed her legs again and leaned back in her seat. "Maybe not touching will help. Say your thing. What's on your mind, Conti?"

I cracked my neck to the side to regain my composure.

"You said you have an idea?" she prompted.

"Right. I do. And it must be important if I'm not kicking these guys out and stripping those little shorts off of you to throw you on my bar like I've been wanting to do since our first date."

She laughed. "Ah yes. A reward for your restraint then, Good Guy," and I bit my cheek and groaned, struggling to stay focused. "What's so important?"

"Play for us," I said, eyes moving over to the other side of the bar. "Tonight. Your songs."

I studied her face for a reaction, but she only raised her eyebrows.

"Alright," I said. "That wasn't a 'no,' so that's a good sign."

"Definitely not a 'no.'" She looked up at me with a smile. "I've actually been thinking about that."

"You have?"

"Yeah, I mean about playing here for just a small crowd. Maybe a lunch gig or something."

I grabbed her face in my hands and kissed her square on the mouth. She laughed after I pulled away, but then leaned in for a deeper kiss. Pulled back and I once again had to remember what I was trying to do here.

"Want to start with a song or two right now? Just the six of us here?"

She was quiet. I could see her wheels turning. Slowly, she started nodding. "Okay. Don't make a big announcement about it or anything. Let me just grab my guitar—"

"I'll grab your guitar for you."

"So chivalrous. Alright."

"Alright," I nodded, rising out of my seat. I had a good feeling about the whole thing. I loved seeing her courage, as I knew this was hard for her. I kissed her cheek, told her not to overthink it. Ran out to the car for her guitar, came back to give it to her.

"Oh, hey! What do you have there, gonna play for us, Ruby?" Lucy said from the other side of the bar.

"That's exactly what we need. A little of our Ruby's beautiful voice to accompany us this warm summer evening," Grayson said in his grandiose way. I was happy, it was just the energy she needed.

But I could see the worry in Ruby's eyes. I grazed my hand along her jawline, pulled her face toward me. Said, "Hey," softly so only she could hear me. The gang all started getting up and rearranging themselves in a little row to have a closer spot to us, and I was worried Ruby might chicken out and play a cover.

"Hey," I said again when I had her attention. "I'm going to sit down with them, but I want you to look at me, okay? Just look in my eyes, don't even worry about anyone else. Like it's just you and me, on my bed, just the two of us."

She nodded her head and parroted, "Look in your eyes. K. I can do that." She chewed on her thumbnail, eyes looking like a million thoughts were running behind them.

"You got this, Nightingale." I winked at her and got up to go take my place with the crew.

My heart was pounding in my chest though. I felt like I had two parts of me at that point. One part of me was trying to steer some conversation with Ruby's mini audience in an effort to keep a casual, light energy. Keep them from staring at her as she warmed up and got herself situated.

The other part of me was stealing glances at her, making sure she was okay. It was the same feeling I would have on a busy night at the restaurant. That split—two sides of me. One doing the cool and calm walk, checking in on certain regular customers that I wanted to make sure felt like a priority. The other side of me all business and worry, fielding interruptions and a million questions from my staff.

But then she started playing. A soft hum at first, eyes closed.

Open your eyes, baby, I was thinking. Come on, open your eyes, Nightingale. It was her music though. Her song, not a cover.

And as soon as she sang her first lyrics, she opened her eyes. Found mine, and rolled into her song. "The Good-est of Girls," the one she wrote on my bed just a couple weeks earlier. I locked eyes with her, leaned forward to rest my forearms on my thighs. Hoping that the more I could close in the space between us, the more safe and secure she'd feel.

My Ruby was so beautiful that night. My Nightingale was singing her very own work, finally. Right here in front of our little group. I knew it took all the courage in the world. She'd close her eyes now and then, lose herself in her music, but I remained firmly fixed in my spot for those first few minutes. Holding her gaze whenever I could see she was starting to get too in her head.

Something passed between us that night, I don't know exactly how to describe it. Really I think something passed between all of us that night. You could hear the whispers from the others as she sang. "Brilliant," from Grayson. A "Holy fuck, she's good," from Katrina. Nods of agreement as we all sat and watched our Ruby drawing us in. All equally captivated in her sound, her lyrics. Trying to grasp and hold onto each and every word and note like they were bits of magic gold.

She ended up playing for two hours straight. Pausing in between songs, chatting with us, laughing with us from up there on her bar stool. Looking more and more relaxed with each passing minute. Asking us what we were in the mood for next, playing a couple bars of a song she was working on. Ruby had our complete and total awe; we were helpless under her spell. It was a side of her so completely different than the quiet, background variety of her I'd seen at her Moon Lounge gigs.

It was right there that night in the quiet depths of summer, Ruby Francesca came alive, the star within her unleashed.

I already knew I loved her, but I *fell* in love with her that night. I think we all did, really, but I *fell in love* with her. *I love you. I love you. I love you,* was all I could think. I fell in love with this person that I knew was under the surface of her, waiting to fly out and away.

I guess you could say that's when the sane part of me shut down, because I was fucked. Caught in her siren spell, and here I am now, getting arrested for climbing on roofs, thinking that was a good idea. I raise my arms and run my hands through my hair. Wonder what in the hell has come over me.

And all the while, Ruby is running around town giving interviews about my big ego. The asshole from her past. I wonder if she even remembers that night, the first night she came alive and sang her songs to an audience that wasn't just me. Is there any way I can remind her of a better time between us, a time when—

"Conti, you're up," a cop says, interrupting my thoughts. "Someone's here for you."

twenty-one

. . .

ruby

WHAT HAS MY *life become*, she thinks to herself, sitting outside the police station. For obvious reasons, she couldn't be the one to go in, and with Grayson now all over the internet, it was too risky for him as well.

So yeah, Ruby had to wake up her dad to go in and get her ex-boyfriend from jail at two o'clock in the morning. Dom was so calm about it, too. Laughing, even. She tried to tell him it wasn't funny, that Joey was a stalker, but Dom was having none of it and said it sounded like an honest mistake.

And here she is now, opening herself to forgiveness of yet another "mistake" from Joey. She hates that she clings to the best pieces of him like this. She should know better by now, right? He's just like she thought, a guy with his own agenda. She knew about that kind of thing all too well.

So why does she keep holding onto hope that Joey really is different?

Her mind thinks back to the beginning. To the way Joey had

helped her in those early days. He seemed more hell bent on getting her past her stage fright than even she herself was.

But she remembers it so well, that first night when she played her own songs for anyone other than Joey or her family. After so long of struggling to break past that barrier of her own inner fears, Ruby couldn't believe the freedom she felt, playing that night with her expanded hodgepodge of friends. Could she even call them that —friends? The only person in that group that she'd known longer than a few weeks was Grayson. And even their friendship had only really begun to take firm shape within the past year, despite four years at school with him. She would wonder about that, what the difference had been. Somewhere deep down Ruby knew that it was her that had finally allowed the persistent Grayson into her inner circle.

Maybe that's what happens when you've reached the right level of time between the traumas of your past and the stable state of your present. We say time heals all wounds, a phrase Ruby never really believed. But maybe it was true. Maybe once enough time has passed, when it's no longer categorized as "recent," that's when a person can begin to shed the skin of protection.

Either way, whether it was time, an eagerness to move on, or Joey himself, Ruby had been finding a new level of courage that summer.

And restlessness.

Performing cover songs had become a bore, and the enthusiasm from Joey had boosted her confidence to a level she knew she needed to explore. Playing that night with her friends—yes, she had decided then that she was ready to call them that—felt more natural than she ever expected was possible. That's when her mind had begun to fantasize about a new mission. Not one of finding a job teaching, but a mission of performing her own music to a crowd.

Ruby would also think about the things Mama Z had told her. How the hell Joey's grandmother had discovered the truth of

Ruby's past, she'll never know. But she had, and when confronted about it, Mama Z assured Ruby that it was far from a mark on her history. Alternatively, she said it was a badge of honor. A moment of victory in an otherwise dismal existence. Mama Z was teaching Ruby so much—a welcomed mentor at the most unexpected of times. For years Ruby had hated the military and the way it had separated her from people she loved. How it later separated her from her dad. But it was the military connection that brought her to Joey's world. Funny how life turns out like that.

But Mama Z was teaching Ruby how to see all of her resilience, and more importantly, power. Yes, Ruby had power, and that summer she was learning how to harness that power to elevate her craft.

Not only that, but they'd discuss Ruby's career. Mama Z had another surprising thing in common with Ruby—an understanding of music. Not just a love of it (anyone can easily love something as fun as a good melody), but a visceral connection to sound.

"Why didn't you run with your dreams of singing?" Ruby had asked Mama Z at one point, over a tea and coffee date at Mama Z's request.

"And live in the eyes of everyone else? Constantly doing what you're told in order to sell more albums and be the face of something in the name of others' greed? No," Mama Z said, dismissing the thought.

"Only if you get really lucky." Ruby was sure she sounded naive, but it's how she felt. Lucky, if she could ever reach that level.

"I could have been lucky." Mama Z responded with such a confidence, it had intrigued Ruby. She sipped her coffee and kept a direct focus on Ruby, her diamond rings flashing in the rays of sunlight pouring through the window.

"How do you know? What makes you so sure?" Ruby asked. She admired the woman's faith in what's possible. Ruby's own mother was usually the opposite and blamed everything and everyone for whatever existence she had.

But not Mama Z. This woman seemed to say, "Throw what you want at me, and I'll transform it into something bold and beautiful." It was almost like Mama Z relished in the challenges of life. She fed off them, as if every obstacle she overcame morphed into a new trophy on a shelf of resilience. She was the ultimate creator in her own destiny.

They worked together in those early weeks of her relationship with Joey and Mama Z was the female role model Ruby never had. They talked about how Ruby could tighten her sound, craft it to streamline into something with both the soul we know and love of great music, and the hypnotic energy that listeners crave.

It was strange to Ruby, the parallel relationships she was forming with Mama Z and with Joey. Her dad was thrilled anytime Ruby mentioned her "makeshift mentor," as she referred to Mama Z. He seemed to feel more and more at ease as the weeks of that summer went on. His girl was finding her feet and her support. Maybe he felt the pressure was off him, who knows. The guilt of his frequent absences of Ruby's childhood, now able to slowly diminish.

But for Ruby, it was Joey that broke through the armor of her heart. Without Joey, there would be no Mama Z in Ruby's world. Without Joey and his playful energy, there would be no thawing of Ruby's mistrust. Ruby looked at him and saw the good guy he truly was. It gave her hope.

Not only that, but Joey had been stirring in Ruby a piece of womanhood she hadn't previously known. He looked at her like someone to be admired and revered. He was awakening things within her body she wasn't sure would ever exist for her. Sex for Ruby had previously been an obligatory part of a relationship. Kissing? Sure, she could enjoy that. But usually the rest was beyond the reaches of anyone she was intimate with.

But Joey worshiped her. He worshiped her body and with

him, she had discovered her own new sense of ownership. Lust and desire that could bring her to places of pleasure. With this new ownership, she had become insatiable at times, much to her surprise. She felt in physical pain when they weren't together. The way she could miss someone so much, when they had only been together hours earlier was unbelievable to her. She'd find herself fantasizing about their moments together, the smell of fresh cotton when she'd nuzzle in his chest. The way her body responded to him, the chills she'd get when he'd run his fingers down her cheek, across her lips. And especially the look of hunger in his eyes.

Occasionally it worried her, the amount she'd find herself thinking about Joey. Was she an addict like her mom, but of sex? Then Ruby would realize the ridiculousness of the thought, laughing at the absurdity of it. She'd be damned if she let her mom's mistakes cloud her own judgment of something so pure and beautiful. Ruby knew the difference. Her mom's craving of cocktails would turn her into a monster. A monster blind to the ugliness around her.

Ruby's obsession for Joey—and his obsession for her in return —it was different. It made her light and airy, brought out the silly side of her. With Joey she had the feeling of coming home, like he was a sanctuary. Her time with him was just *fun*. He could make her laugh until tears streamed down her face. There was nothing Joey ever took too seriously, and Ruby loved that about him.

And as she thinks about it now, sitting in a dark car in the middle of the night, outside of a police station where her dad was inside collecting this man that was once her everything, she knows one thing to be absolutely true.

Whether or not Joey's made mistakes, she knows the obsessive addiction they had for each other that summer did something to her. It helped her break free from her own prison cell of hiding. Free from the torments of her past. Because with Joey, with his unwavering belief in her, with his family and Mama Z and her makeshift mentoring, it transformed Ruby. Transformed her and turned Ruby into—

Well, a star.

"OUT WE GO, LOVER BOY," Ruby hears her dad say as he exits the police station with Joey in hand. She's in the car with the windows down. She looks at the two of them, takes in the sight. *This is my life,* she thinks.

They walk towards the car, Joey looking so sheepish Ruby finds it both charming and vindicating.

Joey gets in the back and her dad slides in the driver's side. He looks at Ruby, says with a smile, "Kid, you sure know how to keep a man's life interesting."

"Don't I know it," she says, a bittersweet smile at just how accurate that loaded statement is.

"Where to?" her dad asks.

"I guess back to the old house to get his car."

"I'm so incredibly sorry, Mr. Francesca," and Ruby can't help but struggle to suppress a laugh.

"What, I bail you out of jail and now we're suddenly formal? Please, Joey. It's Dom."

"Dom. Right. Again, so sorry. Incredibly embarrassed. Dumb decision right there that I'm sure I'll never live down," Joey says. Ruby steals a glance back at him, but he's staring out the window. He looks so innocent. She watches as he sucks his lips in, a move that she always loved because it makes his dimples pop out for a second.

"Young love will do that to you," her dad says.

"That or crazy," Ruby says.

"Shit," they hear Joey mumble.

"Ruby," her dad scolds.

"What? He's a grown ass man climbing on rooftops in the middle of the night. Not sixteen. What were you thinking?"

"I wasn't, alright?" he says, looking at her before dropping his head. "I seriously don't know, something took over my body and next thing I knew I was on your roof. Not wanting to wake up your dad. Only it wasn't your roof. And apparently the neighbor saw and here we are now."

"I know the neighbor that called," Dom says. "She's a nosy old lady that can't keep her head in her own business. She didn't even think you were an intruder, she thought you were the son that lives there. The teenage kid that she's convinced is vandalizing her mailbox and this was her opportunity to get back at him."

"By calling the cops and saying he was breaking into his own house?"

"Oh no, she called and said it was an intruder, alright. Then apparently once you were collected, she called back and asked if they got the kid. She was just trying to get him caught sneaking in the house after curfew or something. They got a good laugh out of that once they figured out what she was doing. And of course, they know it's the old house of Ruby Francesca, so they figured she accidentally caught a stalker. I straightened out the misunderstanding though when I got in and explained that we know you, that it was a harmless mistake. No charges, and hopefully they'll keep quiet." Dom turns to face Ruby. "By the way honey, I'm going to need some tickets or signed memorabilia or something. I gave them some shirts to hold them over, but I may have made some promises."

"Great, Jules is going to have fun with this," she says, referring to her PR manager.

"No such thing as bad publicity though, right?" Dom says. Ruby only groans.

"They can eat at my restaurants for free for life if they keep this quiet."

Ruby had a feeling Jules might actually have a field day spinning this. With all the buzz on the new song and the rumors about her and Joey, she knew it would feed right into the machine that her team would want.

She can see the headline now—

"The Lovesick Ex Returns!"

In smaller letters underneath—

"Hearing Francesca's leaked videos of her viral new song, Joseph Conti attempts a romantic surprise, climbing on what he thought was Francesca's porch to surprise her under her window—only to learn he got the wrong house!"

Ruby wonders if that's why Joey reached out. It had to be the song, he heard it and needed to see her, right? The familiar aches of their passion for one another grow in her belly. A flicker of hope flashes in her, and she hates herself for letting it.

They drive the rest of the way, Dom making polite conversation on Joey's business updates, telling him about friends that have sung their praises of his restaurants. Eventually they pull up next to Joey's car. Her dad turns to her. "Maybe you two should talk some things out?" he suggests.

Joey unbuckles and slides forward in his seat, putting his hand on her dad's shoulder. "Dom, you are a saint, my man. I promise to stay out of trouble and have this be the one and only time you need to grab my sorry ass out of jail."

Her dad pats Joey's hand. "Son, I know you've always taken care of our girl here, and I know you're going through some things. I'm sorry to hear about your grandmother."

"Thank you. Mama Z is holding on strong until the end here, but I know she's ready."

"Well we're here for you, right Ruby?"

Ruby just nods.

Joey thanks Dom again before getting out of the car.

Her dad turns to her. "You need to talk to him."

"What? Why?" she says, baffled. "He climbed a roof thinking it was ours. He's a stalker, dad."

"Like hell he is, and you know it. He's done nothing but support you, Ruby." She rolls her eyes. If her dad only knew.

He presses on. "I know you're going to be up all night with all this. Just go talk to the guy, see what's going on," he says, nodding his head in Joey's direction.

She sighs, knowing he's right. Plus, she can't help but be consumed with vain curiosity over Joey's reaction to the song.

"You're too good for this earth, dad," she says, getting out.

"I won't wait up," he says, and she shakes her head.

Ruby knows what he's doing. Her dad has been more protective of her than ever since her career has taken off. He's made it clear that she needs to be careful who to trust. That's been the theme in their household ever since she was fourteen. As if she needs any more reminders of that. So sure, Dom's putting all his hope in Joey and thinking if she settles down with him, then she'll be safe. It's three years ago all over again, only with higher stakes now, thanks to her rising fame.

She nervously walks over to Joey's car and opens the door to take a seat.

"Ruby, fuck I'm so glad you're here—"

"Silence," she says, stopping him.

Joey backs off. "Fair enough." They both watch as her dad drives off, giving a wave as he goes.

She waits for Joey to move too, but he just sits there. She glares at him. "Did you want to get arrested again, lurking here on the street?"

He smiles, dimples melting her, and she can't help but smile too.

"I was trying not to talk."

"You're an ass. You can drive without talking."

"Not if I don't know where you want me to go."

She furrows her eyebrows, thinking about it. Should she say his place? She definitely doesn't want to have this confrontation with him back at her dad's. But is that presumptuous? Maybe, but it's still the best option.

"Your place," she says. "But don't expect anything," she adds. "You're going to explain what the hell you're doing living up to the stalker joke, and that's that."

"Deal," he says, and they drive off.

A million thoughts are swimming in her head as they move through the night. Anger and hurt, sure, but also there is a surprise flicker of hope that he showed up tonight because of her song. That he heard it and it woke him up to how much they had together. That he knows he made a mistake last year, and he regrets it.

That he loves her.

Could she forgive him? She realizes she already has. So much was insane about their relationship. It started with a hot and heavy summer and abruptly came to a halt with the surprise break that changed everything. The relationship was too new to make major commitments, but too far in to attempt to let one another go. They were stuck in an in-between that they didn't even have time to process.

And Ruby knows too that her own secrets got in the way. She dove in, hot and heavy, but then retreated when the new possibilities of her career presented themselves. A convenient barrier. She was ready to take ownership of that and the way it might have driven Joey away. It's painful to admit, but true.

Because maybe, just maybe, if she hadn't tried to push down her feelings for Joey once her career had taken off, maybe he wouldn't have cheated on her at all.

twenty-two

. . .

mama z

ALRIGHT, LOOK. NO one is perfect. We all have mistakes we would rather not think about, and I'm no different. But you have to know, I'm willing to admit them. Or rather, trying to rectify them, if you will. And one must believe that I had the best interests of my loved ones at heart at the time such mistakes were made.

The Gentleman and I had continued quite the beautiful affair. I will tell you this, our love was and still is very real. I myself could not quite believe it at the start of it all. I considered myself fortunate, really. On the surface I had my husband Artem, working his way to his own fortune one hard day at a time to live out our American dreams.

But underneath it we each had our hidden lives. Artem with who knows who and what, and me with The Gentleman. At some point I'm sure there had been some whispered rumors around town, but we did our best to keep quiet. And mostly everyone respected that. Too many networks had been established for The Gentleman within his career. Too many people involved with their own agendas, secrets, and risks. It was a man's world—a boys club of money exchanges and handshakes over cocktails. Everyone was fighting to claw their way to the top of whatever ladder they had deemed their own, and we had to be discreet.

My ladder was of a more subtle variety. It had to be. You see at some point, I became pregnant with my first child. No stranger to difficult life choices, something like an unexpected pregnancy was small potatoes. Orphaned and tossed around Europe as a refugee with no real home? My formative years. Never knowing who to trust, never knowing which groping hands were waiting for me around the corner? My adolescence and teens. Oh yes, I had experienced some things I dare say I could write a book about. Encounters that might bring you to your knees, begging for it all to stop, believing death might be the better option.

But I've never been anyone's victim. When you've lived a brutal life, it's all you know. There's a choice you must make—you can cry and drown yourself in the tears of the bad hands you've been dealt, or you can pick yourself up and fight.

Now, as a woman, the fight must look rather clever. One cannot get far with physical force when one is a petite little thing with body parts the world loves to objectify, and a mind and voice the world wants to quiet. Oh no. So one must learn a different craft of survival. Thankfully I have always been skilled in this craft. My very own brand of witchery, some might say.

The Gentleman was distraught though when I gave him the news. Oh, I laugh still at the memory. His face! You would have thought I was giving him a death sentence.

"Are you sure it's mine?" he had said. We were at his home one evening and his wife was who knows where. I would like to think she was off having her own glorious affair, but sadly I can tell you that girl had no knack for knowing how to live. Poor thing.

"What a stupid question. How should I know?" I had replied. I had an inkling based on sheer numbers and passion, but in the end of the day it was a toss up.

"My love," he had said. "Please don't trivialize this. Surely you must know?"

"Trivialize the child I'm carrying?" I could see I had hurt him though, so I put my hand to his cheek. Grabbed the cigarette dangling from his mouth to take a drag. Blew the smoke in a slow exhale, never breaking eye contact. "I'm not trying to trivialize. It's just that we would be stupid to think this might not happen. I can say the chances are in your favor, however."

I quite purposely used that phrase, "in your favor." I needed him to understand that this was not to be viewed as something negative. I knew it would cause him distress, sure. You see, his wife was part of a family that was the very lifeline of The Gentleman's career and new found success. They were the owners of a record label who signed all the right artists at all the right times. Throwing fire on that marriage would mean obliterating his own gains.

But I had a plan, naturally.

I returned his cigarette to his mouth and continued. "Inhale, dear. You look ill at ease." I rose from my seat and walked over to the fireplace. Watched the flames dance in the jubilee, blissfully unaware of their own potential for destruction in the wrong setting.

"I *am* ill at ease. If word gets out, I could be ruined, you must know that."

"I know," I had said.

"Is that what you want?"

I turned to him then. "Of course not. You're on the brink of having everything you've worked so hard for. I would never stand in the way of that."

"So what, then? What are we to do?"

He looked so unsure, and I had to laugh to myself at his fear. He could be wonderfully cutthroat in the best of ways. No problem plowing his way to get what he wanted when it came to everything else. Yet with me? I suppose I was his kryptonite.

"The way I see it, we can have it all. I will have this baby and you will have a child—something I know you've always wanted but your own wife is not able to give you. I will raise it with Artem. A family had always been our plan, and now we will begin with that plan. No one needs to know it's yours."

"What if I want to know? To be sure it's mine?"

"What difference does it make? If it's not, will you simply throw me out?"

This got to him, as I knew it would. "Stop that, don't say that. I love you, you know I can't stand it, I'm so lost in your web." He rose to join me. Grabbed my elbows, searching my eyes. For what, I cannot say. Approval, I think. Reassurance, perhaps. His addiction to me was strong, I knew. And mine to him, though in keeping to my craft of playing my limited cards just right, I could never fully allow him to realize this.

I sighed as if bored with his words, though inside my heart swelled. "You poor fool," I said, but I gave him a smile anyway. "You see then? It makes no difference. Nothing needs to change. We can continue just as we always have, our affair a quiet corner of the world, just for the two of us. You be the doting husband to your wife that you need to be, and I will raise this child with Artem. You have no obligations. Our secrets will always be safe with me. You keep your eye on the prize. I would never stand in your way of that."

He leaned down and kissed me, the passion and relief evident in his possession of my mouth. "How did I get so lucky to have found you?" he mused as he pulled back. "What we could have been in another life."

"None of that, darling. This is the life we have been given, and we'll make do with it just fine. Just promise me this," I said. I was sure to run my hands over his body in gentle caresses, jut out my chest just right.

"Anything," he said, his erection growing in my hands, constricted by his trousers.

"When you're long gone from this town, when your career

catapults to the levels you and I both know it will, you will find a way to remain in touch with me."

"It's the only way I think I'll ever survive," he said. I could tell he believed that whole-heartedly.

And we made love there in front of the fireplace, his words echoing in my mind.

He believed with all his heart I was the answer to his survival. Just as he had been the answer to mine.

HERE'S THE THING YOU REALLY need to understand. I imagine it's easy to hear all these confessions of mine and be appalled. But I assure you I was merely taking it all one day at a time. I had no idea what the future would bring for me. Sure, I knew The Gentleman loved me then. But would it last? I had no way of knowing that. I was just as at risk for suffering through life's gambles as the next person. Can you imagine? Holding onto so much, yet never knowing when the door would be shut in my face?

I needed three things: The Gentleman's career to continue just as it was projected to and Artem to blissfully play along with our agreed upon facade of marriage and happy family.

But most importantly, I needed The Gentleman to continue to hold me in high regard.

"What do you think of this sound?" he would ask me when working with a new artist.

"Oh, he's alright. Where did you find him?" I would ask. And I would get the back story of a kid walking into the studio to record something, or a performance he had stumbled across with the hopes of finding his next star.

He had the business sense and the ear, but it was not always enough.

"I need your input, you always know the feel," he would say.

"What would you do without me?" I would tease.

I did my research, I paid attention to the hits, ignoring industry chatter in favor of my own instincts. I learned to convey that information so that he had felt I was indispensable to him. I tried my best to help in whatever small ways I could.

Really though, I think he just needed the friendship.

"You're my good luck charm," he would say. And at some point after years of this, I allowed myself to breathe, knowing I had solidified my own little way in his world.

But that was the biggest unknown back then. It's funny to think about that now. I have the gift of hindsight now, knowing it all worked out even better than I could have expected. But I can't say I was not unsure at times, especially as my pregnancy with Isabella carried on. My belly swollen and my usual confidence coming in and out like waves with a storm wreaking havoc on an otherwise beautiful beach.

I clung to hope and reminded myself that no matter what, I was the master of my own destiny. I would figure it all out.

The Gentleman and I continued to see one another as often as possible, even though I had left my job at the station in the name of trying to keep our affair private. Too many eyes and ears surrounded us, and it was best that I stay in the shadows.

And my heart hurt, I tell you. Unfortunately, an unexpected side effect of pregnancy and motherhood is the emotional roller coaster that comes along with it. I fell even more madly in love with him as the months carried on, and he looked at me like an angel sent from heaven. He had convinced himself that I was mothering his child and a conversation of paternity was never again raised.

Still, I carried on. Month after month, year after year. And like I knew it would, The Gentleman's career took off. True to his word, he always remained available to me, though. I would send him a photo or two of Isabella whenever possible, share my updates. I would give him just enough to ensure his continued interest, but not so much as to sound desperate.

You see the key to keeping a man on the line is to never let him think you need him. Never let him know just how much it hurts to not be in his presence, or the way you cry when you see photos of him in the paper, side by side with a wife you know in your heart should have been you. Living a career you believe in another life could have been the perfect backdrop to your own dreams.

I hope by now you can see then why our dear Ruby Francesca presented such a unique opportunity. That girl had suffered her own injustices, I knew. While life had a different plan for me, I was going to ensure she got everything she ever wanted. She had it all—talent and looks, but most of all, the quiet cunning determination that it would take to get to the top.

"Call your nephew," I had said on the phone to him one evening, that first summer after meeting Ruby. By now, The Gentleman's nephew had stepped into the family business and was the active presence in the industry.

"Why, my love? What do you have for me?"

"A girl. Young and pretty. Writes beautiful songs. Sings them even better."

"There are plenty of them, Zabel. All vying for the same thing."

"This one is special, trust me on it."

"What makes her so special?" he asked.

I had to be careful, though. I knew he would not like my next words unless I presented them just right.

"She's important to someone I love, that's what makes her special. And therefore she is now important to you."

"Oh? Zabel you have me intrigued."

"Good. Because she is Joey's newest girl."

The line was silent. I expected he would grapple with this. You see our lives rarely crossed paths in the physical sense anymore. Too many years had passed with too much going on. Our phone calls were nearly all that remained, thanks to his own curious interest in the family he left behind. He had funded Isabella's schooling and was the angel investor to Joey's first restaurant, but his generosity and involvements were always from a place of complete and total anonymity.

Finally he responded. "Zabel, I appreciate that you want to help this girl. But if she is together with Joey, then perhaps introducing her to my nephew is not the best answer."

"I understand your reluctance."

"I'm glad."

"What if I could assure you that she and Joey would not stay together? That there's no risk of him ever meeting anyone, no risk of exposure?"

"How can you possibly assure that?"

"They have only been dating a few weeks. I don't see it lasting."

"So then why care about this girl at all if she's a temporary fixture?"

This was my moment. I knew that he would be just curious enough to want to hear Ruby's music, (he was a sucker for chasing the high of discovering The Next Big Thing), but that he was forever riddled with the guilt of the life he left behind, and the life he knew I sacrificed in order to allow his own path to remain clear.

"Well, my dear, it's simple." I went in for the words I knew he would be unable to ignore. "She reminds me a lot of myself. And she deserves to live the life that I myself never could."

twenty-three

. . .

joey

"I OWE YOU an apology," I say, turning on the lights in my living room and kitchen. "I owe you a lot of apologies, but figured maybe I'll just start with a general blanket statement on that."

Ruby smiles. Seriously, she actually *smiles* at that, and I'm filled with a little hope. Maybe the interview dig on my ego was just a little something for show. I feel so fucking confused with her sometimes; I don't know what's real between us, and what's all part of the Ruby Francesca Career Plan. I think that's always been a big part of our problem.

She follows me into the kitchen, and I pull out two waters for each of us. She still hasn't said anything to me and I'm dying to know what she's thinking.

I look at her, my Ruby, here in my kitchen. Casually sipping from a water bottle I gave her. She's got on these tight little pink spandex shorts and an oversized sweatshirt, cut so it shows the tiniest bit of her stomach.

I remember that stomach. I remember when my mouth would be on it. I remember a whole lot more than that.

As if reading my mind, she takes her hand and rubs it across her toned belly. "Joey, there's probably things you and I could both apologize for."

"Really?" I try not to sound too shocked at this, but I can't help it. My voice comes out horribly high pitched. I clear my throat. "Let me try that again. Really?" I say with an exaggerated deep baritone.

She laughs, though. "Yeah. Really."

I'm trying to study her face, but she's giving nothing away. I stare at that little button nose and big sapphire eyes on full display, accented by her hair in a messy knot on top of her head, a few strands framing her face. She stares back, unblinking.

I like her like this, all natural and raw. My sights of her have been limited to the dolled up version of Career Ruby. That version of her has been a strange mystery to me. And the longer I've gone seeing that version, the more I've wondered if our relationship ever even existed in the first place.

But here like this, I know it did.

I step closer to her. "Does it feel weird? Being together like this after all this time? Here?" I say, nodding in the space around us. My apartment where so many firsts happened between us.

She nods, and the knot on her head shakes a bit. "Yeah. Weird. But comfortable at the same time," she says, but her eyebrows are pinched together in confusion.

"You're frowning though."

She raises her thumb to chew her nail. And I'm looking at her and she looks so damn vulnerable. My mind can't make sense of this double concept of her. Ruby the Star, and then *my* Ruby. The Ruby that I know and fell for. A young woman with talents, and fears, and a playfulness that matched mine, but hesitations that didn't.

I want so badly to tell her all the things I wish we had done differently. I want to explain myself, explain why I did what I did.

And then I think about that interview jab at me, and I'm right back to questioning everything.

"Say something, Nightingale. What are you thinking?" I step closer as I say this. Grab the hand that she's chewing on, a sign of her nervousness. I grab it and hold it in mine. She doesn't pull away, but she doesn't step closer, either.

"I'm thinking that I hate that I like being here."

That's definitely not what I want to hear. "Why do you hate that?"

"Because I'm scared it's a security blanket for me."

I only nod, not sure what to say to that. I know what she's talking about though; it's always been on my mind with her. I don't know what happened with her and her mom exactly, but I know enough to see the mistrust and fear it put in her, and the way she can hide as a result.

"Ruby. I never, ever wanted to be a place for you to hide away. Too scared and comfortable to reach for anything more." I pull her hand to my lips, I can't help myself. I kiss each knuckle. "I hope you know that. I could never live with myself if I felt like you stayed put here with me because you were telling yourself it was good enough."

I think back to that last weekend she was here in town. One year ago, at my bar, after hours. Place dark, just me there. Ruby came in crying talking about how scared she was, that she worried choosing a life in the public eye was a mistake. That she needed me. I held her as she cried, hating seeing all her old fears resurrected and making her want to hide.

"That wasn't your decision to make for me, Joey."

Just like that, she pulls her hand from mine. Drops it, and crosses her arms over her chest. It makes her sweatshirt raise even further, showing more of her stomach. "Don't you see?" She looks at me with question in her eyes. "You never even gave me a chance."

"A chance for what, what do you mean?"

"Never mind," she says, shaking her head. "It's in the past now, what's done is done."

"Fuck that. It doesn't have to be, Ruby."

To hell with it, I think. I'm done trying to be careful with what I say. I step forward, close the gap between us. Grab her face in my hands, turn her head to look at me.

"Please," I say. I lean down, slowly. Press my lips onto hers. Just once.

She lets me.

Thank God, she lets me.

Reluctantly, I pull back slightly, not wanting to push too far. "Please, Ruby. Tell me there's a second chance here." I kiss her again, her lips so comfortable and familiar to me. Like no time at all has passed. She parts her lips for me, drops her arms and clings onto my shirt.

It takes everything I have in me to be gentle with her right now. But I am. I'm slow and careful in my movements, pausing to check in with her because I'm terrified of pushing too far, pushing her away. Too grateful for this kiss—this chance—but scared of how long it will last. I relish the taste of her mouth. As starved as I am, I savor every piece of her. I bite and pull her bottom lip, then glide my tongue over it, then back in to explore once more.

At some point she pulls back, but stays with her hands on my shirt. I kiss her head, then rest my chin on it, holding her close to me.

"Why did you come tonight?" she whispers.

"You mean to stalk you?" I say, and my chest is warm at the feeling of her small body laughing in my grasp.

"Yeah. Stalker, like I always knew."

"They say to trust your gut."

"I did, remember? But for some reason my dad really likes you."

"He has good instincts."

I kiss her head again. Lean back to look at her. "I came because I don't know how to be away from you when you're so close by." I shrug. It's my truth, and there's not much more to it than that.

"And the song?" she asks.

"Which one?"

She raises her eyebrows at me. "Umm, gee I don't know…The one I'm currently blowing up for?"

My mind's racing back to what Reggie was saying earlier tonight. It feels like a lifetime ago. "I…I have no idea what song you're talking about, Ruby."

She pulls back from me and laughs. "Oh my God, for real? Do a quick search, Conti," she says, pulling my phone from the counter and handing it to me.

"What am I searching for?" I take my phone from her, but I'm nervous now for what I'm about to find.

She opens her mouth to speak, then thinks better of it and closes it. "No. You know what? I don't want to be here when you hear it. Come on, take me home now."

Oh shit, *what the hell just happened?* "Ruby, wait," I say, following after her.

She's at my front door, pulling it open. I reach over her head and push it shut again.

"Let me out," she says.

"Don't run out right now, please."

"Listen, Stalker. I'm not running out, okay? But I also need to not be around you when you hear the song."

"What song? What's it called?"

"I can't even tell you. You'll see when you figure it out."

"But why? Why can't you be around me?" I say.

She turns around and leans her back against the door. I put my other arm up to lean against it. There's fire in her eyes, and I can't tell if it's anger or the same desire for me that I'm feeling for her.

"You remember when I got this?" she says, raising her arm up, pulling down her sweatshirt to expose her wrist. I look at the small, black tattoo. A bird. A nightingale.

"Of course I remember." I had taken her to get it, right before her move to LA.

"You remember what you said to me? That no matter what, you'd be with me. This tattoo was my reminder of that. And I loved that idea. It gave me some security when I was absolutely terrified of what the future was potentially going to bring on me. I was on the verge of getting everything that I wanted, but terrified of what that would mean, exactly. I knew it would be hard, and I'd be facing a lot. And you couldn't be there, because of how things were blowing up for you right here. I couldn't ask you to come with me, because we'd only been seeing each other for a couple months. Weeks, really.

"So I left. Yet somehow, we talked all the time anyways. Sure, we called it friendship at that point. What more could it really be?"

"It was what made the most sense," I say. Even as I say the words I hear how stupid they sound.

"Right. That's what we told ourselves. What I told myself anyway. But you know what, Joey? We both knew that friendship was *not* what this was, that it was more. Yet when I needed you most, you fucked up."

I nod, a gut punch to the stomach at her reminder of it. I pull my arms back from the door. Run my hands down my face. "You didn't need me, Ruby. You were scared and hiding. I wasn't going to let you do that."

"Oh real nice, Joey. Yeah. You cheated on me *for* me, is that it?"

"That's not what I mean. Fuck, it wasn't like that." I'm so frustrated with this whole mess. I need to clear the air with her, but I know it's not a quick fix. That it'll take more than a quick conversation to explain it all away.

Still, I gotta start somewhere. I have to try.

"Look," I say carefully. "We weren't even together, technically.

You were…" I pause because I can feel myself getting angry, and I'm struggling to keep my tone down.

Screw it, I think. I have to say my piece. "You were out dating other celebrities, living the time of your life, Ruby!" I say, arms out wide.

"No," she says, her voice quivering. "It wasn't like that. You don't understand."

"You're right! I don't!" I know I'm yelling now, but I don't care. "I had to sit back and watch you from afar. And it was so fucking painful! Do you have any idea what that was like for me? Seeing pictures of you with these other guys? The latest headlines flooding my phone about who you were seen with, what steamy moment was caught on camera. It *crushed* me," I say, slamming my fist in my chest. "But could I ever admit that to you? No. Not really, not without it wrapped in a joke. Because I would be damned if I'd be that guy that would make you feel guilty for doing exactly what you needed and deserved to live out this dream. I wasn't going to do that to you."

I'm frantic trying to make sense of this and relay what needs to be said. I need her to understand—too many games had been played already.

She's shaking her head, hands covering her face. "This is all so fucked up." Her voice is heavy with emotion, and I wish I had the secret recipe to make it all better.

"What don't I understand?" I ask, my voice softening. "Explain it to me."

"No! That's just it, Joey. You never *let* me explain in the first place," she says. She drops her hands and I see the tears streaming down her face. My heart squeezes in my chest. "I needed you then, and you never let me explain why. You just assumed you already knew what I had going on. Assumed you knew what was best for me, and carried it out. I'm so sick of everyone doing that for me. Everyone thinking they know what's best for me.

"It's my dad all over again. Divorced my mom and had me live with her because he thought that was best. And look how that fucking turned out! But apparently I'm used to following orders, because here I am, in a career where everyone chooses what's best for me."

I move towards her to wipe the tears from her cheeks. I hate seeing her fall apart like this, but I'm trying to hear what exactly she's telling me.

"You know what's funny?" she says, looking up at me. "Your grandmother warned me about all of it. Mama Z, yup. She said she never wanted to live a life chasing a singing dream, because she didn't want to live for other people. She wanted to create her own destiny."

It's the first I'm hearing anything like this. "She did?"

"Yeah. She warned me."

"When?" And it's there again, that nagging feeling that Mama Z has more secrets than any of us realize. But how the hell does that line up with Ruby?

"At the start of it all. As time went on and she'd check in. Email me. She was right, you do live by the rules of everyone else when you're in this. But I felt okay about it, because I was out there, singing my music. And I still felt like I had you," she says, holding up her wrist and showing her tattoo. "And that helped carry me. In those early days especially, having you was everything to me." She wipes her face, tucks the loose strands of hair behind her ears. "Until you made it clear that I didn't." Ruby looks at me, the blue in her eyes even more startling now against the bloodshot red, thanks to her tears.

"Why didn't you tell me any of that? I didn't know, Ruby. I thought...I thought I was just a friend to you, but that you had moved on."

"Next time, try and pay better attention, Conti." She turns around, faces the door. Turns her head back over her shoulder, says, "Can you take me home now?"

I reach for her chin, step around her to face her again. "Next time."

"What?"

"You said 'next time.' Tell me there's still a chance for a next time."

She only shrugs. "Why?"

I look into those blue eyes, her pillowy ruby red lips. I remember that summer when I first fell for her. The start of something that I knew was going to be it.

And I want it back.

"Because," I say, my thumb running along her lips. "I'm not nearly done with you yet."

"Didn't you hear what I just said? That I'm tired of everyone deciding everything for me?"

"Yeah. Alright then," I say, running my fingers along her face. "Tell me this, then," and I run my hand down her arm. I pull back her sleeve to expose her wrist again. Kiss the nightingale.

"Are you done with me?" I ask. I'm scared of her response, but I see it. I see the fire in her eyes. It's hurt and anger, sure. But there's want in there too. Desire and frustration that we were robbed of time, interrupted too soon when we were only just getting started.

She looks down at my lips, then back to my eyes. I move my hand up to cup her cheek. She leans into it and closes her eyes.

"Well?" I prompt.

To my relief, she shakes her head no, ever so slightly. "No, I'm not done with you yet."

"Good," I say.

She opens her eyes, gives me a half smile. "Oh yeah?"

"Oh yeah." I kiss her fingertips. "Cuz I'm only just getting started with you. With my Ruby in July."

She fully smiles now and closes her eyes again. "You have no idea how perfect those words are right now."

twenty-four

. . .

ruby

IT WAS EVERYTHING she wanted to hear. And he didn't even hear the song. Maybe that's better, she thinks. Maybe him coming to her without ever even listening to what she was trying to say is exactly the thing she needs in order to believe him. To trust him. To trust in them both and a future of what could be.

She feels the kisses on her fingers, on her knuckles. Her tender Joey, always so loving with her. She's tense with each of his touches, her instinctive reaction to freeze, a response she hates. But Joey helped before to break down her walls. He may not have known why they were there, but he did. He helped ease her into a comfort with touch, and she can feel in her gut that he can get her there again. He never even knew what a struggle that had been for her.

She squeezes her eyes shut, refusing to let her mind go to darker places of her past.

I feel Joey's kisses. I feel his lips. I feel his shirt in my hand, she thinks.

I smell his soap. I smell the fresh cotton.

Her mind struggles to stay present, but she's strong, she reminds herself.

I hear the hum of silence. I hear the sounds of his lips. Slowly she feels herself sliding back into her body and connecting with the moment, with his touch.

I feel desire, she thinks, victorious at the realization. She focuses on the welcomed ache between her legs.

Desire to be touched by Joey.

She gasps as his hips press against hers, pinning her to the door. Her body responds, and she lifts a leg up to his hip, feeling the roughness of his jeans on her skin. He places his hand under her leg, grabs her other leg and lifts her up off the floor. She wraps her legs around his hips, her arms around his neck.

"What's the song called," he says, carrying her.

"Huh?"

"The song you were talking about. What's it called?"

She can feel the tightness in her chest. It's a confusing mix of wanting to share with him, but nervous with the vulnerability.

I feel the softness of his hair. I feel it between my fingers.

"Don't you want to be surprised?" she asks.

He looks at her carefully. Eyes focused. "What I want, Ruby, is you. That's all that I want, all I care about."

"Oh, is that all?" she says with a laugh. The tightness in her chest eases, just a little. "Then what does the song matter?"

His lips move to hers. A gentle kiss. So tender. So familiar.

"Because you wrote it, and that means it's a part of you." Another kiss. "And like I said, I want all of you."

"You didn't say all of me. Just me." She feels his kisses on her jawline, dotting along.

"Well let it be known," he says between kisses, "that I meant all of you."

"That seems a bit selfish."

"I'm very selfish," he says before moving his lips back to hers.

She leans in to welcome his tongue in her mouth and her belly warms at the feeling of him consuming her.

I taste him. I feel his hands. I feel his firm grasp, holding me up. I taste him.

And the feel of this man brings her a sense of comfort that she hasn't felt in a long time, she realizes. How can she possibly feel so *right* with him? Even after everything? But that's exactly what she feels.

Her eagerness is stirred and she fists his hair in her hands. She bites his lip and is rewarded with his hungry groan.

"Fuck, you make it hard to hold back," he says between their kisses.

"So don't," she says. "Don't hold back." She runs her lips along his cheek, dragging her tongue until it gets to his ear, down to where his jaw meets his neck. She bites again.

He responds just as she knew he would and her back hits the door, forceful this time. Their movements speed up, the intensity building, an unstoppable power.

"Tell me," he says. He takes his hips and pins her to hold her in place, all the while balancing her around him. He reaches behind him and yanks his shirt over his head, dropping it to the floor. She's giddy at the sight of the bare skin of his torso. "Tell me the song name," he says, his voice low and commanding, his hands cupping her face.

"Nah, think I'll keep it to myself."

He groans in protest. "Ruby, Ruby. Trouble, you are."

She runs her fingers along the naked skin of his back as he gently sets her back down to her feet. His fingers graze her stomach as he grabs her sweatshirt, sliding it up and off her body. She leans her head back, feeling the cold of the air, her fingers tugging at his hair as his lips explore her chest.

"You're the one I had to pull out of jail tonight," she says. "Seems like you're the one who's trouble."

"Worth it," he says as his tongue invades the space under her bra. "I'll go to jail time and time again for you if it means I get this." He bites on the cup and pushes it down to replace it with his mouth.

"Yes, fuck yes," she says at the feel of his teeth on her nipple.

"Mine," he says in between kisses and bites on the underside of her breast, his mouth working in possessive movements. He rolls his tongue back over her nipple, moves up to her collar bone, her belly tightening with each sensation. "Mine," he repeats, and she arches her back as the cold air meets the wetness of her breast.

"Yours," she says. Her eyes meet his, his pupils so dilated his eyes look nearly black.

"Mine, Nightingale," he says before he rips the straps of her bra down her arms. Pushes the bra down to her waist. His fingers go to the waistband of her shorts, and he pushes them down her hips, just enough. She's thrilled to realize how badly she wants his touch. This man, the only man able to stir this kind of desire within her.

He presses his hand along her skin, between her shorts and panties. Slips his fingers through and inside her in one harsh push. She gasps, scratching at his neck as the pleasure of his movements rip through her.

She loves his roughness with her. Loves the grip of his other hand in her hair as he tugs her head back and continues his stroking down below, the pulses inside her.

"This is mine," he growls, and she grasps onto his arms. She basks in hearing him claim her. It's what's she's needed. For him to take charge and claim her without pleasantries. Without gentleness.

Her pleasure builds with each of his movements, his hand tight between her shorts and her body. She rocks her hips in rhythm to his movements, and shudders at the impending orgasm threatening to take over. His ownership of her body is everything she wants to feel.

Because it gives her ownership too. His touch is her desire. His claim is her own claim.

"That's right, baby," he says. "Come for me, Nightingale." And she comes undone, putty in the literal palm of his hand. She feels the flush roll through her body, heat creeping through her skin and she presses into his torso, clinging to him. The feeling is nearly too much to handle.

But he doesn't stop. He's persistent in his possession of her as her body trembles. She cries out, her knees no longer strong enough to hold her, and he swiftly drops his hand from her hair to around her waist, catching her before she falls.

Her pulses continue as she relaxes into his embrace. The heat between her legs is a welcomed fire. The pulses continue, slowing steadily, and she opens her eyes to see him staring back down at her. The darkness in his eyes only more intense now. But there's no fear in her, only desire. Only the knowledge that she's exactly where she's supposed to be.

He leans his forehead onto hers. "I've missed you," she whispers, and he shakes his head.

"You have no idea," he says, and she can hear the smile in his voice. "No idea the way I've missed you. Torturing myself with seeing you all over online."

"Stalker."

"Caught me."

"Can't say I'm complaining."

He pulls his head back from hers. She reaches her hand up to his cheek. "What's on your mind, Conti? You look too serious for a stalker that caught his prey."

"I need you to know something." There's something in his voice that she can't quite pinpoint. Urgency, maybe.

"So this is serious," she chides.

"It is."

Her chest squeezes again, unsure what he's about to say. She feels her eyebrows furrow. "What?"

He smiles at her. "It's nothing bad. I just need you to hear this, okay?"

She nods, trying to be brave for whatever he's about to tell her.

I hear the clock chiming. I hear his sighs.

"I lied. Last year. When it all went down, I lied," he says, his eyes locked with hers, his gaze intense.

"About what?"

"All of it."

Her heart flutters at his words. The blossom of hope grows against her better judgement.

"Joey, don't feed me some bullshit because you think it'll fix everything."

"It's not bullshit, baby. I mean it." He cups her face in his hands. "I lied when I said I didn't love you. Or that I never had. It was so fucking wrong for me to say that to you." He leans his forehead to hers. "Of course I loved you. I did from the first time I heard your songs. And then I loved you a little more when you played your songs for me. When you played right here in this apartment, on my bed."

She nods, but says nothing.

"But you know when I really fell for you?"

"When?" she whispers.

"That night when you played in front of our little group." She smiles and murmurs that she remembers that night. "I fell in love with not just Ruby the star, but your courage. Doing something you were clearly meant to do, and fighting past all your fears in the process."

"You made it easy."

"Nah, that was all you, Nightingale." They say nothing and let the memory sit between them in comforting silence. Ruby's mind floats back to the feeling of that night, and how good she felt every time she locked eyes with Joey. A practice she still imagined now and then. When she was in a particularly large venue, the flutter of nerves creeping in, she'd imagine his encouraging gaze in the crowd, cheering her on.

Eventually Joey sighs, his chest heaving with heaviness. "But I lied about one more thing too, Ruby."

She searches his face for what's yet to come. "What?" she asks, not sure she wants to hear.

"I lied when I said I slept with someone else." His words land with a tortured crash on her shoulders and in her chest.

She closes her eyes, because she doesn't want to hear this. It's too painful to hope if it isn't true. She doesn't want to be coaxed into buying another version of the story just because it sounds better. "You don't have to do this, Joey."

"Please, look at me, Ruby." She hears the desperation in his voice. She opens her eyes.

He continues. "There was never anyone else, I swear it. That sounds like bullshit, I know. But it's true. Those whole two years, there was never anyone else."

This, Ruby did not expect to hear. But she realizes just how badly she wants to believe it. She studies Joey's face, searching for signs of deception.

Yet she knows he's telling the truth.

"Okay," she nods.

"Okay?" he repeats, his eyes questioning and hopeful as they search hers. "You believe me?"

She tilts her head to the side. "I do, actually. Yes."

His eyes briefly close in relief.

"And I'll tell you why," she adds.

"Why?"

Ruby sucks in a breath and lets it back out again. "For one, I've obviously let you back in," she says, smiling and glancing down at her naked torso. "So if you were just trying to feed me a lie to get back in my pants, then it seems a bit late for that."

"Sure glad I waited then." He kisses her cheek. "And two? You said 'for one'—is there a second point?"

She nods, reluctant to say the next part. "You said two years.

There was no one else for two years." She watches as realization meets his eyes. "You didn't say three years, you said two."

"I did."

"Because three years would have been a lie, right?"

He nods. "Yes."

As much as it hurts to hear it, she can't blame him. She's not naive. She had stopped talking to him after last year. And she herself had come close to sleeping with someone else a time or two. She had tried, that's for sure. But she never felt comfortable enough with anyone else.

Only with Joey. "Anyone serious?" she asks.

"No, no one serious. Just—"

"Stop," she interrupts. "I don't need to hear it. I just need to know I'm not stepping on someone's toes, here."

"Ruby, I'm not that guy."

"Not you. You're the Good Guy, right?"

He smiles. "Most of the time."

"When it counts."

"When it counts. When I'm not sick with needing to devour you."

She laughs and pulls him towards her for a kiss. And she thinks about how far they've come and how much has changed in these past three years. As much as success and fame have brought her more than she could have ever wanted, she still feels the hurt of what could have been with Joey. The mistakes that didn't need to happen.

As if sensing her regret, he pulls back. Says, "Ruby, I love you, okay?"

She's quiet, because she can't say it back.

"I need you to know that I love you so fucking much, and I've been a miserable dick because of it," he says.

"So it's my fault?"

"No! That's not what I'm saying."

"Relax, Good Guy. I'm only kidding."

They stand there for a moment. Silent. Breath still heavy. She notes with some comfort that she's half naked in front of him, yet feels completely okay with it.

It has to mean something.

"Look," she starts. "I can't say that I'm ready to respond at this point. I can't say that I love you too." She reads his face for a reaction, and sees the hurt in his gaze. But he nods.

She continues. "But I've never been someone who could stand half naked in front of another man like this and feel so *good*. And I'm trying to pay attention to that. It feels significant. Because it's not easy for me to…" She doesn't want to say "trust." It feels trite, and it's more than just that one little world.

"To what?" he prompts.

"To be okay with letting someone into my bubble."

"What can I do?"

"Nothing, I don't think." She tries to find the right words, but everything feels like the wrong tone. "It's nothing that I can explain just yet. I think I just need time. I never let anyone in before you, and I can feel the pull between wanting to dive head first, and wanting to run away.

"But I'm going to try, okay? Not for you, but for me."

"Alright."

"There is something you can do, though," she says.

"Anything."

"Don't be so careful with me. You weren't in the beginning, and it worked. From that time you demanded to walk me to my car. In front of everyone."

"A damn fool."

"I needed it, because I would have never given you the time of day otherwise," she laughs.

"A clever damn fool."

"And you touched me that first night. In the parking lot."

"I did?" he says, surprise punctuating his voice.

"You did. You reached for my hair. After calling me Nightingale."

"I'm so smooth."

"Like satin." She smiles, her belly fluttering at the memory. It had taken her by surprise. Not just the move of his touch, but the way she didn't instantly want to run. "It was the first time I'd let someone touch me like that when I didn't even know them."

"What do you mean?"

She shakes her head. "I don't want to get into it. But let's just say my body for some reason really likes you, Good Guy. And I'm listening to it. Because it feels really fucking good to feel so good."

With that, she reaches for his jeans and unbuttons them.

"You're a puzzle, Ruby," he says with a groan.

"And you're still against underwear, I see," she says as she wraps her hand around his cock, swollen and ready for her.

"Were you wondering?" he asks.

"I'm glad some things never change." She pushes his jeans down and drops down to her knees as she wraps her mouth around him.

"Fuck, Ruby," he groans, fisting the hair behind her temple, the knot on her head slowly coming undone.

She runs her tongue down his shaft, relishing in the velvet softness of his skin. She teases and twists her tongue around and up. Kisses the tip of his dick softly before opening up to take in as much of him as he can. She feels the grip of his hand in her hair as she tortures him with a mix of deep pulls on his cock, and soft tastes with her tongue. Back and forth, going deeper in her throat with each turn. She reaches a hand up to his stomach, exploring his bare skin with her palm while her mouth takes him in.

When he finishes, she swallows quickly and wipes her mouth, smiling with the feeling of power over him. Ruby looks up at him, spent and leaning his forehead on his arm, against the front door. She crawls out from under him and rises to a stand to put her bra back on, pops on her sweatshirt and walks into the kitchen. Rinses out her mouth at the sink.

She finishes and looks up to find him there in the kitchen with her, watching her. His jeans are back in place low on his hips, but he's still shirtless. *He's a fucking God,* she thinks.

"I see all your restaurant success hasn't kept you from the gym," she says.

He dramatically flexes, and Ruby laughs through her pleads for him to stop.

She walks past him and grabs a seat on a bar stool. As she sits, she whispers, "Why did you do it?" and watches as his face falls. "Why did you tell me all those hurtful things if they weren't true?" She tries to focus on his face, and not the sight of his shirtless body.

He sighs heavily. "Because I thought it was the right thing to do, Ruby. That if I pushed you away, you'd continue pushing yourself forward in your career and not go back to letting fear take over."

She nods, but still has the sense that that's not entirely it. There's something else he's leaving out. Even last year, when he said he didn't love her and there was someone else...after they had slept together that night in his office.

And on his bar.

It didn't make sense, and she knew there was something he wasn't telling her. She had tried to confront him, but got no answers then. And it's looking like she won't get them tonight, either, she realizes with bitter disappointment. Her hesitation creeps in all over again.

Maybe opening up the Joseph Conti Jr. chapter isn't such a good idea after all. Yet it's all she wants.

THE COMMENTS FROM HER TEAM fly out of the speakers of her laptop, rapid fire.

"We need to strike while the iron is hot on this."

"Absolutely. There's already buzz on its potential for a Grammy. Everyone's asking when the official release will be."

"When's the soonest you can get in to record?"

"And the music video, we have a few options here, but Ruby we'd love to hear your ideas."

"Simple," she shouts out before anyone else can say another thing.

"Simple?" another voice on the line repeats.

"Yes," she says, glad someone actually paused to allow her to chime in. "Elegant. Emotional. Simple."

As much as she's thrilled with the "buzz" that her and Grayson's performance has generated, she wasn't quite prepared for the overwhelming rush of messages, calls, "emergency" meetings, scheduling, ideas being thrown at her, questions.

"And Grayson's on board with this, correct?"

"He's right here, ask him yourself," Ruby says, a coy smile growing on her face as she looks over to Grayson.

"*I hate you,*" he mouths to her from his safe corner on the couch.

They're on an "emergency" video conference call with Ruby's management team, though Ruby is having a hard time taking them seriously with the concept of "emergency." Natural disasters or war strikes? Sure, let's call that an emergency. But the scramble of determining next moves! Maximizing the momentum! Ruby breaks the internet! She finds it downright funny.

Which she supposes is exactly why she has this team.

She turns her laptop in her lap over to where Grayson is perched, his face contorted into a muted growl. But as she knew he would, he turns on the performance, his face lighting up to an infectious grin once on camera.

"Yes, hello. I'm here! At your service," he says with a salute.

Ruby scoots herself closer to him so they can both be in view of the camera.

"First things first," Jules, Ruby's publicist, chimes in. "I want to nail down the angle on this."

At this, Ruby starts to bring her thumb nail up to her mouth. Grayson swiftly grabs her hand before she gets the chance and gives her a reassuring squeeze.

Jules continues. "The rumors are swirling, and that's a good thing," she rushes to add. Jules knows Ruby needs a little encouragement when it comes to the sideline chatter that runs parallel to the public image they both work hard to fine tune and navigate. "Everyone knows you're back in your hometown now and the cat's out of the bag on Ruby and Joseph Conti."

Ruby feels her heart flutter in her chest at the mention of his name. It's a strange thing having a relationship be out there for public scrutiny—not that she and Joey are even in a relationship exactly. She's thankful that Joey has the attitude that he does, though. He can look at the bright side of most any situation.

But for her? The usual Ruby and Joey puzzle of a relationship in and of itself feels confusing as all hell. Like the first day of school when she started college, maybe. It's where you want to be, but you're scared and there's so much to navigate. You're unsure where to go, what to expect, how to get where, and all the while just trying to take it all in and have as much fun as possible.

Maybe that's the way she needs to think about it. Just have fun with Joey, secrets be damned.

Too bad her heart wants so much more than that.

Grayson, the godsend that he is, beautifully maneuvers in to answer for her. "Jules, love, correct me if I'm wrong here, but perhaps a little mystery is exactly the thing to keep people hungry for more?"

"Yes, I like that," Ruby nods emphatically. "I'm not ready to be putting up lovesick posts or anything. We aren't officially together. I'd rather keep it all quiet."

Jules nods. "Good, okay. So you just keep interacting with fans with gratitude for the support, but stay vague on specifics. Keep them engaged with some info on what they can expect, like plans for release and behind the scenes on the music video, that kind of thing."

"I can do that," Ruby says.

"But pull back on any public interaction with Joseph Conti. No dates out and about because you never know who might be watching. And stay away from his restaurants for now. Try and keep it quiet. Closer to the official release we can revisit coming out with the relationship."

Grayson throws a side glance at Ruby, and she smiles and squeezes his hand once more. She can see the concern in his eyes, and she wonders how she could possibly be doing this life if she didn't have him there with her.

They wrap up the meeting and Ruby closes down her laptop. She looks at Grayson, waiting for one of them to speak first.

"And a star is born," he says with dramatic flair, and she's grateful for the quip.

She gets up and reaches for Rebel, his fur and snuggles the comfort she needs. She nuzzles his head and hums into his fluffy neck. "Where would I be without you two?"

"Come on, let's have it, doll," Grayson prompts. "What's on your mind?"

Ruby considers this. She's relieved at the borrowed time she has with the keep-it-mysterious angle, though she knows it will inevitably be short lived. What she's unsure of is how to proceed with Joey.

That's the thing about living a life in the public eye. It's what Mama Z warned her about. Your life isn't just for you anymore. A relationship and all of its expected complications are suddenly a hot topic of conversation. What might have previously been internal dilemmas of building trust, letting someone in bit by bit and all the other things that come with taking the leap of faith in love—now they have the added bonus of doing so with the eyes of fans and critics and gossip hungry media outlets watching.

It's why they attempted to hit pause on it three years ago. It was too much to throw onto something so new. And yet? Ruby herself took the first steps in reaching exactly this position.

"My head is spinning a little," she finally answers the patiently waiting Grayson.

"Because of work or a certain handsome someone?"

Rebel groans in her lap, as if bored by the topic already.

"The latter."

"I see."

"I mean, it's what I wanted, I guess. Right? It's why I finally put out a Nightingale song. I think I subconsciously wanted to give it another chance."

"What changed?"

She bites her lip as she thinks about this. What did change? Was it seeing him? Probably. The thrill of the tour and a new found confidence in finding her groove in the music world? Yes.

But ultimately it was something else. Something she's grappling with making sense of, something that threatens to yank all of her confidence right out from under her. It's a delicate topic. And one that Grayson is thankfully one of the few people familiar with.

She braces herself as she prepares to get it out in the open. "I heard from him," she says robotically, her eyes lost in a distant gaze.

"I'm not following. Joey?"

"No, no. I mean *him*." She hates to say his name out loud. Shudders to even allow it to enter her mind. Ruby throws a knowing glance over to Grayson, hoping her eyes say enough.

"Oh, fuuuccck." Grayson nods knowingly. "I see." He pats her hand and rubs Rebel's back. "When? How?"

"He—or rather, they—sent me a letter. Here at the house. It was addressed to me and looked harmless enough. I saw who it was from and for whatever reason, I took it. I didn't read it at first, just put it in my bag. I got to it before my dad did I guess, because they say in the letter they'd tried to reach out before."

"When did you get it?"

"I saw it when I popped in to see my dad, right before we went to see Mama Z."

"Oh, Ruby. Why didn't you tell me, love? You've been sitting on this for over three weeks now?" Grayson's voice is gentle, not scolding, but Ruby still feels a little twinge of guilt at having kept it from him.

"I don't know. I think I didn't want to face it just yet. There's something about being back here, though. In LA or while on the road, I'm in this little bubble, you know? Playing a role and escaping. It feels like I have a double life. But then as soon as we cross into the lines of town, it's like the mask comes off and I'm just regular me again. Major imposter syndrome kicks up."

"Ruby, you are exactly who you are. And doing exactly what you were meant to do."

"Logically I know that. And I've worked really hard to get past my own self doubts and disbeliefs of what I'm capable of or what I deserve. Like, really fucking hard."

"But?"

"But...I don't even know. I think a big part of it was that I was nervous to come back. The past year has been this super convenient whirlwind. But I also know I need to reconcile these two parts of myself. Integration, that's what my therapist calls it."

"Ah, yes. Integrate the many parts of ourselves, of course," Grayson says with a mock-serious professional tone.

"As strange as it sounds, I was nervous to be in town and feel all the reminders of my former self, hiding in a corner. I've avoided it, really."

"I get that. It's been a hell of a few years all around."

"And this tour *especially* has felt like an alternate universe." Ruby lifts Rebel in her lap. "This guy right here has been my favorite little buddy, right Rebel? You remind me of everything good in life," she says with a kiss to his head. "You keep me sane."

"So this letter, do you still have it?" Grayson asks and Ruby nods. "Can I see it?"

With reluctance and a sigh, Ruby lifts Rebel off her lap and hands him to Grayson. She retreats to her room and returns moments later with the paper. She holds it by the corner, far away from her, as if a rotting sock that had been worn for a month straight without washing.

Grayson takes the letter from her, unfolding it and begins to read.

Hello, Ruby. Not sure why we bother with writing you anymore since we get zero response. But it's hard to ignore our daughter given that she's famous now. Music going well? We always thought you had talent. We're proud of you and we want to see you. How long will you shut us out? Lots of time has passed, Ruby, and you can't deny that we exist forever.

I'm sober now, have been for months! Todd too, of course, but he's proud of me. Thought you would be happy to hear that. But we miss our little girl. We had so many good times, I hope you remember that. Like that time when we just moved into our apartment, and ordered Chinese and took you to the store to pick out anything you wanted? We came home and sat around on the floor, still waiting on our furniture. You had those cute little stuffed animals that we bought you, and you fell right asleep in your rice! You were holding the new teddy bear and so damn cute.

Well, hopefully you're not too good for us now. That would be a shame to let something like a disease be the thing that keeps you from your family. It doesn't have to be like that, Ruby. I am still your mother. I hope you haven't forgotten that.

Always thinking of you,

~Mom and Todd

"Well okay then," Grayson says, folding up the letter and putting it on the coffee table in front of them. "Does your dad know about this?"

Ruby shakes his head. "No, not yet. I don't want to upset him."

Grayson cocks his head to the side and gives Ruby a look. "How about how it's upsetting you?"

"It's not upsetting me," Ruby insists. "I just think it's funny how they got a few facts wrong, that's all. They left a few convenient details out."

"Mmm hmmm," Grayson nods. "Go on."

She looks at him, eyes narrowed, but he only nods to encourage her to keep talking. Softly, he says, "I'm listening, Ruby."

As if knowing he's needed, the old and slow moving Rebel lifts himself off from Grayson and wanders back over to Ruby, sniffing her before settling in beside her. She smiles sadly down at him.

"Let's see, where to start? Oh, calling me their daughter. I'm not that fucker's daughter," she says, shaking her head in disgust. "Why they're trying to frame it like that, I'll never know."

"Manipulative," Grayson says.

"Well it backfired, because it only freaks me out." She pats Grayson's arm in mock excitement. "Ooo, ooo! Or how 'bout that adorable weekend in the new place mentioned? That was real fun, yeah. Fun how they were broke by then, drank and spent all their money on I'm guessing more than I'll ever care to learn. The apartment was a shithole and the furniture we were 'waiting on' was folding chairs and some free couches and mattresses from God knows where. The gorgeous shopping spree? Ha! The dollar store I'm pretty sure? And my stuffed animals doubled as pillows for a while there. I mean, I was thirteen, not three. Didn't really need stuffed animals, but love that she tries to spin it as some magical memory."

She leans back in her seat and groans. Then pops back up again, remembering something else. "And the music! Oh that was real cute! Supporting my music my ass. *That,* I think pisses me off more than anything. Their only support might have been in hearing the epic fights they'd have and the things I would write as good old inspiration. They sure gave me material, I'll say that much."

"I'm surprised they're still together, based on all you've told me about the beautiful couple," Grayson says with bitterness.

"Please, that part doesn't surprise me at all. Tragedy loves to find company with itself. Fucking toxic magnets, those two are. They hate each other, yet can't live without one another. You know they got married just three weeks after meeting?"

Ruby thinks back to this time with disgust. She remembers how naive she had been at first. She was thirteen, and Pearl, Ruby's mom, had been a miserable drunk at that point for long enough for Ruby to know she had zero hope in any kind of television like mother-daughter relationship.

And then one day, Pearl came home after work with a new energy. She was dancing around the kitchen in a daze saying she'd met the man of her dreams. Talking about how Ruby was going to love Todd, a new waiter at the restaurant where her mom worked. How he'd been the piece they were missing the past couple years. Ruby's sweet, young self had thought maybe this was the answer. That her mom had been heartbroken after her dad left, and that this might be the key to changing things.

Todd Mills was great at first and Ruby bought into it. She remembers the little post-it notes he'd leave for Ruby. The milk-shakes he'd buy her or the surprise candy he'd bring home. Sweets that her mom never liked in the house. Sweet Ruby actually had hope in those first couple months.

Until the day Todd and Ruby were home alone together.

He gave her a hug that lasted just a beat too long. Ruby had been uncomfortable, pushed him away and went to her room where she closed and locked the door. She couldn't decide if she was being dramatic or what, but something about the look he gave her, the way he touched her—it made her feel off.

It was the beginning of the real misery of that household.

When it started feeling normal to have fights leading to cops being called by the neighbors. The long nights where sometimes neither would come home. Those nights started to feel like good luck for Ruby. Soon they moved out of the apartment, into the next one. A building of cracked sidewalks, decaying walls, and broken everything.

Time had a swift way of swooping in to tell Ruby she was right to feel a new suspicion of Todd.

Thankfully for Ruby, the underestimated teenaged girl in her took matters into her own hands.

twenty-five

. . .

joey

I WALK INTO my parents' house, stepping over a few toys. The house is relatively quiet, just the sound of the TV coming from down the hall. As I walk past, I peek down and see some of my cousins' little ones watching TV in the playroom, snuggled in blankets. I debate popping in to say hi, but decide against it, not wanting to disturb their peace by getting them all riled up.

I round the corner to the kitchen and find my mom wiping down the counters. She looks up to see me and smiles. "Hey, kid! Checking in on her?" she asks, nodding her head behind her towards the in-law-suite.

"Yeah. And you," I say with a kiss to her cheek. "Need help with anything?"

She shakes her head no. Throws the spent paper towel she's holding in the trash before heading to the sink to wash up.

I lean against the wall and scan the place. Note with satisfaction that despite the scattered toys, it looks much better.

Guess the initial shock of Mama Z's decline has worn off, and it's almost back to business as usual. I share the observation with my mom, and she laughs.

"I've seen enough people go through deaths of their parents to know that wallowing in the grief for too long does you no good. If she wants to stretch out her last days for all she can, so be it. I'm not going to let it consume me."

I grab a couple M&M's from a crystal bowl and pop them in my mouth. Smile as my mom does the same.

"How's Ruby?" she asks, with a look like she knows I've been talking to her again.

"Good. Why?" I ask, eyes narrowed.

She grins. "Heard you had a little mishap with the police, that's all," she says with a casual shrug.

"Goddamn, news travels fast in this family. Dom told?" I ask. She nods her head yes to confirm. Pops one last M&M in her mouth before pushing the bowl away and back to me.

"Glad it all worked out. You and Ruby, I mean."

I lean back against the counter. "I wouldn't exactly say that. I mean we're talking and we've seen each other."

"So I hear."

I ignore her. "But it's a lot to sort through. Her career took off when we were so new, and things just got messed up and now her life is only more complicated."

"But at least getting the chance to see her again when she came to see Mama Z is giving you both the chance to start things up again, right?"

I look at her, confused. Her voice has this flippant tone to it or something, I can't quite read it. "I mean, it helped get a ball rolling, yeah." I narrow my eyes at her. "What's going on? I know that look. It's the look you get when you win a hand in poker, surprising everyone."

She looks down at her nails, examining them. "It's just that I think Mama Z wanted to see Ruby for exactly that reason."

"What reason? So Ruby and I would see each other and fall madly in love all over again?"

My mom drops her hand. "Something like that. She's had a hand in quite a bit, you know."

"Like what?"

She looks at me and her face softens as she sees my frustration. I hate so much feeling like these women are all buzzing around, keeping things from me behind my back. Friendships with my ex, secret plans to throw us back together again, it all feels like I'm a fucking toy to them.

"Joey, don't look so hurt."

"My life is not a game for your entertainment, you know."

"Of course not."

I shake my head. "I knew it was weird Mama Z was asking for Ruby. Friendship or not, of all the things to ask for in her deteriorating condition, Ruby seemed like a stretch." I look up at my mom. "Why did she even care so much to try and do this? What did it matter to her?"

My mom clears her throat. "Joey, maybe you should know. There's a lot that Mama Z cares very deeply about. And a lot she's..."

"A lot she's what?" I prompt.

"Had a hand in," she says again.

"You said that once already."

"In fact, there's a whole lot more she's behind than you realize." I watch as my mom taps her fingernails onto the countertop, as if debating something. "Joey."

I'm silent, waiting for her to continue.

"It was all Mama Z."

I scoff. "Okay. What now? What's all Mama Z?"

My mom waves a hand around. "All of it, everything. Ruby's career, her break. It was Mama Z."

"I don't understand. What do you mean it was Mama Z?"

My mom looks downright annoyed. I guess whatever the hell it is she's trying to say is hard to say, but her snap in attitude is still unexpected. "Pay attention, would you?"

"I'm trying, but you're making it pretty fucking impossible with the roundabout way of talking!" I turn my back to my mother. Partly out of guilt for cursing, but mostly because I'm boiling and need a minute. I wonder how the hell Mama Z would have anything to do with Ruby's big break.

"Watch your goddamn mouth, Joseph. You do not talk to me that way or so help me God," (I know she's making a cross over her chest), "I will slap those dimples right off your face."

She's quiet and I stare at the dripping faucet of her kitchen sink.

Drip—so much you don't know, Joey.

Drip—pay attention now.

Drip—once a leak starts, you never know how much is waiting to burst.

I turn back around to face my mom. She sighs and perches herself on the arm of the small breakfast nook sofa. "Listen. Mama Z arranged for that rocker guy—"

"You mean multi Grammy winning artist Jamison Spencer," I say, sarcasm oozing out of the words "Grammy" and "winning."

"Yes. Him. She arranged for him to be at your restaurant that night. On a night Ruby would be playing."

I shake my head, scrunch together my eyebrows in confusion. "I need a drink. This doesn't make any sense." I walk over to the butler's pantry on the other side of the kitchen. Grab whatever substance is sitting on the mirrored tray on the marble counter. Pour the amber liquid into a lowball, and gulp. I look back towards my mom and catch her watching me.

She clears her throat. "Are you ready to listen now?" she asks.

"I just...how would Mama Z possibly know Jamison *Spencer*." I clench my jaw because I'm trying to contain my sarcasm and disbelief and anger. Emotions I'm not used to letting consume me like this. And I need to get my shit together so I can get to the bottom of this.

"She didn't know him directly. But she had...a friend who knew the right people who did."

"Her art group friend?" I say. "The one that gets us all the concert tickets and random memorabilia and things?" My mind flashes to images of signed albums, guitars, posters of random bands' albums. I have some of these hanging in my restaurant, but I never gave them much thought. My designer liked them, and I let her have at it when she heard about my grandmother's collection. How deep could some local old lady's connection really run?

I look over to my mom. She bends at the waist in full belly laughs. I mean like real big, hysterical laughing. In a fit. That's the word. A fit of laughter. I'm looking at her in both horror, but also the slightest seeds of absurd amusement.

'Cuz I have a feeling she's about to say some shit that's going to blow my whole world apart. And I can see how much I've probably missed, even if I don't understand exactly what, just yet. But it's there, and now I'm laughing too, because the world is fucking upside down and there's nothing I can do but ride along and enjoy the flips and turns.

"It's not an art group friend, is it?" I say, pouring myself another drink. I have to pause, lean down and rest my forearms on the counter, full laughs taking over my body to the point where I'll spill if I try and hold onto my refilled cup.

"You hear that, Mama?" my mom shouts over to the direction of the in-law suite, mid laugh. "Joey thinks—" she's in full hysterics and can barely get the words out. "He thinks your connection is—" She bends at the waist again and I watch as her back and shoulders tremble from her volcanic cackles. "—some friend from your art, *your art group*." Those last words come out in a pained, strangled whisper of a sob, and I rush over to her.

"Mom, shit, you okay?" I ask, kneeling down in front of her. She has her face in her hands, her head down and all I can do is put my cheek on the back of her head, and attempt to hug her in an awkward embrace. She's sobbing so hard, her back is convulsing under my arms. "What the hell is going on?" I whisper out into the air.

"I'm sorry. I'm so sorry," is all I hear in Mama Z's voice, infiltrating my mind.

"You hear that?" I ask my mom.

My mom's muffled voice comes from below me. "Hear what?"

I sigh in confusion. "She's sorry."

"Sure. Who, Mama Z? Oh good, look at that, she's sorry."

"I'm serious, you don't hear that, mom?"

"I don't know what you're talking about. But if she's telling you she's sorry, tell her, it's a little late."

"You can't hear that?" I ask, a chill sweeping over my body. But I can tell by my mom's lack of reaction that this voice I'm delusionally hearing is for me and me alone.

I give up, try to squeeze my eyes shut and shake out the sound of Mama Z. "Tell me about this not-art group friend," I say to my mom.

Everything goes eerie as my mom abruptly stops her sobs. She pops her body back up straight, throwing me off of her.

"Mom?" I press.

"It's someone bigger than that," she hurls out in a rush, the words all coming out at once, like one giant jumble.

Itssomeonebiggerthanthat.

She sucks a breath in, says, "Someone at the very top of the music industry."

I rise up and back away from her. Look around for the tissue box, find it and hand it to her. "Okay. I don't even know what that means, but okay."

"He owned a company. And that company owned a record label. A label that's been the very life of some of music's biggest names for decades."

An image of a pompous looking white guy in a suit and a mess of rings on his fingers pops into my head.

"He's an old man now, actually just recently passed away, but… but one phone call and he could make things happen."

"Who is this guy?"

"I can't tell you and it doesn't even matter. But they go way back, him and Mama Z."

"Why doesn't it matter?" I ask, because that feels like the biggest crock of shit I've ever heard.

"Because you'll never meet him, he'll never meet you, and the impact he had, the moves he's made, they have and always will remain behind closed doors. Locked away with Mama Z."

There's anger in my mom's voice as she says this. An anger with a life force of its own.

"What impact, what do you mean?"

"One phone call, one email from The Gentleman—"

"The Gentleman?" I say, eyebrows raised probably up to the damn roof above us. "You've got to be kidding me," I scoff. "He's got a code name? A secret catchphrase? The Gentleman," I say, spreading my hands out in front of my face in a dramatic gesture, as if showcasing the words in a neon sign. "Making calls and emails and changing lives," I spit out in my best narrator television voice.

"It's what she's always called him," my mom says, deadpan.

I look at her and drop my hands. "Fine. Okay. The Gentleman." And I look my mom square in the face. "So he's the one that brought in fucking Jamison Spencer to my restaurant. Which both catapulted *me* to the top of the restaurant scene, and shone a big, fat, shiny light through good old Jamison's one Instagram post on Ruby Francesca. Making her a star. Just like that," I say with a snap.

"More or less, yes," my mom says, squaring her shoulders and rising to a stand. Composure regained as if she had never lost it in the first place. "He continued to oversee and ensure Ruby's success, though Ruby doesn't know about that or him."

"Why didn't Mama Z ever say anything? I mean, apart from it

all seeming so unbelievable. Why not admit it? Take the credit?" I cross my arms behind my head, feeling my blood starting to boil again. "Why not tell us the fucking truth?!"

"Jesus, Joey, because she didn't want Ruby feeling like she hadn't earned it!" She sighs and pauses for a beat, hesitant. "But also, Mama Z knew that ultimately," another pause, "it would be the thing to rip Ruby away from you."

Her words land like an axe into my chest. Because it's true. Ruby had to choose—me or fame. She had an opportunity, and holding onto both couldn't be done. It wasn't possible.

Or maybe it was.

I'm sitting here with this gnawing feeling in my gut. My chest is tight and my breath is getting shallow. Something's off, here. Why did I think it wasn't possible to have both? Why not stay with Ruby when she was first signed? I think we both wanted to stay together, I remember that. Sure, it'd be a lot of time apart, but I was ready to fly out to her whenever I could to be with her. Her home base could have always been here in PA; it didn't *have* to be all the way across the country in California, despite the label's recommendation. Right?

That's when it dawns on me. The biggest fucking thing of it all.

That the plan to make sure Ruby took her opportunity, chose her career over me, the sin that I committed in telling her those hurtful things. All against my fucking instincts, all in order to make Ruby doubt us and walk away—

That entire setup was Mama Z's idea.

Mama Z's great push to help me push Ruby.

Mama Z. Who ultimately is the one that secretly got Ruby her big break in the first place, while never telling a soul.

Mama Z orchestrating everything. Not just a sweet little grandmotherly source of guidance, quietly listening to all our problems, chiming in with advice and suggestions here and there.

But a secret mastermind. A puppeteer pulling strings. My life, my *love* for fuck's sake, all just a game to her.

I grab my glass and throw it against the wall. The sound of shattering is music to my enraged ears. The drops of brown liquid, rolling down the wall before me like a mudslide of destruction.

"It was all her, wasn't it?" I say, attempting to appear as if this fact isn't the very thing that has left the darkest of holes in my heart the past three years. "It was her own dream that she never lived out. Mama Z's own misery at never being a star, and we all fell right into her plan."

"It was for her, it was for her…"

"You did it for YOU!" I scream. I turn to look at my mother, quiet in the corner of the room. "I'm right, aren't I?" But she doesn't say anything. She wipes away what I think was a tear from her face, but says nothing.

"…I'm sorry."

But I no longer get chills when I hear it, hear her voice infiltrating my skull. It's Mama Z, alright. Pulse barely kicking just feet away from where I stand, but still the mastermind matriarch of this whole family.

What I don't get is *why?*

"Why would she do that, Ma? It doesn't make any fucking sense. Why would she call in a favor to this guy," (I refuse to use that bullshit code name of his), "help get Ruby her big break, but make *me* do what I did to push Ruby away so she'd never speak to me?"

My mom only sits there, quiet now and staring off into space. She gets up and walks to the window. I'm staring at her back, waiting for an answer, but I have a feeling I'm not going to get it.

"You pushed Ruby away?" she asks, her back still to me.

"Yes," is all I say. She's a smart woman. I'm sure she can fill in the blanks of what that might mean.

My mom sighs and places one hand on her hip, and brings the other to her face. "She had her reasons," is all my mom says, and it only further sends my anger flying.

Reasons or not, I'll never forgive Zabel. Not until I know I have my Ruby back completely. Not until I figure out the impossible way to earn my Nightingale's love and trust, fully and without a drop of hesitation.

No. Deathbed or not, that woman does not stand a single chance of forgiveness until that wrong has been righted.

I HAVE TO GET TO the bottom of this. I'm trying to wrap my head around the whole thing. Mama Z and some secret friend within the music industry. Making this call to get Ruby discovered. It just doesn't add up.

Alright, fine. Mama Z was a wannabe singer once upon a time. Worked at a radio station, I knew that. Never thought much of it.

But to still have contact with this person, yet never tell any of us about it—that's the part that doesn't sit right.

I think about all the memories with my grandmother that pop in my head. Always a strong woman, never shy about sharing her opinions, especially with the girls in the family. She had a soft spot for me for some reason. I could see that even as a kid. Dinners at my grandparents' house when my grandfather was still alive—she'd have the girls get up to clear the table, and want me to stay behind like a prince being waited on. I ate it up as a kid. My little sisters would give me shit about it, and I'd tease them that it's the benefit of being the older brother.

Mama Z loved my sisters too, I know she did. I think she just had higher hopes for me. Saw me as someone who could make her laugh, someone with career plans that she admired. Mama Z loved that I wanted to open up a Mediterranean restaurant since it was a tribute to her roots growing up with a hodgepodge of cultural influences.

And Ruby—man I loved how much Mama Z loved Ruby, right out of the gate. Gave me some seal of approval that I was right about this girl.

So why the hell would she push for us to end it? Not just once, but twice. That's the thing I can't make any sense of.

I'm sitting here on Mama Z's hospital bed, sick not just from the smell of looming death in here and the Chanel perfume attempting to mask it, but something else.

"The Real EmZee, you've got some explaining to do," I say. I get a little hum from her, but nothing else. Not even the strange whispers of her voice in my head are coming through. I wonder if it's me, if I'm subconsciously blocking her out.

I try again to get what I need to say off my chest. "See Mama, I know your little secret. Yup, that's right. I know it was all you behind helping to get Ruby discovered."

My heart starts pounding in my chest, a bubbling up of so much happening at the thought of my girl. Of her career. Of all the shit she apparently had been going through that I realize I have yet to even fully understand.

"I suppose you want a thanks then, huh? I'm supposed to come and thank you now, is that it? Thanks for helping my girl," I say with sarcasm.

I lean in closer to her ear. "Except you didn't just help her, did you? Oh no. You took it a step further. And you told me I was going to lose her anyways, so I needed to let her go."

If disgust looked like a substance coming out of a person's voice, mine would be oozing black tar. And let me tell you, it takes a lot to piss me off. Yet I'm sitting here kind of high off this feeling of rage I have. All because of the actions of some little old lady.

I lean back, drop her hand from mine and rise. Start pacing around the room. "Where are those voices I'd been hearing, huh Mama Z? Quiet suddenly, here in the hot seat?"

I pause in front of a shelf in the room. Pick up a picture frame, a photo of Mama Z and my grandfather, snuggled up together. They're in front of my mom's Christmas tree. I recognize the manger setup on the fireplace mantle beyond. My mom had gone to Catholic school as a kid and picked up the religion with a fierce-ness, despite Mama Z's agnostic stance.

As I look closer at this photo, you can see my grandfather leaning in, his arm draped around his wife. But looking closer, Mama Z has a fake smile, I can see it now. Her body's turned slightly away from him. Her smile not reaching her eyes.

And it dawns on me. I point the photo towards Mama Z, despite her closed eyes. "This photo's all bullshit, isn't it? You prob-ably never even really loved good old Artem. My grandfather." I study his face, see the love in his eyes for his wife.

"This gentleman of yours, was he your lover?"

"Loved both."

I hear the strange voice in my mind and instead of giving me chills, it just makes me sick. Fills me with a bitter taste in my mouth that only infuriates me.

"That's what you want me to know?! That you loved both?!" I raise the photo in the air, ready to slam it to the floor, but hold back and merely give the air a half-hearted, restrained punch. Sigh and gently return it to the shelf.

"What other things have you been hiding from this family, huh Mama Z? And why the hell did you drag Ruby into it all?" I step back closer to her, but remain standing beside the bed.

"Because while maybe on the surface you calling in some favor from an old flame may have looked sweet, it's the shit you pulled afterwards that I'm struggling with. Do you remember, Mama Z? Remember telling me I had to let my girl go? Let her find her dream, or else she'd spend the rest of her life resenting me? Oh yeah, you made a whole lot of sense to me back then. I fell for that shit, no problem. Knew my grandfather wasn't faithful to you." I scoff at this. "That was no family secret. Figured 'Poor Mama Z. She knows what she's talking about, I sure won't do that to my Ruby.' You're good, old gal. I'll give you that," I say, wagging a finger at her.

I turn away from her, resume my pacing. Run my hand through the back of my hair. Stop as my next thought creeps in.

"Here's the crazy shit—you did it *again*. Last year, when Ruby came back to me. Struggling, and I came to you. You! For advice," I'm laughing through this part, "and you said to let her go, don't let her hide behind me. I said I didn't think she would if I was by her side. And you turned it all around, said her career was too new, and it was more important now more than ever that she keep her head in the game. You told me letting me go would be the best way."

I put my hands in my pockets, throw my head back and laugh. "And the best part! Oh fuck, I haven't even gotten to the best part. Now sit back, you're going to love this. When I said I didn't think we could stay away from one another, Lord knows it hadn't really worked for those past two years so far, you said—do you remember it? Remember Mama Z? You said, 'Tell her something where she'll have no choice but to let you go. Tell her you've found someone else, and you're in love.'

"I thought you were kidding at first. I really did! Thought how funny my Mama Z was. But you were dead serious, weren't you? And I always thought you had everyone's best interests at heart. So I listened. Figured she's old and wise, she must know.

"And I followed through. Mostly." I lift an arm and run my hand along my jaw, remembering it. "See I couldn't quite bring myself to say I was in love with someone else. That was just a step further than I could take it. But I did tell Ruby I had been with someone else. And that I didn't love my Nightingale, and I never had and never will. Convinced her we were just a summer fling, caught up in the newness of it. Yup. Sure fucking did. Can you imagine? That sweet girl's face? You know she spit in my face the next time I saw her?"

The strangest bit of affection floods through me at the memory. I had almost forgotten about that part. My girl, not going down without a fight. I think I fell in love with her even more then.

I sit back on the bed with my grandmother. "I should have

known right then that she had ten times more fight in her than I ever gave her credit for. But I have a feeling you already knew that, didn't you? So again, why? Why work so hard, convince me with such unquestionable persuasion that I needed to let her go?

"Was it so you wouldn't lose me? Is that it? Scared I'd go follow my girl around the world, the steadfast love along her side following her career? And then what, you wouldn't have me here to joke around with you, give you all the fucking *attention* you apparently never felt you got enough of!"

"Joey!" My mother comes bursting in through the door. "What are you doing, I hear you in here shouting!"

Was I shouting? I hadn't even realized.

"My God," my mom says, bustling around the room and making strange adjustments to things. Tucking in Mama Z's blankets tighter around her body, fluffing up pillows, shifting the random flower arrangements everyone keeps sending. The woman's not even dead yet, but the room looks like a floral shop.

She turns back to me. "What has gotten into you? You think she's going to rise up and fight back? Tell you everything you think you need to hear?"

I open my mouth to respond, but shut it again. I don't even know what exactly I'm after.

My mom stares at me for a beat, eyebrows raised, waiting on me to say something.

"I'm just trying to understand where it all went wrong, so I can make it right," I say finally.

Eventually my mom breaks eye contact. I watch her as she moves over to some drawers in the room, pushing things aside and rummaging around. My anger pulls back a bit, replaced by a little curiosity. And maybe a little bit of hope that she's got the answer I'm looking for, right in the old dusty time capsules of Mama Z's bureau.

My mom pulls out a yellowed piece of paper no bigger than the size of an index card. I watch as she stares at it for a moment, silent and face unreadable. She reaches a hand up, mindlessly scratches at her neck. I cross my arms over my chest impatiently as I wait for her to explain.

Eventually she breaks the silence, clearing her throat. Says, "You said you and Ruby talked, right?"

I hadn't told her the whole story, but I nod my head. Say, "Yeah. We talked. It's a start." My mom only nods. I continue. "I'm going to get her back, Ma," I say, not caring how crazy that potentially sounds to her. "That's all I want."

"You love her?"

I nod, take a step closer to my mom. Look her square in the eyes. "More than I've loved anyone before in my life. I know how that sounds. We weren't even together that long before her world completely changed, but there's something there between us. And I went about it all wrong." I dart my eyes over to Mama Z, then back to my mom. "I thought I knew what was best for her and I pushed her away."

As much as I want to blame Mama Z for all the things I'm not saying right now, I know that it's not fair to. Because ultimately, I'm the one that pulled the trigger.

So all I say is, "I'm trying to figure out how to convince Ruby to let me back in."

"And she's been agreeable so far?"

"I'd say she's open to the possibility. But holding back." I look down at the floor. "Rightfully so," I whisper.

"Do you know anything about her past, Joey? About Ruby's stepfather?"

I shoot my eyes up to look at her. "Her stepfather? What stepfather?" I say. Ruby never mentioned a stepfather, that's for damn sure.

My mom sighs, big and deep and laced with sadness and something else. Takes a couple steps over to me. Says, "I know you want answers, and in time they'll come."

"Okay, and?" I say. There it is again, that feeling that there's so much more to the story here that no one's telling me. A puzzle I'm supposed to solve when I only have half the pieces.

"For now, why don't you start here." She hands the paper over to me.

I glance over it, unsure what to expect. It's a newspaper article that dates back ten years. The headline reads "Fourteen-Year-Old Girl Stabs Stepfather in Self Defense."

My eyes move across the paper, trying to skim through and decipher what in the world this is. Words jump out at me like "apartment with mother" and "molested" and "knife hidden in nightstand." I look a little closer. Read through about the alleged sexual abuse of the girl on two occasions, and the girl's plotted attack as a response.

"What the hell is this, mom?" I ask, my stomach dropping. I raise my fist to my mouth, biting hard, fighting the urge to vomit. "This was Ruby's stepfather? Is that what you're saying?"

She nods her head. "Yes. It was something Mama Z found, shortly after you and Ruby met."

"How?"

My mom shakes her head gently, "I guess she went down a rabbit hole to dig up information. She found records of Ruby's dad, Dom. Then her mom, and then the mom's remarriage to someone named Todd Mills, and eventually that led to this," she says, pointing to the article in my hand.

"She never told me," I say, still unsure how to process this.

"It's a hard thing to share, sweetie," my mom's voice says quietly. "Can you imagine?"

"Yeah, but—If I had known, I could have..." my voice trails off, not sure where the thought is going. Treated her better? Been more gentle, more careful? She'd hate that, I already know. Ruby would hate me thinking that's what she needed.

Which is probably exactly why she never told me about her past in the first place.

Still, I'm struggling to absorb this information. Ruby, my

Ruby. Suffering as a kid, not just from an alcoholic mother, but from something even worse. And Mama Z, somehow knowing that about her when I didn't. For some reason, I can't get past that. Maybe it wasn't my business, but still. I wonder how my grandmother could sit there and suggest I hurt this girl like that, when she knew all the shit Ruby had already been through.

"Don't do that to yourself, Joey," my mom says, her voice an unbearable attempt at soothing. "You can't change the past, no matter how much you wish you could. And look at Ruby, she made out okay. She's stronger than most."

I'm just staring at her, stunned. Holding my breath, afraid that if I breathe out, then what I'm hearing is more real.

My mom goes on. "Bad things happen, and I'm sure the last thing Ruby would ever want is for something like that to follow her around and define her. It's just a thing that happened to her. But it's not her whole story, okay? That may be hard for you to understand, but please, try to keep that in mind. The last thing she needs is for you to treat her like she's not capable of anything and everything."

I hand the article back to mom, unsure what to do with the putrid paper. I'm hearing her words, trying to put this all together, but all I can think about is my girl.

My girl that was so skittish in the beginning. Hitting me with a flashlight when we first met. Hiding her music online behind a fake name, never showing her face, but wanting so badly to break free of a prison that I now know was put upon her at the hands of some monster.

I think about the strangeness of how she was with me. Going from so on guard to completely in. Then back on guard again and I never quite knew what to expect.

I think about what she told me the other night. How when I reached for her hair that first time we met, how she was okay with it. And that meant something to her. I was someone she felt comfortable with, and I never even knew just how delicate that was. Or what a gift it was.

And then I think about that article.

She stabbed him. My Ruby stabbed her monster.

I'm mixed with this strange concoction of pride for my girl, and disgust that she was ever put in that position in the first place.

And then rage. Now the rage comes, hot and violent and I'm fuming wanting to know where the fuck this guy is now. I ask my mother if she knows, trying with all the force in the world to keep my voice steady.

"That's the thing, sweetie. I'm giving you this now because I know you're trying to fix things with Ruby. I don't know exactly what happened with you two last year, but I can tell you this."

I swallow, a golf ball in my throat that I'm trying to keep down. "What?" I say.

"Last year," my mom starts, "when Ruby came back into town—"

"Yes, what about it?"

"It's when the stepfather got out of jail."

twenty-six

. . .

ruby

THE TIMING SEEMS like a giant "fuck you" in Ruby's face. An email now somehow making its way to her private email right there into Ruby's phone. From a not so clever email account, username "millsmans555." She stares at it, shaking with the sight of the words on the screen. Just nine words to evoke terror.

"I know you're in town. We're not through yet."

That's all it says. It's all it needs to say, and she's heard those words before. The last four—*we're not through yet*—years ago, slurred and hot on her cheek, drenched in the foul smell of cheap booze and teeth that probably hadn't seen a toothbrush in days, maybe more. He said those words countless times to her, until the one time when Ruby knew it was going to be his last. She knew it had to be, before things got any worse.

Ruby thinks back to last year, the first time she had heard from him, right after he was released. Knowing he was getting out, she had decided to pop back home to be with family—both her dad and the makeshift family of Joey's clan. But shortly after she landed, an email had come. It was from a different account, but had the same subtle little jibes, saying he'd heard she's here.

A letter from her mom is one thing, more an annoyance than anything else, but the emails? They fill Ruby with disgust.

Just like last year, Mills seems to keep track of any cheap celebrity buzz alerting the media of when she's in town. It's like he gets a thrill out of messing with her. He's quiet as a mouse when she's on the road or in LA, but the minute she's back home? He can't seem to resist fucking with her. It's as if the proximity is his own personal invitation to taunt.

She drops the phone on the couch, turns away and raises her hands to her face. Ruby smirks, thinking how sobriety as a free man clearly proved to be more than he could handle for long.

She should tell her dad about this, she knows. Or Grayson.

Or Joey.

Her mind goes to Joey and how she'd even begin to explain it all to him. The man her mother Pearl had married and the hugs that made her uncomfortable. About how they then escalated to "accidental" times he ended up in her bed instead of his own, and how that turned to—

Her head and body involuntarily shake, and she wills herself to dismiss the thoughts and memories. She'd had plenty of therapy to help cope through that with the best therapist her dad could find. It had worked, though she knows seeing this resurrect will demand some more frequent sessions in the very near future. There's only so long she can avoid it, when it's here attempting to weasel its way back into her world.

"You alright, honey?" her dad says as he walks downstairs and into the living room.

"Huh? Oh, hey," she says. Facing this at this moment is the last thing she wants to do.

"You look pale—you feeling alright?" Dom walks up to her, puts a hand on her forehead.

"I'm always pale, Dad."

"You take after your mother like that," he mutters, and they both startle at the unexpected mention.

Pearl had long been a name dropped from their household, only reserved for when it was absolutely needed. Her steadfast commitment never failing in her claims denying Ruby's story. Claims that Ruby had attacked Pearl's husband unprovoked.

Well, at least until Ruby started getting famous and suddenly Pearl was trying to change her tune and expecting forgiveness. But Ruby and Dom both knew all she was really after, and some bullshit apologies were never going to fly with Ruby.

Dom had asked Ruby at some point, years ago, if she wanted to attempt any kind of relationship with her mom. She imagines he was torn with wanting to respect the right for a daughter to have a relationship with her mother, and wanting to rip the skin off his ex-wife's body for her complete neglect of their daughter. Not to mention Dom's own guilt at having left Ruby with her.

Ruby would have none of it. She remained adamant that a relationship with her mom was never going to happen. The woman was dead to her.

"Yes, but I have your pretty blue eyes, don't I, Dad?" Ruby says with a light-hearted smile and quick kiss to her dad's cheek.

She hates seeing the guilt on his face. It's not his fault he married the wrong woman, one who, at the time, seemed like his perfect match. She later dissolved into misery, blaming military life and claiming that she missed home. She convinced him that he caused Pearl pain in his efforts to simply provide for his family and serve his country.

"That voice of yours comes from my side too," Dom says.

"See? All the best parts. All from you."

Dom is quiet for a moment and gives Ruby a half smile. "Your pale skin is beautifully yours though, too." And she wonders how many other contact attempts have been made that Dom has kept from her. She wonders if they're now subconsciously popping into his head.

Yes, Ruby knows she needs to address this, sooner rather than later. If not for her, then for her poor father and his eternally worried mind.

But first, she wants to see Mama Z.

twenty-seven

. . .

mama z

OH IT'S A beautiful thing these last days of life, I tell you. I have floated through tulip fields, made love to both my lovers countless times, dined with Cher and sang softly to my children and grandchildren. All of the best moments of my life, right here for me to experience again, as if in a dream.

My visitors seem to have grown tired of my continued battle. What was a daily party of no one ever leaving my side mere weeks ago has now dwindled down to a single person sitting with me now and then. I can feel the absence in their presence, though. They're here but do not want to be. Bored perhaps. I cannot say I blame them. I would be bored as well.

I tune in and out, listen for anything interesting, but mostly my ever so loyal family seems to have forgotten they are even in the company of a dying woman. I feel their discontent when here. The next person up on the sign up sheet for the task of keeping me company. Funny how grief can settle into annoyance like that.

Joey though, my Joey. Oh he's mad at me alright. Even without his words, I could feel it. You see, each person that steps into this room brings with them a unique essence. An aura, if you will, though I was never the superstitious type to buy into that kind of thing. Cannot deny its existence now though having experienced it, can I?

Isabella's presence brings with it the strongest grief. I feel the hunger in her bones from her lack of appetite and I smell the earthy scents of rain after a storm. Her tears, both shed and unshed. I see hope bloom in the form of a flower anytime I make a sound or attempt to move my body. Hope in my darling daughter, emanating off her. I'm pleased with her hope, foolish as it is. We both know I shall not return. But her hope and the love fueling it satisfies me, nonetheless.

She was seventeen when I told her about The Gentleman. I never did give her a direct answer on whether or not he was her biological father, for I myself did not know. Isabella was my spitting image, much to my relief for both my lover and my husband's sake. It was a convenient foot in either world that I was able to maintain.

Still, when Xavier's mother became pregnant with him, at the seed of my dear husband Artem, I felt Isabella should know of my own lover. I was mourning our relationship, I suppose. It was a turning point, you understand. The affairs that had marked our past two decades needed to come to an end. Too much to risk with the life we had so carefully built. Artem's business was thriving, we finally had money beyond our wildest dreams. The Gentleman had also reached a level of success that made him more and more of a distant figure in my life.

It was time to grow up, once and for all, and my depression was bitter and suffocating with this realization.

"This is my father?" seventeen-year-old Isabella had asked, after finding me crying on the floor of my bedroom. She always did have that motherly instinct. She stroked my hair with such love, my young daughter, not quite a woman but no longer a girl. She was trying to understand.

I had been clutching the sole photo that I had of The

Gentleman and myself. Him dashing in a white suit jacket, me in a red pencil skirt, blazer, and flower hat. He had bought me the outfit from Paris, and I felt as dazzling as the rarest of gems. Arms linked, smiling into one another's eyes. The happiest I had ever been, I might say.

But in a moment of weakness, I had slipped and allowed Isabella to find me on that floor in my room, heart heavy with pain and loss as we now had this other battle upon us. Artem's secretary, pregnant with his child. A woman scorned as he made it clear he would not be leaving his family for her.

We decided then that enough was enough. It was time to end our affairs.

I had rolled over onto my side, legs curled up, hugging my knees to my chest. "I don't know, darling," I said honestly in response to Isabella's question. "But he believes he is your father, and I'm not sure I have ever really wanted to know for sure either way."

She should have been furious, I know I would have been mad as hell. But Isabella's always had a more gentle spirit than mine. Fierce when it counts, believe you me, but she saves it. As I look back now, I recognize the immense power that kind of emotional control holds. I admire her for it.

"Does Daddy know?" she had asked.

I nodded, a few more tears rolling down my cheek and into my hair. "He does." What more could I say? How could I possibly explain the years of our indiscretions? The understanding that Artem and I had, the life we had designed for ourselves that had far more secrets behind closed doors than anyone would have ever imagined.

Isabella lay down on the floor beside me, wrapped her arms around me, and allowed me to weep in her cradled embrace. The poor child, learning of her father's affair and new half sibling on the way, and now her mother's long time lover. A man that might very well be her biological father. She had no idea how he had funded Isabella's schooling in the early days before Artem's business took off. Or how he had quietly inquired year after year about the potential daughter he would never know. It had to be torture for her to learn of these things.

That's the thing about family secrets. They are loud demons—creatures layered with coverups and lies. Omissions and deceit have a way of crawling out when one is not looking. They are spiders that escape their corners, spin new webs and catch the innocent passerby off guard with their crooked legs that offer horrific and unexpected speed.

I let this spider out in showing Isabella that photo. Her mother with a man who was not the man she knew as her father, but was clearly her mother's great love.

I *wanted* her to know.

Because I could not stand the pain in that moment, further amplified by the pity from the family in learning of Artem's affair. They looked at me as a saint for forgiving him. "Poor Mama Z," they thought. "She's so sweet to take him back and to welcome this new baby that is not hers."

It disgusted me.

I needed someone to know that my tears were not for Artem's unfaithfulness, but for my own sacrifice and broken heart. It was a crippling stab to the heart, yes. But it was a dagger I had placed there myself. This, I needed Isabella to know.

Because I was nobody's victim.

BY NOW I HOPE YOU recognize that I have always had well calculated plans. Those plans have not necessarily been easy ones, I tell you that. I have been faced with obstacle after obstacle, choice after cruel choice. Life is what you make it, though, and I can truly say I have zero regrets.

Except for one.

"Holding strong, I see, Mama Z," croons that beautiful voice of

Ruby. I'm delighted that she has returned once more. My darling Joey's little Nightingale.

She brings with her a river of bars of music, divine in their tune. There is grief mixed in, notes in a lovely minor chord, but coupled with something else. Acceptance and gratitude, perhaps. She loves me, I can feel that. But there's something else there as well.

"The asshole is trying to contact me," she confides. There it is. The other bit, the off key thing I could sense.

I know who she means. And while I may be nearly dead, my pulse quickens as I hear her words. I could have figured this day would come. Men like that never can live without having the last word. I want to tell her to be careful, to tell Joey, so she can unload this burden. No sense in carrying it all alone. Ruby needs to understand the importance in this.

How I wish I had conveyed that to her before.

How I wish I could have had more time with her, but such is life.

My time is quickly coming to an end, I can feel that. My concerns for Ruby have limited outlets. My grip in this life is shifting to a grip on fine particles of falling sand. Not much left to hold onto, I'm afraid.

I do, however, have some hope. I have decided to leave Ruby a small package that she'll receive upon my death. Her presence here now assures me she's worthy of it. She can do with it what she will, and I do hope it will help her lean on those who love her.

I attempt to infiltrate her thoughts with my own—a very much welcomed and unexpected talent I have discovered in my dying days.

"Allow him to love you," I urge. *"Being strong also means allowing yourself to be loved."*

Ruby says nothing, but I feel her body tense. The river of music freezing, midair. I'm frightening her, I fear.

I try again. Try to speak out loud these words that she needs to hear.

"Joey," I manage.

There's a glow of light in her now. A yellow humming, and the flow of her song begins again. "Did you speak?" she asks me, disbelief in her voice. The river of music swells, the beat and tune changing to a cadence of drum beats, quickening in pace.

"Joey!" she calls out, and I hear my grandson's footsteps, distant beyond the room.

But I want Ruby to hear this without him present. I try again. "Let him...love you," I breathe out. "Let Joey...love you."

She squeezes my hand. A gesture of understanding. *Allow him to love you, Ruby. Care for you. Be strong when you don't want to be. Let him...let him...let him..."*

It's a lightning strike when Joey enters the room, his energy such a force. Too big for this space. I try to use it.

"Together," I say out loud.

"She's talking! Does she usually talk?" Ruby whispers.

"Sometimes, though not much lately." Joey is beside me now, I can feel it. He grabs both our hands, Ruby's and mine. "Mama Z, we're listening. What is it?"

Now is my chance. It's the final task of mine before I leave this world to await whatever fate lies beyond.

"Be together," I say. "You be together."

I hear Joey huff in disbelief, but a warmth radiates despite himself. The lightning of his anger softening. "Me and Ruby, huh?"

"I could hear her," Ruby says. "Like before she spoke out loud, I could hear her—"

"In your mind?" Joey finishes for her. I let go just a little more, relieved that they are finally sharing the gift of my invading messages.

"I know it sounds crazy."

"No. It doesn't, I hear her too sometimes," Joey says, his voice quiet. The lightning has evaporated, just as quickly as it came, replaced now by his own tenderness and hope. It brings me relief.

I would not want our last hours together to be tainted by his anger with me for my mistakes. I do not expect understanding from him; my choices may not be the same ones another would make. But I do hope for his forgiveness. Deserved or not, it's a desire of mine.

"What the hell is that?" Ruby says, and I'm beguiled once again at the reaction to my mind-entering powers. Me! The non-believer in everything other than what is within my tangible control! It is ironic.

"I don't know. But I thought I was losing my mind."

"Be together," I whisper again. I'm too tired to say more.

"Together...together..." I repeat over and over again to their receiving hearts.

I can see it, there is the river of music from Ruby. Now moving towards Joey. I see them both in my minds, swirls of notes and color, mixing around them. A glorious sight of love between these two spirits.

It is the love that I felt once too.

Not the love I had for Artem, though I did in fact love him as well. That came in our later years. By ceasing our affairs, we put a halt to our avoidance of one another. It allowed my husband and I intimacy neither one of us thought possible. Fifty plus years of marriage, with our last thirty stronger with each passing memory we finally allowed ourselves to build.

But the love emanating now between my Joey and his Ruby—it is the kind of passion and love I was blessed to have in those years of my 20s and 30s.

In the late nights under buzzing lights of a radio station. Sounds of music creating poetry, an atmosphere that echoed the forbidden feelings in our hearts.

Or in the dark and smoky corners of The Gentleman's house.

In front of the crackling fireplace. His debonair smile, a gaze of lust and love held firmly on me. Our naked limbs, intertwined. His hands on my growing belly. Tender kisses to my navel. The baby, kicking beneath the warmth of his palm. The swell of pride in his face at the feeling.

I can feel it now, his love wrapping its arms around me. The smell of his cologne as I nuzzle his chest. The safety I never knew I could feel. A sense of belonging. A sense of home created each and every time we would reunite. I feel it all now.

And when I truly felt the love at a level I never knew existed—the one and only time he held baby Isabella, during a brief hotel stay in New York.

Twenty-four hours of the three of us, never leaving our suite.

We were a makeshift family, pretending the outside world did not exist. Limbs coiled together. Making love while our baby girl slept in the cot in the next room. His hand on my postpartum belly, followed by his kisses, eliminating my insecurities of my changed body. Him worshiping me.

Me finally believing that I was worthy of being worshipped. All from his touch, his love.

Perhaps the best twenty-four hours of my entire life. And I'm reliving them again, here and now. His call to me a distant, soothing voice I'm moving closer to.

My Gentleman. My home.

twenty-eight

. . .

joey

I CLOSE THE door of my apartment behind us, leaning against it with a sigh. I scan my eyes around the space. The exposed brick wall, the black couches of my living room. Monster TV hanging high and proud, the vintage shuffle board table. Dark hard wood floors, all surrounding the open kitchen area island.

I bought the apartment right before meeting Ruby. Hoping to God I'd be able to continue to afford it, still high on my dreams of my first restaurant taking off with success. I thought I had everything I ever wanted.

I never realized how empty it could feel in the months after knowing the space with her in it.

"Are you okay?" Ruby's melodic voice says to me. I back away from the door, take a step closer to her. Watch as she licks her lips, both of us unsure what to say now.

We both know that tonight will likely be the last time we see Mama Z alive. Her breaths were coming further and further apart after she spoke those last words to us. My mom and aunts are with her now. But I couldn't stay. And Mama Z didn't want me to, I had heard her voice.

"Leave me now, go and be together," she had said.

Ruby heard it too.

I drop my keys on a nearby table. Step over to Ruby, sweep her hair off her shoulder. I run my hand down her arm, watch as her skin covers in goosebumps. Try and ignore the taunting call of her nipples hardening under the fabric of her dress. I run my hand back up her arm, and I can't help myself. I circle my thumb around a nipple, smile as she sucks in a breath. I dip a finger in underneath the fabric along the neckline, tormented as I realize she has on no bra. I growl in frustration and appreciation. Graze my finger along her skin, my dick throbbing at the sound of her responsive purr.

"Okay, yes. I think I'm ready for you now," she says with giddy energy.

"Should I call Taylor to join us?"

She smiles, remembering our joke, and shakes her head no. Tells me this is just for us, and grabs the waist of my jeans to pull me close to her, nearly closing the space between us. I pull my hand back from its exploration of her chest, run both hands up along her neck.

God, I've had nothing on my mind these past few days but this skin. Her hair, her lips. It's taking all the restraint in the world for me to not throw her down on the floor right here. To feel her clawing at me, begging for me.

I settle for a kiss. Gentle and slow, I lace my hands and fingers in her hair, my thumbs stroking her cheeks. I want to tell her that I love her, that I'm so glad she's here and that I'm never letting her go.

But first, we need to talk.

So I pull back and let out a groan, frustration at needing to hit pause on all the things I want to do to her body right now. I grab her hand and walk us towards the couch. I sit down and lean my head back, waiting for Ruby to join me.

But she releases my hand. Walks over to my mini bar.

And pulls out two lowball glasses.

I furrow my eyebrows in confusion. I've never seen Ruby drink more than a beer at the most. And that's usually without ever finishing it. Generally she just sips to try it.

"I'm not really sure what I'm looking for here," she says, her voice bashful as she scans the liquor options. "But I think a drink is in order."

I smile and lean my head back against the couch again, interlock my fingers behind my head as I watch her. "Take your pick, Nightingale. You can't go wrong with anything sitting up there."

I watch as she scans the various options, picks a bourbon and pops the top off. Takes a whiff before pulling back with a look of surprised satisfaction. Ruby pours the liquid into each glass, slow and delicate in her movements. She has on a navy blue sundress, and I've never been more glad for summer weather and the display of her bare legs as she moves.

She walks over to me with both glasses, hands me one but remains standing above me. She taps my glass with hers, says, "Happy birthday, Good Guy."

"Happy anniversary," I say. And she nods and we both go to take a sip.

I pause midway, watching her as she tips her glass back like it's a delicate potion. She allows the slightest bit of liquid to escape past her lips. Swallows and parts her lips, and I'm hot with jealousy of the glass and its experience in her hand, on her mouth.

I reach forward to her thigh, touching against my knee. I caress the bare skin, watch as chills erupt on her, followed by a breathy escape of my name.

Eyes closed, she takes another sip, a bigger one now and I watch as her face twists with the bite of it. But then she licks her lips and hums in approval.

"Good?" I ask.

"Better than I expected," she says, eyes still closed. "Warm and sweet."

"It's strong though, be careful," I say, mindful of the fact that she's not used to drinking. Not that I know of, anyway. It occurs to me that her drinking habits may have changed in the past couple years and I hate that I wouldn't even know.

"Do you drink now?" I ask, my thumb spinning small circles on her thigh.

"Not really, no. A champagne toast here and there. Nothing more. Don't like the loss of control," she says, and for some reason I'm relieved to hear that.

Having her stand here in front of me like this is torture. Her bare legs a tease, her hair falling loose, rolling over her chest, dangling ends by her waist. I want to yank her body on top of mine, have her straddle me so her dress is forced further up her body.

But I know I need to wait. I haven't asked her about her stepfather yet. And for some reason it feels like something I need to bring up, because I can't stand the thought of any more secrets being kept between us. I need her to know she has my trust, and I hers.

We each take one final sip, and she takes our glasses and sets them down on the table beside me. She sits down next to me and I wrap my arm around her, pulling her to my chest. I kiss her head, and she slides a hand under my shirt to rest on my side.

"Think she'll hold off 'til after midnight?" she asks.

I laugh. "God I hope so. I'd rather not share today with her death."

I can sense Ruby's smile on my chest. She lifts her head up and looks at me. "That would be kind of mean."

"So fucking mean," I say, running my thumb along her mouth.

She parts her lips and I can tell she's waiting for me to kiss them, but I don't. I can't again, not yet. Not until she tells me about her past. Not until that last bit of wall between us is down.

It's a truth she spoke about with my grandmother, and I

wonder if she thinks I knew about it all along. Does she think I had been aware? That I had any idea of all she had been through, yet did what I did to hurt her and push her away anyways? It breaks my heart to think she might, and I need to clear the air with her.

"What's on your mind, Conti?" she says. "I'm giving you my best kiss me look, and you're not making a move. It was Mama Z's orders, remember?" Then she frowns, drops her face into my chest. "Shit, I'm sorry," her muffled voice says.

"Shhh, no," I say, lifting her chin back up to look at me. "No, I've come to peace with that. She's been suffering these past few weeks, months really. It's her time, I'm okay with that. You have nothing to be sorry for."

She nods, but looks unsure.

I run my hand along my jaw, trying to figure out where to start. "Ruby, Mama Z had something in her room that I want to talk to you about. An article."

I study her face for the light of recognition, but she only drops her head back down to my chest. I adjust my body to pull her even closer to me. Kiss her head and take in the smell of some kind of flower. Rose or lilac maybe.

"What was the article about?" she asks.

I run circles along her arm, wishing to God I didn't have to say what I'm about to say. "It was about a badass girl. A fourteen year old."

I feel her head nod gently in my chest and her body tense. "And what did that badass girl do?"

My heart's beating out of my chest now, I'm raw with emotion and I scoop up her entire body to sit in my lap. She curls up on me, sinking into my chest. "That badass girl stabbed the man that was supposed to be a trusted person in her life," I say, surprising myself with the emotion in my voice.

She twists and wraps her arms around my neck, and I'm relieved at her response. "I'm sorry I never told you," she says into my neck.

"Stop that, you have nothing to be sorry about," I say. "That was your story to do what you wanted with. You don't owe me an apology."

"I'm not sorry for you, I'm sorry for me," she says. "Idiot," she adds, and I smile and press my cheek to her head.

"He didn't know what he had coming, trying to mess with you, did he?"

"No he did not."

We sit like that for a while. At one point she pops up to reach for the remote beside me, tells me to put on some music. I turn on the system, reach for my phone.

"What do you want to hear?" I ask. "Annie Lennox? Little Bird?"

"Always a winner. And actually my own personal hype song, especially when this all went down. Those lyrics fueled my fight." I give her a little comforting squeeze. Think back to when I first called her Nightingale, and she told me "Little Bird" was her favorite song. "But really anything terribly upbeat and pop-y will be delightful and the perfect backdrop for what I'm about to share," she says, and I laugh.

"You're as surprising as ever, you know that?" I say. I set up for a hits station to play.

"Well you'll love this story, then. That article got a couple things wrong." I wait for her to continue, to explain what she means. The sounds of a current trending song fill my apartment.

"It wasn't just the two incidents, I have no clue where that came from. That always bothered me for some reason. Like if this story had to be out there, at least get the facts straight." She lets out a big sigh, and continues.

"His name is Todd Mills, and he and Pearl got married real fast. Too fast, obviously, though believe it or not they're still together now."

"True love," I say.

"The truest."

"What was he like?" I ask, though the words are bitter in my mouth.

"Awesome, actually. Fun and funny. He seemed great at first. And then...less awesome. They partied like rockstars together. And fought like rockstars too. Dishes flying and epic fights that got physical, usually ending with one or both of them storming out of the house.

"Then one night I woke up to him. In my bed." She sucks in a deep breath with this, in and out. Brings that thumb of hers to her mouth.

"You don't have to tell me about it if you don't want to," I reassure her. I don't want her to have to relive it. I just want her to know that I now know. It feels important to have that truth out there.

"No, it's okay," she says to my surprise. "I want to tell you about it. It feels better to talk it out and clarify and tell the story like it actually was."

I nod because I'm not really sure what else to say. I have no idea what it must be like to carry around memories like that. But if I can at all relieve some of the burden, I'll listen until the end of days.

She continues. "So there I am, disoriented, just feeling a random hand up my pajama shirt. I thought maybe it was a dream or something and was stunned once I realized exactly what was happening. Like, I completely froze, not sure what to do. Just feeling like this can't be happening, no way this is happening. I was pleading in my head to let this not be real.

"But it was. I don't think I've ever been so scared. I didn't know how to react or what to do. I just knew I needed to get out of that bed somehow. I ran through a million scenarios in my mind of the best way to react, none of them seeming right."

My heart hurts listening to her, imagining what that moment must have been like, and having no clue how to get out of it. I'm surprised at how much it *pains* me to listen to it. Gripping, gut wrenching pain.

Anger is easy.

It's the way I hurt for her that's hard.

"At some point, I jumped up. I don't even think I thought about it. I shouted for my mom, running out of the room, but she was passed out drunk. I flew into the kitchen, turned on every last light, like maybe if it wasn't dark, then that would take away his power or something, I don't know.

"He stumbled out after me, but he was just laughing and apologizing that he was in the wrong bed. I wanted to believe that so badly. Somehow standing there in that dingy kitchen, all the lights on and out of the situation, I figured it's easier to just believe him. He was drunk, it was just a mistake."

Mistake. The word hangs in the air around us, a phantom cloud of bullshit. I'm holding my breath listening to her, thankful to have her open up to me like this, but enraged at the thought of this bastard. I'm too scared to say anything, not sure how my voice will sound.

"But then it happened again," she says, her voice heavy with emotion. "The fucking bastard did it again, and I could no longer pretend it was all just some mistake. I hated him so much for that, Joey, for not taking the out and giving me that, at least. I don't even know how to describe it. I know it sounds crazy, but more than anything, I hated that he couldn't just let it be the first story. It was like he had crossed this threshold now, and there was no going back.

"Because now this was a *thing*," she says, her voice dripping with disgust, "and I *hated* that this was a thing, forever a piece of my history. He did that to me, and I had no say in it, that's what's so awful about it."

Her voice gets softer. "It's like you're a part of some crime, a driver in a getaway car when you had no idea that's what was happening. But now you're in it and there's no erasing it. There's no rewind button to get you back to your former innocence. You had no say in it at all."

I hear Ruby sniffle, but I can't tell if she's fully crying. She raises a hand to wipe at her eyes, throws her head back to look at the ceiling, and I watch as she blinks away tears, fighting them with all her might.

I want to tell her it's okay, that she can cry. That I'm here to catch each and every one of her falling tears.

But I also know my girl, and I'm guessing her tears are the last thing she wants to give this guy. So what the fuck do I say? How do I help her in this?

I just listen.

"I told my mom the next day, but he was smooth and ready with his answer, claiming he was just drunk and didn't know where he was.

"The next time it happened, it was the same thing. My mom told me to stop being dramatic, but I could tell she thought about it. She knew the truth of what he was up to, and in some sick ways I think it made her jealous."

"Sick," I repeat.

"She'd tell me I was luring him in, that I needed to stop dressing a certain way, that I was asking for trouble. Here's what's fucked up —I actually listened," she says, a soft drop of her clenched fist into my torso. "I started wearing the baggiest clothes I could find, never wanting to show skin. I locked my door every night and barely slept, scared of what might happen.

"And then one night, I woke up to him over top of me, completely naked. I must have been out cold, sleep deprived after weeks of this, and he somehow got in even with my door locked."

"Too drunk to be held accountable for which bed he ended up in, yet not so drunk to mess with a lock," I say, my teeth clenched. My whole body is tense, I realize, and I soften my grip around her, scared I'm crushing her.

"Yeah, exactly."

"So then what happened?" I say, despite all the tightness in my chest, feeling the hotness in my ears as I think about this fucking scum of life bastard. A coward, hiding behind a drinking problem as a convenient cover for tormenting innocent girls.

"He was in the middle of pulling down my shorts and underwear, and I was frozen in fear. I was scared to move, scared I wouldn't be able to free myself from his grasp. I kept my eyes shut, figuring as long as he thought I was asleep, I could catch him off guard when I tried to escape, like I had before."

I squeeze my eyes closed, my mind wandering into that room with her and this piece of shit. Imagining the scene, imagining myself tackling him down, ripping him to shreds with my hands around his throat. The face of his mugshot from the article is clear in my mind as I imagine taking the life from him with my bare hands.

"At some point I took my chance, kicked him as hard as I could, and ran out of the room. I ran to my mom and shook her as hard as I could to wake her up.

"It was a near escape of him fully raping me, though I knew it was only a matter of time and that I needed to get out of there. I reached out to my dad who was overseas at the time and told him I needed him to come back and get me. He wanted to know why, but thought I was just in a fight with my mom or something. I couldn't tell him. I just couldn't get the words out, so I just said that her drinking had gotten so bad that we lost our apartment and were living in a dump somewhere and that she couldn't take care of me anymore.

"And then I had to wait."

I look down at her. Ruby's eyes are wide and staring straight ahead, locked in on some unknown vision, like she's in a trance. "Those next couple of weeks while I waited for my dad were the scariest of my entire life. I was barely sleeping—a zombie in school. A zombie in life. I did everything I could to avoid being alone with him. I would stay late at school whenever I could. I locked my door every night and wore jeans and a belt to bed. It was just a ticking time bomb."

I watch as she blinks, darts her eyes around the room as if coming back to reality. It's such a strange thing, to have to watch someone you love sharing a memory with you that you can see they're fighting to take control of, as if maybe in telling it this time, the story will change.

Except that it doesn't. I can see it in her eyes, read it on her face. The bitter realization that yet again, as always, the story has the same ending.

But there's braveness written on her face now. A shift in her expression, as she snaps out of her horrific reverie and continues on.

And she actually *smiles*. A smile that nearly chills me to the bones. "So I started sleeping with a knife next to my bed, and I'd imagine what might happen, how I'd wake up and fight him, the way that I would do it so he'd never see it coming. I'd mentally prepare for how I'd fake sleep until the right moment to strike." Ruby looks me dead in the eyes—blue flames of fire staring back at me.

"I wanted him to come back in there, Joey. Just so I could do it. Just to feel a blade go into his stomach and watch as the terror took over him as I stabbed him and twisted the knife with all my might. I was so ready, and I needed to win that fight." Her eyes narrow and her pupils dilate, filling the space of her beautiful blue irises with beautiful onyx.

"And I got my chance."

I stare back at her, my Nightingale. Falling out of her nest. Her sleepless nights, her plan of attack that she never should have had to make.

An attack plan that she not only made, but executed. Flying away in escape.

She leans back into me, resuming her position of her head on my chest. Says, "I'm nobody's victim." A chill sweeps over my body. Because just as Ruby says those words, I hear them in another voice too, at the same exact time.

The voice of my grandmother, Mama Z.

twenty-nine

. . .

ruby

LIBERATED, THAT'S HOW she feels. Sitting in the nest of Joey's lap, a weight has lifted at having told her story.

She meant it when she said she was sorry she hadn't told him sooner. It would have helped her. Joey never did realize the gains he was making in allowing Ruby to feel that level of intimacy with someone. He's the one and only person she could crave in a physical sense. From that first night they met, exactly three years ago to the day. His birthday.

She's always wondered about why it was him that she felt such a connection with. At sixteen she lost her virginity. It was with a boy that seemed nice enough, and she was eager to have other hands on her body that weren't her stepfather's. The boy made his awkward thrusts on top of her, and Ruby reached a conclusion that sex was going to be something she would never enjoy, her body too tense in a knee jerk reaction to touch. It saddened her to realize.

But something shifted in the air the night she met Joey. She had been working in therapy to learn to be present within her body.

With time she became more and more comfortable, but had never reached any real comfort when with someone else.

Until Joey. He had called her Nightingale, and he couldn't have stumbled across a more perfect name. She always related to that little bird in her favorite song, and here he was calling her Nightingale. Accidentally channeling that, turning her struggles with insomnia into something sweet, instead of a defense she had never been able to shake. It stirred something in her.

Or maybe it was the dimples, the charm in his smile that she found incredibly sexy. The banter that felt so natural with him.

Maybe it was the fact that her first contact with him was her flashlight to his head, she thinks with a smile. That sense of power allowed her to soften, just a little. This guy, a gym rat that looked like he could lift a car, keeled over at her hands. He could have snapped in an impulsive reaction at having been hit.

But he didn't.

And then later that night when he reached forward in that dark parking lot, the sounds of the restaurant behind them, a merriment backdrop. His hand in her hair.

She liked his touch. Even thinking about it now makes her hungry for him. She hums at the thought.

"What's on your mind, Nightingale," Joey asks.

"Just fantasizing about you."

"I knew it. You find me irresistible, don't you?"

"Have you listened to the song yet?" she asks.

"Oh I see. You get off on your music, is that it?"

"Maybe a little," she says.

He sighs. "No. I'm waiting because I need to hear it with you. Though gotta say, it's been pretty hard to avoid, which is saying something considering it's not even been released yet."

Pride swells in her. "I know, I'm kind of liking the build up."

"So vain."

"This job really does have a way of inflating your ego," she says.

She dots little kisses on his neck, and delights in his groan and the feel of his erection under her.

"Speaking of ego, you really think mine is that big?"

She laughs, knowing he's referring to the interview in Chicago. "Maybe we're both perfectly vain with big egos."

"Mmm, I like that," he says, and she drinks in the vibration of his voice in his chest.

She repositions herself to wrap her legs on either side of him, straddling. She runs her fingers through his hair. "You're sexy, Conti."

His hands run up her thighs, lifting her dress up and over her ass. She whimpers at the feel of his fingers gliding along her panties, inching their way in. "And you're going to be the death of me," he says. He moves his hand to the front, pushes aside her panties and runs his fingers up and down.

She grips her hands tightly in his hair, arching her back and grinding her hips into his touch. "Good. I like knowing I can kill you at any moment," she whispers.

At this, he throws her off him, onto the couch, pinning himself on top of her. She giggles under him and looks up at the wolfish grin on his face.

And then his face falls serious. "Tell me this is okay," he says.

She shakes her head. "Don't do that, Joey. Don't treat me like something you need to be all delicate with."

He leans down and kisses her, then pulls back. "Ruby, I'm never going to be a guy who forces himself on a girl without making sure it's okay. That has nothing to do with anything other than…fuck, I don't know. Trying to be respectful." He drops his head onto her chest, and she laughs at his frustration.

"Always the Good Guy." She squeezes her legs to pull his weight down onto her and moves her hips as she arches her back to grind into him.

"I warned you," he growls.

"You did."

"Say it, Ruby. Tell me I can fuck you."

"You can fuck me," she breaths out from under him.

"Good. That wasn't so hard now, was it?"

She lets out a moan, closing her eyes as his mouth works on the sensitive spot on her neck, her hips writhing under him. His tongue explores her skin, slowly dragging along her jaw before moving up to her lips. He bites her lower lip and pulls it back before releasing it with a pop. Her need builds at his slow torture.

She feels his mouth by her ear. "Now I want to hear you beg," he growls.

Her belly does a flip at the sound of his commanding voice in her ear. "Please fuck me," she breathes out. "Please, please."

"Good." He rises up to kneel, she hears him pull his shirt over his head. She opens her eyes to admire the sight of him.

"You're really strong, aren't you," she says with a smile, gliding her hands over his stomach. "Aren't you supposed to be a chef? I don't think chefs have abs like this."

"I pay people to chef for me," he says, pulling the straps of her dress down her arms. Her breasts spill out, and he wastes no time putting his mouth on them. Her hips ache with pleasure and need.

And she realizes she hasn't had to do a single mental exercise of centering. No senses work, no effort to focus on sounds or smells or sights. She's fully present in her body with him, with none of the usual work she's always had to do.

It's a surprising revelation, and Ruby wonders if she loves him. She does, she realizes. She has probably from the start, since that first summer together.

And here she is now. Fully vulnerable beneath him like this and consumed with heat radiating from both their bodies. She's never felt more alive and wild with raw lust. It's delicious.

He rises to a stand, and she watches as he undoes his belt buckle, his eyes dark as they hold her gaze. He unbuttons his jeans, and she smiles as she sees his cock spring free. Bubbles of anticipation knowing it's all hunger for her.

"I really love that you're opposed to underwear," she says.

"Have you been thinking about it?" he grins, and she nods yes and giggles. "All this time, fantasizing about me and my...freedom, haven't you?"

She shrugs. "Maybe a little."

He steps out of his jeans and resumes his position on the couch, kneeling between her legs. He pulls her dress down her body, leaving her panties on. He drops his head down between her legs and inhales with a groan. Then turns to the side and bites her inner thigh. "I could live right here and never need to see the light of another day," he says. His tongue explores the soft skin of her inner thighs, and she suppresses a giggle.

"I think I'd be okay with that."

He rubs his nose up and down, over her panties, the subtle scratch of the lace amplifying the sensation as heat floods between her legs. He continues his teasing, biting and licking all around her sex.

Eventually he bites the waistband of her panties, working to drag them down. His hands finish the task, stripping her completely. She watches as his eyes scan over her body in appreciation.

"My God, you are so beautiful," he says, staring down at her. His words are tender, but he's looking at her like he wants to devour her.

She notes to herself that he himself looks like a God, hovering about her like this. The low lights illuminating around him, causing a silhouette of his massive torso.

Her ears perk up as the song playing in the background ends, and the next one is one of hers. One of her breakup anthems, to be precise, "Telling Time." The lyrics begin...

I only leave when you say it's time
I only bleed when you cut this vine
I only love when I'm clearly blind
I only sing when no one's in line

When will I learn, to finally tell time

They both glance over to his speakers. Ruby looks back at Joey, wondering if he realizes the inspiration behind the song. There's concern in his eyes, and she feels herself wanting to reassure him.

"You know this is my second most popular song," she says.

"I did know that, yeah."

"Don't look at me all guilty like that, Conti. I should be thanking you for such good material." She grins and hopes he sees that she truly does only feel grateful. "I'm not holding any grudges, so don't make this weird."

He laughs. "Alright, if you say so."

"I say so."

"Well then let me ask you this. Do you like to fuck to your music?" he asks. He lowers himself back down, trailing his tongue down her belly. Down, down, almost to where she wants him to go.

She moans in response, pushing her hips up, begging for his tongue, his hands, his anything on her.

He continues to tease her and touches everywhere but there. "Well, Nightingale?"

Her eyes flutter open. "I've never actually had sex to my music before," she says with some embarrassment. "I haven't been with anyone since you."

To his credit, he doesn't miss a beat. He keeps at his mission, though maybe with a little more intensity now. "Well then you're gonna come right here, right now. To your song."

"You have less than three and a half minutes," she whispers, though humor is quickly fading as her pleasure builds.

Finally, he buries himself into her, his tongue gliding in all the right ways—up and down, combined with gentle nibbles and sucking. And she can't deny it, this with the backdrop of her music is *hot*. She's blind with stars behind her eyelids, and within two minutes she's coming undone, clawing at the couch cushions and crying out his name. She's writhing beneath him, right along to the swelling of her music, until she can no longer stand it, and she pushes him away.

"I need you inside me," she says as she pulls him down onto her.

"Condom," he says.

"Fuck the condom, I'm on birth control. Unless you've been without protection before?"

"Always with protection. And tested, I'm good."

She's relieved, and surprised at how badly she wants him bare. "Inside me then. Now."

He leans back down on top of her and brings his mouth to her ear again. Whispers, "Beg for it."

"Please. Please, fucking please be inside me," she cries out. She's aching with the need to be filled by him.

Maybe it's her music playing. Maybe it's being back in this apartment where so much happened for her. So much growth.

"That's my girl," he says. "Open your eyes," he commands, and she does.

His dark eyes are staring down at her with intensity. He holds her gaze as he pushes himself into her, spreading her open. She cries out in pleasure and pain, just as her song comes to an end.

"Fuck, you're tight," he breathes out.

She inhales at the unexpected soreness of having him inside her, after so long without sex. "Breathe, baby," he soothes, and she lets out a slow breath. "That's it. Relax," he says, and she joins him in his movements.

She notes how good it feels, how right it is to have him joined to her like this. Sex with him had always been good, and she wonders if half her avoidance of it recently had been because she feared no one could please her like this. Joey seemed to know just how to work her body to respond in all the perfect ways.

Maybe she knew no one else would compare.

But she's relishing in every feeling and every tingling sensation as they move together right here, on this couch, in this space.

Even if her mind is not always sure about what's right, she decides she's going to trust her body. It's never failed her. It's always been accurate, whether to warn her of danger or to tell her something's worth exploring. She realizes how powerful she is when she pays attention to her body's signals, and that's more comfort than she'll ever need.

She reaches another orgasm, and Joey pulls out of her afterwards. He repositions them both so she's back to straddling him, tells her he's not ready for it to end. She lowers herself onto him and assures him she's not either. That this doesn't have to end.

Not making love to him, not being with him.

None of it has to end.

He cups her face at this and they pause their movements. "I love you, Ruby," he says.

And she says it back.

LATER THAT EVENING, RUBY WAKES up with a startle. A nightmare disturbed her otherwise peaceful and much needed slumber. She was being chased by a creature of some sort, talons the only discernible feature. Reaching for her, the rest of the figure hidden under a hooded cloak. A grim reaper, maybe.

When she stopped to turn and face the creature, convinced outrunning it was not possible, the creature vanished. A cloud of dust or smoke the only remains of its existence.

In the distance from behind a tree, out stepped a woman. Mama Z, only she was much younger than the Mama Z Ruby knew.

She raised a finger to her lips, an indication of silence, and Ruby froze in her tracks. Mama Z then retreated back behind the tree only to reappear a moment later directly beside Ruby. She whispered in Ruby's ear, "I am Queen Zabel, married in the name of forging a destiny. Scholar of the arts and the magic of creative enlightenment. Woman of power."

In a flash, she disappeared again, leaving behind the shadow of a voice. "Traitors must be killed through truths."

Which is how Ruby woke up, mere moments ago.

She untangles herself from Joey's arm and grabs her phone, wincing at the harsh brightness blinding in the dark space of Joey's bedroom.

Another email. One simple line. Thirteen little words that yank the air right out of her lungs.

"You robbed me of a decade of my life, you lying little cunt."

Ruby's heart sinks. She knows this will only continue. The monster is growing, just as it had eleven years ago. As a child, Ruby remembers holding onto hope that it was all in her head, that she was overreacting to a situation. That a hug was just a hug, and not a forewarning of more sinister acts to come.

She knows better now. These emails are not nothing. They will continue until the words are no longer safely behind a screen, but leaping off, ready to attack. Haunting her in the night, in the flesh.

She needs to be ready.

thirty

. . .

joey

MY GIRL DESERVES Eggs Benedict, I decide.

My girl that loves me. She told me so, and I thought my heart was going to burst out of my chest at the sound of those words.

I should have told her I loved her a long time ago. I should have told her that last year, when she had rushed into my restaurant after hours one night. We'd made love on my bar, a fantasy I had had for the previous two years. And afterwards we moved into my office, not saying much. Just the two of us in the dark and empty space. I remember breathing in the scent of her hair, wishing we could freeze that moment because we both knew it was temporary.

She had cried in my arms at one point, and I thought I understood why. Thought it was the stress of her growing fame, wreaking havoc on her and that's why she had come to me.

But no. I know now it was more than that. It was because of that disgusting piece of shit.

I clench my jaw as I watch the butter melt before me, thinking of the regrets I have in how I handled everything. How I let my own selfishness in needing to ravish her stand in the way of allowing her to say what she needed to say. Instead, I thought I was saying goodbye that night. Setting my Nightingale free for her own good.

I jump as I realize I just cracked the egg in my hand, my fist reflexively squeezing not just out of disgust at the asshole that fucked with her, but at the asshole in me that fucked up everything with my girl. What I wouldn't give to take that back, to do that whole night and the next day over again. The next day after, talking to my wise old grandmother, my heart torn in thinking I needed to help push Ruby along. What I wouldn't give to undo all that.

In the past now. My girl has given me a second chance, undeserving as I am. And I'm going to spend the rest of my life making it up to her, making it right.

First, I need to wash the sacrificial egg off my hand.

"Mmm, whatcha making?" Ruby says, walking into my kitchen. She looks positively adorable in a t-shirt of mine. Hair a wild mess, loose around her face and shoulders.

I steal a quick kiss before returning to my bowl, whipping up the egg yolks and lemon juice for the hollandaise sauce. "Eggs Benedict," I say. It occurs to me I have no idea if she even likes Eggs Benedict. Maybe I should have gone with pancakes.

Thankfully she reaches up to her tippy toes to plant a kiss on my cheek before slapping my ass. She heads over to the counter and takes a seat on a bar stool. I lift the melted butter to start the task of slowly pouring it into the egg concoction while mixing.

"I really love having a boyfriend that can cook," she says, and I nearly drop the butter in and ruin the whole thing. I catch myself and examine the egg yolks, relieved nothing has curdled.

"Please repeat everything you just said slowly and clearly so I can freeze this memory into my head, Nightingale, or I don't think I'll ever be able to breathe again."

She laughs, says, "I think we've wasted enough years avoiding making this officially what it is, don't you?"

"One thousand percent fucking hell yes," I blurt out in a rush. "I just really wish I wasn't doing the single most delicate and careful thing right now in making a hollandaise sauce where one wrong step and I'll end up with curdled egg yolks instead of the silky sauce you deserve, because there are a thousand things I want to do instead."

"Like what?"

My cock stirs but I do my best to ignore it. "Oh, I don't know, like kiss you long and slow and watch your face as I tell you I love you and hear you say it back to me."

"Is that all?" she asks with a coyness in her voice. "Not throw me against a wall and jam your dick into me too?"

There she is, my frisky little Ruby. Goddamn, I love her.

I laugh. "Fine, yes. That might have crossed my mind too." I'm nearly done mixing in the melted butter, and not in all my years of cooking, when semi famous guests came into my restaurants or known critics that I was trying to win over have I ever been so eager to see a meal complete.

"I really love that you're standing here cooking in nothing but pajama pants, Conti. It's pretty fucking hot, not gonna lie."

"Maybe next time I'll just be naked."

"Yes, please," she says. I hear her slide off her seat, feel her hand on my back. "Can I help you?"

"Have you ever poached eggs before?"

She shakes her head no. I kiss her nose, tell her to sit her ass down then. "So bossy," she says.

She doesn't usually drink coffee, so I signal to the pantry. "There's tea in there if you want," I say. She saunters over to it, bends down to rummage around the shelves, and I groan at the sight of my shirt inching up her legs, teasing me with the slightest hint of what I'm pretty sure is her bare ass.

For a man with a dying grandmother, I'm feeling like I'm on cloud nine.

"Any word on Mama Z?" I swear she can read my mind.

"No, nothing. I'm going to pop back over after work today," I say. I hate that I have to leave her, but I have a million things to do if I want to be able to relax later this evening with Ruby.

"Keep me posted." She shuffles around the kitchen, opening cabinets and making herself at home. I love seeing her here so comfortable like this. At ease. It's definitely a different energy than she had three years ago. I can tell her confidence has soared, and I'm flooded with relief and pride in my Ruby, having finally found her groove.

"What's your plan today?" I ask, sliding the eggs into the boiling water. I walk over to the toaster to pull out the English muffins. Assemble the Canadian bacon on them.

She sighs. "Well, my hibernation officially needs to come to an end, apparently. They want Grayson and me in New York to record."

I smile at this. One, because I'm glad she doesn't have to go back to LA for that. But two, because I know what she needs to record. I was telling the truth yesterday when I said I haven't heard the song yet.

But I did stumble across the title. "Nightingale in July," I say.

She's steeping a tea bag in her mug, and pauses. "I thought you didn't know."

"You've gone viral, Ruby. As much as I tried, it was impossible to avoid learning the title."

"Such patience. Not curious to listen to it?" she asks, an eyebrow raised. "Though better, probably. The label's eager to get a proper recording of it out, hating the number of fan phone recordings floating around."

I assemble our plates, pour the sauce over the poached eggs, and walk over to her. "Any chance I can hear straight from the star?"

"I think it could be arranged." Ruby looks down at her plate, moans in appreciation, and cuts into the silky pile of food. I can't help but watch her as she takes her first bite. She closes her eyes, appreciation clear on her face. She moans again and my thoughts are carnal as I watch her.

I've never been happier to have a skill that can bring this girl so much pleasure.

"Still like having a boyfriend that can cook?" I ask.

"Shut up and let me enjoy this," she says, eyes still closed.

I laugh, kiss her cheek and then her forehead. Whisper in her ear, "Anything for my girlfriend."

I PRACTICALLY SKIP INTO WORK, I'm so high off of Ruby Francesca. I get pulled in a million directions, put out fire after fire, the price I have to pay from being so caught up at my grandmother's bedside these past few weeks. But nothing can bring me down.

"Why the grin?" Lila asks me as I make my way behind the bar. She bartends for me twice a week, and I had forgotten she'd be in today. It's been over a month since we last slept together, probably closer to two. Still, I feel a twinge of guilt.

Never shit where you eat. It's what I get, I guess.

Lila leans forward on the bar, resting her weight on her forearms. It's relatively calm for the moment, and in the past, a rare, slow night would have meant a fast, heated fuck in a dark corner somewhere. I try not to let my mind go back to any memories of that, but Lila's giving me that wicked look, like that's exactly what's on her mind.

Like she wants to eat me alive.

I used to love that look. I'd escape in it.

Now I'm pretty sure it only scares me.

I clear my throat. "Hey. Just thinking of something funny, that's all," I say. I feel out of sorts around her, worried my usual approach will come off flirtatious, and that's *definitely* not what I'm going for.

"It wouldn't have anything to do with Ms. Ruby Francesca,

would it?" she says like she knows damn well it does, and doesn't give a shit.

I casually slap my hand on the bar with a "None of your business," and walk back to my office. I swear though, I can feel the laser heat coming off her eyes and into my back.

I get settled in at my desk, happy to escape the talons of Lila. My mind goes back to what Ruby said last night. She hadn't been with anyone since me last year. It might be wrong of me but I'm thrilled to hear that. Not that I would have expected it. It just makes me feel a little shitty that I couldn't say the same thing.

I'm guessing it'd be a challenge to know who to trust when you're in a world like hers. Never knowing if someone likes you for you, or for your rising fame. Even 'round here I've had girls throwing themselves at me, apparently turned on by my minor Z-list celebrity status as owner of two popular locales. I can only imagine what it's like on Ruby's end. I'm instantly jealous at the thought of some dickwads making calculated moves on her. It's gotta be hard for her, but I'm selfishly thankful it means she's simply kept to herself.

I don't deserve this girl.

The night flies by in a blur, and I'm proud of the incredible restraint I've shown in not checking my phone a million times for anything from Ruby. Just a few texts letting me know she and Grayson were getting settled and she'd be off the radar for a bit. I've been tempted to cheat and Google the song, but I know it'll be so much better when I hear it from her.

I should do something special for her when she plays it for me. Though I also kind of want us naked for that experience. Hopefully that's not asking too much.

I hear a tap at my office door, and Lila walks in, two shots in hand.

"Got something for ya," she says, shutting the door behind her. Mini skirt showing legs for days.

Oh, shit.

I gotta be cool with how I handle this. My status with Ruby is not supposed to be public knowledge yet, and even we ourselves only just made it official, finally. But Lila's not the kind of girl that gets turned down.

"You mean you got me my own booze from my own bar?" My tone comes off arrogant, but I don't give a shit. She needs to know this isn't happening.

She sits down on my desk, next to where my arm is resting. Naked thigh revealing itself as her mini skirt rides up. I pull my arm back and cross my arms over my chest. Lean back in my chair to create some distance.

"Come on," she says, voice all seductive pleading. "I'm bored. You're always so good at fixing that." She juts out her bottom lip in a mock pout. Green cat eyes devilish in contrast to the attempted innocence of her pouty mouth.

If this were a movie and any man were watching me turn this woman down, they'd be throwing shit at me on screen.

"I don't pay you to be bored, Lila. Go find something to do."

"Mmm, moody Joey is fun," she says. "At least take a shot with me."

I sigh. Unwind my arms and reach over for the glass closest to me, but she pulls it back before I get to it. Tips her head back and throws the contents down her throat. Puts the empty glass on my desk, and licks her lips like a freakin' porno crew is in here filming. She takes the other glass and starts to bring it to my mouth, but I turn away.

"Quit fucking around, Lila" I say, rising to a stand, impatience building.

She grabs my crotch and takes the other shot, keeping a firm stare on me. I'm holding in a breath to attempt to keep down my quickly rising irritation with this woman, reminding myself that I brought this on. Broke the cardinal rules—don't fuck with the Bar Bods, just like Katrina says.

I look her square in the face. "We're not. Doing this." I grab her arm that's on my crotch. Lift it off and drop it in her lap. "So get back to work."

Let the record show that I should be given a medal.

Actually scratch that, I should be given a kick in the ass because clearly I am one.

"Oh, you got it bad, huh big guy?" she says, shaking her head as she rises.

I clench my jaw, feeling instantly protective at the subtle mention of Ruby.

"Does your darling Ruby know anything about the fun you and I have had?" she taunts through fluttering lashes.

She's just trying to bait you. Don't fall for it.

"Do you like working here, Lila?"

"Not particularly in this moment, no."

"Got a real easy solution to that problem."

"Oh relax, big guy. Just trying to have a little fun, that's all." She leans in closer to me, the smell of my tequila on her breath. "Our little secrets are all safe with me."

She starts walking away, though. All I can think is that her sister Lucy—hell, all of us—have been wildly underestimating sweet little sister Lila.

"I hope that girl knows what she's got," she says, opening my door.

"You done?" I ask, voice steely.

She throws her head back to laugh. "With you? Yes. I moved on to Kenny the wine guy anyways," she calls over her shoulder with a grin, and I allow myself to relax a little.

Figures. Hopefully that solves that problem.

"So what was this, a test?" I call after her.

"Something like that. Just a little fun." She starts to walk out, but then turns back around once more.

"Oh hey, one more thing…"

Jesus, is there no end with this girl?

"Yes, Lila?"

I guess my voice is coming out anything but friendly because she throws her hands up, says, "Chill, for fuck's sake. I get it, you've made your choice clear."

"Good. Then what is it?"

"Just a weird interaction I meant to to tell you about. Some guy walked in the other day asking for you. Katrina said he came by yesterday too."

My hackles are up instantly. There's something about the way Lila says it that comes across as off key. She's got her arms crossed, her eyebrows are pinched together. Her cool demeanor from just a second ago now gone.

"Who?"

"Said his name was Mills."

And just like that, I'm walking around my desk to stand in front of her. "When exactly? What did he say?"

"Jesus, Joey. Calm down, you're freaking me out. You know him?"

"Not exactly. Just of him. Nothing good."

"Well that tracks," she says with a shrug and a shiver. "He was creepy as fuck. Looked like shit, too. High or something maybe, I don't know. He just asked for you and said he'd be back."

"If he comes back, and I'm not here, call me immediately. And tell everyone he's not welcome here, alright?" I fist my hands at my side, clenching my jaw. What the fuck was he doing here?

Guess that's the problem with fame. It was something Ruby feared. This bastard is out now and apparently back to his old habits looking to start trouble. And now Ruby and I are in the public eye with nowhere to hide.

"Who is he?" Lila asks.

As much as I want to warn her of this piece of shit, I sure as hell am not going to expose Ruby's past.

So I answer as honestly as I can. "Someone that doesn't deserve to walk this earth."

thirty-one

. . .

ruby

GRAYSON REMOVES HIS head phones, announces, "Ladies and gentleman, I think we've got it."

Ruby beams at the high fives and applause from their small audience in the studio. Water bottles, tea mugs, and the occasional can of spiked seltzer flood the surfaces. It was a successful day, and Ruby has a feeling this new single is going to be just as big as everyone is saying.

"Thank you everyone," she says to the group, dragging out the "one" in "everyone" while hopping up and down in a dance.

There's nothing quite like the feeling of a completed recording, and this one feels about a million times even more special. There's buzz about it being worthy of a Grammy nomination. She tries not to imagine it, but the fantasy creeps in. Having your songs reach the Billboard charts is one thing. But a Grammy? Even just to be nominated would be the ultimate dream come true for her. A validation of her as an artist.

She's held onto hope before, trying not to feel crushed at the lack of recognition. Her team reminding her that she's just starting out, that "Good-est of Girls" was a song stuck in everyone's minds, that everyone loves her work, and having a hit single is a hell of an accomplishment.

But she wants more. And while her breakup album compliments of Joey Conti was good, she has a feeling this next one will be her best yet.

It's so much better to create when fueled by love, and not a mask worn out of protection.

They head back to their hotel and Grayson and Ruby collapse on the couch in her room.

"You hungry?" Grayson asks.

"Yes, but not really interested in gearing up in disguise," she says. It's a strange thing to get used to, being recognized on the street. In Garden Springs it's easier. A small town where people aren't necessarily expecting to see anyone famous, even though it's public knowledge that it's been Ruby's hometown for years.

But in New York, she gets a lot more random fan recognition, requests for selfies, and autographs. Nothing too extreme, but right now with leaks of the Nightingale in July performance going viral, she's nervous to head out. Especially with Grayson, as together they are even more likely to be stopped.

"Room service it is, then," Grayson says, getting up and walking to find a menu. "The usual?" he asks, and she nods. Cobb salad, her go to. He places their order, then returns to her side.

"Soon I'll need to be *your* assistant, now that I've got you performing with me," she teases.

"No. One and done on this one. I'm featuring on a song, nothing more," he says adamantly.

"I know, I know. I thank you, though." She and Grayson both know the unique aspect of his cowriting with her is a big part of the angle the team is pushing with this single.

"So what's next, love?" he asks, knowing her mind is only flowing with more ideas and lyrics bubbling up now that the well has been tapped into yet again.

"I'm just dying to see what else I come up with for this album. I have a feeling the best is yet to come."

"Even better than Nightingale in July?"

"More like, the dressing and accessories for Nightingale in July."

He nods. "I like it. Can't wait for the ride."

She turns toward him and leans back on her side with her elbow on the back of the couch to prop her head in her palm. "I have this strange feeling like a part of me has been holding back. And now that Joey and I have finally figured our shit out, I can really let loose. Is that crazy?"

"For an artist to be inspired by love? No, doll. I think that's a concept that every artist in the history of the universe has tried to convey."

"I love him, Grayson," she says with a grin. It feels good to say it out loud.

"I know you do. I can't say I blame you, easy on the eyes, that one."

She nods, still grinning.

But then Ruby remembers the other bit in her world that needs to be addressed.

"I have to tell him that Todd's reached out to me, though." Grayson contorts his face into a grimace at the mention of her stepfather's name. "Got another email from him."

"You didn't block him?"

"Can't. I feel like I need to know when he sends them and what he says to see if this thing escalates, which I guess it kind of has already if I'm getting multiple contact attempts."

"You think he's after money?"

"My mom? Sure."

"But not him," Grayson finishes for her.

"His emails read more like a man scorned, looking for revenge by way of tormenting me. A sick power play obsession."

"Oh Ruby, you need to let everyone know what we're potentially dealing with here," he says, his voice serious now. Professional mode turned on. "This isn't a crazed fan. It's personal. We're going to need to stay ahead of that." He pats her knee. "I say that as Grayson your friend. You're pretending to be cavalier about it, but I know you. I see fear behind that mask."

She groans and flops back on the couch, wishing Rebel were here with her. She left him at her dad's and is now regretting it. "Would you be a dear and take care of that for me?" she asks out of the side of her eye. She catches Grayson furiously typing away on his phone.

"Already am, love. I've got you."

"Thank you. I'm honestly not even worried about that side of it. It's Joey I'm dreading telling."

"Why? That man looks like the perfect built-in body guard. Think his protection extends to me?"

She gives Grayson a gentle kick to his leg. "Hands off, he's mine. But yes, you know it does."

"So what are you worried about?" he asks. "And tell me quickly, because we have about ninety seconds before my phone starts blowing up with calls on this," he says, waving his phone in the air.

"Not worried, exactly. I just hate that we are giving this thing a real shot, and now the Todd Mills storm is coming over it, threatening to downpour. I just don't trust him to go down easy, here, and I'm not sure how this ends. I doubt he'll stop on his own accord, but he hasn't done any official threats that I could report at this point."

"Harassing emails is enough." And at that, his phone rings. "Let me take this and we'll figure this out. Don't go far," he says, and she rolls her eyes at him.

She decides to distract herself by texting Joey. She misses him already, and is grateful she and Grayson will be back in PA tomorrow evening. She was given a little grace time so she could churn out as much as she can of her next album. The goal is to release in the fall. She has a couple songs ready, but with Nightingale in July the new star of the album, Ruby wants to revisit some themes.

She imagines herself writing in Joey's apartment. Is it too soon to use it as her personal PA crash pad? She has the feeling he'll be just fine with it. It's not like she's asking to move in, she has her own place in LA.

The reminder of that makes her heart sink, just a little. Though truth be told, she feels like she's spent less time there the past three years than what would warrant calling any place a "home" anyhow. And hasn't she done enough rubbing elbows at this point? Her hope is that with this single, she'll have solidified her career to the point where she can have her home base wherever she wants.

Ruby looks at her phone, getting ready to text him, but he beat her to it. Joey's words leap off the screen.

> J: She's gone. It's the end of an era.
>
> J: How did recording go?

She can't help but smile in appreciation of him asking about recording. As if that's just as important as the loss of his grandmother.

Yes, she absolutely loves this man.

"Well there you have it, folks," Ruby mutters with a sigh. She realizes her heart aches at the thought of not being there with Joey tonight. She imagines the family all together at the house, reminiscing and sharing their favorite Mama Z stories. They'll be making arrangements for the funeral, passing around tissue boxes, and making the necessary phone calls.

She tries to pinpoint the feeling stirring in her. It's not quite sadness, or at least not *only* sadness. Like Joey said, it was her time. Mama Z lived a good and full life and would not want to be a hundred years old, her body continuing to fail on her. Ruby thinks about this and realizes she feels the same way.

The feeling swarming through her includes something else.

Gratitude, perhaps. It's gratitude to have had a woman come into her world at such a strange time when Ruby was trying to find her next moves, unsure how brave she could possibly be. Mama Z, Joey, his whole family and crew provided the briefest glimpse of a support system for her. One Ruby had always longed for but never felt she had. Sure, she had her dad and grandmother before she passed.

But the Derian and Conti family tree was a massive oak, with branches robust and solid, multiplying in every which way. It housed a collection of characters within, all bringing forth their unique personalities and contributing to the system as a whole.

It felt like home.

So no, the sadness she feels for the loss of the matriarch of that tree is not the only feeling. With it is the gratitude of having known her at all. And longing at not being there with Joey right now.

AFTER THE PAST TWENTY-FOUR HOURS, Ruby feels a flood of relief at driving up to Joey's restaurant. She'd undergone a flurry of phone calls and meetings to share her concerns regarding her stepfather and outline steps to ensure any emails are shared to watch out for threats.

But mostly, there was a whole lot of lack of regard for his potential as a threat. It seems everyone feels he's just a money hungry ass, seeking whatever he feels Ruby's success might have to offer him, and nothing more. In short, they weren't taking it super seriously, nor did the police feel there was enough of a threat to take any steps. It felt like a lot of empty "We've got you" promises with no real follow through.

Maybe Ruby was overreacting. Maybe Todd would get bored with a lack of response, and this would all fizzle out.

Maybe she knew deep down that was bullshit.

Still, she couldn't bring herself to bring it up with Joey. Not now. Not with Mama Z's recent passing and all he surely has on his mind. Grayson and her dad had her back, and for now that felt like enough.

With Rebel in hand, Ruby locks the door of her old hatchback, her baby that she can't bring herself to sell, despite its age. Like Rebel, that hatchback holds a piece of her heart. It's a comforting constant in her life that has been with her through so much. She smiles to herself, remembering the first time she officially met Joey, right there at the trunk of her car with him trying to be chivalrous and her jumping in attack.

"Who knew, right?" she says to Rebel's panting face. It's nearly midnight now, as she's been keeping a low profile to avoid unwanted attention. She had been texting Joey, knowing he'd be here late finishing up work. He gave her the combination to his apartment, expecting her to meet him there when he finished. But she didn't want to be alone so she figured surprising him after their brief time apart would be fun.

The dark street is relatively quiet and she's happy to have Rebel in her arms as she makes her way up to the back door of the restaurant, as she can't help but feel spooked.

Just nerves, she thinks.

She refuses to allow fear to consume her and keep her from living her life. Still, the hair on the back of her neck is standing up, and it has nothing to do with the gentle summer breeze. She quickens her steps to the door, eager to knock and step safely inside.

Three gentle taps and a quick text to Joey saying she's outside, and she's more than a little relieved when the door swings open.

"What the—" Joey starts to say, but he pulls her inside and crashes his lips to hers before he can even finish the thought. She smiles against his lips, kicking the door closed behind her.

When they finally break apart, Joey looks down at Rebel. "Old buddy still kicking, I see," he says, patting Rebel's head.

"I hope it's okay I brought him. I missed you both."

"Whatever you need, Nightingale. No one's here, and I know the owner," Joey says with a wink.

God, I've missed that face and smile, she thinks. All of her spooks from a moment ago are magically melting away.

With a hand on her lower back, Joey guides them both through the kitchen and to his office. She thinks back to last year when she came to him to this very space late that night. It feels so much better this time, even with the menacing emails and pressures with work. Somehow, this time, everything feels just as it should be. She's opened her heart to Joey, and with that things have finally fallen into place.

"Are you thirsty? Hungry?" Joey asks as he sits in his office chair, and Ruby and Rebel take a seat on the couch.

She shakes her head. "No. I just missed you and didn't want to wait around at your apartment all by myself. I thought I'd surprise you instead."

"I can't pretend to be mad about that, especially because I've been rushing through and half-assing everything in a hurry. Maybe now I'll actually get a few things done," he says, eyes moving across his computer screen. She notes the circles under his eyes, and figures he must be exhausted.

"Do you have a lot more?" she asks. She settles Rebel down next to her and curls up her legs.

"A few emails, an accounting misstep I'm trying to get to the bottom of, a few other things. Should be less than an hour. You sure I can't get you something to eat?"

"Nah, I'm good. I've got some lyrics I want to get down, so I figured we could work together," she beams. It feels so good to say that, "work together," her and Joey. Both in their career stride, and now both finally falling into the relationship neither of them could stop from happening.

She grabs her notebook out of her bag and begins writing up the song concept that had been floating around in her mind. A song about back and forth, pushes and pulls. She has yet to find the proper descriptors for it, but the concept is forming, waiting to land in the right place. Maybe here she'll be able to push past the block.

They work for a while in silence. Ruby scribbles away and tries not to be distracted by the muscles in Joey's forearms, which are twitching on his desk with each subtle move he makes. She spins around an idea, watching him.

Ripple and roll, tensions constricted
I'm here waiting for the toll
It's the sight of power
Happy to pay when I know it's my hour

Not terrible, she thinks, and a tune starts to form in her mind. She smiles to herself, loving the way her block is slowly moving aside, right here in Joey's presence. He seems to light the fuse that ignites her creativity.

Firework from a spark

Joey's phone interrupts their silence. He looks down at it, says, "Shit, I gotta take this." He rises out of his seat, answering the call. Ruby watches with curiosity, wondering who's calling him so late. She must have concern on her face because he locks eyes with her and smiles with a wink. He pulls his phone away from his ear to say "Be right back," and heads out of his office, swinging a right to head to the main dining area.

Ruby looks down at Rebel with a sigh. "No rest for the business owner, I guess."

She goes back to her notepad, but she's itching to play the tune forming in her mind. Despite every bone in her body telling her not to head out to her car right now, she finds herself rising out of her seat. "Be right back, Rebel. I need my guitar." She hadn't wanted to bring it in earlier and risk disturbing Joey, but she has a feeling he'll be okay with it. "Nothing to be scared of, right?" she assures the unaffected Rebel brightly. "I can't stop living my life."

She heads left out of Joey's office, through the kitchen and out the back door. She's humming her new tune along the way, partly out of holding it in her mind and partly to help calm her growing nerves. With a glance around her surroundings, she confirms there is no one around. No shadows lurking in corners, just the steady buzz of street lamps softly illuminating the empty sidewalk. She keeps a random key on her key chain locked between her fingers, pointing outward. Just in case.

Still, a chill rolls through her body, followed by a sick feeling at the pit of her stomach.

"I hear the buzz of street lamps," she whispers into the empty air. "I feel the crooked pavement of the sidewalk." She hates with all her might the growing fear in her belly and the flush of sweat on her palms despite the chill that remains on her bare skin.

She sees a shadow move ahead and she stops dead in her tracks, ears alert and listening. Blood is pulsing in her ear.

I hear something rustling, she thinks, lost between her grounding exercise and confirmation that she does in fact hear something. *This was a bad idea.* She thinks about Joey and how long he'll be on his call and if he'll come looking for her. She feels frozen in fear, glued to this sidewalk and unable to move.

And then with a burst, a black creature darts out before her, carrying something in its mouth. A stray dog, rushing away from her, looking more scared than she herself even is.

She laughs as relief washes over her and shakes her head to herself. Still, she quickens her steps as she makes her way to her car, happy it's just a few yards ahead. "Okay, no more randomly roaming the streets alone at night," she says to no one. It's as if she's bargaining with the universe. Forgive her of this dumb choice, and she'll be smarter next time. Just as long as this turns out all right.

Except something's not right. Her car is in front of her but there's something on her windshield she can't quite make out. She takes a tentative step closer, squinting.

A teddy bear is tucked under her windshield wiper. Mindlessly, she takes another step and sees that its mouth is slashed open with stuffing spilling out in its place. A ribbon is wrapped tightly around its neck, with a note tucked beneath it.

Against all better judgement, she reaches for the bear and gulps as she sees the familiar handwriting. With a shaking hand she reads the note.

"You never could keep your mouth shut, could you? Enjoy fame now, little cunt. It won't last if you can't sing."

A threat. *This is a threat, right?* she thinks. Her eyes dart around, scanning for movement or signs of life, but there's none. Eerily alone, with a slashed teddy bear for a companion.

She feels tears prick behind her eyes, threatening to blur her vision. "Fuck youuuuuuu!!!" she screams out into the night, crumpling the note in her hands. She refuses to sob, choosing instead to suck her breath in, then out again. In and out, in and out, her breathing is hard and fast. But she's not sobbing, she notes.

Footsteps come up hot and fast behind her, and she turns around just in time to slam into the wall of Joey's chest.

"Ruby!" he yells, cradling her head and pulling her back to look at her. "What the hell are you doing out here?" His eyes scan all across her face, down her body in frantic examination. "Are you hurt? What's wrong?"

She can't speak though, for fear that the tears will come tumbling out. Her body is shaking and she can only tilt her head behind her, directing Joey towards her car.

He keeps his hold on her and looks over her shoulder. She looks down to the ground, unable to watch as his face takes in the sight.

"The *fuck*?" With one hand still on her, he takes a step closer to the car. He returns his attention to her, snatching the crumpled note from her hand. She dares to peek at his face and watches as his eyes move quickly across the paper. His head darts up and around, scanning their surroundings for signs of something.

But the street remains silent.

He looks back down to her, his eyes dark and cold, demanding an explanation, maybe. Or something else.

"I...I was getting my guitar and I found this," she blurts out. "I think it's from him. From Todd," she says, her voice a trembling squeak.

"You *think*?" he says, his eyes wide with disbelief.

She nods her head in short, choppy movements. "I mean I know. He's been sending me emails."

"For how long?" he says through gritted teeth, his voice clipped. Body rigid.

"A couple weeks now. Nothing too bad at first, but he's getting more angry. I told Grayson and the team, and we talked to the police, but there was not enough proof of anything threatening."

Ruby watches as Joey lifts a clenched fist to his mouth, his other hand grazing the back of his head. He says nothing, the air thick with all the things not being said. She sees the tension radiating off his body, looking like he wants to burst out of his skin as he takes in everything she just told him.

She knows the feeling.

Finally, after a few agonizing moments, he snaps. "Jesus *Christ*, Ruby!" he shouts, slamming his fist on the roof of her car. She jolts at the unexpected force of the move. "Why didn't you fucking tell me?! *What were you thinking?!*" Joey's usual kind eyes are now black with rage.

She watches as he turns his back to her and raises his hands to the back of his head, snaking his fingers through his hair to squeeze in tight fists. Even from this angle, she can see his rapid breathing, the rise and fall of his shoulders and expansion of his torso.

Reflexively she giggles, but her heart is pounding. The sound is a betrayal, a complete contradiction to the fear she's still feeling.

He turns back to face her, his eyes clouded with anger. "You think this is funny?" he yells at her. She shakes her head no, and watches as he registers the tear rolling down her cheek and his eyes quickly replace fury with concern.

He takes three quick, long strides towards her and envelopes her against his chest, threading his fingers through her hair. She inhales deeply, trying to center on the scent of his soap, the fresh cotton of his shirt.

I smell soap, I smell my Good Guy. I feel his arms. I feel him wrapped around me. The thoughts are a rapid blur in her mind, behind her tears.

"I'm sorry…I'm sorry," he breathes into her hair. "My Nightingale, Ruby, I'm so sorry," he continues. His voice is barely a whisper. And she cries into his chest, all the fears she's been holding back since receiving first contact from her stepfather and all she's been carrying. It's all surfacing right here on this dark street. Wrapped in Joey's arms.

He continues his soothing apologies, kissing her between each statement.

"I should have told you," she croaks. "It's just, with Mama Z and everything finally settling with you and me, I didn't want to bring this into it."

He continues his kisses and soothing strokes on her back, rocking her in his arms.

He speaks softly. "Baby, baby. My God, I can't protect you if you don't *talk* to me, Ruby. We just went through this…you gotta talk to me. I don't give a flying fuck what I have going on." He grabs her shoulders and pulls her back. "Look at me," he commands.

Reluctantly, she meets his eyes, not wanting to see the worry in them. "You are my number one, Ruby. Don't you understand that? You are my everything, my whole goddamn world. And I need you to learn to get over that 'It's all fine' bullshit and Let. Me. In. Do you hear me?" his question demanding a response as he gives her a gentle shake of her shoulders.

She nods her head yes. She knows he's right and hates that she's been so stupid in avoiding these conversations with him.

That's what happens when you've shared your story and not been believed. You start to think no one wants to hear your stories at all.

But she's done with that shit.

Joey says nothing and continues studying her face, searching for something. Eventually his gaze drops to her mouth and he closes his eyes. He pulls her back towards him for one more embrace. They stand like that on the street, her body eventually steadying its trembles in the warm comfort of his arms.

At some point he releases her to grab her hand and says, "Come on." They take a step forward to head back to the restaurant.

But then he stops short to point towards the car and the evidence. "This," he says, his finger an accusatory instrument in the direction of the mangled bear. "Maybe *this* is the fucking *proof* they need." He spits the words out in venomous disgust, his voice laced with anger.

And so much more.

It's the fight that she wished her mother had all those years ago.

It's the seriousness she wished the police had earlier today.

It's the advocacy her dad had when she disclosed to him the truth at fourteen years old. And he did everything in his power to make sure Todd Mills got the maximum sentence for his crimes.

But even more than all of that, in Joseph Conti's voice is a promise. One that says everything Ruby needs to hear about his commitment to her, to being by her side. To having her back and to loving her despite all the volcanic shitstorms that may be raining down ashes upon them.

In Joey's voice, she hears only unfiltered, unhinged, and unstoppable raw, ferocity of love.

thirty-two

. . .

joey

I

T'S A STRANGE thing, being here at Mama Z's funeral. In a historic Catholic Church on the outskirts of the city. Flowers everywhere, people in dark tones of navy blue, black, and charcoal. Suits and dresses, all looking elegant.

Ruby's team offered us to have actual bodyguards in attendance for her, which I found incredibly amusing. And no, not just for her stepfather, though the police apparently paid him a visit after we reported his ridiculous teddy bear threat. What kind of fucker sends a teddy bear like that? I almost feel sorry for his lack of creativity, the sick fuck.

But with Mama Z's obituary and public announcement of funeral arrangements, we had to think about fans and paparazzi showing up. I'm just laughing because Mama Z would absolutely love that. We assured them that we'd have it handled, no muscle necessary when there was plenty of that right here in the Derian clan. So far it's not been an issue, just a couple cameras waiting when Ruby and I walked up.

In a surreal moment in my life, I had to be part of a meeting of when to make a "public" appearance. All to announce to Ruby's exponentially growing fan base that we are in fact a couple.

We decided Mama Z's funeral, with the stone backdrop of this gorgeous church, was the perfect time to allow a few photos of Ruby and me arm in arm.

I gotta admit, I kind of love the attention. I feel like a star by proximity. The hardest part was not grinning like a fool when I'm supposed to be in mourning. Ruby and I planned the whole thing out, having a blast with the drama of it all. We walked through how I'd help her out of the sleek, black SUV and pull her up to wrap my arm around her in warm comfort. Allow those flashes of lights for their sought after photos to finally give credibility to the rumors.

Strange, the things fans want to see.

My girl handles it all like a champ, though. Such a natural. I think I'm not too shabby with it myself.

Seems to have done the trick. We're inside the front hall of the church now, and my cousin reported the cameras are gone. Might have another attempt to catch some tears when we leave, but we'll make our way out a back exit for that.

After the strange little burst of excitement from our entrance, I'm back to the realization that we're here.

At my grandmother's funeral.

I remember being sad when my grandfather died, but this feels like something else. There's grief, sure, but more than that, I feel like Mama Z has just leveled up in a way, and is now sitting high on a throne, watching us all from above. Call me crazy, but I'm almost happy for her.

I'm standing here talking to a guy I can't for the life of me place, but I know I've met him before. Older dude, and he keeps calling me "Little Joey," telling a random story of me as a kid, running through the house naked, apparently not a care in the world.

It tracks.

"I'm going to use the bathroom," my girl says real quick in my ear. I can tell she's trying not to interrupt my conversation, and I'm not having that. I need her to know she's never an inconvenient interruption, so I grab her hand and pull her close to me before she gets the chance to quietly retreat. I give her a squeeze and introduce her, practically glowing as I say the words "girlfriend" to the dude in front of me.

"Looks like Little Joey made out okay," the guy says. Old people are so odd, but he seems kind enough.

I let Ruby go with a quick pat on her ass. She saunters off, throwing me a look over her shoulder that says, "You're trouble."

I suppress a groan as I watch her walk away, her beautiful ass pulling my attention away from the poor guy that is now committed to explaining to me his former career in accounting or insurance or some shit like that.

Xavier walks up to join us, looking polished in a black suit, complete with beard trimmed and long hair pulled back in a low ponytail. It's a stark contrast from the years of him in an army uniform, hair short and face clean shaven. His look now suits him.

He puts a hand on my back. Says, "Sorry to interrupt, mind if I grab Joey for a sec?" Insurance guy waves a hand and Xavier steers me away.

"No need to save me, I had it," I assure him, but I quickly register the look on his face.

"We have a situation," he says. My body instantly goes tense, because I have a feeling I know what this is.

Not only did we need to think about likely paparazzi visits today, but I had a feeling a certain piece of shit might get some ideas as well, testing the limits despite getting a warning from the cops.

Sure enough, Xavier steers me outside to the front steps, where my skin instantly crawls at the sight of good old Todd Mills.

I had told the family a most basic variety of the man, knowing that they didn't need to know all the details beyond "Watch out for this guy, he's not our friend." What was left unsaid didn't need questioning and this family of ours understands that. Ruby didn't deserve to suffer any more humiliation than what that bastard had already put her through, and I was going to see to it that her privacy was kept.

But as I lay eyes on this miserable excuse for a man, I have the urge to shout out to the world "Pedophile!" and take a seat just to sit and watch with pleasure how this family would tear the guy to shreds.

"He says he's looking for you and Ruby and he looks like the guy you described," Xavier explains, snapping me out of my fantasy.

I pat his back reassuringly. "I got this," I say.

"You sure?" The look my uncle is giving me is all the combat vet in him, springing to life.

"Sure," I say, giving him a nod. "Hang back just in case, but sincerely doubt I'll need you," I say with a smirk as I look at the coward, a scrawny little creep that just *looks* like he preys on innocent girls.

I walk up to him, my heart beating in my chest with a fury of energy that I'm straining to contain. I flash him a smile, reach out my hand and say, "Hey, fella'! Joseph Conti. Heard you were asking for me."

"Todd Mills," he says, and he reaches for my hand to shake it. I surprise him in return, giving it a hard squeeze, not letting go as I put my other hand around his shoulders. "Let's take a walk, shall we Todd Mills?" I say with all the sales charm in the world, oozing out of me in ribbons of fresh caramel.

I thoroughly enjoy the pure, rigid terror I feel from this guy's body as he realizes he clearly made a mistake here. I shuffle him around to a quiet corner, tell him he has about twenty seconds to explain what the hell he's doing here.

He stammers through some sorry explanation. Says, "Just giving my condolences."

"Like hell you are," I say through gritted teeth once we're safely out of view from anyone else. "Now tell me just what in the fuck you think you're doing here, so I can release myself from the grasp on your filthy body and get back to celebrating a woman that was a thousand times more man than you'll ever be."

"Look, I just thought you should be warned. You're with Ruby, right? That girl's a liar, and you can't trust anything she says," he says, his body twitching, like even *it* can't stand his words.

I could snap this guy in half right here, right now. But I'm breathing slowly, reminding myself to stay in control. Not let this asshole bring me down with his own sinking ship. "A liar you say, huh? Is that why you're wandering around town, stalking her, threatening her with nasty notes and twisted gifts that show exactly just what a sick little shit you are? Because *she's* the liar?"

And he smiles. This piece of shit actually smiles, stale booze on his breath, his teeth rotted like a glimpse inside his rotted soul. "She'll hook you, watch out. Got you too, huh? She'll make you think you got something special. Did the same shit to me!"

I could puke in this guy's face right here and now with what he's saying.

"You thought you had something special with a fourteen year old child, is that what you're telling me?"

"Shoulda' seen her at fourteen, sure as fuck coulda' passed for eighteen. *Felt* more like eighteen too," he says.

I snap, seeing nothing but red.

I slam him against the stone wall of this holy church that I know my grandmother would be laughing at, and I bring my arm right up against his throat, pinning him as hard as I can. Bring my fist back for three hard punches to his stomach, maybe more. I'm blind with fiery rage and feel a force flowing through me, a tingling sensation filling my blood, heating me to lava. I watch as he reflexively tries to keel over with each blow, but is unable to with my arm pinning his throat to the wall.

I release him far too soon for my liking, scared if I don't stop now I never will. I remind myself that a murder charge is not what Ruby really needs from her man.

I back away, just in time to escape the vomit that spews out of his mouth. Clench and unclench my fists as I continue to step away from him, my arms straight out by my side, still ready to strike.

But he's down on the ground now, rolling to his side in the fetal position.

I glance around us once more to check that the coast is clear. I only see Xavier, just around the corner, looking casual like he has no idea what's happening. But I know he's got one eye on us, keeping watch.

I step up to the piece of shit. Crouch down next to him. Pull out the handkerchief from my suit's front pocket. Toss it at him and say, "Looks like you could use this."

I lean in closer to him. "I know you're not as dumb as you look. I also know that you *know*, if you so much as say her name again—"

"Let me guess, you'll kill me?" he says, snatching up my handkerchief.

This fucking guy.

I shake my head and smirk. "Not at first. But I can guarantee you'll be begging me to."

I rise up, spit in his face with a smile, remembering when I last saw Ruby one year ago. After I had said all those dumbass things, and she had asked to meet up again.

All so she could spit in my face.

Still smiling, I turn around and walk back over to Xavier.

"Better get in, almost time," I say, straightening my tie and cracking my neck.

"Why'd you give him your cloth tissue thing?" he asks, turning and walking back into the church with me.

I shrug. "Don't know. Guess because I'm a gentleman."

<hr>

I GET IN THE FOYER, scanning the crowd for my girl. I have no idea how long I was outside for. Only a few minutes, but it feels like years and I need her by my side.

I look towards the hall with the bathrooms and see her standing there talking to my aunt Malia. And roll my eyes as Malia grabs her cell phone to snap a selfie with Ruby. "Really?" I shout across the crowded foyer, not caring that people are now looking at me, confused. Ruby gives me a sideline glance that's trying real hard to contain a giggle, and I level up my love for my Nightingale just a little bit more.

I watch with admiration as she makes her way over to me in this fitted gray dress of hers that is threatening to make me want to miss Mama Z's funeral. I extend my elbow out to her, and she loops her arm in mine. We file over to the side with the family, preparing to make our way in as the guests take their seats, waiting for the funeral to begin.

"Put away those dimples," she whispers with a tease. "You shouldn't be grinning at a goddamn funeral."

I can't help it, I'm fucking bursting with happiness right now. "Not gonna happen," I lean down and say, keeping my eyes straight ahead.

"Why are you so happy?"

"Oh, you know," I shrug. "Just thinking that the next time I walk down an aisle—"

"It'll be me on your side but wearing white?" she interrupts with a laugh. *Why the fuck is everyone trying to finish my sentences today?* I think.

"No, Nightingale. It'll be you in my arms, carrying my bride in whatever goddamn color she wants to wear."

She throws her head back and laughs, but I think I catch a little glisten in her eyes. "Quit cursing. We're in the house of God," she whispers.

"Don't worry. Mama Z would fucking love it."

thirty-three

. . .

ruby

SHE TWISTS AND turns the cocktail napkin under her finger, mindlessly spinning it on the bar top. There are a thousand music notes in her ear, none of which she can make any sense of. She feels guilty for thinking it, but Ruby's happy the day of the funeral has finally arrived. The past couple weeks have felt like nothing else could exist.

She had found herself an unexpected aide in arrangements and various tasks, as it seems like Joey's sisters, aunts, and cousins were more of an annoyance to Isabella than help. Ruby had offered Joey's mom to lend a hand, more just out of politeness, but surprisingly Isabella had taken her up on it.

Joey seemed so happy to have her there, too. Pride was etched all over his sweet face. Plus it gave him more time at work without the guilt of feeling like he was leaving his mom to everything. Together, Ruby and Isabella had cleared out Mama Z's room, sorted through what to keep and what to give away. At times, Ruby worried she was overstepping. Shouldn't family be here for this? At one point she had blurted that exact thought out to Isabella, but she merely laughed like that was a funny thought.

For a family so close and so committed to Sunday dinners, gossip, and endless birthday parties and events, they sure knew how to disperse when it came to any real work.

"Please," Isabella had said. "I'd rather be the one in charge of this without hearing all the opinions and cleaning up their tissue messes."

Ruby was startled at her candidness. *Guess no family is perfect, even the perfect looking ones*, she thought. It gave her some comfort to know that.

"It seems like you and Joey were the closest to Mama Z," Ruby had noted.

Isabella had been putting neatly folded clothes in a box and paused to contemplate Ruby's observation. "My immediate reaction is to want to tell you no, that she loved us all equally, but I guess that's not really true."

"So what made you two so special to her?" Ruby asked. She hoped her voice was coming out in a friendly, teasing tone, but she wasn't sure.

Isabella resumed her folding and filling of the box. "You'll see, Ruby, that as you get older, you find less and less reason to try and hide who you really are. The expectations and status quo change with time, and eventually you realize everyone has their dark secrets. Maybe you just get desensitized to it," she said with a shrug.

Ruby was taken aback and confused. What the hell was any of that supposed to mean?

Her expression must have given her away, because Isabella laughed. "Mama Z wasn't always so obvious about the fact that Joey and I were her favorite, but in her later years it's a little like she just didn't care anymore to pretend otherwise." She rose up from her kneeled position on the floor and walked over to another box. She pulled out a thick, mustard colored envelope package, and handed it to Ruby. In large print on the front, Ruby could see her own name.

"Here," she said. "Mama Z wanted you to have this."

Tentatively, Ruby took the package. "What is it?"

A warm smile filled Isabella's face. "Answers. And some things she wanted you to have. Open it later, though. I'm not sure I can cry any more today."

And so Ruby had taken the package, stuffed it away in a drawer at Joey's place where she was keeping a few things. She hadn't touched it, unsure of what to expect.

But now, standing here at the funeral reception, she's itching to be done with this whole day. She wants to settle in for the night back at Joey's and see what Mama Z had in store for her.

The bartender hands Ruby her soda and she turns away, scanning the crowd. She sees her dad chatting with Xavier, Reggie, and Reggie's mom and grandmother, and she smiles at the warmth she feels knowing he too has found a place here in this family.

It's strange all that has occurred these past few weeks. It feels like another life when she was in and out of her tour bus, on stages, in sound checks, random hotel rooms, hair and makeup and costumes and people peppering her with questions and information.

Now here she is, back to normal life, only it isn't the normal she knew from before. She feels like overnight she grew a massive and chaotic family, just like how overnight she grew a massive and chaotic career, fanbase, and success.

She absolutely loves it.

"Why, if it isn't the famous Ruby Francesca," Lucy says, stretching her long arms out for a hug.

"Lucy, hi!" Ruby warms at the brunette's radiant smile and embrace. "I've missed you, is that weird?" Ruby says as she pulls back. The two had lost touch over the past three years, which saddens Ruby. She remembers warming to Lucy right out the gate when they first met.

"It's a little weird," Lila says, sliding in between the two women. Her voice comes across off-pitch, somehow. "Considering you're the great Ms. Francesca." Ruby narrows her eyes, wondering if she imagined a bit of a condescending tone. Something about the way she emphasized the last syllable of Ruby's last name. Like "Sca" was a joke, as if it didn't belong with the rest of the word. Unlike Lucy's hug, Lila only offers Ruby a limp hand shake, giving off the vibe that touching Ruby were something she'd rather not do.

Ruby looks up at Lila. Both sisters are tall, but the blonde Lila towers over Ruby by nearly a foot. Ruby straightens her spine to stand a little taller. "Hi, Lila."

"Don't be rude," Lucy says, pinching her sister's arm, though based on how thin Lila is, Ruby wonders how Lucy managed to grab a hold of anything at all. "Ignore her, she has a strange chip on her shoulder these days."

Lucy waves down the bartender and puts in her drink order before getting pulled into conversation with another guest—an older woman Ruby doesn't recognize. Apparently Lila doesn't know her either, as she remains poker faced and firmly in her spot. Ruby feels like a kid getting abandoned by their mother, left standing alone with Lila.

Ruby scans Lila's outfit, a stylish blouse and slacks combo that looks straight off a runway. Her long, platinum hair is neatly coiled in an oversized bun on top of her head. She hates how naturally gorgeous this girl is. How can someone have that caramel complexion, yet still pull off platinum hair? "I love your blouse. Is it designed by your mother?" Ruby asks.

Lila and Lucy's mom is the esteemed fashion designer L. Delphi-Ray. It was a backhanded compliment, as Ruby had heard once that Lila had a particular dislike for living under the shadow of her mother. She's not sure why she felt the need for the subtle jab, but something about Lila is rubbing Ruby the wrong way.

"No," Lila says, looking away as if bored. "Though I've seen some of your costumes. I really don't know how you do it, all while up there singing like that." Her cat eyes remain staring away, the one in Ruby's view crinkling as she lifts the side of her mouth in a smile. "You're so brave, I could never do that."

"It's all about the confidence," Ruby says to the side of Lila's lovely face. "Not everyone has it."

With that Ruby turns on her heels and walks away, not sure what exactly is ruffling her feathers with this girl.

Ruby decides Lila Ray isn't worth her energy.

<hr>

LATER THAT EVENING, WITH HER dress stripped off in favor of a towel wrapped around her, Ruby pads her way across Joey's room to her drawer. She retrieves the package and wonders how much longer Joey will be in the shower. She smiles, curious if he'll have enough hot water left since he had decided to interrupt Ruby's shower. It was well worth the interruption, but she had hurried out after, eager to see what Mama Z had left her.

She carefully opens the package, sits down on the floor to get comfortable. Ruby finds a note along with another smaller package inside. She unfolds the note, dated from April of this year, just a few months ago.

My dearest Ruby. My Joey's Nightingale.

When you came into my life, I thought I had accomplished all I ever wanted. I had risen up from nothing, made a life for myself that fulfilled every wish I had that amplified the opportunities given. Few know all the details of that life. Some secrets are better left going down with the grave.

But you waltzed right in my art studio, unabashed and brazen. Ready to tackle the Meddling Matriarch, and my oh my. I admired that.

In short time I had reached out to you after that first meeting, apologizing for my lack of tact. Mind you dear, I am not one to apologize unless absolutely sure it is necessary, so I do hope you recognize the meaning of that.

I explained to you that I had stumbled across a little newspaper article, passing it across the table to you, and you looked at me with startled eyes. I reached my hand over to you and assured you that I held you in the highest regard. For you had done what no one should ever have to.

And what I once had to do as well.

I told you that secret of mine, one I had believed I would take to the grave—that I myself had stabbed a man with groping hands. And I told you that while my perpetrator was safely tucked away six feet under and in a land left behind across an ocean, I admired you even more for staying right here in this town, only a few miles away from the prison where he was serving his time.

I knew that you had a fire and spirit that I could see would be an unstoppable force in this world.

What I did not share with you that day is something else. I did not confide that I had a connection to a certain man that could make all your dreams come true. Ensure you would be discovered and catch your big break. Yes, it was me that pulled the strings to have you seen that night in our dear Joey's restaurant. Not even Joey knows that.

This secret I kept because I never wanted you to feel like you had not earned that break in your own right, and I still worry even now that in telling you this, you may mistakenly believe that. Please do not. No one in this life achieves success without the scaffolding of others, and we are pompous fools if we try and convince ourselves otherwise. But your talent and your volition are the very reason you are where you are, and no amount of assistance could have brought your success without those traits.

But yes, I had a play in things. I do not tell you this in hopes of any gratitude, (I'll be long gone once you read this. What good would that do me anyhow?). I tell you simply so I can clear the air on some things. I made a few mistakes along the way in my efforts to lift you up. The first of which has to do with the demise of your relationship with Joey. Hear me out, as I do hope you give my Joey the chance he deserves; here is why he does.

You see, my connection in the music industry also happens to be my former lover. The Gentleman, I've always referred to him by that so as to protect his privacy. He is very famous, as you'll soon see. He died just a few days ago (he lived to a ripe old age, so no sadness necessary), and I do fear that with Artem's passing several years ago, and now with my lover's passing, I am not far behind. My heart can feel it.

Now is the time for you to look at that second envelope, dear, for inside you will find something else...

Ruby rips open the other envelope and pulls out its contents. A yellowing stack of handwritten papers, word after flowering word of poetry.

Songs.

Written by Mama Z.

And yet, the most notable aspect of this second envelope is not the dozens of songs apparently written by and held close to Mama Z's heart, but something else.

A photograph, taken in the late sixties or early seventies, maybe, Ruby's not sure. From what Ruby can tell, it's a young Mama Z—an Armenian Jane Fonda, just like the version of her Ruby had seen in her dream. She's gorgeous and grinning, her arm is linked with a man in a suit and white jacket. Ruby flips the photo over, and gasps as she reads the back.

The words, "The Gentleman," and the names of the two in the photo.

Zabel Derian, and none other than perhaps one of the most revered music moguls of all time—

Evander K. Legado.

The uncle to a current power house of the very label Ruby has been signed with since the start of her catapulted career.

And the thing is, he's smiling right down at Zabel.

Flashing dimples Ruby recognizes all too well.

Ruby drops the photo in her lap to pull her hand over her mouth.

Joey could be a dead ringer for The Gentleman—Mama Z's apparent lover. And in fact, Joey looks similar to The Gentleman's nephew, now that Ruby thinks about it. There's not a doubt in her mind of what that means.

That man in the photo, music legend Evander K. Legado—

is Joey's grandfather.

thirty-four

. . .

ruby

RUBY TAKES IN this information, attempting to allow it to absorb.

The Gentleman, as he was referred to behind the closed doors of Mama Z's heart, is Joey's grandfather.

Is she crazy to draw this conclusion? Only one way to find out, and she scrambles to read the paper labeled "Letter to Ruby continued…"

So my dear, have you figured it out? Have I sufficiently shocked you? I do wish I could be there to see your face, I must say.

Yes. The Gentleman is in fact Isabella's biological father.

Though I did not know for sure if that eldest daughter of mine was his or Artem's for many years.

Until along came my favorite grandson, Joey. And what might have been a fading love for me (The Gentleman and I had by that point in time ceased to see one another in person), it re-bloomed as The Gentleman received an unofficial confirmation of his paternity. The true biological father to Isabella, and now grandfather to a grandson. There was no denying it when The Gentleman could have spit Joey out himself.

So when I had asked my dear former lover, still a longtime part of my heart, to call in a favor and give you the break you deserved, I had to do so with assurances. A quiet guarantee that Joey would never meet him or his nephew, lest we risk exposure of our secret.

It's why I urged Joey to keep you at a distance, convincing him it was within his little bird's best interest to fly away solo. And when you returned to town last year, after the receiver of your knife was released from his sentence, I feared once again that I would need to press for Joey's distance from you.

I told him to forge a lie that he had fallen in love with another girl.

Now my dear, you are not the faint of heart, and I have a feeling a hatred for me might feel like a natural and just response. Maybe I deserve it, who knows. You may feel what you wish about me and these acts. My own feelings will not exist in the flesh soon enough. My work on this earth is done, save for this one final matter.

Forgive my dear Joey for his betrayal. He committed the crime only due to his unwavering trust and faith in me, and out of his love for you.

It broke his heart to push you away and set you free. You must know that. But please believe that he did so thinking he would sacrifice his own happiness, just to see you live your dreams.

That is the kind of man my grandson is.

And it is the kind of man a woman like you deserves.

Be together with him. Allow him to care for you, as I hope you know he will with a steadfast loyalty like no other. I have truly never come across a more loving spirit, and I only wish to see you build a life full of memories with him.

Your star may be rising, but it will inevitably fall. All do. Where will you be when that happens? Who will be by your side, holding your hand, caressing your cheek, looking in your eyes like you still are and always will be the brightest star in the universe?

These are the only questions that really matter.

I love you, my unexpected kindred spirit.

With love, guts, music notes, and Ruby Red poppies,

~Zabel

P.S.—Yes, I wrote all this music. Is it any good by today's standards?

Do with it what you will.

The tears are streaming down her cheeks as Ruby reads this declaration of love and confession from the enigmatic Mama Z. And an ache in her heart forms at wishing they could have had one more afternoon together.

One more coffee and tea. One more painting soiree—sweet, testing spirits of the Artist Challenge at heart.

One more glimpse into the secrets of this woman's soul. A soul that Ruby has found to be a most unexpected treasure map of how to navigate the turmoils of life.

And one more lesson of how to consistently absorb and receive love, even when love feels supernatural. Ruby wishes she could ask Mama Z—how do we take the love that lands in our laps, drink it in for all we can? Despite our better judgements or questioning, resistant minds? Though after a beat, Ruby realizes this letter and these confessions are exactly that very attempt.

This right here is Ruby's "one more" from Mama Z. And she resolves to have it be enough. It has to be.

She holds no anger for the matriarch's misguided advice to Joey. Because Ruby knows all too well that we don't always make the best decisions when we're in situations that require cunning maneuvers. Or that we feel we can only navigate with the most cunning of acts. And so, Ruby forgives Mama Z's indiscretions and closet full of spider webs.

Ruby leans back against the dresser, teary eyed at the sentiments, all these revelations, yet unsure what to make of it all.

The question of Legado—does this mean Joey has no idea? Zabel said she didn't want to expose her secrets, meaning no one knows this truth? She furrows her brows in confusion, feeling completely at a loss. Surely Isabella must know, if she's the one entrusted to give this package to Ruby.

Or does she?

The other thing that strikes Ruby is Mama Z's mission. First the one to keep Joey from meeting Evander and his nephew Marcus. It's true, they eventually would have crossed paths at some event or another, and their similarities might have been obvious.

She thinks about what the future holds for her and Joey, and how that might still in fact happen—that Joey and Marcus will likely eventually meet. All it takes is one photo to be snapped together, a random person makes a comment on the striking resemblance, someone else runs wild in hopes to get a hot story, etc. etc. She figures they'll cross that bridge if or when they get to it. With the original adulterers now gone, how much could it really matter?

But the second mission is also weighing on Ruby's mind. Her mission to right the wrong and ensure Ruby and Joey got back together. The efforts she took to convince Ruby that Joey was in fact innocent in his crimes, and deserving of another chance.

What Mama Z didn't know was that Ruby didn't need her help in believing in Joey. Letter or no letter, something about Joey always stuck with Ruby throughout this past year. As if she felt it in her bones that he was good. That they had something real. That there was some misunderstanding somewhere along the way. She had thought maybe things ran off course due to the timing of everything. She remembers how when he told her he was with someone else, how he didn't love Ruby and never could, Ruby felt something was off about it. The words were too harsh, too out of left field for Joey.

Except when she asked to see him one more time, determined

to get answers, she found only hurt and pain in Joey's eyes. It should have comforted her, given her the confirmation that she was looking for in feeling that something wasn't right.

Instead, it pissed her off even more. So she spit in his face and walked off.

And yet? The look in his eyes, it always stuck with her. Not fury, especially after her crude act. It would have been so much easier if he had yelled at her, called her a bitch, anything other than give her that look.

But he didn't.

It's why when Grayson gave her word that Mama Z was on her deathbed, asking for Ruby, it felt like the sign that she had been looking for. A reason to reawaken the Joey chapter.

So no, Mama Z didn't need to go through all this work to convince Ruby to find forgiveness and faith in Joey. To see all the good in him and believe in his love for her.

Ruby felt his love in her heart all on her own.

thirty-five

. . .

"WHAT'S THAT," I ask, rubbing my towel through my wet hair. I'm looking at Ruby, sitting on the floor of my room, still wrapped in her towel after our shower. In her lap and on the floor around her is a mess of random papers.

Her eyes are wide as she looks up at me, like I startled her. But her expression quickly shifts to a smile.

"You're yummy and distracting. Waltzing out here all naked like that."

"Good. That was my plan." I finish drying my hair and wrap the towel around my waist, moving closer to her. Scan the contents of the papers around her. "Seriously, what's all this?"

She looks up at me as if she's not sure what to say.

"Hey, you alright? Is it something from that asshole?" It better fucking not be. I'm really hoping that after our little run-in today, he'll give up on whatever the hell he's after. I debated not even mentioning him showing up today, don't want to further stress my girl out, but on the other hand it feels like upfront communication is probably the best way to tackle the situation. Easier to stay one step ahead if we're all on the same page.

Thankfully, she shakes her head. "No, nothing like that."

I'm relieved, but still. Now's as good a time as any to mention his little appearance. Might as well rip off the Band-Aid.

"Well, he showed up today," I say. I'm hoping it comes across as no big deal. Like, so and so popped in, said hi! All good, nothing to see here.

"Of course he did. Where, the church?"

"Yeah, outside the church right before the funeral started. I hate that I even have to tell you that," I rush to add.

"Alright." I watch as she nods her head, absorbing. "Well, there's that. We figured we'd get some attention today, right?"

I crouch down in front of her. "Some more fun than others, but yeah." I grab her chin and pull it up to look at me. "Hey, you good? I don't want you worrying about this, alright?"

And then I see that wicked little grin of hers sweep across her face. "You kicked his ass, didn't you?"

I can't help but grin right back at her. "Maybe."

"I knew it! That's why you were so happy right as we were lining up to go in, I knew something was up," she says, poking me in the chest. "Tell me everything," she says. She brings her hands in front of her and starts making small, excited claps like a kid about to see her new puppy. "Tell me, tell me, tell me."

"You seem awfully excited to hear this, Nightingale," I say, sitting down next to her. I pull her close and stretch out my legs, cross one ankle over the other.

"Did you hit him?"

"Do you want me to have hit him?"

"Fuck yes," she blurts out with zero hesitation.

I kiss her head. "Well, my little firecracker, I think you'd be happy. Xavier saw him, came and got me. And I took old Mills on a sweet little tour around the side of the building."

"A nice field trip?"

"He definitely seemed to learn a thing or two, so yeah. A threat to stay the fuck away or else. Couple solid punches to the gut, enough for him to toss up his lunch."

"Gross."

"Don't worry, I got out of the way in time."

She nuzzles her face into my chest, kisses my bare skin before settling back to rest her head on me again. "My hero. Hardly a fair fight, I'm guessing," she says.

"Too easy, really. Though not gonna lie, I keep fantasizing about killing him."

"Don't worry, me too. It's normal," she says. And then she pops up to look at me, eyes wild and excited. "I remember something I randomly heard before. How in jail, other inmates eventually learn who the creeps are, and work to make their lives a living hell." She shrugs. "It makes me feel kinda warm and fuzzy to know he got his karma."

"Karma's a bitch."

"Only if that's what's deserved."

She leans back against me and I think back on today. From the looks of the guy, he definitely seemed to be running from some demons by way of shit much harder than booze. What a shame, what a waste of life. Put on this earth to do nothing but cause and be surrounded by suffering. I wonder what that guy's story was, what led him down his fucked up path.

And then I think about Mama Z and all she went through as a kid. I don't know the half of it, I'm sure. But maybe that's why she and my grandfather struggled to be faithful to one another. Maybe suffering inevitably leads to morally gray life choices, some worse than others. It's hard to make sense of. I mean, I know I've had it good, but I like to believe that even if I hadn't, I'd still find a moral compass stronger than secret affairs and other shit.

Or maybe that's more credit than I deserve, who knows.

Then again, look at Ruby. My girl went through hell, and she's got integrity and spirit stronger than anyone I know. So there's that.

Maybe some people are put on this earth to give us hope, show us what could be. Model our abilities to be decent human beings, no matter what.

"How are you so *good*?" I ask her.

"Good?"

"A good person."

She laughs. "Joey, I just told you that I take comfort in knowing Todd was probably raped to all high hell while serving his sentence. I don't think I'm that good."

"Yes you are," I assure her.

"Sucker. Got you fooled."

I smile. Take a deep breath, glad to hear how okay Ruby seems. My girl, strong as fuck. I hate that she ever has to be, but I'm impressed nonetheless.

I want nothing more than to make sure she never has to be strong all by herself ever again.

We sit together for a while, just leaning against my dresser. Ruby and me. As crazy as the events of the day have been, I feel content and at peace.

Eventually I nod over to the papers on the other side of her. "So what's up, doing a little light accounting over here or what?"

She sighs, like a real big kind of sigh. "So," she says, lifting her head up from my chest, pulling away from me. "There's something I have to show you." She picks up one of the papers and hands it to me.

I take it, scan my eyes over and notice the handwriting. The perfect cursive, all slanted and elegant. "Alright. Definitely not taxes," I joke. "Mama Z?"

"Yeah," she says, biting her lip. I'm skimming over, concentrating to read the tight cursive. "They're songs. Mama Z's songs she wrote," Ruby explains. "Your mom gave me this package," she says, lifting up a large, yellow envelope with "Ruby" written across it in Mama Z's handwriting. "And there was a letter in it from her and a photo."

"Huh," I say, feeling happy that my grandmother left something for Ruby. "That's awesome. I knew she used to dabble in a little songwriting. She'd sing us lullabies she wrote when we were little. I never realized she was as into it as she was, though."

I think back on the whole secret lover in the music industry thing. The anger there is gone, but I still feel confused as fuck—like the woman had a whole other life I never knew about. Then again, that probably shouldn't surprise me, knowing how tough the old bird always was. I'll probably never truly know all the secrets she had.

"They any good?" I ask. "The songs, I mean."

Ruby nods. "Yeah, actually. I'm thinking of working some into this next album. It would be pretty badass to release songs from the grave. I'll tweak and it'll be a cowriting thing. Mama Z gave me permission to do with them what I want. I wonder how the royalties on that would work?" she murmurs.

"So what you're saying is, you'll be contributing to my inherited estate," I say with a grin. "The family is going to love you that much more."

She laughs. "Buying their love."

"Yeah, it's probably the best way to win over their hearts."

"More money, and all problems disappear."

"You'll make us a fortune. Buy us a chunk of land and build a Derian compound."

"Multiple pools," she says with a serious face. "A tiki bar."

"We'll name it 'Zabel's Nightingale,'" I say, sweeping my hand in front of us as if showcasing a sign.

Ruby settles her head back into my chest, and I shuffle through a couple of the songs. It feels like a final opportunity to learn some things about my grandmother. I think about what a strange thing it is, going through a person's belongings, yet they no longer are here. It feels invasive in a way. Like these songs are all souls waiting to be adopted, but there's no one to answer you when you have questions about them. There's been no more voices from her since she's been gone. No more guidance. Just the pieces of her left behind, lost objects with no real home.

It's like the objects we hold in our possession are given a life when we are alive. But what about after? The heartbeat of everything feels like it stops right along with the owner. When I had been in her room, her blankets suddenly felt out of place. The glass jewelry container by her bed felt strange and foreign, despite the fact that it's an antique I can remember her having for years. With the life of her zapped out, all her possessions had a feeling of abandonment with them. Eerie, in a sense.

I release Ruby from my grasp and start to get up. My ass is killing me from the hard floor, and I think I've had enough of emotional pushes and pulls for one day.

But Ruby grabs my arm to stop me. "Wait, hang on," she says. I watch as she rummages around the papers and lifts up a photo. Hands it to me.

"Have you ever seen this?" she asks.

I take the photo from her, scan the yellow hue cast over it.

My stomach drops at what I'm looking at, though. A chill sweeps over my body. Heart starts racing.

Because in the photo is me.

Except that it's definitely not.

"What in the…" I say, but there's no words behind the rest of my statement. I peel my eyes away, blink a couple times and glance over to Ruby.

"Look at the back," she instructs, and I turn the photo over.

Read "The Gentleman" and two names I never in a million years thought I would see together.

My heart feels like it's threatening to break out of my chest. This can't be for real.

I drop the photo, unable to look at it anymore. I get up, legs feeling weak. I try and take a step forward, but I'm frozen, my feet glued on the carpet. All I can do is turn my head down to look at Ruby.

Her face is full of all the answers that mere seconds ago, I didn't know I even needed. Subtly, she nods her head.

"The Gentleman," I say, pointing down at the photo.

"You knew of him?" she asks.

"No. I only just learned about him a couple weeks ago. My mom told me about him." I gulp, because I'm not sure if Ruby knows that's who got her her big break.

She lifts up one of the papers, says, "She explains it all in here. He's behind my—my everything, I guess. He and Mama Z were um, you know." She lifts up her thumb to chew on her nail.

"I know."

Lovers. Mama Z's secret affair. A whole other life that happened behind closed doors, before I was born.

Before my mom was born.

The famous Joey dimples I've worn with pride my whole life, learning early on the attention they brought me. A feature that no one else in the family had. Just a fun little thing that hard wired me to grin as my default.

"There's no fucking way," I breathe out. "Is he my...?" I let the question hang in the air between us, because it's obvious the answer.

Ruby rises up to a stand. Paper still in hand, she wraps her arms around my waist.

My head spins at what exactly this means.

"Does my mom know?" I ask.

But I already know the answer. It all makes so much sense now. It's why my mom got so upset when she told me about him. It's that piece I knew, I just *knew* was missing, but couldn't quite figure out.

We stand in silence, arms wrapped around each other while I attempt to let this strange information sink in.

My grandmother.

And the famous Evander K. Legado.

My mom. His daughter.

Making me this guy's biological grandson.

I'm fucking *Evander K. Legado's grandson.*

No I'm not. That's crazy.

I start laughing, and then pause. Eventually eke out a "What the..." as another wave of shock and realization washes over me.

My mind has a million bizarre thoughts running through. This can't be for real.

What a strange fucking day.

Ruby unwraps her arms from around me. Grabs my hand and places the paper in it. "Read this, Good Guy. It's all in here," she says.

And with that, she walks out of the room, leaving me standing alone with answers to questions I never knew to ask, and a mountain of mysteries around my feet.

***

"IT EXPLAINS A LOT," REGGIE says, baby Ronnie bouncing in her lap. I'm almost dizzy watching Ronnie with yet another signature giant bow on her head, bobbling around and full of baby giggles.

"How so?" I ask. It's been over a week since I found out about my biological grandfather, and you can imagine the hushed but dramatic conversations we've been having ever since. My mom made me promise not to tell anyone other than my little sisters. Too many people in the family. If they all knew, it would spread like wildfire. And with Legado being such a high profile figure, even dead, we don't want to risk being the next great entertainment business scandal.

But Xavier was the one I insisted I be able to share with, and my mom agreed. So naturally, that means Reggie knows now too.

Xavier walks over, hands her a plastic cup that says, "Hot Wife" written on it. I laugh at what strange and surprising humor he has. Seems like something I would do, actually.

Reggie grabs the cup from him, laughing at the label. "Nothing says classy like wine in a plastic cup with 'Hot Wife' scrawled on it. Thanks, babe."

Xavier takes a seat at our table. "Nice hat," he says to me, referring to the obnoxiously large paper cone adorning my head. It's my cousin Max's eighteenth birthday, and I'm guessing Max wasn't thrilled at my aunt's insistence on throwing him a party. He was probably hoping to go sneaking drinks with people his own age, and now he's looking miserable sitting off in a corner with little James holding up a toy train to his face.

I return my attention back to Reggie. "Seriously, how so? How does a secret affair, a surprise bloodline that my mom apparently knew about since she was *seventeen*," I say with exaggerated emphasis, "explain a lot?"

Reggie shrugs and hands Ronnie over to Xavier. She leans forward and rests her elbows on the table. "Because. Think about the way your mom always tried to make sure Xavier was included in the family. The illegitimate half brother, but she took a particular liking to him."

"And?" Xavier prompts. "What's that got to do with anything?"

"Don't you two fools get it? Isabella knew what it was like to be the product of a secret affair, even if she couldn't tell anyone. She must have felt a little like an outsider after finding out. Knowing the dad that raised her, the biological father to her sisters, wasn't actually hers. And she at least had the luxury of it all being a secret."

"Not exactly a luxury," my mom says, taking a seat next to me.

"How do you always know when we're talking about you?" I ask, putting an arm around her with a squeeze to her shoulder. I note with relief that it's not quite as bony anymore. The woman is finally eating again.

"It's a mom thing." She sips on her own plastic cup, pulls it back with a grimace. "What is this?" she asks.

"A very fine wine," Reggie says. "Very fine to wine enthusiasts under the age of twenty-one."

We all laugh, because we're pretty sure Aunt Malia only insisted on this party because she was assuming Ruby would come. Once she found out Ruby would be back in LA recording, it's like she gave up on making a whole lot of effort, but it was too late to cancel.

I think back to my own eighteenth birthday. I, unlike my cousin, was all for a family party. My mom and Mama Z went all out, photos of me in various awkward stages of life everywhere. All my favorite foods, there was even a damn photo booth complete with various trophies of mine as props, and popsicle sticks with my senior photos pasted on top. And that's in addition to a DJ and a dance floor. It was pretty epic, actually. As much as I want to be mad at my mom for keeping this secret from me my whole life, it's hard to be when she's always been such a rockstar to me and my sisters.

And as for the grandfather I never knew? I wonder if he ever felt regret for his decision. The daughter, grandson, and grand-daughters he never got to know. Was his career success worth it?

My sisters, speaking of, couldn't care less once they learned the truth of our grandfather. Maybe it's a guy thing, who knows. Maybe because they were never as close with Mama Z and our grandfather Artem as I was. Both men are gone now anyways, so I guess you could say it really is all buried in the past.

At the end of the day, though, how upset can I be at the whole thing when that biological grandfather of mine had done all he could to ensure Ruby's success? For that, I'm both grateful and disappointed at never having the chance to meet the man.

Who knows. It's all still a mixed bag of emotions for me.

My mom clears her throat. "I mean, I suppose it was a luxury in some ways, yes," she says to Reggie. "But not others." She looks over at Xavier, her half brother who in fact isn't her blood brother at all, since they didn't actually share a dad.

Which also means he's not my biological uncle.

My mom continues, looking at Xavier. "You knew the truth about your conception from the very beginning. And I felt fiercely protective of you and making sure you felt like one of us. It did help me learn the silver lining in having the secret. At least I didn't feel the need to fight to be accepted as a true part of the family, because it's all anyone knew." She looks around to the rest of us. "But I had the burden of knowing there was a man out there that I would never meet. That was always made clear to me, and I hated that."

"So you wanted to meet him? Even though he chose his career?" I ask.

"Sure, I was curious."

"Did you ever try and reach out to him?" Xavier asks.

My mom shakes her head no. "To me, I knew who my father was, and it was the man that took care of me. *He* was there to raise me. He taught me how to play soccer, cheered for me at games, yelled at me when I was a stubborn ass—that was my father. The Gentleman felt like a foreigner to me. And I understood, it was a choice he had made. He was in the public eye, had a whole complicated life he was living as a result of being in the public eye. I imagine it wasn't always an easy choice, but it was the right one for him. I think at some point I realized that it was easier *not* meeting him, than risk doing so and wishing we could have had more of a relationship."

"I guess it's what you make it though, right?" Reggie chimes in. "Look at me—a dad and twin brother that died when I was three. Xavier and you," she says, nodding to Isabella, "the products of affairs. But hell if this Derian family doesn't suck everyone in that crosses their path and makes them feel right at home." She smiles, and I watch as the words "Hot Wife" scrawled on her cup tip over as she takes another sip of her wine.

"Even when every bone in your body wants to tell you you don't really belong," Xavier adds. I take in just how funny he looks, saying something so serious but with baby Ronnie and her giant bow in his lap.

I grin. "This crazy crew just doesn't let that happen, do we? Pretty sure that's all Mama Z's doing."

"Cheers to Mama Z," my mom says, and we all raise our red plastic cups in reverence to a woman that knew exactly how she wanted her life to go, and how to make whatever was thrown in her path work to her advantage.

She may have made some mistakes along the way, but she did it with grace and a fierceness that was unstoppable.

Her tribe was everything to her. For a woman that grew up without a real one of her own, she sure figured out how to create one for the rest of us, blood or not. Planned or unplanned.

And for that, I've got nothing but gratitude in my heart for the great Zabel. For her determination to create the destiny she wanted. Sometimes the real things you need in life are whatever can offer you consistency and safety. The constants we can rely on when shit around you is going crazy. And you can't ignore that power, or pretend it's something you're immune from needing. I guess we like the comfort in telling ourselves we're fine without, but it catches up to you eventually. Did with me anyways, to the point where I ended up so desperate for the thing I knew deep down should be my constant, that I wound up on a strange porch roof in the middle of the night, like a damn jackass.

So yeah, Mama Z's a real badass. Because even though I know she had bigger dreams for herself, she ultimately created a different destiny. A meaningful one. I'm grateful as all hell for that destiny to have been something as steadfast and constant as the Derian family clan.

But I'm even more grateful to myself for finally making a few demands of my own.

the glitter & notes press

. . .

AND THE GEM HERSELF, RUBY FRANCESCA, SLASHES THE DEMON OF HER CHILDHOOD!

Ladies and gentleman, the sparkling Ruby Francesca has stunned us once again—this time in a rare exposure of her past. In an exclusive interview with reporter S. Right, she discloses the childhood sexual abuse of her stepfather, Todd Mills, and the courageous attack that ultimately sent him to jail, and set Ms. Francesca free.

S: Why now, why share your story here today?

R: I was scared for many years. And I thought my past was something to be ashamed of. Abuse is something that can mess with your self concept. I logically knew it wasn't my fault, but still the feelings of never being safe end up creeping in.

S: How did you move past that?

R: Therapy. Good therapy, for

starters. But also I found that in sharing my story, I made connections with other women who had similar experiences. It feels a whole lot less lonely, or less like something's wrong with you when you realize you're not the only one. It's also much easier to see your past as just a little piece of the story when you can openly share and let it out. It's not everything, it's not the whole tale, just one small part. When you hold it in, the story feels horribly big and consuming. It becomes a secret that keeps growing and growing in your mind. But when you let it out and talk about it, suddenly it shrinks, and that's been really powerful and liberating for me.

S: We're incredibly grateful you've had the courage to share your story here. What's made that important for you, to not just share amongst your trusted loved ones, but to go public with it?

R: Because it's time to stop hiding. People like Mills exist in this world, and their power stems from manipulation and faith that people will hold onto their monstrous secrets out of fear and shame. It's time to put an end to that, and stories like mine too often go untold. I'm lucky to have a lot of young people that look up to me. If I can help even just one person feel the slightest bit of hope, then it's worth it.

S: Is it hard to share like this?

R: [exhales deep breath] Um, yeah. I'd by lying if I said this was easy; it's not. But I guess that's the point, right?

S: Model the courage and bravery.

R: Exactly.

S: What do you want people to know? What's your message to them?

R: Don't sit back and think you're the problem or question if you did something to deserve this. Take a stand. Fight. Tell someone. Make sure your voice is heard. And above all else—make sure you know that YOU are a fierce warrior, capable and deserving of anything and everything. Never let anyone rob you of that. Fear doesn't have to stop you. Instead, let fear be the fuel to your fire.

S: And for Todd Mills? A message for him?

R: You know a couple years ago, I might have had absolutely nothing to say to him. I would have avoided even thinking about that.

S: And now?

R: Now I can sit here and say that I'm sorry for whatever life did to him to make him the way he is. I spent a lot of time feeling angry towards him. But all anger does is further weigh on me. So instead, I've learned to dig deep, and find some semblance of forgiveness.

S: How did you reach that?

R: Look, the forgiveness is just as

much for me as it is for him, let's be honest. I mean I'm cool, but not that cool. [light laugh] I guess I just realize the value in support. When you've been through hell, as long as you have support to lean on, there's a lot you can manage to survive and come out stronger. A wise woman once taught me that. Someone like Todd Mills just never had any support. From the little I know of his childhood, I know that much to be true.

S: Does that excuse his actions?

R: Are you for real right now? Is that seriously your question?

S: You're right, I apologize. What I mean is, how does that help you make sense of his actions?

R: I don't know if it helps me make sense of them—it just helps me keep the focus on him as the problem, and not me. He had his own struggles, he had no sources of support, and he made the choices to avoid dealing with that and instead drown out his pain in poisons. Those are facts, and when I keep those facts in focus, I can eventually land on some field of forgiveness. And that's where I feel my own greatest power.

To read the rest of this exclusive interview, visit G&NP online

thirty-six

. . .

joey

I SLIP OFF my suit jacket, sweating already. Drop it over the back of the trendy velvet maroon of the hotel suite chair. I kind of like that chair, actually. I wonder if red velvet is a thing. Maybe it's something to consider for any restaurant facelifts.

Who am I kidding? Velvet would never work in a restaurant.

Still, I'm enjoying the old Hollywood glamour of this suite.

I lean against the wall and take in the sight. Watch as the makeup artist puts finishing touches on Ruby's face. I think about the whirlwind of the past few months. The song release, followed by the album release. Sale numbers that skyrocketed, far surpassing any of Ruby's other albums.

Landing my Nightingale the coveted platinum. I was so proud when we got the news.

Ruby nearly fainted. I literally had to hold her lifeless body up when the call came in.

And oh yeah, our little virus Mills? Landed himself back in jail. For—get this—robbing a fast food restaurant. Or attempting to, anyhow. Couldn't even get the job done without getting himself caught. Go figure. Luckily, we've had no further word from him or Pearl. I may or may not know that Dom stepped in and set Pearl straight, but you didn't hear that from me.

But all that seems like a lifetime ago as I watch Ruby under the lights of the makeup artist's setup. Here she is, my Nightingale, looking downright out of this world gorgeous. Like something from a dream.

I've gotten used to seeing the dolled up version of her, I will say. But it still feels odd to see the process happening. She's got these clips in her hair, with tissue paper or something crazy like that to keep from ruining the 'do with the pressure.

The makeup artist sweeps one last brush stroke across Ruby's cheeks, announces that the look is complete.

I gotta admit, I'm catching my breath at the sight of her. My Nightingale.

I watch as the clips are removed, a few more finishing touches to the sweep of her dark curls, enhanced by some magic by the hairdresser.

"In you go, love," Grayson says as he drags her gown towards her. He himself is in this tux that looks every bit like the rockstar he's clearly meant to be, though he still holds firm on his preference to be behind the scenes.

Ruby undoes the belt of her silky robe, full swell of tits out on display even with the random people in the room. She's got on these panties that I picked out for her, I told her they were good luck. White lace, and amazingly she agreed.

It's weird seeing your girl naked in front of other people, but she handles it like a champ. I love how comfortable she is in her skin.

I love even more knowing that that skin is mine.

I walk over to her, offer up my hand as she steps into the waiting gown. I don't even know how to describe this thing to you, but it's gorgeous. Red and silver, lacy and sparkly, and I can't even begin to imagine coming up with something like it. It's art.

Designed by our very own L. Delphi-Ray, believe it or not. Better known to us as Lilith, she is mother to Lucy and Lila. I can pretty much guarantee Lila and Ruby will never exactly be friends, since I get the sense that Lila now sees *me* as the one that got away. Guess dating a star will bring on some jealousy, and yeah, I'm eating that shit up.

But Ruby and Lucy have struck up quite the friendship these days. It was actually very cool of Ruby to let Lilith dress her this evening. She's a great designer, but not one of the big couture design houses who had offered to dress Ruby. She held firm though that Lilith would be designing her look tonight.

I'm learning some crazy shit since being thrust into Ruby's world, and particularly since she's leveled up big time with her latest album. She's nominated tonight for a couple things, but the one we're pretty sure she's got a real shot at is for Song of the Year.

For "Nightingale in July." Apparently the complexity of the harmony is all the rage, and with Grayson as cowriter on that, he's having a pretty hard time continuing to pretend he's still just her assistant. It's sweet though. We're all about to hear a whole lot more from Grayson, just as it should be.

"Would you," Ruby asks me, her head over her shoulder indicating for me to zip up her dress.

"Don't worry, handsome," Grayson says. "You can drag that zipper back down again later this evening."

I don't even say anything, because I'm feeling all kinds of things right now, sliding this zipper up my girl's bare back. Knowing why she's wearing this dress, where we're all about to go, the hard work she's put in to get here. Her creations, this song, this album, my very own grandmother's words woven in. It's surreal, and I've got a strange sort of feeling bubbling up in me.

Grayson must catch sight of it, because he puts a hand on my shoulder, locks eyes with me with the subtlest of nods, as if to say "you got this." I finish zipping, grin and grab his face and smack a kiss square on his lips.

Ruby bursts out laughing. "Well shit, am I about to lose my man to Grayson right now?"

Grayson looks hilariously caught off guard and stunned. Eyes wide, he finally starts blinking rapidly after a moment. Says, "Ruby, we can no longer be friends. I think I'm in love," and we all just grin like a bunch of idiots, so happy in this moment. "In another life," he says to me and I nod and tell him absolutely, I'll hold him to it.

"Well? Shall we?" Ruby says. And off we go, to the biggest night in music.

The Grammy's.

LISTEN, CALL ME VAIN, BUT I think I'm a natural on the red carpet. Sure, they came here to see Ruby first and foremost, but throw a mic at me, and I think I make those interviewers' jobs pretty easy.

"Well he's just a natural in front of the camera, isn't he?" one says, mid laughter.

Ruby leans into my arm, says, "Oh, he's taught me everything I know, I assure you," and I plant a kiss on her head, careful not to disturb her hair.

"And apparently a kissing fool," Grayson chimes in.

I can't help it, I know I'm not supposed to look at the camera, but I do, throwing in a wink.

We make our way through the crowd, a strange hodgepodge of gorgeous celebrities, dotted with random people dressed casually, cameras and microphones, a crowd behind a railing thing, throwing their phones up to snap pics. Not much can top all this excitement. There's noises and voices and snaps and flashes in every direction. It's hard to even know where to look. I just want to be everywhere all at once.

Reluctantly, I let go of Ruby's hand now and then. Watch as

she steps up and poses for photos, people calling out her name and telling her to turn here, turn there. She slips one leg forward, hand on hip. Looking like a goddamn model and I'm amazed at how emotional I end up feeling, watching my girl. She's commanding on the red carpet with all eyes on her. I gotta blink and look away, the sight too much to see.

My Nightingale.

I'm overcome and biting my cheek because I'm a goddamn man and not going to be crying when I look fucking smashing in my tux and a glisten in my eye is not a look I'm trying to add.

Every once in a while, they want me in a photo too. Now, that's when I *really* feel like a million dollars. Ruby's right, the both of us are vain as hell.

But when I hear those words "Joseph Conti, wrap your arm around her!" I pop in for a moment, so happy to have a recharge in the touch of her. Grin and grab Ruby's ass as subtly as I can. Gotta hand it to her, she never even skips a beat, her pose and sultry look held perfectly still for the starbursts of flashes before us, even with me messing with her.

And then I like to step back, do a dramatic gesture up and down the gorgeous Ruby before applauding with appreciation. Hear a few "We love you, Joey!" calls from my very own little fan base, and I blow fantastical air kisses back at the crowd.

All in all, when it's all said and done and we've made our way through, I can honestly say we crushed that whole red carpet thing.

Yet it only gets better.

I mean the music, the performances—my girl included. God, she was unbelievable.

I could barely breathe the entire time she was up there. I'm so damn *emotional*, it's fucking wild.

It's like all the best moments in life, all the best feelings and experiences and things you learn and things you realize you still have yet to learn—all wrapped up in one night.

Maybe it's the music. I'm understanding this ancient form of art in a way I never had before.

Music has a way of pulsing through your veins, attaching itself to you and never letting go, changing you while simultaneously breathing in new life. The heartbeat of what it means to live.

To love.

It's a little like I never truly understood or appreciated it before now. But everything I've been through these past several months, every moment that has passed between my Nightingale and me, looks that say more than words, touches that whisper declarations of love—they've brought me to this new place of limitless euphoria.

And I'm never letting go.

Finally though, the moment comes. Red carpet gone, now sitting here, watching as awards are announced and dreams are coming true.

And up next—award for Song of the Year.

This little table here in front of me feels like the only thing keeping me from fainting, so I can only imagine what's running through Ruby's mind. So many amazing artists here tonight, and Ruby is right up in the running with each of them. Partially thanks to Mama Z, which is even more wild. I can't quite wrap my head around the strangeness of it. While I miss her like hell, I know my grandmother is having the time of her life wherever she is, watching this all.

Maybe with my grandfather.

I hope they're proud.

Amazing what love can create, when you give in to your heart, even when the world is telling you not to.

But it's time now. We hear the words, feel the thick tension in the arena. My stomach feels like a gymnast is in there doing party tricks just to see if I can keep my champagne down. I'm clenching my jaw so hard I'm wondering if I'll have any teeth left in the morning.

I look at my Ruby. Take in the sight of her face. Her pouty, red lips and summer sky blue popping under a thick hood of lashes as she locks eyes with me. Although surrounded by cameras, her face remains impassive, but I see the fire dancing in her eyes. The nerves. I see the emotion and intensity that she's working so beautifully hard to keep still. I can practically hear her reciting her grounding phrases in her head.

"*I see you, Nightingale,*" I mouth to her, ever so slightly.

"*I feel you,*" she mouths back, squeezing my hand. Moments like this have passed so often between us, but never before have I felt quite like I do now. Reverence and pride for my girl, this shiny star right here by my side.

Up at the mic, the umpteenth celebrity artist of the night, getting ready to announce the award. Envelope in hand. Words filling the silence.

And my heartbeat. I feel it, I hear it. A drum in my chest.

"And the Grammy award..."

I hear the words like they're far away, off in another realm. My mind laser focused on nothing but Ruby. My Nightingale's pulse drumming along. A ripple I feel in the soft skin of her wrist, beneath my thumb.

"...for Song of the Year..."

The rise and fall of her chest. I see the tiniest bit of red at the tops of her ears. I give my girl's hand one final squeeze, knowing in my gut I'm about to have to let it go.

"goes to—"

acknowledgments & thoughts

(I know, I apologize for leaving you hanging like that. But you have to admit, it's better this way, right?! Answers will come in the next book, I promise.)

More importantly though, thank you for being here and bravely hearing this story. Both Ruby and Mama Z have experiences that are unfortunately not uncommon. To anyone that could relate in any way to them—YOU are the true warriors. As I say in the book, that's just one piece of your history, and far from the whole story. I hope more than anything that I did this tale justice, and you were able to cheer for yourself right along with these characters, imagining your own victorious, metaphorical "dagger," because a fight like Ruby's is generally not how the situation goes. I grappled with how I wanted to tackle such a sensitive topic. Ultimately, I decided we all deserve to live vicariously through a different ending where justice is actually served.

You are my world, readers. As long as you're here and wanting to read my stories, I'll do the best I can to deliver and give you endings to love that just might sit with you even after that last page. If you or anyone you know needs support, please check out https://rainn.org/resources or call 1-800-656-HOPE (4673).

Our fierce Armenian Mama Z was a character inspired by my paternal great aunt. She and my grandfather were small children when the Armenian genocide began, and they were separated during forced deportation, eventually landing in an orphanage after World War I ended. Aunt Naomi did not know her exact date of birth, something that always stuck with me, and so, this story began to find its subplot. Like Mama Z, my great aunt was a small but mighty woman, living in Germany and Bulgaria until she traveled to the United States when she was twenty. Aunt Naomi passed away in 2015—at the age of 104!

By now I'm sure you can gather that great characters fuel my love of writing. But I could not do this alone. As an indie author, you are tasked with forming your own team of eyes to help fine tune your work. The book you hold in your hands is, I feel, of pretty incredible quality, even without the industry masterminds a big publishing house would offer. And it's because of a few dear friends that selflessly volunteered their precious time and minds to help me tweak this beautiful final product.

Jacqui Muller, you somehow have become my developmental editor, and it's pretty awesome. This book has more dimension as a result of your wisdoms! You feel all the bits that need tweaking, and the result is infinitely better because of it. Your brain is stellar.

Jen Denver, you saved these characters from being boring every time the therapist in me got in the way and I would go "Can't they all just get along?" You reminded me that no, no they can't all just get along because that means no conflict, which means yawns. And let's be honest, Lila came to life largely thanks to you.

Catherine Skeans, how you juggle a million things and still manage to have the patience to proofread and find the TINIEST of errors, I just don't know! But it's pretty freakin' amazing.

Carly Pinato and Meg Sponseller!!! You babes are the real deal. My cheer squad, the life of the party gals, you bring the life in *my* parties/stories. I feel your love for my characters just as hard core as I love them. Meg, thanks for saving the blurb. And Carly? Oh, I'm bringing you your Simon in the next book :)

M. K., thank you for letting me pick your brain on all things restaurant ownership!

To my man, Matthew...It's so fun tweaking tales with you and getting your feedback. Never thought you'd read so much romance, huh? Your seal of approval on my male voice POV is strangely exciting.

And as always, to my four babies—thanks for letting me be horribly behind on laundry so that I can write. And for being the best kids a Mom could ask for so that I'm able to hide away, glued to a laptop. And for your zillion, adorable ideas you throw at me to help with the social media you see me tumbling my way through.

about the author

A believer that life is all about the great stories we live to share, Vanessa Zian loves helping people find the heart and ah-ha moments in their own tales. Her two loves are romance novels and tapping into underlying emotions.

When she's not writing or reading romance, Vanessa works as a therapist, helping clients heal through the powers of introspection. She writes with the same goals in mind—to find value in the conflict and strength of character in beautiful stories, and to celebrate our happy endings.

Vanessa lives in Delaware with her childhood crush-turned-husband, their four kids, and their rescue pup Mikka.

And lots of high heels.

Readers—please consider leaving a rating or review! As someone brand new out here, it's not only so appreciated, but vital to helping me keep writing.

Love her or love to hate her—Lila is going to meet her match...and be put in her place.
Read all about it in the next Dog Tags & Lace book, *Mine after October*
Join my newsletter where I will randomly ask for character name ideas, offer therapeutic tidbits, share sneak peeks, etc! Visit
vanessazian.com
Email: Vanessa@vanessazian.com

facebook.com/VanessaZianWrites

instagram.com/vanessa_zian

tiktok.com/@vanessazian

www.ingramcontent.com/pod-product-compliance
Lightning Source LLC
Chambersburg PA
CBHW030118310726
48970CB00004B/1312